DRAGON FIRE
— AND —
OTHER NONSENSE

BETHANY MEYER

To Poiema. You are Archer's human village.

Satyrs
Nixies
Eri
tree people live here?
castle
no one lives here.... Why not?

weird seraphs
far
seraphs
Humans
Danna's house
centaur valley
(VERY busy)
MANGHA
mangh... everywhe...
(border patrols)
mangh...
MANGHA
HERE
TOO
BEARS

GLOSSARY AND TERM GUIDE

Aethan (AY-than) — A centaur of the valley.

Aro (AIR-oh) — A coastal country wherein eight different sentient species live in harmony.

Caihu (KYE-hoo) — A prophetic centaur, now considered mad and irrelevant. Deceased.

Cohn (CONN) — A centaur known for her strategy and cunning.

Crowned Head — The ruler and king of the manghar.

Dorana (dohr-AH-nah) — A centaur of the valley, wife to Aethan.

Eland (ELL-and) — A young centaur with red hair, still in apprentice training.

Eri (AIR-ee) — One of the biggest cities in seraph territory, well-known for its riches and beauty. Burned.

Fair Folk (FAYR FOHK) — A race of small, nomadic agricultural people. About three apples tall.

Farris (FAIR-iss) — A scholar and a centaur friend of Cohn.

Frutelken (froo-TELK-ehn) — A common household drink of the seraphs, with a fruity, spicy taste.

Geniss (GEHN-ihss) — One of the archivists in the centaurs' valley.

Gint (GIHNT) — An elderly dragonkin; a librarian.

Heather Stone — A magical stone used to cast spells for the protection of Aro, currently split into eight pieces and given to each race in Aro for safekeeping.

Hessen (HESS-ehn) — An important family in the seraph city of Tor.

Hirim (HEER-imm) — a red-haired centaur of some small importance in the centaur valley, and Eland's father.

Kanri (KAHN-ree) — A satyr girl tasked with protecting the Heather Stone.

Leshy (LESH-ee) — A race of people with the appearance of trees on legs, with glowing yellow eyes. The protectors of the forest.

Lif (LEEF) — The younger sister of Wick, also known as Reesa.

Manghar (MANG-harr) — An aggressive and terrifying race with the appearance of giant bats on two legs.

Martook (MAR-took) — A dappled centaur with long hair. Sometimes too enthusiastic.

Nin (NIHN) — General and leader of the Scorch army.

Nixies (NICKS-ees) — A race of pale green people with many teeth, dressed in armor and sea findings.

Ongel (ON-gehl) — A centaur with dark skin and hair, commonly a mentor figure to centaur apprentices and messengers.

Ryga (RYE-gah) — A dragonkin; a scout for the Scorch army.

Sanlar (SAN-lar) — The nixie queen's general and leader of her armed forces.

Sasha (SAH-sha) — Archer's horse, usually found inside his unfillable bag.

Seraphs (SAER-affs) — The winged people.

Skorffv (SKOR-fah-veh) — An old seraph word meaning -1. The moment between flying and falling. -2. A moment where failure is imminent but anything is possible as the inevitable has yet to happen.

Telf (TEHLF) — One of the princes and leaders of leshy territory.

Tinor (TEE-norr) — A centaur with grey hair, a mentor among the centaurs.

Tor (TOHR) — One of seraph territory's richest and most important cities. Burned.

Transmogrification (Trans-mohg-riff-ih-CAY-shuhn) — A leshy's ability to change his or her appearance into something different, usually used as a defense mechanism. Irreversible and normally discouraged by the leshy.

Valoren (VAL-oh-ren) — One of the archivists in the centaurs' valley.

O N E

Burning Skies

THE WORLD WAS DARK.

And hot, so hot.

And *heavy*.

An unseen weight crushed Archer's right wrist, pinning it flat against the ground.

Archer tried to tug his hand free. His fingers flexed and scraped against the grit of dry earth and broken grass, but the pressure on his wrist pinned it in place.

No. No, stop.

Archer tried to lift his head. The same weight pressed down on his nape.

Trapping him.

Panic lanced through his veins. He thrashed.

Why's it so heavy what is it get it off get it off!

The fighting only shifted the crushing burden. Knives of pain dug into his hand as the pressure increased.

Stop moving, stop moving! Breathe.

Breathe.

Archer forced a single shuddering inhale. The air tasted like soot, and his heavy exhale against the ground wafted dust into his eyes. Archer winced. Grit crunched in his eyelids.

What is this thing?

His eyes scrunched tighter shut on the grit as he tried to reorder his thoughts.

Clues, find clues.

The weight above him pressed down like the weight of three dozen muscled manghar. His head throbbed and his lungs ached and something jabbed into his ribs in a strange, tingly way that he hoped wasn't the sign of a light impaling. Broken wood?

Ah.

His eyes opened, refocused on the dirt.

I pulled Fowl under the stairs. The stairs came down on top of us.

This is part of the stairs.

Light poked through a small tunnel in the rubble, casting shadows across the textured earth.

Lift the whole thing. Just push it up.

He steadied himself.

Then he *shoved* with all his strength. His back pressed against the solid wood of the stairs. His shoulders trembled under the weight. For a long, terrible moment, it wouldn't budge.

Archer jammed the joints of his wings against the wood and heaved like Atlas bearing the world.

Finally, the wood lifted by a mite, and Archer's blood surged with terrified glee.

Something unseen crackled toward him through the

rubble.

Archer froze, but knew he couldn't stay still long or the stairway would crush him. He heaved the wreckage higher, dragging his knees forward into supportive pillars. He crouched awkwardly to avoid tearing off his trapped hand.

The hurried footsteps crunched closer, and Wick's voice hissed, "Hold on! I've got to get some leverage!"

"I *can't* hold on," Archer replied through gritted teeth, "or it'll break my back."

Wick made a straining sound. Suddenly, mercifully, the load lightened as Wick lifted. The crack of light widened. Fresher sooty air rushed in. Archer's hand scraped free, the wood scraping away strips flesh and leaving bloody gashes.

Archer scrambled on hands and knees toward the grey light and the too-short legs of the pants that Wick had stolen from him. Splinters stabbed his palms. The knee of one pants leg caught on a nail and tore free in the same heartbeat.

"Hurry!" Wick grunted.

"*Trying.*" Archer skittered free like a four-legged beetle.

Wick dropped the wrecked stairs behind him, spraying clouds of soot in every direction where it fell.

Archer checked his injured hand front and back. Scrapes and beads of blood, but no broken bones. Even when he lifted his shirt to check on his stabbed ribs, he found only a few bleeding scratches.

"Archer." Wick staggered closer, clutching a sore shoulder. "Are you all right?"

"Yeah. Yeah," Archer repeated, swiping away the soot surrounding his eyes. Wick looked to be all right; a blood-encrusted scratch across his temple and down his cheek was the worst of it, and a few light burns across his forearms where he probably tried to cover his head from the fire. Stupid. Like something Fowl would do.

Fowl.

Panic again ripped through his mind like lightning. Archer flew to his feet, dry grass stabbing at his palms. He lurched forward and grabbed Wick's grimy shoulders. "Where's Fowl, Wick?"

"I don't know yet," Wick said in a tone so calm it could only be fake. "Let's just—"

He's buried. He's lost under all the rubble. You were too slow again.

Archer spun, scanning the piles of the rubble for anything person-shaped. For a leg or an arm or a feather sticking out.

In a pile of charred wood behind the stairwell, something moved.

Archer lunged toward it, hopping around the pile of sharp wood and a few smoldering patches of grass. A blackened hand pushed the splintered planks aside to make room for a head of dark hair, tangled and grey with soot. Archer wrapped his hands under a beam and heaved it higher, making room for Fowl to crawl out arm over arm. Free, Fowl fell back into the grass, clutching his ribs with a crumpled wince.

Dropping the wood, Archer rushed to his brother's side, but Fowl held out a hand to stop him.

"I'm fine." Fowl groaned and sat up. The wince on

his face unfolded a touch, but the pinch at the corners of his eyes remained the same.

Archer hesitated, realizing he didn't have a clue what to say. Worry hovered in the wings of his consciousness, but Fowl would never accept his help. "That doesn't look fine, Fowl," he said at last.

"It is fine, now quit your worrying." Fowl pulled himself upright using the beam that Archer had dropped and forcibly straightened his spine.

"You can—you can walk, can't you?" Archer said. "We just had a stairway fall on us and all, so—"

"I said it's fine," Fowl snapped. "Now, stop—"

Something in the treetops snapped, raining flaming branches behind Wick's head. Archer flinched.

The dragonkin are still here.

In the corner of his eye, he saw Fowl's glassy eyes staring into the flames as they fell.

"We need a place to hide," Wick said worriedly. Looking first up and then down the street, Wick pointed through the drifting smoke toward the smoggy glow of the sun. "We'll go that way—I think I see the opening to a cellar. We can hide there."

"Not good enough," Archer said. "We need to get out of the city, now."

"No." Fowl broke in. "We can't leave yet."

Archer turned to his brother. "Fowl," Archer said shortly. "We'll have cover in the forest, but here in the city, they'll find us. We need to get out."

"We haven't looked through the house yet." Fowl's face was an iron wall. Immovable. "I didn't get a chance while I was recovering."

"There's nothing left," Archer insisted. "It's all burned by now."

"You don't know that." Fowl's eyes moved away from Archer to Wick. "You can go on without me if you want, but I'm not leaving Tor until I get to look through the house."

Archer stepped closer, fumbling at his side for the mouth of his bag. "Fowl, I will stuff you in this bag and carry you out of the city myself—"

"Try. It won't work." The soot-smudged tips of Fowl's wings lifted slightly, a reminder that while Archer could not fly, Fowl could take off any time he liked.

Take off and leave Archer behind.

Archer gritted his teeth.

Wick's hand grasped Archer's shoulder, stopping the words in Archer's throat. "Fine, Fowl, we'll go to the house. But we've got to move, right now," Wick said, his voice firm but urgent. "We're out in the open; we can't stay here. We'll figure out the rest when we're safe."

The rest.

The dead parents. The home turned into ashes. The return of the dragonkin.

We'll figure it out later.

Archer flexed his hands. Later sounded better than now. If he was lucky enough, he could keep later-ing it forever, and he'd never have to face it.

"Archer. Fowl," Wick said, more firmly this time. "We're going, right now. Come on."

Ducking the flaming leaves that fell on every side and casting fearful eyes cast to the sky, they set off into the smoke. Archer followed Fowl, darting from shadow to shadow through streets that he no longer recognized, until the shadow of a vast tree fell over them.

Fowl looked up. "This is it."

Every glittering window of the Hessen home had been smashed in. Many of the walls crumpled into the shell of leftover structure, allowing soot to sprinkle and blow through the gaps they left behind. The paint of the remaining walls peeled away in blackened strips, and the stairs had given out, several steps still swinging from the chain railing and clattering in the breeze like ominous wind chimes.

The tree groaned within the blackened rings of the house, itself stripped of swaths of dense bark and foliage and twigs until only the trunk and the thickest bald branches remained.

Fowl glanced first up the street, then down, with the wind pulling dark strands of hair across his face. Then he pushed off the ground and soared up into the layers of the house.

Archer watched his brother vanish with his fingers drumming against his thigh.

Wick scanned the street. "Do you want to go up with him? There might be something left."

"Nothing I want." Archer paused. Still, Fowl had gone up there alone. . . . What if something found him? "I can keep him company, I guess."

"Good. I'll scout ahead that way." Wick pointed further up the street, through piles of smoldering debris. "I won't go far, but hopefully I'll spot a safe path, or at least a place to hide for a while."

Archer nodded. "If anything, you know, sees you, just

scream like you're being murdered."

"If anything sees me, then I *will* be murdered," Wick said. "That should make it easy."

"Yeah. Don't get murdered."

Wick slipped down the street like a broad-shouldered shadow, and once he vanished into the smoke, Archer gripped the remaining tree bark and crept up the stairs of his old home. The steps that still held shuddered under each inching footfall. His heartbeat pounded as he wondered which turn of the tree trunk would reveal something waiting on the other side.

But each rotation revealed only more empty stairs.

Archer paused at a gap in the stairway three steps wide. Faint clatters floated down from above: the sound of Fowl rifling through the wreckage. Archer pulled back and leaped the gap. His heels struck the far side with a resonant *boom*, and the whole stair shook.

Archer crouched, clinging to the bark with one hand and the flimsy chain railing with the other. The smoky chasm below looked almost hungry.

The shivering of the stairs faded away into nothing. Archer stood, trying to swallow the fear that lingered like a bad taste in his mouth.

He clambered up the rest of the steps to the first floor of the Hessen house. His legs burned.

"Fowl," he called, in a voice too soft to be a shout and too loud to be a whisper. "Where are you?"

"Further up," Fowl's voice called back, louder but disinterested.

After a moment of wandering, Archer found the remains of the second-story stairwell. It failed to collapse under him, so at last Fowl came into view, his hair and feathers blowing in the wind. His back faced toward Archer.

Now within reach of his brother, something stopped Archer in his tracks.

Fowl doesn't want you here.

As suddenly as the thought appeared, Archer slapped it away.

Too bad. If he didn't want me to follow him, he shouldn't have come up here.

He tiptoed to avoid most of the splinters and stopped a few steps shy of Fowl's side.

As if burned, Fowl leaped forward a step and strode toward another part of the house.

Archer often wondered if in another life, he and his brother would have been friends.

"Archer, would you climb back down?" Fowl sighed without looking back.

"I don't see a problem with it," Archer said. "You're up here."

"Because I have wings that work."

The statement came out so sharp that they both paused. A hundred stinging retorts came to mind, but Archer swallowed them to join the banished fear in his stomach. If they fought now, he'd never convince Fowl to get out of Tor.

At last Fowl just shook his head. "I just meant that I didn't ask you to climb up here with me. I just wanted to look."

"I know," Archer peeped. But honestly, even if Fowl had *specifically* told him not to, Archer still would have climbed into the house. Some parasite living inside his brain kept whispering that Fowl would escape at the first opportunity. Archer crept as close to the edge as he dared, planning to keep an eye out for dragonkin, but every second of silence sounded like Fowl flying away for good. Even as he watched the treetops for danger, Archer kept glancing back to make sure Fowl was still there.

When Archer's eyes weren't locked on Fowl, they swept over what remained of Tor. Nearly everything on the street had been reduced to the same colors: charred black, ashy grey, or if it was still burning, red and flickering. Chunks of houses lay in heaps where they had fallen. In the center of the road far beneath Archer's feet, a broken frame burned around a painting of. . . something. It might have once been someone's face.

A muscle inside Archer's chest tightened, and he wondered if the sensation was a feeling or a vacuum created by feeling nothing at all. The two seemed nearly the same.

Below, the flames flickered merrily. Archer nudged a piece of wood off the ledge and watched it tumble to the ground below.

He'd thought that they had finally done it.

After all the effort to collect the Heather Stones and stop the Scorch, after gathering the people of Aro and earning their trust, they'd still failed. The dragonkin had only vanished for a few days. And after, they'd come back with more fire than before, and what remained of Tor had gone up like so much kindling.

Fowl climbed higher through the rubble.

Archer followed him. A splinter stabbed one of his

bare feet, and he hissed. Ahead, Fowl sighed deeply but didn't speak.

Finding a stable enough stump of wood, Archer sat and swiped the splinters off the sole of his foot. Looking up, he said, "Fowl, I don't think we're going to find anything here."

"Then don't look," Fowl responded hastily.

"Fowl. We're wasting our time, and we need to get out of the city. There are still too many dragonkin here." Archer paused, but Fowl didn't respond this time. "Everything is gone. Maybe there was something left after the first attack, but I can guarantee you that the second wave got everything else. We're looking through a junk heap."

Standing in part of what used to be a stairwell, Fowl didn't turn, but his shoulders tensed. "Just because you're glad to bury our parents," he said in a low, measured tone, "doesn't mean that I'll give up on them. You're not their only child."

"I'm not—" Archer snapped, then bit down on the words. He lowered his foot to the ground then spoke again. His voice still came out more forceful than he meant it. "I'm not giving up, okay? I'm just trying to get us both out of here alive."

Not a minute later and a few feet higher, Fowl stopped short. Crouching, he plunged his hands into the rubble. Archer winced watching him.

Nearby, something crackled and crashed, and the hair on Archer's nape tingled. Was it a dragonkin?

"Fowl, we should go."

Fowl lifted a piece of charred wood and heaved it to

the side. Something glinted in the pile of rubble.

The flap of wings echoed up the street. Archer shot to his feet and leaned around what was left of a doorway to peer out into the street.

Just as he did, a trio of dragons touched down just two houses away, their claws crunching through the charred wood that littered the street. The collars of flame streaming from their heads pulled downwind. Two of them poked their claws through the wreckage, but the third lifted a long snout the size of a bar stool and appeared to be sniffing the breeze.

Archer's body tensed. They weren't downwind from the dragonkin, but if the wind changed, their luck was up. "Fowl," he hissed. "There are dragonkin out there."

"Give me a minute." Fowl dug deeper into the pile, and something clanked loudly.

The dragonkin's head twisted, turning down the street toward them.

"*Fowl!*"

The clanking grew louder. Too loud. Archer snatched Fowl's arm. "We've got to go right now or we're going to get caught."

Fowl tried to shake free. "Let go!"

Something flew free of the rubble with a snap, leaving only half in Fowl's hand. It was a silver locket, one of many gifts from their father, which Archer only remembered their mother wearing on birthdays and to dinner parties. The broken chain swung wildly from Fowl's fist now only supporting the locket's back and the miniscule portrait inside.

Fowl turned angry eyes on Archer. "Are you happy

now?"

Archer took another glance down at the dragonkin. They were crawling away down a side street, rapidly vanishing into the smoke and wreckage. "Whatever. Just forget it. We're getting out of here before they come back."

A voice in his head that sounded too much like Wick's asked, *Is* whatever *really the best you can do?*

"Look, I'm sorry," Archer mumbled hastily. "Please, let's just go."

"Oh, shut up. I know you aren't sorry." Fowl slipped the chain into his pants pocket, next to his right hand. He didn't look at Archer.

Together they scrambled back down the broken stairs. On their second journey around the tree trunk, Archer spotted Wick's dirty blond hair bobbing up the street, dashing between piles of wreckage in quick bursts.

They reached the bottom of the stairs in one piece. Fowl scanned the street for dragonkin before they crossed, and Archer took Fowl's brief distraction to glance back at the smoking house. Even now, no sad and soggy feelings surfaced. After all, it had never been *home*, only house. The only feelings within reach were relief to be out of the wreck and an agitation to find safer places to be.

On the other side of the street, Wick waved them into the shadows with him. "You saw that group of dragons, right?"

"Yup." Archer frowned. "That was way too close. We've got to get out of the city."

"Agreed." Wick looked from Archer to Fowl, then back to Archer. "Did you find anything up there?"

Fowl huffed.

"There wasn't much to find," Archer said quickly. He glanced toward the sky; still clear. "We should get moving now, before they get back. Did you find anything while you were scouting?"

"The smoke gets thinner that way," Wick said, pointing back down the road southward. "The streets looked less. . . less damaged, too."

"Less destroyed?" Archer asked.

"I thought about saying *wrecked*," Wick corrected, more patiently than Archer deserved. "But then I thought it would be in bad taste. All the same," he added, looking from Archer to Fowl, "I think we should go as far south as we can today. We might even make it somewhere safe before tomorrow morning."

"I've got a better plan." Fowl broke in.

Fowl, of all people? With a plan? Archer's eyebrows rose.

"Those things will see us in the daylight," Fowl went on, in a dull, exhausted tone. "I have a friend who lives south of here; if we can make it to his house, we can stay until it's night and escape under the cover of darkness."

"That. . . does sound better," Wick admitted. His fingers tapped on his thigh. "Archer?"

"Which friend?" Archer asked, after a moment's hesitation. But he already knew. Of course, it would have to be the mess of precise features and blond curls and sharp edges that was Astor Reynold, Fowl's closest friend.

"It's Astor," Fowl said, confirming Archer's dread, then added hastily, "You'll just have to get over it."

"I will, if you'd give me a minute." Archer's fingers

twitched, itching to wrap around Fowl's neck and shake. He stuffed the betraying hands into his pockets instead. "Let's just go before something sees us."

Wick's eyes traveled between Fowl and Archer a few times, then his mouth tightened slightly. Archer knew that look to mean that Wick had discarded whatever he had been planning to say. "We'll go, then. Lead the way."

The three of them started down the road at a quick pace, sticking close to the piles of rubble and keeping to the shadows as much as they could.

Navigating through the city was no easy task. Between the thickness of the smoke and the great number of fallen tree limbs and debris, the streets had taken on the look of another city. One that Archer couldn't recognize.

Stepping carefully through the sunset-colored remains of someone's stained-glass window, Archer wondered again what the strange empty feeling was in his chest, and why it wouldn't leave.

Archer checked over his shoulder again for Fowler. His brother walked quickly with his head down, bits of dark hair slipping free from his hastily tied ponytail and whipping around his face in the hot wind. Fowl never spoke on their journey, didn't even look up from his feet. His injuries from the first Scorch attack were still not healed, and the bandages wrapped around his midsection gave him a strange stiff bulk under his shirt.

Archer remembered with a cringe how Fowl had clutched his midsection as Archer and Wick had dragged him out of the wreckage. Who knew if Fowl's injuries had reopened in the scuffle.

What if—

Archer clamped down on the fear and put it away, deep inside. What was he doing worrying about Fowl? Fowl was the older brother; he was supposed to take care of himself. Even if something *was* wrong, Fowl wouldn't be coming to Archer for help. He'd probably rather go to anyone else.

They were on their way to an "anyone else" right now. That proved it.

Archer double checked both directions and crossed another street. Behind him, Fowler and Wick skirted the same burning branches and piles of smoldering leaves. The fires grew smaller the further they went from the ruined Hessen home, but it could always get worse again. Astor's house could be swallowed in flames.

As though thinking about the dragonkin had summoned something, a shadow swooped low overhead. All three of them started and crouched as the dragonkin went overhead.

What *did* the Scorch want? Whatever they were up to, it sure looked a lot like an organized plan. If they only wanted to get some mindless killing in, they wouldn't have aimed straight for Tor like it was the throat of the enemy. What was more, they wouldn't have left anything standing. If they only wanted death and destruction, they would have just torched all of Aro in one go and left it to burn, right? But it looked like they had left more city standing than Archer had thought. So, what was the plan? Were they looking for something? Something other than the Heather Stones?

They finally reached an area where the smoke

thinned. The streets behind them had been so dense with smog that they could only see a few dozen yards at a time, but Archer could now see as far as the end of the street through the hazy air. The smog that remained stung on his dry eyes, and the grit clinging even to the inside of his shirtsleeves ground against his skin like sandpaper.

Archer didn't spot any dragonkin, either, but he didn't want to take any chances. He kept to the shadows with Fowl and Wick close behind him.

In single file, they darted down the street, clinging to the trees and sheltering under the protection of branches. Pain began to creep up Archer's neck. Every anxious look over his shoulder seemed to wind the tension in his shoulders even tighter. Archer rolled his neck to loosen it. The triple cracking sound from his spine echoed through the trees and earned him a harsh look from both Wick and Fowl.

"Sorry, sorry."

A long time later, they reached what Archer thought might be the right street. Like all the others, it had lost many landmarks and gained heaps of scorched debris, but as they got closer to the huge oak, Archer caught a glimpse of a vibrant blue-green door through the wafting smoke. Singe-marks darkened one of the walls and blazed in stripes up the trunk of the tree, but despite all of it, Astor's house still stood. Shutters—blue, like the door— clamped shut across every window. Pots of flowers, now charred and empty, clustered around the base of the stairs—stairs with a solid wooden railing.

Archer paused, and Wick gave him a questioning look.

Archer nodded at Astor's house. "That's the one."

"It's still here," Wick murmured. "That's a good sign."

"If we can get inside without being caught, it'll be a really good sign." Archer checked left and right, then darted across a clear part of the street toward the stairs.

He hurried up the steps with Fowl behind him and Wick bringing up the rear. Archer noticed, not for the first time, how deathly silent the city had become. No bird sounds, no chatter of crowds, no rustle of leaves; only the creak of the stairs beneath their feet and the breathing of Fowl and Wick behind him. Halfway up, a harsh, hot wind blew up the street from the direction they had come. Archer told himself not to think anything of it as they rounded the trunk of the tree. But when the staircase circled around to face the street again, he looked again anyway.

Three dragonkin swept through the trees, trailing smoke and flame from their wings, headed in Archer's direction.

"Get down!" Archer hissed. He yanked on Fowl's sleeve and grabbed the railing for balance as he crouched.

All three of them pressed as close to the steps as they could and stayed still. Archer tried to avoid the eyes of the dragonkin as they soared closer with his heartbeat pounding in his ears, too loud for comfort.

Had the dragonkin seen them? Their course never wavered. Archer tightened his hold on Fowl's sleeve and tensed to run.

Then the dragonkin swerved around the tree and flew off into another part of the forest.

As if they were all of one mind, Wick and Fowl stayed frozen beside Archer for a long moment. The breeze rippled Fowl's sleeve in Archer's grasp.

Archer stayed still as a tree for three deep, shaky breaths, listening. The breeze whistled by his ears, louder than ever in the silent city, but no flap of wings shook the stillness. He took one more look down the street. Nothing moved but the drifting smoke. Archer rose from his crouch.

"Come on, let's go!" He beckoned as he raced up the stairs, Fowl and Wick close behind him. The locked shutters of windows bounced past one by one. Reaching the top of the staircase, Archer pounded on the heavy turquoise door with the side of his fist.

AFTER ONLY THREE KNOCKS, the door opened. On the other side towered a strong but disheveled-looking seraph with an angular face and a tousled mane of honey-colored curls.

The seraph's mouth tightened. "Archer."

"Nice to see you, Astor. There's no time, let us in." Archer pushed past Astor and into the house with the others close behind him. Once Fowl and Wick were safely inside, Archer snatched the door from Astor's hand and slammed it shut. Then he pressed his ear to the door.

For a moment, no one moved. Archer listened carefully for the sound of crackling wood or the beat of wings. For the sound of anything at all burning. But it seemed the dragonkin weren't coming back.

Archer stood back from the door. "All clear."

Everyone's shoulders slumped with heavy relief. Fowl's brow unclenched. Wick leaned back against the wall and took a deep breath.

"Fowl." Astor slipped past Archer to trap Fowler in a rib-crushing hug. "I'm so sorry about your mother and father."

That's fine, don't worry about me, Archer thought to himself. But then, it wasn't as if he had been. . . *close* to his parents. Or with Astor, either. Fowl and Astor had been nearly inseparable friends even before Archer had left seraph territory. On the other hand, Archer's primary memory of Astor involved biting him very hard on the arm.

Archer stared into the shadowy hallway behind Astor's back and wondered if anyone would notice him escaping up the stairs and never coming back.

"How is your family?" Fowl asked. "Did everyone in this part of the city escape?"

"My family's fine," Astor said. "But the lizards are nesting near here, so my parents went to stay with the cousins, since the eastern side where they live was barely touched. I thought more stragglers might come through from your side of the city, so I stuck around a few days longer."

"We're sorry to impose on you," Wick said. He pushed off the wall and extended a hand to Astor to shake. "We're still trying to leave the city, but there are too many dragonkin out at the moment. We'll try again after nightfall."

Astor seemed to receive Wick better than he had Archer. Gripping Wick's hand, he gave a bit of an easy laugh. "It's not even close to an imposition. This is exactly why I stayed behind." He leaned closer to the windows and flicked a curtain aside to peer out. "It's not safe out there."

"Not to assume the worst," Wick said, "but the dragonkin seem to be burning everything. Don't you think it's only a matter of time before they come for your house, too?"

"I thought of that, too. I'm planning to join my family in a few days; I only stayed in case anyone else needed a helping hand." Astor frowned. "You keep calling them dragonkin. Dragonkin are just. . . fairytale things. Right?"

A flicker of irritation burned between Archer's ears. "Yeah, fairytale things. Fairytale things that look just like those," Archer said, pointing out the window. "If I've learned one thing from the seraphs, it's that sometimes older history gets buried inside songs and stories. I think they're dragonkin, so that's what I'm calling them."

Astor glanced over his shoulder into the living room, where a violin rested in a corner. "There is a lot of history in songs. A *lot*. But on the other hand, some people really are just superstitious."

The irritation chilled into a cold spray of anger. Archer tilted his head, his hands clasping tightly together. "It was my mother that taught me that. If you're disrespecting my dead mother, you'd better not be."

Astor glanced at Fowl. "I didn't. . . I wasn't thinking. I'm sorry."

Sorry, but not for Archer. Archer stared coldly at the back of Astor's curly head as Astor peered out the window again, and wondered how hard it could be to kill Astor in his sleep.

Wick caught Archer's eye, and Wick frowned

slightly, shaking his head. A warning. Archer decided that his plans to murder Astor would have to wait, at least until he knew he could kill Astor on the first try.

"Anyway, we'll be traveling by night," Wick said quickly, probably trying to steer the topic away from Archer's outburst. "We should all get some rest while we can."

"If anyone's hungry, there's food I can make in the kitchen," Astor said, and took off down a nearby hallway. Fowl soared after him, leaving wingless Wick and Archer behind.

Archer turned toward the shadowy stairs at the back of the house. "I'm going to get the best bedroom before Fowl can beat me there."

"We should get going again just as soon as it's dark," Wick said. "This street won't stay safe forever. And I want to get to the valley as quickly as I can; I don't have a clue how bad it is there, and I'd like to help, if they'll have me."

"That's us, always in the middle of the action," Archer said. He cast another look toward the stairs, then hesitated. *Fowl. . .* He faced Wick again. "Fowl might want to stay here. He's always been close with Astor."

Wick's head tilted. "He would let you go without him?"

Archer shrugged. "Pretty sure Fowl likes Astor a lot more than he likes me, brother or not."

"You could ask if Astor wants to come with us," Wick suggested.

Archer's lip curled.

Wick smiled slightly. "If you want to keep Fowl with

you, you'll have to make plans that help both of you. Tricky, isn't it?"

"What are you talking about? I've got tons of practice looking after *you*," Archer said, shaking his head. "Just imagine where you'd be without me."

"Oh, it would be awful. I'd be working the job of my dreams, dripping in unimaginable success. Perfectly comfortable and uninteresting. What misery."

"And burnt to a crisp, too." Archer sighed. "I'm going to bed."

"You're not hungry?" Wick asked.

"No." Not after running into Astor again.

"Well, I am. And I'm curious what food there is here that I haven't tried."

Leave it to Wick to stay obsessed with his new sense of taste even in the middle of a warzone. "Figures. You should see if he has any desserts." Archer forced half a smile. "Well, I'm sick and tired of this territory, and the sooner I go to bed, the sooner we'll be leaving, so good night."

Wick's brow wrinkled slightly. "Are you okay?"

For half a heartbeat, Archer considered the offer Wick was making. He could talk about. . . about what? Even he didn't know how he felt. Since his mother's body had been found in what remained of his old house, Archer hadn't been able to make up his mind if the clenching feeling in his chest was some kind of sickness or. . . or something bigger. Something more frightening.

Without a name to call it by, what was there to talk about? Archer put a wall between himself and the vacuumous squeezing feeling in his chest. If he kept building up the wall, the sensation would eventually become a distant memory.

Wick was still looking at him.

"Of course I'm okay. When am I not?" Archer bounded up the dark stairs before Wick could answer.

Archer collapsed facedown on the nearest quilt and stared into the concerned eyes of a teddy bear on the rug below until sleep fell on him like an assassin. He slept deeply, so deeply that dreams never reached him. When he opened his eyes on the watery moonlight leaking through the shutters, his head felt just as full and heavy as if he hadn't slept at all.

"Night time," he muttered to himself, dragging his body into a staggering walk. "Time to move."

It was far too early. . . or too late. The house was still black and cold and deathly still, but if Wick and the others weren't already awake, they'd have to be soon.

Archer rubbed his swollen eyes as he slipped out of his room and into the chilly hallway. Looking down the shadowy hallway of closed doors, he realized he didn't have the first clue which room Wick was staying in.

He tried three or four wrong doors and after eventually getting a pillow thrown at him by a crabby early-morning Fowl, a creak floated down from the top of the hallway. Wick's voice, still thick and raspy from sleep, drifted down after it. "Stop making a ruckus. I'm right here."

"What possessed you to take the room at the other end of the hallway?" Archer demanded as he padded down to meet Wick.

"Don't talk so loud, the others are still sleeping."

Wick rubbed at his eyes with his palms. "I went to bed late, and I didn't want to disturb anyone else, so I took the room at the far end. What did you need?"

"We need to figure out how we're getting to the valley without getting torched, for one thing." Archer remembered to lower his voice. He went on, quieter. "There aren't as many dragonkin around here, but that doesn't mean we're safe."

"I know." Wick leaned back against the wall and crossed his arms. "The good news is that I haven't heard a sound from outside since the sun went down. I don't think there are many dragonkin up and about. We've got a chance to leave, right now."

Leaning against the wall opposite Wick, Archer nodded.

"We'll fill your bag with as many supplies as we can and we'll start out for the valley within the hour," Wick said. "We just have to ask the other two if they're coming."

"I. . . want Fowl to come with me," Archer said. He shifted his footing uncomfortably. "I'm not going to leave him here, even if it's with Astor."

"What if I want to stay?" Fowl demanded, appearing in the hallway without a sound. "I don't get a choice?"

Archer noticed that the locket they had found in the rubble now hung around Fowl's neck. With the front half missing, the miniature portrait of their family stared out at Archer with frozen, empty eyes. Ochre and Willow sat poised in matching chairs with their sons standing behind them. Fowl's hand rested on Willow's shoulder, but Archer's hand only clasped the back of Ochre's chair. His hair had hung down into his eyes then.

Even then, though, he wouldn't have touched his father with a thousand feet of fishing line.

Archer crossed his arms tighter, but couldn't look Fowl in the eyes. "No. You and me should stick together."

Mounds of Fowl's untied hair fell into his eyes as he tilted his head. "Since when are you the one making the choices for both of us? I'm the older one."

"Then how about you start acting sane, huh? Instead of dragging us both back into a burning building." Archer pushed off the wall and faced Fowl at last. He raised his chin to meet Fowl's eyes and found a storm there. He held his ground. "Until this whole thing with the dragonkin is past, you're sticking with me. I decided that," Archer snapped. "You're coming to the valley with me if I have to drag you along by all that hair on your head."

"You're not making my decisions for me."

"Well, if I let you make your own decisions, we both know where you'd be. You'd be back in the husk of the house, waiting for someone to come home and make it all right again." Archer took a step closer. "You know you would. You've already proved you can't look after yourself, so I'm doing it for you."

The door behind Archer opened. Archer spun around, nearly elbowing Astor in the ribs. Astor caught his elbow in time. Unlike Fowl or Wick, Astor looked so crisp and wakeful with his sharp eyes and unrumpled clothes that Archer wondered if he'd gone to sleep at all. "Fowl," Astor said, "Look. I'm planning to go, too. Even if Archer is being a little twit, it's not safe here in the city." He turned to Wick. "You're going to the valley, where the centaurs are, right?"

Wick nodded.

"It's safer there, Fowl. I think I've done all I can here anyway, so I'll see what help I can lend over there."

Archer's blood still boiled over being called a *twit*, but he watched Fowl to see what he would do.

Fowl frowned, but broke eye contact with Archer. "Fine." Fowl turned away, taking the eyes inside the locket with him. With the portrait no longer staring at him, Archer's tense shoulders loosened a tiny bit.

"We've got an opportunity while the dragons seem to be inactive," Wick said. "If we're all going, we should move now."

No one disagreed.

"With the lot of us it will probably take about four days walk," Wick went on. "We'll have to take supplies for our travels from the house."

"Do you think it would be safe enough for Fowl and me to fly?" Astor asked. "We might be harder to spot in two groups."

"I wouldn't risk it," Wick said with finality. "Up in the sky, you'd be too exposed. Besides, we may need your speed to scout ahead."

What is it with the winged people wanting to leave the rest of us behind? Archer thought to himself. *Astor just wants to abandon us.*

But now they had a plan, so Archer followed Wick to the kitchen for food.

The house transformed into a flurry of activity as they gathered the supplies they would need for their journey— fruits and vegetables, bread, bottles of drink, blankets, bandages and ointments, in case the worst did happen. Astor stood at the center of the activity in the hallway, directing Fowl and Wick to whatever they asked for with a flick of his wrist. Archer stood a safe couple of paces away. As Fowl and Wick handed him bundles and jars, he stuffed them into the unfillable bag without a word.

In the corner of his eye, Archer could see Astor's head turned toward him, watching.

"That has got to be the strangest bag I've ever seen," Astor said as he caught Archer's eye. "You've put so much into it but it never even changes shape. It almost looks empty."

Archer jammed another pair of blankets through the opening, where they vanished.

"Where did you get it?" Astor asked after a moment.

"Somebody gave it to me."

Astor's thicket of eyelashes narrowed to a thin line. "Did that somebody *know* they were giving it to you?"

Archer rolled his eyes. "I didn't steal it. I told you, someone gave it to me. It's mine."

The next thing to worry about was defense. Through the library doorway, Archer watched Fowl heft a heavy poker from the fireplace and slap it against his palm. Moments later, Wick passed by carrying a pair of kitchen knives, wrapped in a towel.

Astor cast Archer a sidelong glance. "You'd better find something to swing."

"I was about to," Archer snapped. He took a quick right-and-left look around the hallway. No pokers, no clubs. Only statuettes on the windowsills and a waist-high vase of wilted fern fronds. He peered through the window and spotted just what he needed on the porch—a break in the handrail.

"I'll be back," he said shortly to Astor, then realized Astor had already disappeared.

Now only accountable to the hallway shadows, Archer grasped the brass knob of the door and tugged. The dry smell of ash filled his nose as he stepped out onto the porch. He squinted into the darkness. No dragons yet.

He gave the broken railing a push. Then, when it didn't give, he delivered a kick, and the railing shifted at last. Archer gripped one of the spiraled newel posts and pried it free.

He bounced the wood in his hand. Heavy enough. He swung the post. It made a whipping sound through the air.

"Archer!" Wick gasped. He fell against the doorframe and swiped a hand down his face. "You scared me. What are you doing outside?"

Archer hefted his post with a smirk. "Getting something to swing."

"The railing?" Astor's voice said, his tone either curious or judgmental. Archer noticed with annoyance the tooled belt Astor had on, and the wide hunting knife hanging from it.

With supplies filling the bag and some means of defense filling every set of hands, they slipped out into the cold night. As they hurried toward the other side of the city, they still saw no dragonkin. Leftover flames and smoldering trees told them that the dragonkin couldn't be far, but as they crept through the shadowy streets, no dragonkin appeared.

"Maybe they sleep all night," Astor muttered to Wick. "That could be helpful."

"Traveling by night again, just like we used to," Wick said. "Eh, Archer?"

"Yeah." Stepping over the remnants of someone's tree swing, Archer's mind was preoccupied with wondering if he would ever miss the place that hadn't been his home. Then he wondered if he was even capable of missing it.

Or if something was very wrong with him.

His walking pace accelerated. The sooner they left the city, the better.

Passing through into the forest, they saw that the dragonkin hadn't set fire to everything, as Wick had guessed, but mainly the cities. Occasionally they skirted a broken branch or a patch of grass still burning, but it seemed on the whole the forest seemed to be in much better shape than Tor.

It occurred to Archer that their clothes would smell like ash for days.

As they walked, Archer and Fowl remained separate. Sure, occasionally they spoke briefly: "Watch out for that branch," "We'll be stopping in an hour," but Fowl didn't come to Archer of his own accord, so Archer didn't go to Fowl for anything either.

The sun rose, and their luck held. No dragonkin appeared. They stopped in the afternoon and took turns keeping watch while they recovered a few hours of sleep. Only Archer managed to sleep soundly with the sun so high in the sky, and so far, no dragonkin had appeared since leaving the city, so their nighttime travel plans transformed back into daytime plans.

On the second day, they stopped for dinner and rest for the night, and Fowl spoke to Archer for the first time on the whole journey.

As Archer dug through the bag for their nightly ration of food, Fowl crossed their campsite and sat cross-legged beside Archer. His wings, both bigger and brighter than Archer's, draped across the ground as he sat. In the corner of his eye, Archer saw that the locket was tucked away inside the high collar of Fowl's shirt.

Good.

"It. . . would probably be better if we talked about it," Fowl said at length. "It might help."

Sasha rammed her nose against Archer's hand insistently.

Archer brushed Sasha's nose aside so he could see better into the bag. "What's the *it* that should we be talking about?"

"Archer," Fowl said. "It's just you and me. Our parents are gone. We don't even have any grandparents left, and neither of our parents had family. It really is just us now."

Archer found the knotted pillowcase that held their bundle of food and tugged it out of the bag before sitting back on his heels. "Do you think talking about it would make either of us feel better?"

"Maybe."

Archer thought about it some more, his fingers kneading the pillowcase. "Do you think I have anything to say that would help you?"

"Maybe not." Fowl looked down at his hands with empty eyes. Of the pair of them, Fowl had always had the nicer eyes. They were like their mother's eyes had been; dark and deep, like they were burdened with unique wisdom.

Archer didn't have those eyes. He had the eyes like their father, blue and hard like a knife's edge.

Archer hated his father's eyes.

"You know," Archer said, "now that the house is gone, and now that he's gone, that's the end of Father's legacy. His empire is over."

"One of us could always rebuild it, I guess," Fowl said.

Archer shook his head. "No, leave it. It's a good thing. I always hated all his influence."

Fowl's eyes snapped up to Archer's face. "He hasn't been dead for ten days, and you're not just fine, you're glad he's gone."

Archer thought about backpedaling. But it would be a lie to say he hadn't meant it, and apologies wouldn't fix a thing. "Me and Dad weren't friends, Fowl."

"We weren't *friends* either, Archer. He was my father. And he was good to me. He let me do whatever I liked so long as I showed up to smile and wave when he asked, which is a lot more than you can say for yourself."

"He let you do what you wanted because he actually liked you," Archer said dismissively, emptying the bundle of food onto the ground. Something ate at the pit of his stomach. He hoped it was hunger. "All he ever did for me was yell at me to do better, jump higher, be more perfect. Last time I looked, I was a kid then. Kids aren't very good at perfection." He shook his head. "Whatever. Forget it."

"You never listened, not to anyone—That's why he

was angry. *I* learned a lot from him. He shaped me."

Like a hammer shapes copper. Batters it.

Archer rummaged more aggressively. "Shaped you into what? A yes-man? I'll pass."

Fowl narrowed his eyes, inspecting Archer coldly. "Maybe if you'd bothered to learn from him, all of this wouldn't have happened."

The sick feeling in Archer's stomach deepened even as he forced indifference into his glance toward Fowl. "What are you talking about, Fowl?"

Without hesitation, Fowl said, "Well, if you ask me, clearly all of this is your fault."

THREE

The Heavy Weight

DRIPPINGS FROM the refilled canteens soaked into Wick's shirtsleeve as he trudged back to camp. The murmurs of Archer and Fowl's voices floated toward him through the trees.

Good. They're finally talking.

His footsteps slowed as he neared the large elm where they had built their little camp. He wondered if they would want him to hang back while they talked things out.

Then Archer's voice cut through the trees, loud and sharp. "My fault, huh? How do you figure that?"

Ah.

An argument was predictable for Fowler and Archer, but Wick still had to squash his discouragement. The tension was already unbearable, and a fight would only make it worse.

Squaring his shoulders, Wick stepped into the camp.

Fowl leaned toward Archer. "You tell me. You let all this happen. If you had learned how to properly cast the spell the first time, the Scorch never would have come here. If you had learned anything from your first round of thievery, you would never have stolen from the leshy and shot down your alliances, which nearly killed us all again. And if you'd learned a single thing about our father, he would have never shut you out of the house in the end." He paused, letting his words settle in.

Wick wondered if he should step in.

Then Fowl delivered the deadly blow. "And as if all that wasn't enough, both our parents are dead. And we'll follow them soon, too. All because you just can't learn."

Wick watched Archer's hands first curl into shaking fists, then go completely still.

"I guess it's my fault that Father hated me, too," Archer said in an empty tone. Wick knew that tone well. It was the calm before the storm, the coil of the snake before it struck. Archer was just warming up.

It would be wise to intervene before Archer got the chance to try anything.

"Archer." Wick took a step toward them, unsure what to say but sure that this had already gone too far.

Fowl straightened, his eyes locked on Archer. "It wouldn't surprise me." Then he rose stiffly and walked into the woods. The tips of his feathers dragged on the ground behind him like the tails of a long robe.

Archer immediately scrambled up to follow him, but Wick caught his arm. "Don't. You want to take Fowl with us, and you can't do that if you drive him away."

Archer shook off Wick's hand, but he didn't chase Fowl. Instead, he snatched a slice of bread from the heap of supplies and jammed it into his mouth, chewing viciously.

Time passed, and Fowl didn't return to the camp.

Wick distributed dinner as the sun disappeared. Astor declared he was going to look for Fowl, only to return minutes later, reporting that Fowl was fine. But Fowl didn't reappear with him.

Toward the end of his watch, Wick finally spotted Fowl walking back from the forest. Without even looking at Wick, Fowl lay down at the edge of their camp and went to sleep.

For the rest of their journey, Archer and Fowl didn't speak at all. Wick had barely seen them speak to each other before, but since their argument, the Hessen boys wouldn't so much as look at one another. Archer seemed unwilling to discuss what had happened, so Wick left it for the time being. There would be plenty of time to talk about it later.

On the third night, Wick once again took the first watch. His sleep across the previous few nights had been restless, fearful that dragonkin would find them in the night. Exhaustion made the watch a struggle. Very soon, he decided that sitting down was a mistake, and he got up to dig through Archer's bag for something to chew on. He crouched beside the bag, setting Fowl's fire poker beside him. If he ate something and kept circling the campfire like a vulture, he could stay alert more easily. Of course he could.

As he sifted blindly through the unfillable bag in the dark, his eyelids grew heavier.

Find something quickly, he told himself. *Or you fall asleep here and now, and then where will we be?*

Just find something.

"Wick!"

Wick's eyes snapped open. He had fallen asleep in a crouch, a lump of bread from Archer's bag clutched in his hand. A shadow leaned over him. He scrambled backward, fumbling for the fireplace poker and finding nothing.

The shape followed him. "For goodness' sake, Wick."

As the glow of the fire fell over it, the shape gained more definition. The red light gleamed on the ridges of barky skin and cast shadows across a face draped in black cloth.

"Were you supposed to be watching the camp?" Twill whispered, looking around at the sleeping bodies of the others. "If you are, I think your method might be bad."

"I know, I know." Wick scrubbed at his tired eyes. "Twill, what are you doing here?"

"I'm going to centaur territory." Twill sat cross-legged across from Wick, just close enough to the coals that he could pick out her shape in the firelight.

Wick struggled to understand. "In a mask?"

"Glowing eyes are very noticeable in the dark, and if I can't see the dragons in the dark, they shouldn't be allowed to find me, either." Twill tilted her head. "I don't know about you, sleepyhead, but I plan to get to the valley alive. What are you doing with a lit fire?"

"The fire!" Wick leaped up and stamped at the fire with his heel. Everyone had fallen asleep directly after dinner, and he'd been tired enough to fall asleep sitting up. . . In their fatigue, every one of them had forgotten the fire.

"I could see the glow for a quarter mile," Twill went

on as Wick killed the last embers. "The smoke trail is probably worse than that."

Wick rubbed his forehead and watched the last of the smoke vanish between the branches above them. He turned his gaze back to Twill, perched by the fire with her hands clasping her crossed ankles. A breeze ruffled the folds of the hood across her face.

"Lucky you had the bonfire, though," she said. "Or I wouldn't have tracked you down."

"What happened in the village?" Wick asked. With the panic about the fire now evaporated, his brain had settled back into a muzzy haze. "Is everyone all right? My parents?"

"They're fine." Laughter entered Twill's voice. "Look, you're going to fall asleep sitting up. Just go to bed. I'll keep watch, and I'll tell you anything you want in the morning."

Wick wanted to protest, but his human body begged him for rest. Even the mention of sleep made his head feel heavy. Between Twill's calm dismissal and the traitorous exhaustion of his new human body, he gave in. "Fine. We'll talk about everything as soon as I wake up."

"Perfect." Twill turned around and faced the forest, ignoring Wick completely.

Wick had just enough consciousness left to pull his blanket toward him and wrap it around his shoulders before the darkness claimed him.

At some point in the middle of the night, he woke enough to hear someone stir and Archer's voice say, "Gah! Where did you come from?"

Wick considered getting up to explain, but only for a

moment. Archer would be fine. He slipped off to sleep again.

When the morning came, Wick woke to the sound of voices and the smell of mushrooms cooking on the fire. Warmth from the fire pressed against his back. As he sat up, tangled in the blanket, he saw that all the others had congregated on the far side of the fire to talk. Everyone but Fowl seemed very engaged in whatever Twill was saying.

"Good morning," Wick croaked.

Twill twisted around. "Awake at last. No wonder you were falling asleep sitting up last night; you clearly needed that."

Wick swiped at his bleary eyes. "What happened to no fires?"

Twill pointed the fireplace poker at Astor, who said:

"There's already smoke rising right over there." He gestured to the forest to the west, where Wick could see other smoke rising through the trees. From smoldering branches, no doubt. Astor wiped his mouth with his thumb. "They might have noticed the firelight in the dark, but I doubt the lizards will even notice our smoke now."

"You should eat some of those," Archer said, leaning around Twill to point at the mushrooms blackening by the fire. "You slept through the rest of breakfast, and we need to start walking again soon."

Wick nodded and reached for some food. He ate steadily as they packed up their little camp and kicked earth into the remaining coals of the fire.

"So, why are you going to the centaurs?" Wick asked

Twill as they continued further south in a long line. He stooped to avoid a branch.

Beside him, Twill ducked it, too. Now that the sun had risen, her makeshift mask of black cloth hung around her neck, where it swayed with her movements. "I want to find out what's going on. No one in leshy territory understands what's happening, and nobody cares about finding out, just about surviving." She stepped up onto a log blocking their path and looked down at Wick. "Our people only watch out for their own, so their plan is just to lay low until the danger is past."

Wick felt a worried crease forming in his brow as he took a large step over the log. "That sounds like them. Did the dragonkin burn much?"

"Not much, the first time," Twill said. "That surprised me when I got home. But thinking about it, I don't think the dragons could find the leshy towns. They can't be very visible above the trees. By my guess, only one or two dragons passed over, and they only burned the treetops."

"But the second time?" Wick prompted.

"The second time was much worse. Your mother's garden is gone. My garden is gone. You'll be glad that the museum is still standing, but those lizard things were angry the second time. They burned a lot of the forest, for no reason, I guess. Then they found the town, and since no one put a stop to them, they just burned things until. . . until they were done burning it, I'd guess." She shrugged, but Wick saw the tension in her posture.

The destruction of their village bothered her more than she let on, of course it did. Who could blame her?

Wick braced himself and asked the most important question. "No one. . . no one died, did they?"

"No. Luckily. Your family is all right, and so is mine. I checked on both of them as soon as I was sure the dragons were gone. They're scared, but scared is better than dead, isn't it?" Twill paused. "The last I heard, most of the royal family made it out alive, as well. I don't know if you care."

"Of course I do," Wick said, surprised.

"Don't *of course* me," Twill responded quickly. "You don't have to care. I know I wouldn't. They took away your job, your prospects, your home, and let's not forget that you can't even call yourself a leshy anymore, thanks to them."

Wick winced. "I don't think I could forget it if I wanted to. That was the worst day of my life, no question about it. But if Archer can consider himself a seraph but not *one of* the seraphs, I think I can do something similar with the name of leshy. Technically—factually—that's what I am. I'm just not a part of the leshy people anymore. I can live with that, I think."

Twill turned to Wick, and her eyes were sincere. "You shouldn't have to live with it. The things you did were radical, not wrong. You were trying to help them while they were too busy doing nothing, and they repaid you with banishment."

"I know. But if I stopped caring about everyone who had ever wronged me, I don't think I'd have any people left." Not even Twill. He thought of the last time he had visited leshy territory, when he had gone to visit Twill and she shouted at him for hiding things from her, or the time before that, when she had warned him to run instead of helping him hide. "And besides," he added, "even if I did stop caring about them, I wouldn't want them dead. Would you?"

Twill considered. "I don't know."

"Twill, come on. You wouldn't want them dead."

"I don't know!" Twill protested. She flung her hands up in the air. "Maybe I would. Maybe I should become a vigilante, too, and once they banish me, we'll find out."

Wick laughed. "I'm not a vigilante."

"Try felon," Archer called back from ahead of them.

"There you go," Twill said, pointing toward Archer. "Felon. And if you ever want to do something else radical just to get back at them, count me in."

Wick shook his head. "I don't think it will ever come to that."

"Anyway," Twill went on, "once the dragons moved on to who knows where, I figured the centaurs would probably have some answers, so I started walking."

"There are probably others who did the same," Wick mused. "I wonder how many people the centaurs have seen in the last few days."

"I guessed I'd find you there, too," Twill added. "I knew you were probably on your way to the valley, if you weren't there already. And if I didn't find you there, I planned to give it a few days."

"And if I still didn't show up?" Wick asked, teasing. "Would you just curse my name and go home?"

"No. If you didn't show up," Twill said, turning her head toward Wick, "I would have assumed you were dead."

Early in the afternoon, they reached the base of the

mountains and began the ascent. The forest surrounding the centaurs' valley seemed fairly quiet. Every few minutes, they passed more piles of fallen branches and gently smoldering leaves, but where Wick had feared they would find nothing but destruction from one horizon to the other, he found that most of the trees remained standing, and only once did they pass a patch where all the vegetation had been reduced to stalks.

As far as Wick could guess, most of the damage was leftover from the first attack, when the dragonkin had tried to stop them from taking the stones to the cavern.

As they hiked over the mountains, they met a small group of human men. The humans appeared delighted to encounter other travelers. They exchanged pleasantries, and Wick learned that human territory had received its own fair share of damage. In true human form, though, the men reported that their people had fought the dragonkin tooth and nail. They had taken down over a dozen dragonkin in their town alone, and already, their village had begun to repair the damages.

As the men continued their travel, passing Wick and Archer's party at a rapid clip, Wick found himself in wonder at the nature of the humans. They were, by nature, resilient almost to a fault. They threw themselves into battle and harvest alike with a smile and a song, and an extra cheer once the work was done. They were as hardy as the satyrs were resourceful or the nixies were enterprising and strong.

In fact, considering their insistent independence, Wick found himself surprised that any humans would come to the valley at all. The situation in human territory had to be more dire than the men had let on.

"Let's hope it won't be too crowded in the valley," he said quietly to Archer as they neared the top. "The valley usually gets a lot more visitors in times of crisis. I've never known them to be overrun before, but there's a first time for everything."

"You're telling me it can get even busier?" Archer frowned. "Every time I'm in the valley, it's already too crowded."

"It does tend to be active. The centaurs are the highest authority in the country, and as such they can provide anything people might need," Wick said. "People trust them for solutions and answers. When things go wrong, people come here."

With that, they reached the top of the pass. Wick hadn't planned to stop. But as the valley came into full view, his feet stopped moving.

Disaster stretched across the valley.

Half the pavilions by the lake were half burned or knocked down, and the great golden statue with the open arms had toppled into the edge of the lake, where he splayed half-in, half-out the water like a helpless corpse. Long strips of trees down every side of the valley had been ravaged, leaving only charred stumps that shed ash each time the wind blew.

And then there were the crowds. Wick recognized groups from nearly every territory, of every age and from countless regions. They crowded in every available space. They perched on the porches of houses built into the mountains and thronged near the storage buildings. They sat in groups around the main hall, waiting to be seen or to speak to someone or just waiting for answers. Wick could scarcely spot five feet of open anywhere in the valley. As he watched, the group of men that had passed them on the mountains trickled down into the crowd, heading for the main hall.

"Oh." Archer gazed down into the valley with the stiff posture of discomfort. "This isn't normal, right?"

"No." Wick shook his head. "I've never seen it like this."

"But if you think about it, when was the last time we had a disaster like this?" Twill asked, appearing over Wick's other shoulder.

Wick glanced back at her. "What do you mean?"

"Honestly," Twill said. "We've never had something this bad happen in any of our lifetimes. Usually the centaurs see everything coming, and they take care of it for us so that nothing bad ever gets the chance to happen. This time, though, no one had any warning, and everyone's homes burned all at once. It makes sense that everyone's panicking."

Not technically true: someone had predicted this. Caihu had. Wick's heart weighed heavily. In all of Aro, only one person had listened to Caihu's warning, and that had been Archer. Even Wick had refused to believe it at first. No one believed that the Scorch was really coming.

No one could deny it now. Wick surveyed the disaster in the valley, listening to the mumble of the anxious masses drifting up the hill. This was the result of Aro's mistakes.

"We can't stand here forever," Archer said. "I don't know about you, but I want to know what's going on."

Wick nodded. "There are more answers down there than up here."

Their group started the steep descent down the slope. As they neared the milling crowds at the bottom, Wick made a last-minute decision. "Stay here," he told the rest of the group. "Archer and I need to find Ongel before we do anything else. Stick close to the path, and wait for us." He waved to Archer, and together the two of them waded into the crowd to find Ongel.

"Do you know where he is, or are we just going for a merry wander like everyone else?" Archer asked, pressing in close behind Wick in the crush of people. Wick accidentally ran into the broad back of a manghar woman and quickly backed up.

"So sorry. Excuse us, ma'am." Wick skirted around the woman and the other manghar with her. "I can at least start with a few likely places. If he isn't in the hall or his study, then yes, we'll have to wander a while until we find him."

They made as direct a line as they could for the grand hall. The crowds thronged thicker around the hall, but Archer took the lead, elbowing through and spreading both wings to clear a path. Wick followed behind, making apologies.

When they reached the door, Wick found a familiar red-haired centaur attempting to direct the throngs. As they approached, Hirim said, "I'm sorry, but it's already overfilled inside—" He stopped, and his eyes widened, full of both shock and relief. "Wick. You're safe."

"We're trying to find Ongel," Wick said, raising his voice above the noise of all the people.

"I think he's still inside," Hirim said. "But I don't know where."

"We'll find him." Wick slipped around Hirim and through the heavy gold doors of the main hall. Inside, dim light filtered down from the high windows and dappled the polished stone floor between the crowded footfalls of everyone inside.

It seemed they had used the shelter of the main hall as a hospital. Blankets covered the floor from wall to wall any way they could fit. On every blanket rested a different invalid—centaurs with bandaged flanks and burned faces, humans clutching their children as they slept, dozens of harrowed-looking fair folk sleeping in communal piles.

It made Wick wonder how many other rooms in Aro had been made over into hospitals. Libraries, bedrooms, feast halls. The patients here had to be only a small percentage of the total. And many worse than wounded.

Several centaurs and a few others that Wick recognized as messengers moved through the patients, applying new bandages, delivering water, making sure that the injured were comfortable. Ongel was not among them.

"Come on," Wick murmured to Archer. "If we can make it to the other end, we can check the offices and storage rooms."

They shimmied their way between invalids and caregivers down the length of the hall. The cacophony outside the doors echoed through the quiet of the hospital. Wick and Archer slid past a closed door. Just as they had passed by, the door opened, and from it emerged a towering black centaur, braids swinging as he spoke to someone exiting the room behind him.

Wick's heart leaped. "Ongel!" When Ongel didn't hear him, Wick stepped quickly over someone lying on a blanket and caught Ongel's huge forearm.

Ongel turned, and his face broke into a smile of relief. "Wick! You're safe."

"We are. And I'm glad to see you safe, too," Wick said. "But we need to talk."

"Then let's talk." Ongel looked around, then reversed back into the room he had come from. His companion raised a hand in farewell, then crossed to the door of the Great Hall and disappeared into the valley.

Wick and Archer followed Ongel through the door of what appeared to be a small library. Between Wick's broad shoulders, Archer's wings, and Ongel's horse body, they had to cram into the last inch of the tiny room, but it was dark and quiet, and the seclusion from the crush of people brought Wick enormous relief. The books lining the walls lended a pleasant muffling to their words.

Ongel reached down to hug Wick. "It's so good to see that you're safe." He reached for Archer as well, and to Wick's surprise, Archer hugged Ongel back.

"We came to see if you had any idea what's going on, but it looks like all of Aro had the same idea," Wick said. His mind swirled with all the things Ongel might say.

"People started flocking in the day after the Scorch returned," Ongel responded. "And they haven't stopped coming since. We're running out of supplies and room, and still people are waiting for some kind of explanation."

"Then you don't have any idea why the Scorch has returned?"

"None."

Archer crossed his arms and looked around. "You have all these books; isn't there anything in them about the Scorch?"

"None that we've had the time to find so far," Ongel said. "I've heard talk about some papers that could give us more insight, and we've begun the search for the papers in the records, but with all the people we're providing for, there hasn't been much time. Everyone's getting little to no sleep, and the workload each day is only increasing."

Archer's lips pursed in a way that told Wick that he was going to say something stupid. "Can't you just run them all off?"

Wick reminded himself to stop Archer the next time he made that face.

"They don't need to stay here; they can go somewhere else where they aren't such a burden," Archer said. "Sure, their homes might have burned, but there are other places they can go. The valley can't deal with all of them and find solutions for the Scorch problem at the same time."

"Dispersing the refugees across several other cities would certainly reduce the strain on the valley," Ongel said. "Some of our messengers have been sent to nearby cities already. We're still waiting for their responses, but I think we can count on their help."

"I'll bet you've already sent out summons to have the stones brought back here, as well," Wick said. "In which case, everyone just needs to hold out until the stones arrive, and then the Scorch will be beaten back again."

"If it's enough." Archer looked first at Wick, then at Ongel. "The barrier spell worked before, but it didn't last.

Shouldn't we try something more powerful?"

"Boys," Ongel said, his voice so dull and tired that Wick looked at him in surprise. Ongel's brow weighed heavily over his eyes. "The valley hasn't yet made this public, but I trust both of you to be discreet: the stones are already here."

Already. The stones were already in the valley.

"As soon as the Scorch reappeared, all of the nations sent the stones to us immediately. Even the leshy sent their piece. We've been keeping them locked in the holding room ever since they arrived."

Worry tickled at the back of Wick's brain. If all the stones had been in the valley for days, and the Scorch was still running rampant through the land, it could only mean one thing.

Ongel looked toward Wick as he confirmed Wick's fears: "The stones are unresponsive."

A shivery tingle ran down Wick's arms. They couldn't use the stones, their one line of defense. They were helpless.

Archer's brow creased. "There isn't a fake again, is there?"

"No." Ongel shook his head. "When the stones first arrived, we tested them all to be certain they were the real ones. And once we had them all in the chamber and on the pedestals, they lit up like before. But the barrier never went back up and the Scorch remains here." He paused briefly. "We've held several meetings to discuss our next move. The Crowned Head sent a message to suggest going to war. If we can't get rid of the dragons the usual way, they're willing to use other means. They've sent to the nixies as well, but their queen hasn't yet responded."

Wick's mind spun. "All that in so little time."

"Indeed." Ongel's wide face looked more somber than Wick had seen it in a long time. His features seemed to sag, adding decades to his age. "What strange times these are."

Archer turned to Ongel. "What do *you* think is the best thing to do?"

Wick paused in surprise. Archer wasn't usually one to rely on anyone, even Wick. Even his own family. But here he was, asking for Ongel's opinion without even a hint of reluctance.

What had happened between the pair of them in the time Wick had been in leshy territory?

"I think that first we need to know why the stones won't work," Ongel said. He looked at Archer, and then at Wick, his hands clasped in his lap. "Not only are the stones essential to prevent. . . Well, to prevent what's been done already, but they're integral to Aro's general safety. Not to mention their cultural and patriotic significance in every territory. If they've lost their power after all these years, we need to find out why, and if their power can be restored. In the meantime, we have to look after one another until we get out of this."

A wise and reasonable course of action, well-thought out, and careful to avoid leaving anyone out in the cold.

That was the Ongel Wick knew and loved.

Archer leveled a palm back and forth. "I would have gone for something closer to what the manghar said. Hit 'em hard and fast."

That got a laugh out of Ongel. "I thought you

would."

"Except that it would never work," Wick said, frowning down at the tiled floor. "Everyone knew the Scorch was coming the second time. We were ready, we had all of Aro's finest warriors, and even then we barely held out until the barrier spell was cast. One of the dragonkin even made it into the Heather Stone chamber."

Archer's head whipped around. "It did?"

"I thought I'd told you." Wick sighed, still thinking. "My point is, we can never hope to outfight them or outrun them. If we're going to stand even a tiny chance, we need to find a weakness to exploit."

Inwardly, Wick cringed at his own words. They sounded like someone else's words, someone vicious and calculating. But the dragonkin had already struck while Aro was down, and they would do it again. They had no other choice but to respond in kind, or face annihilation.

Ongel nodded. "My thoughts precisely. We have no way of spying on them, so our best chance would be the records here in the valley; they go back for centuries. Logically speaking, there should be more than enough written on the Scorch to give us a game plan."

"How should we do that?" Wick asked.

"Hirim thought Eland could help," Ongel replied. "A lot of Eland's training has been in keeping records and creating documents; that will be his expertise once he's done his training. If there's anything to find in our library, he'll be the one to track it down."

Thank You For Not Understanding

PLANS FELL INTO PLACE.

Wick would find Eland, and then Eland and Wick together would comb through the library and learn what they could about the stones and the Scorch. Archer would take the rest of their group and set up a base camp outside of the valley so they wouldn't add to the crowds.

"Staying outside the valley would make it a long walk to the library, though," Wick mused. "Is there a corner of the cavern where we could set up base camp? Or would that be against the rules?"

"The rules aren't the problem," Ongel answered. "The problem is that the cavern is already full."

Wick paused. "It is?"

"Indeed." One of Ongel's hooves stamped, like a nervous tick. "The cavern is officially a ceremonial site for the Heather Stones, but the cavern floor can be used as an emergency bunker. We're using it as extra space for the refugees."

Archer's eyebrows rose. "They're crammed every-where."

"Yes." Ongel rubbed his head. "I hope the surrounding cities will be generous so that the valley can get some rest again."

"We can at least help by removing our group," Wick said, reaching for the doorknob. "Archer will get them out of here. I'll see if I can find Eland, and we'll start on the records right away."

◇

AS ARCHER WOVE back through the throngs, he asked himself how he always got these kinds of tasks while Wick was off doing more interesting things.

Well.

He didn't *really* want to be the one sorting through files and documents, especially since he doubtless couldn't read half of them anyway, but anything sounded better than looking after Fowl and his changeable moods.

Archer tucked his wings in tight to squeeze past a group of satyrs and hoped he didn't know any of them. Running into an old enemy was the last thing he needed right now. Even in a time of crisis, plenty of people would put aside their differences to end Archer Hessen.

Finally the others came into sight. "Come on," Archer said, "we're going to set up camp outside of the valley. There's too many people here already without us taking up room."

"Because we're taking up more room than the

thousands of other people here?" Twill asked dryly.

Maybe Twill wasn't so bad.

"Mr. Hessen."

Archer's stomach clenched, and he stopped mid-stride. *Mr. Hessen.* It was his name, technically, but it felt unfamiliar and stiff, and sounded altogether too much like someone addressing his father. His temper prickled at the voice: old and husky, but loud. Familiar.

It was the grey-haired centaur with the beard. The one who had said such rotten things about both Archer and Wick.

Tinor.

Archer's fingers gripped the smooth leather of the bag strap on his shoulder as he turned to face his least-favorite centaur.

Tinor hung back a few paces. He towered inches above even Fowl and Astor's heads, his hair blowing across his robed shoulders. He didn't seem malicious; actually, judging by the slumped shoulders and the clenched brow, he seemed more. . . unsure.

Archer swallowed. "What do you want?"

Twill's eyes flickered toward Archer, but if she had something to say about Archer's harsh tone, she kept it to herself.

Archer took a breath and spoke again. "If you're looking for Wick, forget about it. I won't tell you where he is."

"I wasn't looking for Wick," Tinor admitted, shaking his head. He took a few cautious steps closer, his hooves heavy on the densely packed earth. "I was just looking for you."

Archer pulled back half a step. "You—why? What do you want with me?"

"I heard that your parents were taken in the first attack," Tinor replied.

"Yeah, they were." Archer put on his best empty face. "What about it?"

Fowl made an irritated noise behind Archer's head.

Tinor reached into a deep pocket of his silver robe and withdrew a packet of envelopes bound with twine. "I had correspondence with your father for years. A few of his letters mentioned you, and I thought you should have them."

Letters from their father? About Archer? A nervous laugh exploded from Archer's mouth. "Why would I want those?"

Tinor hesitated, then extended the packet again. The ends of the twine swayed between his fingers. "Take them. Whether you read them or burn them, I'm giving them to you."

Archer's fingers twitched on the leather strap. Tinor watched. His hand didn't drop.

Finally, Archer snatched the packet of letters. He stuffed them under the flap of his bag before he had the chance to hesitate. "Anyway. We've got to go." He spun on his heel and started back up the path, waving for the others to follow him. They climbed back through the pass. They didn't need to go too far; the other side of the pass would be good enough, if they could find enough level space to set up camp.

Fowl had gone back to stoic silence. He didn't say a word as they hiked up the mountains, no matter what sort of thicket Archer led them through. The silence could have been a sign that Fowl was still angry, but Archer didn't want to open up that conversation any more than he wanted to reach his hand inside a wasp's nest. He left Fowl's silence alone.

When the first piece of level ground came into view, Archer said, "Here's good enough," and threw the unfillable bag down. No one argued.

The looks of the ground had been deceiving, Archer realized as he set up his bed near the edge of the clearing. It definitely still slanted. That meant he had to choose which end he wanted downhill. For the time being, he didn't care. He tossed the blanket across the ground in a folded-up heap and sat on it.

"You have it all rumpled," Fowl said as he laid out his own bed a few paces away from Archer's. Archer noticed with a twinge of annoyance that Fowl had carefully chosen the most level part of the clearing for his bed.

"Well, I'm not sleeping on it yet, am I?" Archer demanded. "It doesn't matter."

Fowl shook his head and flicked over a corner of his own blanket to make it flat. Meticulous, as always.

The camp would be about a half hour's walk to the valley, but Wick probably wouldn't mind. So long as he was being helpful, Wick probably wouldn't mind anything. Archer had yet to find out what it was about helpfulness that Wick liked so much.

Something crackled in the treetops. Archer looked up. The shadow of something big passed overhead, but in the darkening sky he couldn't be sure if it was a dragonkin or just another manghar headed for the valley. He took a few steps into the trees, trying to follow the shape with his eyes.

"You know, Fowl's struggling," Astor said behind him.

"Yeah?" Archer kept studying the sky. The thing, whatever it was, had disappeared. Drat.

"He could use our help."

Archer turned to Astor. "Tell me something I don't know. Fowl's going through plenty, sure. But last time I looked, he and I had the same parents, the same city, lived in the same country that's about to burn. What makes Fowl's problems special?" He shouldered past Astor and walked back to the camp.

He just barely caught Astor's response.

"At least Fowl cares."

Archer slumped into his makeshift bed face-first and lay there a moment.

Wick had started doling out tasks again, Fowl was moody, Astor wanted to tell him what to think—they all needed to lay off. And Tinor, giving Archer an entire pack of useless letters from his father. . .

The letters, at least, could go in the fire.

Archer rolled onto his side and reached into the unfillable bag. He found the pack of paper in an instant, already slipped free of the loose twine. Archer flipped through the envelopes mindlessly. From Tinor to Ochre Hessen, from Ochre Hessen to Tinor. . . every envelope read the same.

The handwritten date of the oldest one came in right around the time that Archer had been in seraph territory with Wick, arguing about scales of one to ten in the window.

Why had his father been writing letters to Tinor? And why would they have mentioned Archer?

Archer huffed out a sigh. "Fine."

He flipped the envelope open and slid out the uppermost inch of the thick stationary.

His father's handwriting appeared, his script heavy and ornate as the bars of an iron gate.

Most respectable Tinor,

In regards to my son, Archer—

Archer slapped the paper face-down on the blanket.

He wasn't just mentioned in his father's letters to Tinor. He was the *subject* of their letters.

"No, thanks," he muttered to himself. "I don't need that today. Or any day."

He shuffled the envelopes back into the unfillable bag, then slung an arm across his face. His name, written in his father's hand, still burned behind his eyes.

For the next few days, nothing really changed. Wick returned late each night and left early each morning, helping Eland with the records and the library. The rest of them often went to the valley to help the centaurs with the refugees, but most of that boiled down to distributing blankets and food, nothing interesting.

Ongel worked to contact the nearby territories so the throngs could be redistributed. From what he told Archer, the satyr safe houses were the top choice, but it would take some time for the messengers to be back with answers.

Fowl ignored everyone, which made Astor visibly

worried and Archer uncertain how to feel. After all, Fowl wouldn't talk to him, but at least they weren't fighting. Fowl mostly sat by himself and read the precious few books he had carried away from Astor's house. He didn't bother anyone, but he also didn't interact without being forced.

Archer couldn't decide if it was better this way.

The first line of the letter lingered in his mind like the smell of smoke lingered in the air. No matter how hard he stuffed it down, he couldn't stop the curiosity from resurfacing. No. Not curiosity. The sensation worming its way into his mind had a nastier taste.

Falling onto his blanket on the third night, Archer stretched an arm into the unfillable bag, feeling for the crinkle of envelopes.

His fingertips found the texture of thick, expensive paper. Archer steeled himself.

It didn't matter what his father had said about him. Or even *thought* about him.

But somehow he knew that the queasy feeling in his stomach wouldn't leave until he knew what the letters said.

Archer rested a wing over his head as a shelter against the chill and the prying eyes and opened the first letter.

His father's iron-shaped handwriting appeared once again. A smell wafted from the letter: a strong, spicy scent almost like frutelken. An instant later, Archer realized what it was: his father's cologne.

Almost as though Archer's father stood leaning over his shoulder.

Archer's back stiffened. He took a breath. *It's just a*

stupid piece of paper. Quit stalling and read it already.

The words seemed to leap from the page.

In regards to my son—

His father had entirely skipped the paragraph of unimportant news and pleasantries and raced straight into the part about Archer. He must have been eager.

Respected Tinor,

In regards to my son, Archer, I assume you mean to find a weakness in him. You only asked if I had heard of his reputation of robbery, but I, too, have heard about the rapidly vanishing Heather Stones. I know that the thief is my son.

I suppose you asked me about him so that you can find a weakness and stop him before he has more Heather Stones. Since he is untrackable—I can speak to that personally—I recommend you focus on thwarting him only once he is already in the valley. Archer is not a man of strategy, however, I still suspect he'll go to the valley last. There would be no point in stealing every Heather Stone if he didn't mean to cast a spell, which is something he can only do from the valley.

What his plan is, I don't pretend to know. Archer plays his cards close to his chest, and throws out a smoke screen of sorts when asked direct questions. Even under torture (which I do not suggest), I doubt he would give up anything rational.

However, be wary. His ignorance and foolishness is entirely an act. My son is an incredibly clever and intelligent young man, and driven, as well, on the occasion that he finds something he wants. Since he seems to have put his mind to stealing Heather Stones, there will be almost no stopping him. He honors no creed and fears nothing, so far as I can tell. He is wild enough to look death in the eye and demand a deal. It is impossible to threaten or bribe him.

All I can suggest to stop him is to overwhelm him with numbers and strike as quickly as possible, to give him no time to react.

Under no circumstances may you kill him. I may be only a humble seraph lord, but I have many friends who have many methods. Any creature who kills my son will regret it.

He may be a foolhardy boy and an enigma, but Archer Hessen is still my son, and I find that he burns quite bright. He is truly my son. One day, I suspect that he may be even a greater man than I am, and build something fit to inspire the nation. I assure you, it is well worth it to let Archer Hessen live.

But first, keep him from setting our world on fire.
I look forward to news of your success—or failure.
Yours in anticipation,
Ochre Hessen of Tor

The edge of the paper quivered in front of Archer's face. The hand that held it drooped to the ground.

"What on earth," he muttered.

His father had thought he was. . . . What? Clever? Driven? At some point in his life, Archer's father had experienced a positive emotion toward him?

Unless it was all lies.

No.

Archer ground his knuckles into his forehead, hearing the paper crackle in his fist.

His father couldn't have gained anything by lying to Tinor about Archer's qualities. If he wanted to get the valley's favor and move up in the world, he would have given them a real plan, or even a real weakness. He would have gotten somewhere just by saying, *hit the bad wing, it'll hurt,* or *ask the manghar, they're happy to volunteer.*

If Ochre hadn't been after the valley's favor, did that make his opinion. . . the truth?

But what sense would that make? Ochre had always hated what Archer's reputation did to the family name. He'd said so enough times while Archer had been home. Before the fire.

One day, I suspect that he will be an even greater man than I am.

"What does that *mean,* Dad?" Archer growled. He rifled through the letters, casting away anything sent from Tinor. He didn't care what Tinor had to say. The next post date leaped out at him: the same day that he had been thrown in manghar prison.

This letter was much shorter, written on a piece of thick card. The size of it looked more like a note than an important letter.

Most honorable Tinor,

You misunderstand. I wrote acknowledging Archer's qualities not as a proud papa, but as a man assessing a rival power. I pride myself on shaping my boys into only the strongest men, and Archer is no different just because he is rebellious.

I only meant to warn you about his strengths so that you could prepare for them. I also think that if it should ever be appropriate, the valley would benefit from an alliance with Archer. I've always thought that he would be a powerful person to have on one's side. I've also thought anyone who could ever gain his loyalty would be the only person in the world able to pin him down.

The letter ended abruptly, with no signature.

Archer paused. He tapped the card on his palm, first slowly, then harder and harder as he thought.

His father *could not* be the person who suggested the centaurs work with him and Wick. He'd suggested that they. . . pin him down. Like a butterfly in a case. Like a prey animal.

"Wow." Archer threw the card the same way the other letters had gone. "That just made it so much worse."

He ripped open the final letter addressed from his father. The posted date read as only a few months ago, right after Archer and Wick robbed the valley. From their first day in jail.

Most gracious Tinor,

Thank you for the news about my son. I'm pleased to hear that his foolishness caused no damage to the valley or to the Heather Stones.

I have no particular inclination to see him in prison, and I doubt he wants to see me. As you might have heard, he does not hold anyone from seraph territory in high regard.

Do be warned: I doubt your prison can hold him for long. He seems to slip through bars like a liquid through a sieve.

If he returns to Tor after his escape looking for refuge, perhaps I can finally return him to sanity and propriety.

Yours in obligation,

Ochre Hessen of Tor

Maybe that was the angle, then. Maybe his father had been using Tinor all along, to track what Archer had been doing. He'd seen the Heather Stones as an interesting test, a way of gauging who Archer had become.

He wouldn't stop saying "my son." Like Archer was something that he *owned*. Like Archer was a thing he had any right to.

Archer's fingers twitched. He swept up the papers and pitched them all into the campfire. The orange flames flickered and surged brighter as the envelopes curled and withered beneath them.

Watching over the knobs of his folded knees, Archer seethed.

"What are you burning?" Wick lowered his bag to the ground at Archer's side.

Archer shook his head. "Just some garbage." His voice sounded empty even to his own ears.

"I see your father's name in there," Wick said, keeping his voice low. "Don't you think Fowl would have wanted to see those?"

Archer snorted. "No, he wouldn't. Trust me." But from the twinge of regret in his gut, Archer knew Wick was right. The letters might have proved to Fowl that their father was a snake.

A smarter snake than even Archer had realized.

"I think," Wick said slowly, "that you need to talk to Fowl. About anything. I haven't seen you two talk to one another in days."

Archer groaned and dropped his forehead onto his knees. "Why?"

"Because it would help you both to communicate *somehow* without arguing. He's all you've got now, Archer." Wick paused and chewed the inside of his cheek.

"You got him all the way here," he said finally. "Don't lose him now."

Wick left the firelight, and a moment later Archer heard the thump of Wick's collapse into bed. Archer seethed for a moment more, now for a different reason, then forced himself to get up and walk to Fowl. Fowl lay on his side, faced away from the fire with an open book clutched in his hands like a lifeline.

Archer sat a few feet away from Fowl's blanket, just out of arm's reach. He tucked his legs up and folded his hands on top of his knees. Then he hesitated.

So, what did you think of our father, Fowl? You know, he thought he sculpted both of us into versions of him. Pretty cool, huh?

No. Archer swallowed the lump of anger clogging his throat. He needed a safer topic if he wanted even a chance of Fowl talking to him.

Archer cleared his throat awkwardly. "So. They're finding places to send the refugees. Places all over Aro. Safe places."

Fowl cast Archer a tired look and went back to his book.

The talk was already not going well.

Too late to quit, though.

"I dragged you here," Archer began painfully, "but I never asked you what you wanted. I guess that's not very fair. If. . . if they found a safe place to stay in seraph territory, would you want to go back?"

Fowl fully looked up at last. "Why does it suddenly matter to you what I want?"

Archer's temper flared, but Wick had specified *no*

arguing if he wanted to talk to Fowl. He pushed the anger down.

"Because, Fowl." His words still sounded clipped, but at least he hadn't snapped. Yet. "Like it or not, you're still my brother, and whether we hate it or not, we're stuck with one another. Our parents are gone. You're all I have left, and I'm all you have left. Either we join forces or we both choose to be alone in this inferno." He took a deep, shuddering breath, suddenly realizing how the question terrified him. "It's not fair to drag you around, so I'm asking you: Do you want to be here. . . or do you want to go home?"

Fowl thought. His dark eyes reflected the firelight as he inspected individual leaves above their heads. At last he spoke. "I don't think I want to travel that far again so soon, so I don't think I'll leave just yet."

Archer's breath came a little easier.

Fowl had chosen to stay put more than he had chosen to stay where Archer was, and there was no saying that this was where he *wanted* to be, but it was a start.

"Archer," Fowl said as Archer began to get up. "Do you. . . do you miss them at all?"

Archer paused, now kneeling. The empty feeling in his gut returned. "I. . ." *I don't. I won't, and I can't.* "Not yet," he said at last.

Fowl turned away, making a noise of disappointment and frustration.

Archer swallowed quickly. "Do—do you?" he asked, hating how small his voice sounded.

Fowl's wings pulled an inch closer to him, like they could wrap into a protective layer around his shoulders.

"Very much."

The empty pit in Archer's gut widened by a mile.

Archer nodded and got up, realizing he needed a long walk, right now. Away from everyone else. "I'll be back," he said to no one in particular, and walked into the darkness.

No one stopped him.

Trekking across the lip of the mountains, Archer could catch glimpses of the valley between the trunks of the trees. He had never seen it at night, not clearly. The last time, he'd looked down on the valley during a raging storm with a thieving scheme embedded in his brain. No time for sightseeing. But on a clear night like tonight, the valley looked like a small city, or a puddle full of stars. Torchlight from the pavilions flickered across the mounded shapes of people sleeping on the ground. Chilly moonlight glinted on the lake, illuminating the outline of the fallen statue.

Somebody really needed to fix that statue.

Archer glanced up at the sky. It seemed strange how the stars hadn't changed, not during his time wandering alone, not since meeting Wick, not since the fire that took down Tor. Despite how fast the world had changed, despite the fire and the death and all the conflicting kinds of pain, the stars hadn't budged an inch.

How dare they stay the same.

Something darted overhead, temporarily blocking out the stars. With it came the smell of ash.

A dragonkin.

Fear shot through Archer's veins. The creature was too close to the valley, and much too close to their camp.

Definitely too close to Archer.

He hid under the shelter of a tree. Years of not dying at the hands of the manghar had given Archer a nearly foolproof strategy: put enough branches between you and the flying thing and nine times out of ten, it won't see you.

This was the tenth time.

Something collided with the top of the tree, shaking it down to the trunk. Despite the fear buzzing in his veins, Archer tried to stay still. Stillness was his second strategy. Nearly everything hunted by motion. If he stayed still, and didn't make any noise, the thing wouldn't notice him, and it would go away.

It didn't go away.

The tree at Archer's back started quivering again, now in small, controlled bursts.

Something was crawling down.

Too late to stay still. Too exposed to hide. The fear in Archer's veins told him to *run*.

He bolted. A crashing sound came from the tree as the dragonkin he still hadn't seen took off once again. It was chasing him.

Archer knew he had to shake the dragon. If he couldn't, it would catch him, and then who knew what would happen.

Well, he knew.

Stop thinking about that, stupid! Just keep it away from the valley!

No matter what, he couldn't let it get too close to the valley. Wick was there, and Ongel.

Archer tore through the trees, keeping the sharpest

eye out for anything that could help him lose the dragonkin. He could still hear the snap of wings behind him; it hadn't lost him even with Archer's zigzag path through the trees. What if the dragonkin had some way to see in the dark, like the manghar?

He spotted a place where the trees crowded closer together and dove for it. For a moment, he wove between the trunks at top speed, burying himself in the density of the branches. Then he stopped short and crammed himself tight between two trunks. The speed of the movement took even him by surprise.

Within seconds, the sound of wings and the gust of wind that came with it passed directly above the treetops. The faint shadow hesitated for a moment, then it flew on.

Gradually, the air stilled, and the sound of wings faded into buzzing silence.

Archer's head dropped back against the trunk. His chest heaved. His heart pounded in his throat. Why was he so scared? Nothing ever scared him like this. Not walking on the edge of cliffs. Not running from nixies with swords and spears. Not even his almost-execution in manghar territory. Nothing, *nothing* had ever flooded his vision with this kind of white-hot terror.

The memory of Tor's smoking ruins flashed before his eyes. The burned Hessen house.

I can't burn, I won't burn like—

Archer swallowed hard and flexed his hands a few times to stop their shaking. He forced a slower breath.

Just shake it off. Get back to camp; make sure the dragonkin didn't find them, too.

Make it through another night, that's all he had to

do. And he'd tell Ongel about the dragonkin in the morning.

He just hoped there weren't more of them.

Burning Lizards and Their Hazardous Side Effects

THE SUN ROSE on the seventh day of searching the records, of combing through every document near the first appearance of the Scorch, and Wick had still found nothing.

Well, not quite nothing.

Reading through Aro's ancient history, piece by piece, was one part dry and unexciting, and three parts strange and unfamiliar. At times, even conflicting.

Every few chapters, Wick frowned at the page.

How have I traveled so much of Aro without knowing any of this?

How had he never known that the fair folk had once lived together, until a nation-wide famine had struck Aro, and the fair folk were forced to scatter and forage rather than starve?

How had it escaped his notice that the nixies and the satyrs hardly spoke to one another, despite being neighboring territories? That the satyrs had never forgiven the nixies for their decades of relentless pillaging?

Why had no one told him about the severe retribution the valley had demanded from the nixies, so severe that it had turned satyr territory into one of the wealthiest territories in Aro?

How had he never learned that just two years before his birth, the centaurs had been so preoccupied with visions concerning a fire on the border of leshy territory that they had nearly missed the flooding in the center of it? Flooding that could have wiped out the entire royal family?

Wick recorded all his findings in a little deerskin notebook borrowed from Eland, planning to ask Ongel about his discoveries after they survived the Scorch.

But survival came first.

Their mission seemed simple enough. They just had to find something, anything, to use against the dragons, or if not that, anything that would tell them why the Heather Stones refused to work correctly.

Simple. Just not easy.

Wick speculated that he and Eland must have gone through an entire bookshelf of records already, and so far a single scrawled footnote had been their only clue.

Wick rubbed his sore eyes. "I'm beginning to wonder if there's even anything to find."

Eland looked up from his current sheaf of notes. Carefully, he set the papers down on their table and reached for a journal. "I'm wondering the same thing. Even if it was just mentioned in passing, the information should be here. It's almost like the story is erased."

"Or gathered together into some drawer we haven't opened yet." Wick scrubbed at his eyes again.

"Sorry," Eland said. "Candlelit reading isn't for the faint of heart. Or the dry of eyes."

"I didn't have eyes that got tired until I changed form," Wick said, blinking hard to moisten his eyes. It didn't relieve the pressure on his throbbing brain. "How do people put up with this?"

"I think they use common sense and stop reading," Eland said with a small laugh, picking up the journal again. "Do you think we'll do that?"

Wick smiled. "Not likely." He moved his crackling sheaf of papers to the side. "Those were useless as well. Time for a new pile." A stack of books, references they had already discarded, teetered.

"Wick," Eland said suddenly. "Look at this."

Wick's fuzzy mind cleared in an instant. He leaned over Eland's shoulder to read the open page.

During more experiments with the Heather Stone, I found that it isn't necessary to have all the pieces before casting a spell. They are, indeed, powerful enough to be used in smaller numbers or even alone. I've successfully cast several spells, including the spell that forms a protective barrier, with as few as three pieces.

"Three pieces?" Wick turned to Eland. "That's not possible. When we tried to cast even small barrier spells with only three stones, it never worked. How did this centaur manage it?"

"Earlier, he stated that the pieces were. . ." Eland turned back through the aging pages. "The manghar stone, the seraph stone, and the leshy stone. Maybe he had a different combination from you? Or maybe his experiments made using the stones easier for him."

"I once read everything available to me on the stones, ages before all this. I never saw a study like this one," Wick said, taking the journal to study the entry himself. "Whoever this centaur is, it seems that he was trying to learn more about the power of the stones. Are there more studies like this? More recent ones?"

"No. These notes were written before the Heather Stone was split up and distributed. He was the only person who ever tried tests like these. Until Archer started gathering them, no two stones had been in the same room in centuries."

The stack of books on the table tilted dangerously, and Wick and Eland lunged to catch it. When they had righted the stack again, Wick asked another question:

"You're saying there have been no studies of the Heather Stone since these? No one has looked into them at all?"

Eland frowned. "What are you getting at?"

Wick leaned back. "Archer keeps speculating that Aro's safeguards—the visions, the stones, the spells— might be failing us because they're finally losing their power." He wet his lips. "I don't like it, but the longer this goes on, the more I wonder if he could be right."

"But how could that be?" Eland asked. The flame of their candle sputtered, sending spinning shadows across the side of his face. "The stones were *just* in the holding room. They should be stronger than ever. And all great seers have to die eventually, but we've never lost all our seeing power at once. Not even now."

"I know. I know." Wick rubbed his forehead. "I just can't stop thinking about it." A faint sound caught his attention. "What's that?"

"What?" Eland stopped still to listen. "The walls here are thick. They muffle everything."

They listened. Then Wick heard it again. Faint, muffled by the thick walls, but still recognizable.

Eland turned to Wick with wide eyes. "Those are screams."

Leaving the records as they were, they dashed through the rows of shelves. Wick tore up the ramp with Eland close behind him and raced to the open doorway. As he reached it, squinting against the brightness, he saw.

The valley crawled with dragonkin.

Hot wind rifled Wick's hair and stung his face as he stared out at the pandemonium. Throngs of refugees scattered in every direction. Seraphs and manghar took off like flocks of birds. Crowds of satyrs mixed with hordes of fair folk as they raced for the cover of buildings. Human mothers clutched children to their chest while their husbands followed them, gripping weapons and watching the sky. On the far side of the valley, a satyr woman stumbled, nearly dropping her curly-horned babe. Meanwhile, the dragonkin alighted on roofs, on trees, on the ground amid the crowd as it shrieked. Ruffs of fire streamed, blazing, from their necks and heads. A group of nixies and humans snatched up weapons and tried to beat back the nearest lizard, but it threw them back with a single swipe.

These dragonkin seemed even bigger than the ones Wick remembered. Most of their heads reached as high as the upper levels of the pavilions, and their bodies curled between the trees and rocks with serpentine ease, all flaming wings and long, whipping tails.

Wick couldn't tear his eyes away from their gleaming teeth.

A human man and woman, each carrying a child, made a dash toward Wick and Eland in the doorway. Eland waved them in as Wick kept a sharp eye on the nearest dragonkin. The family raced into their open arms.

"Are you all right?" Eland asked.

"No. Why are those things here?" The woman let her daughter slide down to stand and pulled aside the child's burned sleeve.

"I don't know." Eland cast searching eyes around the room. "I'll find water for that burn."

While Eland was distracted caring for the wife and child, the husband joined Wick at the doorway. He tugged on his red beard, slowly, worriedly. "Thank you for helping us."

"Of course." Wick took another glance at the man. The curl of his mustache seemed familiar. "I met you in the pass, didn't I?"

"You did," the man responded with a somber nod. "I remembered you as well. It's good to stand by a man I respect."

"Agreed." As Wick peered through the doorway, over the mountains soared the biggest dragonkin of all. Its size dwarfed even the dragonkin below. Its shoulders could have barely fit through the mouth of the Heather Stone cavern, and his head could have easily reached above the highest roofs of the valley.

Even from far below, Wick saw what appeared to be war paint spread across the leathery skin of its chest. Once over the mountains, the dragon's flight angled down. It dove for the valley headfirst. As the shadow fell over the valley, everything but the dragonkin scrambled for the mountains.

The huge dragonkin landed with a crash that shook the ground. Wick grabbed the door doorframe as the very foundations of the library jumped and crashed. The man beside him fell to his knees. Wick hauled him back up by the arm.

Screams echoed through the valley.

"Silence, all of you," the dragonkin hissed.

A masculine voice, deep and whispery like sudden wind through the treetops. A voice that carried weight. Every scream fell silent.

The dragon's neck curved in a broad arc as sunken eyes swept over the valley. Not a soul dared move a muscle. As the eyes of the dragonkin passed over the library, Wick noticed the war paint over each of its eyes, a slash of blue from its brow to its chin. "I am General Nin of the Scorch," the dragonkin announced. "I come to you with an ultimatum."

Wick's hand tightened on the doorframe. An ultimatum.

The dragonkin wanted to make some sort of deal.

"We've shown you what the fire can do," General Nin declared, "Now, it's for you to decide when you surrender.

Today, our armies leave your land."

Wick blinked. They were leaving? What kind of threat was that?

"Only our scouts will stay to monitor. We want your Heather Stones," Nin continued. "All of them. And we *will* get them, but how we get them is entirely up to you. You can give them up freely, or we'll burn your land to the ground and pick the stones from the ashes. You'll have a month to make your choice." The head of the dragonkin snaked closer to the library, eyeing Wick and the human man beside him. Despite the fear shaking his heart, Wick met the piercing gaze. Even through the fear, it struck Wick how familiar those eyes looked. He knew another harsh stare like it.

"Or, if you like," the dragonkin continued, his eyes at last sliding on past the library, "you could choose now. From where I stand, it looks like an easy decision. Either way, we get the stones, but it's your choice whether you live or you die."

A thick tension filled the valley.

Wick's mind raced. There had to be a catch. Giving up the stones had to have consequences, consequences that the dragonkin were hiding from them.

"Any takers?" the dragonkin drew out the *s* on purpose, making it *takerssssssssss*. Wick couldn't be sure, but it sounded like it was mocking them.

Wick's eyes darted around the valley. No one moved yet, but someone would soon. Someone had to. If any of the refugees spoke first, out of foolishness or fear, Wick feared the consequences would be irreversible.

As the dragonkin's head twisted toward the crowd of

humans and fair folk huddled in the trees across the valley, Wick decided he had to move now, before he couldn't move at all.

He darted from the library doorway. His legs almost didn't support him, and at first he stumbled. Catching himself, he bounded a few more steps and shouted, "No!"

The dragonkin's head whipped around, and the green eyes fastened on Wick. His neck stretched out, longer and longer, until his face hovered level with Wick's. From the doorway of the library, the air had felt hot enough, but here, mere feet from the dragonkin, beads of sweat dried before they could roll down his face. Wick thought his eyes would shrivel in his head

"No. . . what?" Amusement colored the dragonkin's voice.

Wick's tongue stuck to the roof of his mouth as he opened his lips to speak. His hands trembled by his sides. "N-no. You can't have the stones."

"And why not?" General Nin asked calmly. "You only have to hand them over, and no one will be hurt."

"I don't believe you." Wick's breath came in frantic puffs. "It can't be that simple. Why do you want the Heather Stones? What—what for?"

Slowly, gradually, the dragonkin tilted his head to the side, just a little too far. As though its neck was broken.

Wick knew a fear-mongering tactic when he saw one.

"Why does it matter?" the dragonkin asked.

Wick's resolve solidified into an iron bar in his chest. His voice steadied. "Because people only refuse to explain their actions when they can't justify those actions."

"Agreed."

Wick nearly jumped at the voice. The human man from the library stood beside him, his eyes alight with fight and fury.

"You can't have the stones," the human man spat. "We'll never give them up without a fight."

"You can't have them. You can't have anything that belongs to us!" a voice shouted from the trees. Other voices joined it. Gradually, the throngs of the valley raised their voices to refuse the demands of the dragonkin.

"You offered us time," Wick said. His hands closed into fists at his sides, steadying the racing of his heartbeat. "A month. We'll take it. But until then, you can't have any stones."

Nin's long snout crinkled into something of a smirk. "You can't learn to defeat us in that time. There is no defeating the Scorch."

And there was no stealing the Heather Stones. "I'll take any time I can get," Wick responded levelly. "While your scouts are here, may we speak to them?"

"You *may*," the dragonkin general said, in the same slow, drawn-out tone. It drew its head back, its eyes never leaving Wick's face. "But you won't gain anything from them. They won't be friendly to you."

Wick matched the general's steely gaze. *Pretend you're Archer. You feel no fear.* "Like I said, I'll take my chances. Thank you."

"I wouldn't take any chances if I were you." The dragonkin's mouth curled. "The scouts will be watching. If any of you try to attack them, or plot with them, or even escape your land, you will be killed."

A manghar leaped forward. "Leave, beast!" he cried,

and pitched a handful of powder into the general's face. The general's ruff of flame lit the powder, and it went up in a flash.

General Nin's head reared.

"No!" Wick forced himself further forward. "Now is *not* the time to attack!" he bellowed to the manghar.

If they provoked the dragonkin now, Aro would be ash within hours.

Nin's head swiveled toward the manghar, who rummaged through a pouch at his belt. Searching for more explosive powder.

"General!" Wick shouted, and the huge head of the dragonkin swung toward him instead.

Wick's heart beat faster, pounding in his ears. "I'm sorry. We apologize. We still want the month to decide. Please, give us time, like we agreed." He prayed that the foolhardy manghar had not thrown away their only chance.

If he had, Wick stood a mere stone's throw from the general's face. He would be the first to burn.

General Nin blinked, slowly, deliberately. The war paint covering his eyelids appeared and then disappeared as his eyes opened. A placid expression smoothed his features. "Very well, then. We'll still give you the month to decide. Perhaps you'll change your minds." It paused. "Or not. It makes no difference to me."

With that, General Nin spread his wings. The heaving of them flattened the grass as he rose into the sky. The dragonkin perched on the surrounding mountains followed suit. Together, they rose to join Nin and soared away as a unit, leaving the valley behind.

The air cooled, but the smell of ash lingered, and so did the silence.

Wick closed his hands into fists to still their tremors. Then he cast his eyes into the crowd for the manghar that had thrown the black powder.

Explosions and Enchantments

ASH-COATED BAT WINGS floated through the crowd and away from Wick as he chased after them. "Wait!" he shouted, but the manghar didn't seem to hear him.

The crowd of people pressed in around Wick.

"Does this mean that the centaurs have a plan?" a fair folk man asked, jabbing up the brim of his hat with his thumb.

"They do," Wick assured him. *Or they will.* "They'll look after all of us. Don't worry."

He increased his pace to chase down the manghar, but a hand caught his arm. "Wick, what's going on?" a female voice demanded.

Wick turned and found the delicate white snout of Kanri, the satyr girl who had accompanied Wick and Archer on their last journey from satyr territory. Her fur looked more rumpled and her eyes more glassy than when he had seen her last.

"Do you speak for all of us now?" Kanri asked, her tone as sharp as broken glass. "There are a lot of people who won't like you taking charge. I hope you know that."

"I'm not taking charge." Wick fought down the mountain of frustration forcing its way up his throat. "All I meant to do was buy us more time before we were burned alive."

Before Kanri could respond, Ongel appeared over her shoulder. "Kanri, why don't you lend me a hand with some of these children, and you can ask me anything you want."

Kanri paused, then nodded. "Fine."

Kanri and Ongel hurried toward the sound of crying children. Wick searched the landscape for the ashen wings again. The manghar had paused a dozen yards away. Wick dashed toward him before any more distractions could appear.

Five steps shy of the manghar, he slowed his pace and took a deep breath. *Be calm. Assess the situation.*

The wings of the manghar sagged subtly, the grey membrane loose. A ring of metal looped through the knuckle of each wing and three wrapped the cartilage of his right ear. A craftsman? Perhaps one of Crowned Head Theodore's men. The muscles of his back and arms seemed uncharacteristically wiry for a manghar, though they were partially hidden under the faded pine-green tunic that slouched across his rounded spine.

Wick circled to the manghar's face and noticed two things, one after the other. Firstly, the barrier that had stopped the manghar walking was Astor. Heads together,

Astor and the manghar discussed something in low, hasty tones. Secondly, Wick noticed the shape of the manghar's face itself. His greying muzzle was slimmer than most, his eye sockets deeper, his ears placed further back on his head.

He was not one of the Crowned Head's men. This manghar was from the southern colony.

All Wick's knowledge of manghar was rendered useless. The southern colony was as good as an independent territory, and from what little Wick had heard of it, he knew only that the culture was vastly different from manghar territory proper.

He had no choice but to play by ear.

Wick installed himself by Astor's side. Before he could plan what to say, Astor turned to him and thrust a palm full of black powder before Wick's eyes.

"Wick, look at this. This is what he threw at that lizard. It's an explosive powder. Powder that he invented!"

"Not invented," the manghar corrected in a hasty, nasally voice. "Borrowed, really. Discovered it in leshy territory."

The flash of light. The puff of drifting smoke. Of course it had looked familiar. Wick took a pinch of the powder and rolled the gritty texture of it between his fingers. "This is what we use to make fireworks, I think." Then he remembered himself and looked up at the manghar. "And you threw this at a dragonkin."

"Had to prove it would work." The manghar nodded quickly. He tapped a fat pouch on his belt with the back of his hand. "I made a lot. Brought it here to help protect the stones from them things."

Wick rolled his fingers again, and the black powder fell through his fingers into the stubs of grass. "Well, I think you chose the wrong time to use it. If Nin hadn't already agreed to a temporary truce, your powder could have got us all killed." The manghar's eyes watched him earnestly. Maybe he would be willing to listen. Wick hesitated, then switched gears. "But I think this could be useful in the right situation. Talk to the centaurs about it and see what they think."

"Wick," Astor said, in a tone so serious that Wick stopped short. Astor pointed out toward the crowds. "This could take a while to calm down. Until the centaurs have a chance to talk to Gregory about his explosives, do you think it would be all right if he and I did some experiments? This stuff could be just the weapon we need, and we only have a month. That isn't long."

Wick hesitated. *I already spoke for the valley once today. Can I really make the call on what weapons we build?*

A month, though. Astor was right, a month was hardly a long time. And currently, they had no safeguards set in place.

"Experiment, yes," he said at last. He gave Astor a hard stare, then Gregory. "But until you speak to the centaurs and have their permission to make weapons for them, it's your personal experiment. You *have* to speak to them about this. And Gregory?"

"My friends always called me Greg," the manghar said quickly.

"Greg." Wick hoped that friendly terms would make Greg more likely to listen. "It would be best to keep future explosions out of the valley."

"What explosions?" Archer peered over Wick's shoulder. "Is that what all the hoopla is about?"

"Yes and no," Wick said. "Astor and Gregory—Greg—want to experiment with some explosives. Do you want to help?" He winced, immediately regretting offering Archer explosives.

Luckily, Archer made a sour, wrinkly face. "Not if Astor's in charge. No, thanks."

Astor gave Archer a sidelong glance. "I wouldn't give you explosives even if you wanted them. No offense."

"There is offense," Archer corrected.

Wick silently agreed with Astor. "Twill knows a thing or two about building fireworks. I would ask her about it." He turned to Archer. "You can help me find Ongel. I want to know what the valley's plans are."

"Hang on," Archer said to Gregory, making Wick pause. "You said your friends *called* you Gregory. Past tense. Did the Scorch take your friends from you? Is that why you're after them?"

Wick stiffened at the insensitive comment, but as he glanced back, Gregory hardly blinked.

"They're dead; long dead. But the Scorch burned my city's graveyard, and the trees that marked my friends' graves are all gone now." Gregory's knuckles tightened around the pouch of black powder. "That won't go unpunished."

Less than three days later, messengers arrived from the surrounding territories, bearing a familiar story: dragonkin had announced their ultimatum in every major city. None of the interactions had been nearly so dramatic or tense as it had been in the valley, but none of the other dragonkin had proposed to take an offer then and there. It seemed that the other dragonkin had been strictly following orders, whereas General Nin felt free to do as he liked.

As Wick had expected, the valley now had to discuss how to proceed. And, as he had feared, there were some who thought that sacrificing the stones wasn't the worst option.

"Did I do the right thing?" Wick asked Ongel, shortly after the fair folk had gathered and declared that if given the choice, they would willingly give up the stones. "Maybe the fair folk are right. It's a gamble, but at least giving up the stones gives us half a chance of survival." Wick leaned against the wall of Ongel's study, frowning at the floor and picking at his shirtsleeve.

"You bought us time," Ongel said. "Any of the refugees could have spoken out rashly and doomed us all. With the extra month you bartered for us, we can make a decision together."

He leaned forward and rested his elbows on the table in front of them, bumping aside one of the plates they had used for their luncheon. "But I have to assume there's a reason they want our surrender. It may be for their own convenience, of course; they don't want to scour the whole country for the stones after we're all dead. Maybe it really is an act of mercy, but something doesn't feel quite right."

"I agree," Wick said. But as usual, his head was spinning, full of questions he had no answers to. "I just hope that we can find something in the records that will help us, so that when the time comes we can make a decision that we know is right."

"Well, between myself and the other mentors, some sort of plan has been formed," Ongel continued, folding his hands on the table.

Wick glanced up, surprised. "Really?"

"Wick, are you familiar with enchanting magic?"

"I know of it," Wick responded. "But not much about it."

"What's enchanting magic?" Archer asked, appearing at Wick's elbow so suddenly that Wick jumped.

"Don't *do* that," Wick gasped.

Archer grinned. "If I didn't I wouldn't have any fun." His expression darkened. "Between Fowl and Astor, I'm not allowed to have any fun anyway. Or a moment's peace."

Ongel's horse legs adjusted, and he changed the position of his elbows on the table. "Enchanting magic is a sort of secondary ability for the centaurs. Those of us who aren't seers often have the gift of enchanting instead. I am one of the enchanting centaurs."

"I didn't know that," Wick said slowly.

Ongel shook his head. "It never seemed to be very useful, so I didn't see any purpose in showing pride in it."

"Huh." Archer squinted slightly. "So, you can change things into other things and stuff like that?"

"No. Enchanting isn't nearly so glamorous or fast. It can take months or years of building layers for an enchantment to become potent. The strongest we have are the enchantments on the holding room. They make it immune to other magics, even other enchantments cast by the centaurs, and enchanted objects kept inside the room are charged with more magic. That's how the holding room works."

Wick scrunched his eyes shut as thought. "If I remember right, enchantments can't change the shape or nature of anything or give it life of its own. The job of an enchantment is more to create a certain effect, isn't that right?"

"Yes, that's exactly it." Ongel glanced at Archer. "Am I making sense to you?"

Wick could almost see Archer's brain dissolving out of his ears. "Not even a little bit," Archer said.

"For example, the effect of the enchantments on the holding room is to keep intruders out and to recharge magical items kept there. There are enchantments on eyeglasses to prevent the wearer from headaches. Some homes are enchanted to keep burglars out, although those take years to build up. Which leads me to my point." Ongel took a breath. "I'm taking as many of the other enchanting centaurs as I can to some of the nearby cities. We'll put down some protection enchantments around their outskirts to keep the dragonkin out for as long as possible. No matter what decision we give the Scorch in a month's time, we don't know how they'll react, so it's wise to take defensive measures."

"Can the valley spare all of you?" Wick asked with a frown. "There are still hundreds of refugees here."

"We received many positive letters this morning," Ongel responded. "The nearby territories are taking all the refugees. After I leave with the other enchanters, the refugees will be split up and sent to the surrounding territories. Thank goodness."

Still, the strain on the valley would hardly be lessened

for a few days yet. "Will you want our help?"

"The valley will have a lot of work to do for a few days, but the end is in sight. I suspect they'll be fine." Ongel turned to Wick with a somber slant to his brow. "You should stay with Eland in the library. We need to find something."

"So, you'll be leaving again," Archer interrupted.

His flat tone made Wick turn to him in surprise. He had never seen Archer so reluctant to part with someone. But Archer wore that empty, vague expression that he usually put on when something was wrong.

Wick resolved to talk to Archer about it later.

"I am leaving," Ongel said. "But not for long. Once the enchanting is done, I'll return to the valley right away."

"Sure," Archer said, but Wick couldn't tell if he meant it.

"When are you and the other enchanters leaving?" Wick asked Ongel.

"Tomorrow, at first light. It should only take a couple of weeks to do what needs to be done."

Frutelken

ARCHER TRIED TO LEAVE with Wick, but Ongel stopped him. "You seem upset. Is something wrong?"

Wrong? Of course nothing's was wrong. How could anything be wrong when one of the few people I can tolerate is leaving again?

"I'm not upset." Archer kicked at a crack in the floor, but missed and kicked the air instead. "I'm fine. Why?"

Instead of answering Archer's question, Ongel said, "I'll bet you didn't know that enchanting has to be practiced, just like any other skill. Without practice, the enchanter gets rusty, so a lot of us keep what's called a totem. A totem is a small object enchanted with some less potent effect, which enchanters add to every few days or so to keep our skills in practice."

Archer wondered where this was going.

Ongel reached into the pocket of his tunic and produced a stick the length of his hand with a small cluster of pinecones at the end. "This is mine. It's nothing too special, but it's helped me a few times and I think it may help you, as well."

Archer waited, looking at the cluster of pinecones instead of Ongel.

When Archer didn't speak, Ongel cleared his throat and went on. "Essentially, it's an object of comfort, for a peaceful mind and clear thoughts." He beckoned to Archer, who reluctantly held out his hand. Ongel placed the branch in Archer's palm.

The instant Archer's hand closed around the branch, an odd feeling washed over him. His shoulders loosened, and the worry cluttering his brain faded from a roar to a background hum.

After the uncertainty of the last few weeks and the constant strain of dealing with Fowl, the release was overwhelming. Archer nearly staggered. He stared down at the stick, baffled. Why on earth would the centaurs favor their stupid visions when they had this kind of sorcery at their disposal?

"It isn't for times of crisis," Ongel said gently. "It would make you ignore the danger, but under stressful circumstances, it does the trick. I'm leaving it with you while I'm gone."

Archer's eyes narrowed as suspicion took over. "Why? What would I want something like this for?"

Ongel's brown eyes, circled in the creases of time, looked on Archer kindly. "You've looked like you needed comfort for some time now. Your face made me worried when I said I had to leave." Ongel reached out, but Archer pulled away.

"Like you said, you'll be back. It doesn't matter,"

Archer said. He considered handing Ongel's totem back to prove it, but his heartbeat jumped at the thought and his fingers rebelled, tightening around the stick instead. "Maybe Fowl could use this, though. He hasn't been doing so good." He hesitated. "Thank you."

"You're welcome," Ongel said hesitantly. Then he added, "And I'll see you again soon."

"Yeah." With his fist still clamped around the totem, Archer left the room.

"Archer!" Wick beckoned from the far end of the hall. By his side stood the hunched manghar with the rings in his ears. The one with the exciting explosive powder.

Archer sidled over, tucking the stick into his pocket so that Wick wouldn't see it. Without the stick in his hand, tension washed over him like a wave.

"The valley gave Greg permission to build a prototype," Wick said. "I thought you'd like to see what he and Twill are cooking up. It might improve your mood."

Archer stuffed his hands into his pockets. "I'm in a *great* mood."

Wick's mouth quirked. "The line between your eyebrows has been deep enough to plant a tree in. Come on. You'll like this."

Gregory led the way between the beds of refugees and through the hall's huge doors. Twill waited for them by the steps outside.

"Oh, good, you got Archer," she said. Her eyes glinted in Archer's direction. "You'll like this."

She took a roll of paper from the crook of her elbow

and unfurled it where Wick and Archer could see it. "I took inspiration from the way we make fireworks back home."

"I thought you might," Wick said, leaning over the paper to inspect it in the dimming sunlight.

Archer squinted at the paper. Twill and Greg's design looked clean and simple—just a small, round canister full of powder with a long fuse.

Archer's eyes narrowed further as he scanned the rows of meaningless numbers lining the bottom of the page. "Why's it so small? It won't do much to a dragonkin."

"It will," Gregory said, short but firm.

"It definitely will," Twill agreed. "Greg's black powder is much more powerful than the stuff we use for fireworks."

Gregory sniffed with nonchalance. "Experimented with the formula."

Twill tucked the flat sheet beneath her arm again and made a ring with her hands. "A pod this big could take out at least one dragonkin. Or more than one of us, so we have to be careful."

"Speaking of careful," Wick said, "Greg, how did you keep from blowing up your entire territory once the dragonfire came down?"

"I kept a fireproof safe. A big one." Gregory worked his jaw. "Too big to carry here."

"Can you build another one?"

Gregory shook his head. "Not in time."

"And you're keeping this stuff . . . where? Up there, somewhere?" Archer asked, waving at the mountains.

Gregory pointed north, where something white fluttered between the trees. Maybe a tent?

Archer's head tilted. "If you don't have a fancy safe or anything, what will you do if the dragonkin find it?"

Wick's eyes widened, and he sent an anxious look toward Twill.

Archer made an explosion sound under his breath.

"Like I said," Twill said crisply as she rolled the page of plans back into a tight tube. "By being careful. Very careful."

The following day crawled by. Archer wandered the valley aimlessly. Eventually he looked up and saw a group of centaurs climbing out of the valley with packs on their backs and weapons in their hands. At the head of their group was a dark-skinned centaur with a head of long braids.

Archer watched as they climbed higher and disappeared into the trees. Ongel never turned to look back.

Soon after, the rest of the valley went to work dividing up the refugees into four main groups—one going to nixie territory, one going to satyr territory, and two going to different parts of human territory. Archer, wandering around making himself useless, was snatched up as extra help. He thought he recognized the centaur in charge; she had the same copper skin and neatly braided hair as the woman centaur from Tor.

With effort, Archer extracted her name from the recesses of his brain: Cohn.

Archer spent the rest of his day sending refugees this way or that way, returning anxious lost children to equally anxious parents, and writing hash marks in a little book that Cohn had handed him. Next to her delicate, crisp marks, Archer's lines looked like harsh gashes.

He folded the book in half so he couldn't compare them anymore. The spine of the book made a horrible cracking sound.

With the refugees divided and tallied, the process entered its next stage. As per his instructions, Archer took his little book of tallies to the storehouses, where another centaur compared the numbers to the remaining stock of food with concern. Archer wondered where on earth they would get more supplies after the refugees bled them dry.

Archer cleared his throat awkwardly. "Anybody going to human territory won't need much. They aren't going far, and the humans always have a lot of extra food stored up, anyway."

The centaurs scratched his forehead, then his expression eased. "That's more than half the refugees, too. That will make a difference."

They unearthed as much food as they could spare—too much, in Archer's opinion; the refugees had leeched long enough—and divided it according to Cohn's instructions. From there, they assigned leaders to each refugee group and entrusted them with dividing their group's rations.

In Cohn's words, they could supply food for the refugees, but making the food last was up to the refugees.

Chaos began again as the groups started the walk to their new sanctuaries.

By evening, the crowds had thinned considerably. Archer found he could walk across the valley without tripping over someone, and see from one building to another without heads getting in the way.

But with no refugees to nanny, Archer realized he once again had nothing to do.

He decided not to go back to camp and the foul moods of Fowl and Astor, so he stayed in the valley, opting to try a batch of frutelken. If he could just get it right this time, a sip of hot, spicy fruit drink might fill the empty feeling in his stomach.

He knew well enough that their supplies were depleted after the refugees, but after all his hard work, Archer supposed he had earned one small batch of frutelken. And besides, something in the air told him tonight was the night. Maybe a miracle would happen and he'd finally get it right.

With enough digging through the sparse storehouses, Archer was able to find all the supplies he needed. The milk smelled strangely sweet, but it would do.

The supply houses also boasted a tiny kitchen buried in the back, essentially only a stove surrounded by countertops and cabinets painted green. It wasn't big, but since Archer didn't have a handy little house somewhere in the hills like the centaurs, it was perfect. He deposited his supplies on the countertop and dug through the drawers and cabinets to find the pots and pans he needed.

For half an absentminded second, Archer wished he had a jug of his mother's frutelken to compare. Then he remembered.

There would be no more of his mother's frutelken. Not ever again.

The thought made him feel all funny in the head.

Archer propped Ongel's comfort branch against the back of the stove for company while he stoked the fire. The flames blazed a little too hot and caught his fingers, and Archer hissed as he clutched his smarting hand.

Once he got the fire going steadily, Archer started chopping fruit to go into the pot. All the extras, the peels and the cores and pits, he piled to the side. Maybe Wick would find some use for them. If not, they'd stay there to rot. The knife felt strange and unfamiliar in his fingers, the handle thicker and the blade longer than the one from his mother's kitchen. It didn't cut quite the same.

"What are you doing?" Wick's voice asked from the doorway.

Archer glanced back and saw Wick leaning in curiously.

"Trying my hand at frutelken again," Archer replied. He remembered to watch the knife, just in time to avoid losing a fingertip. "I didn't feel like going to sleep yet."

"Me either. I'm still not used to needing all this sleep." Wick moved closer and surveyed Archer's carnage across the counter. "I either sleep too much or too little. I can't seem to find a balance." He looked over at Archer and paused. "You have juice all over your shirt."

Archer looked down. The front of his white shirt had turned a sort of orange-brown. Looking at it, he became aware of it sticking to his stomach. "I don't think I have any extra clothes left."

"You can probably borrow something from Eland." Wick's fingers tapped on the counter, then stopped. "Are you okay?"

"Yes," Archer responded, too fast. *Drat.*

Wick caught the slip. "I don't think you are. Not since you lost your parents and your home." He paused. "Both homes."

Archer leaned forward and took a whiff of the pot. It didn't smell nearly spicy enough. He pushed past Wick to grab the spices scattered at the other end of the counter. "It doesn't bother me, really. I never liked living with my parents, and I never actually lived with my grandparents. I just liked it there."

"Still, losing all of that can't be easy," Wick insisted.

Archer swallowed violently.

Why did everyone insist he needed comfort when he wasn't sad? Why was Wick always so pushy when he thought something was wrong? Why couldn't anyone just leave well enough alone? Archer hacked into another peach with too heavy a hand. The counter shook from the force of the knife.

"Archer?"

"I'm fine!" Archer snapped. "I feel *fine*. Nothing is wrong. Can't you just accept that?"

Wick blinked at his outburst, but recovered quickly. "No, I can't. I've never known anyone in the world to lose everything you have and then be *fine*."

Archer stabbed the blade into the cutting board, where it stuck, quivering. "I haven't *lost* anything, Wick. My parents and I were never close. I think the strongest feeling my mother felt for me was tolerance. I can't even tell what my father thought of me. I could care less about their house, and I gave up my grandfather's house by choice." He gestured sharply to the stove, for no reason in particular. "I said I'm fine, and I am fine. If you're waiting for me to shut down, like Fowl is, keep waiting." Archer scooped up the whole double-handful of spices he had measured and dumped them into the bubbling pot. The frutelken would probably taste too spicy now.

"Archer, really."

Archer spun around to face Wick. "Really, what? Sorry if you're expecting me to be a mess of grief. Maybe I should be, but I'm not. Even if my parents never missed me when I was gone and never cared if I visited, maybe I should still feel terrible that they're dead. Maybe I should feel responsible for what happened to the house. Maybe I should feel *something*, but let's face it, I don't."

As he spouted words, Archer watched Wick's face go from surprised to alarmed to piteous. It only made him angrier.

"As usual," Archer snapped, "I'm the messed-up screw-up of a son who can't just get it right. I can't even lose someone the right way. I'm just the same as I've always been." His voice broke, and he blinked, feeling a prickle in his eyes. How had he let himself get so worked up?

"You're not messed up, Archer," Wick said quietly.

"It doesn't matter." Archer turned back to the pot but didn't stir it. He stared into the bubbling tawny drink. "Just change the subject. Please."

The following silence could have crushed a mountain. The density of it was suffocating.

"Just change the subject," Archer repeated, with less force this time, and continued stirring the pot. The mix smelled almost right. Maybe he hadn't put in too much spice, after all.

"All right." Wick leaned his back against the counter and crossed his arms. "I think Ongel will be all right. The dragonkin have as good as promised they'll be out of Aro until our time is up, so he shouldn't be in any kind of danger."

Archer nodded.

"I am worried about my people, though. Twill said they're all right, but no one has heard from them. They haven't responded to any messages." In the corner of his eye, Archer saw Wick cast his eyes toward the floor. "I just hope I'm not the reason they won't reach out."

Archer didn't know what to say to that. "Maybe they just don't want to be a burden," he managed after much too long.

"Maybe."

Archer heaved the pot of frutelken off the stove and onto the counter. "Want to try it?" he asked, looking over his shoulder at Wick.

"I think I would try snail slime if it would get my mind off the leshy," Wick admitted. "Are there any glasses in these cabinets?"

Archer opened every cabinet, but it appeared that the centaurs had not stored a single glass. He did find a stack of wooden bowls. "We'll use bowls, I guess." He handed one to Wick, then dipped another into the pot of fruit drink. Steaming overflow dripped down the side of the bowl, narrowly missing his fingers.

Wick dipped his own into the pot as well. "Cheers."

The drink was still piping hot, but Archer took a cautious sip all the same. Immediate disappointment shot through his heart. The pot had smelled spicy enough, but after tasting it, he could see the volume of spices he had added only made the mixture bitter, and somehow the fruit added almost no flavor.

"Excellent. Another waste of my time." Archer set the bowl down and walked out of the storehouse.

Archer walked back to their camp and curled up under his rumpled blanket. After a few minutes of tossing and turning, he took the stick Ongel had given him from his pocket, and calm washed over him again.

He fell asleep tangled in his blanket with his back to a tree and the comfort stick clutched to his chest.

The next morning a familiar smell woke him. Face pressed against the ground, fingers clenching the rough stick, he struggled to identify the scent. So sweet and fruity, but with a heavy layer of something else. . .

Frutelken.

Mother?

Archer sat bolt upright. His bleary eyes weren't ready for the sunlight, and he winced as he tried to spot where the smell was coming from.

Only a few yards away, the source of the scent hung over their fire. Wick leaned over a bubbling pot, stirring carefully. As Archer watched, Wick consulted a bit of paper by his side and nodded to himself. Then he picked up a stick lying on the ground beside him and poked at a few packages cooking at the edges of the fire.

"What are you doing?" Archer rasped, scrubbing at his eyes with one hand.

"You can't smell it from over there?" Wick asked absently. With a deft turn of the stick, he flipped over a few of the things cooking on the coals, revealing their blackened undersides. "I thought this might improve your mood." Wick reached for a stack of bowls at his side and used one to scoop up some liquid from the pot.

Archer got up and edged closer. His eyes narrowed at the slip of paper. "I know that handwriting. Where'd you get it?"

"Your mother gave it to me," Wick said calmly. "After you wouldn't take it, she gave it to me, just in case you changed your mind."

Archer drew back until Wick's torso blocked out the recipe. "I still don't want it. It's cheating if someone else gives it to me."

Wick moved his elbow out of the way as the bowl threatened to spill. "Good, because I'm not giving it to you. I'm just making a batch for us to enjoy." He held out the bowl. "Now, drink this before I make you."

"Whatever." Archer snatched the bowl out of Wick's hand, nearly sloshing it. The frutelken poured steam, even in the humid morning air. Barely sparing time to blow on it, Archer took a cautious sip.

Fruity. Peachy. Thick and hot. Enough spices to nearly overwhelm the flavor. Frothy. Perfect.

Archer looked down at Wick again, about to say something, but forgot what it was as he saw Wick's face. Lips pressed tight together, eyes screwed almost shut, Wick was on the verge of laughter.

"What?" Archer barked.

"You look like you might melt into a puddle," Wick said with a grin. "Really, I've never seen you look this happy."

"Shut up. I'm always happy." Archer took another long, slow sip of the frutelken, relishing the flavors as they melted in his mouth. "It's the best taste in the world," he said quietly.

Wick scooped up a bowl for himself and took a sip. "It's pretty close to hers, if I remember right. I'm glad it came out well." Still holding the bowl, he prodded the packages cooking in the coals again.

This was the part where one usually said something.

"Thank you," Archer managed stiffly. "It's better than anything I've made."

"I'm glad it helps."

Archer shifted uncomfortably, then sat down on the ground by the fire, holding the bowl of frutelken close to his chest. "And. . . I'm sorry that I yelled at you."

"Everyone's on edge," Wick said. "And you're dealing with things I could never hope to understand. Maybe I pushed too much. Still. . . thank you for the apology." Wick took a sip from his bowl. "I'm starting to see why you like this drink so much. It's just the right balance of sweet and spice."

Archer nodded. "Imagine drinking it your whole life," he said into the bowl as he took another drink.

A sharp inhale came from the other side of the camp. Fowl's head jerked up. When his eyes lit upon Wick and Archer by the fire with their bowls, the light in his eyes died again. "Ah," he said in a small voice.

"Sorry, Fowl," Archer said. "I thought the same when I woke up and smelled it cooking." Archer held out his hand to Wick, who dipped up another bowl of frutelken. With a bowl in each hand, Archer crossed the camp and gave one to Fowl.

"Thank you," Fowl said quietly. As he took the bowl, his free hand slipped something into his shirt pocket. Archer only saw a glint of silver, but it had to be the locket. Fowl must have taken to sleeping with it clutched in his fingers.

Archer returned to the fire. Wick was telling Twill about the leshy situation as she stood in the sun, arms crossed, absorbing the energy she needed for the day. Across the camp, Archer could vaguely overhear Fowl talking to Astor.

"I was just dreaming about them, and then when I woke up and smelled this, I thought. . ."

"I know," Astor said. "But nobody meant to. They didn't know."

Fowl said something else, even softer, and Astor replied, "But you can't live like that, Fowl, you know that. You'll lose your mind dwelling on a fantasy."

"Still." In the edge of his vision, Archer saw Fowl's head sag lower. "They were alive there. I'd. . . almost prefer the fantasy."

Just like that, the glimmer of happiness brought about by the frutelken blew out like a spark in the wind.

You Can Run (But You Can't Hide)

THE CROWD IN THE VALLEY had shrunk to a fifth of its size now, with most of the refugees returning to rebuild their own villages, or off to the neighboring cities. The workload for the valley had returned to a manageable amount, and many of the centaurs were finally able to get the rest they needed. Eland's father, Hirim, greeted Wick with more energy than he'd displayed in days.

While work with the refugees had lightened, remaining work still loomed. Storehouses had to be restocked somehow, rations divvied out in the meantime, more letters sent to the leaders of the other territories. A decision had to be reached about the dragonkin, and until Ongel and the rest of the enchanters returned with news, the valley would have nothing but time to think about it.

If the enchantments did the trick in the other cities,

they could work for the valley, too. And the leshy forest. And a thousand other places.

But in the meantime, Wick and Eland had been summoned to inspect a dead dragonkin with their mentors.

"Do any other territories have a plan yet?" Wick asked as they passed the Great Hall.

"The manghar aren't declaring war, at least for now," Eland said. "I know that much. The nixies might cause trouble; their queen led an attack when the Scorch delivered their ultimatum, and she was injured pretty badly."

"I hadn't heard about that." But, of course, the nixies had tried to attack the dragonkin. Fighting for their lives came to them as naturally as breathing.

"We got word about it yesterday," Eland went on. "The nixies haven't announced yet if they would go to war alongside the manghar, but while Queen Frey recovers, her general is running the kingdom. It's hard to say what he'll do."

"I don't remember him being very friendly." Most of what Wick remembered of the nixie general involved daggers. Daggers at throats, specifically. "He might be the type to go to war."

"The problem is that they could never win, even with the nixies and the manghar working together," Eland said with a shake of his head. "The Scorch are too many. That's why we need to find *something* useful in our research. If we can't use the Heather Stones to drive them away again, we'll have to fight for it. And right now, we have no chance."

Cohn waved to them from behind a copse of trees, her long hair whipping across her copper face. Wick waved back, and he and Eland hurried to her. With her stood Hirim, the stern face of Fariss, and Ongel.

"You were nearly late," Cohn warned in a low tone. "But not quite. Martook is about to begin."

Martook, a fair, dappled centaur the age of Hirim and wrapped in a leather butcher's apron, gave Wick and Eland a friendly two-finger salute and a smile. Wick didn't remember ever seeing him before. The creamy fabric of what might have been a bed sheet fluttered behind him as it draped a large and bumpy shape.

"You're just in time." Martook unwrapped a cord from his wrist and used it to bind back his mass of tangled black hair.

"You see," he said as he smoothed back mounds of hair, "I started studying this dead one shortly after the first attack. Most of their dead were blown away by the barrier spell, but for whatever reason, this one was left behind." He finally succeeded with his hair and drew the sheet away from the dragonkin corpse.

The first thing that jumped out at Wick was the size of the creature. It couldn't have been more than five yards from nose to tail, much smaller than the soldiers he'd seen days ago, and without the flaming ruff and towering posture, its sprawled shape seemed even smaller.

Second, he noticed the long cut down its neck and torso. All blood from the dissection had been wiped away, leaving the cut clean and pale, but the glimpse of slick organs within made Wick's stomach clench.

"Four limbs—two legs and two wings," Martook said.

He bent beside the dragonkin corpse and stretched out one of the wings. "The wings have three claws and one opposable thumb claw for dexterity. Their hind legs seem to be mostly useful for takeoff and landing, not for long-distance walking."

"Any weaknesses?" Farriss inspected the dragonkin with his arms crossed over his chest.

"The ear holes and the underside of the chin seem to be the most sensitive," Martook responded. "The hamstring of the leg isn't well-protected, either. Now: let me show you something really interesting."

"Their fire is naturally secreted through glands in their skin." Marook circled the dragonkin, pointing to features of the corpse as he described them. "Especially in the head and upper torso. From what I can guess, they must be on fire their whole lives. Which leads me to the most interesting part. Look at the torso: what do you see?"

Wick edged closer and crouched beside the dragonkin's wing. The torso of the creature looked frail without fire to cover it, the muscles strangely wooden.

"Why are there so many scars?" Eland asked.

Martook pointed to Eland. "Exactly. The skin of the head, the neck, the shoulders—everything that would normally be on fire—is covered in scars on top of scars. The dissection didn't get me far, but I can tell you one thing: these creatures are always on fire, but they aren't prepared to withstand it."

◊

"KEEP UP, we're almost there," Archer said, stepping

over a fallen log.

One of the centaurs had heard about their group staying in the woods and immediately offered them space in his home. Wick had tried to insist that they couldn't impose, but Archer had slept too many nights on cold ground and put up with Astor's snores for too long. He had accepted the offer on the spot.

Wick worked in the valley, Archer had the task of moving their camp to the nearby house. Packing up hadn't taken long; all they'd really brought were weapons and cooking utensils and their blankets, plus Fowl's few books. In all, packing up their camp had taken a quarter of an hour at most.

Their host's house appeared over the rise, two levels of red-painted beams with a massive front porch and a narrow railed ramp leading down toward them. The trees gathered so closely around it that it looked almost out of place in the forest.

"This is it, I guess," Archer said to the others. He got a better grip on the mess of blankets tucked under his arm. "Come on."

As Archer set foot on the base of the ramp, the centaur man appeared in the doorway of the house, all sinewy height and billowing chestnut hair and wide youthful grin.

"Welcome!" he exclaimed.

Archer scrambled for something Wick would say. "Thanks for helping us out."

The words sounded awkward to his own ears, but it only made the centaur's smile grow as he leaned down to give each person a warm hug. "Of course, of course!

Anything for friends of Wick's. He's been nothing but helpful to the valley since the day he came."

Archer smirked. "Tell him that sometime, would you? He won't take it from me."

"I will." The centaur paused and clapped his hands loudly. "Let's get on to introductions. My name is Aethan, and my beautiful wife, Dorana, is caring for our new baby in the house. We'll be in the front bedroom, which is the door to your right as you enter. That room is the only one that's off-limits. The rest of the house is yours, though I wouldn't go down in the cellar, since snakes tend to find their way down there. I don't think we'll see one another much, since most of the time I'll be in the valley, and Dorana will be with the baby."

"We'll be in and out a lot, too," Archer said.

"Precisely." Aethan's expression grew slightly sheepish. "Good thing, too, since I nearly forgot about the baby when I invited you all here. Dorana is delighted to have you, but she's asked all of us to keep our voices down near the house. Our little one wakes up easily."

Twill glanced at Archer. "I can keep my voice down if you can."

They filed up the ramp into the centaur house.

"All the guest bedrooms are up the ramp past the sitting room," Aethan called from the doorway.

As everyone made their way up the ramp and chose rooms, Archer found himself silently staggered by the scale of the centaur house. The *size* of everything! Granted, the furniture in the valley was all a little too tall, and the doorways were usually a little wide, but this house wasn't like the valley. It was built for centaurs and no one else. The ceilings were nearly as high as the ones in the seraph houses Archer had grown up in, and Archer nearly fell down the single high step from the doorway.

The beds at least weren't so tall, but their shape was altogether unfamiliar, less like a bed frame than an expanse of dense cushion scattered with pillows. Archer could spread both wings on the bed and just barely touch open air on each side. Every room had either a lounge or a sofa for sitting and shelf after shelf of books.

Once he had hurled his blanket across the bed and emptied a few things from his bag into a corner of the room, Archer realized he had nothing else to do.

He considered just staying in his room.

But no.

He should probably make sure the others were doing all right. At any rate he could find someone to be astonished over the huge beds with him.

And someone had to claim a room for Wick.

Some time later, once Archer got everyone settled in, and the fist of tension in his chest had squeezed too tight to ignore anymore, he concluded he needed a breath of fresh air. A walk, by himself, would solve it. Archer told Fowl where he was going, then he told Twill, too, in case Fowl forgot. Then he left with his bag slung over his shoulder. A quarter mile from the house, he wondered why he had brought the bag; he didn't need it. He entered a clearing, and the bright sun beat down on his scalp.

Something rustled in the bushes to his right. A rustle too big for a rabbit or a wandering fair folk.

Archer froze. Could he stay still and hope that nothing spotted him? Or would it be better to run?

A scaly head emerged from the bushes, eyes fastened on Archer.

Archer dashed for the edge of the clearing.

Before he made it five steps, something grabbed Archer's leg, and he smacked face-down into the leaves. The musty leaf scent filled his nose for only a second before the dragonkin pulled him backward.

"Let me go!" Archer bellowed. He scrabbled at the ground for leverage. "Your general said you'd leave us alone until the month was up! Let me go!"

The claws dragged Archer back until he lay sprawled before the dragonkin. With its claws still clamped around Archer's calf, the dragonkin calmly asked, "If I let you go, will you run?"

"Uh, yeah!" Archer tried to pull his leg free. He only succeeded in twisting face-up toward the dragonkin. Up close, its eyes looked a lot like everyone else's: round black pupil, multicolored blueish iris, a bit of white at the wrinkled corners.

"I didn't stop you to hurt you," the dragonkin said. The voice surprised Archer. Masculine, for sure, but it sounded much smoother and more even than General Nin's. Then, hot breath blew in Archer's face, making him wince. "I only want to speak with you," he continued.

"What, to talk me over to your side or something?" Archer demanded.

The corners of the dragonkin's mouth lifted slightly. "Yes."

"Well, too bad!" Archer picked up his other foot, the one that wasn't in the dragonkin's grip, and swung it into the lizard's snout. The dragonkin jerked back in surprise, and his grip on Archer's leg loosened.

Quick as a snake, Archer slipped free and raced for the other edge of the clearing. Halfway there, he realized he couldn't hear anything chasing him.

"I just thought you'd wonder why the Scorch is back so soon," the voice of the dragonkin said behind him. "And why your visions can't spot us."

Archer hesitated for a fraction of a second, nearly stopping at the edge of the clearing.

It was a trap, he knew that. The dragonkin sounded reasonable, almost suspiciously reasonable. And it could only be saying things.

Still. . .

For a heartbeat, Archer thought of what they could learn from this dragonkin. He could ask about the dragonkin plans or how they operated. But then he remembered the teeth.

He kept running.

As Archer dashed, breathless, up the steps of their guest house, Wick opened the door. "Bad news," Wick reported.

Archer's relief spoiled into apprehension. "Now what?"

"Come inside. I'll explain to everyone at once." Wick shot Archer a tired look. "Wish me luck."

Once everyone in their group had huddled in the wide sitting room of the house, Wick began his explanation. "Ongel and the other enchanters returned this morning."

Astor's brow furrowed. "They've only been gone a week."

"Yes." Wick took a deep breath. "They only made it to one city in human territory. It took them two days to cast protective spells on the city, and just as they were about to move on, some dragonkin scouts arrived."

"Is Ongel all right?" Archer blurted.

"He's fine," Wick said quickly. "They're all fine. According to Ongel, it was like they wanted to prove a point. The dragonkin flew over their heads and passed right through the protective spells."

Tension thickened in the room. Fowl's shoulders hunched toward his ears. Beside him, Astor glared at the floor and raked a hand through his curls. Twill's posture barely changed, but Archer watched as something about her seemed to uncannily tense up.

Astor spoke before Archer could. "So, you're saying the enchantments didn't do anything at all, not even to slow those things down."

Wick's mouth tightened. "Yes. From the sound of it, the dragonkin flew in like they never even noticed the spells."

"Great." Archer crossed his arms.

"But that's not all," Wick added reluctantly. "After Ongel arrived, we got a messenger from the satyrs. The mineral and herbal spells they put up around their safe houses had no effect either. They found a dragonkin basking on a roof like it hadn't noticed a thing."

Twill's eyes, focused somewhere near her feet, lifted to look at first Wick, then Archer. "It sounds to me like they know the spells won't help, and they're trying to prove it to us. It's a power move."

"So," Astor said, "this means we can't shield ourselves

at all?"

"The centaurs are meeting now to discuss it," Wick said, "which is why I'm here for now; I have to wait until the meetings are over to return to the valley. Otherwise I'd be doing more research to help. I'm sure the centaurs will come up with something," he continued uncomfortably, "but yes, this is a bad sign. The enchanters' and the satyrs' spells were our strongest magic, after the Heather Stones."

"Wick," Twill said in a pointed tone, "are you going to tell me why we haven't tried the Heather Stones yet? Or rather, what went wrong, because I'll bet we already tried."

Wick hesitated, then sighed. "We did try. The stones arrived here only days after the Scorch returned, but for some reason they wouldn't respond." He shifted uncomfortably on his feet. "Until we find out why, we won't be able to use the Heather Stones."

The air in the room seemed to bristle as the tension worsened. Archer watched his brother. Fowl seemed contemplative.

"And if you don't find anything, then what?" Astor spoke calmly, but Archer saw the tension in his posture. "Do we just sit and wait for the inevitable?"

"Nobody's sitting around," Archer said. "If I know these people, they'll go through every option there is before they quit. Trust me, they're unstoppable."

"So are your dragonkin," Astor returned pointedly.

Fowl stood, and everyone paused. The tilt of Fowl's shoulders was sharp, resolved. Archer couldn't see his eyes.

"I'm going, then."

Astor's head swung up. "You're sure?"

Fowl nodded quickly. "Someone has to do it."

"Okay. Wait up." Astor sprang up, too, and followed Fowl toward the door. Archer's eyes darted between them as his heart raced faster. While Archer had been busy distracting himself, Fowl and Astor had concocted some plan of their own.

That couldn't be good.

Archer lunged after them. "Where are you going?"

"Out," Fowl said shortly. He shook out his wings as he strode toward the door. "Someone has to find a way out of the country before the dragons burn us all." Astor opened the huge centaur door, and Fowl forged ahead through the doorway.

Archer chased them down the ramp, practically treading on Astor's heels. "They won't just let you run. Nin warned us; they'll find you, and they'll kill you!"

Astor reached the bottom of the ramp and turned, hair swinging across his face. He clutched a rail in each hand, blocking Archer's path. "Archer, listen. We'll be all right."

A scoff ripped from Archer's throat. "Right. This is idiotic!"

"It's not," Astor said, in a voice so even and calm that Archer's vision nearly turned red. "We'll be alright. As long as we fly fast and low, nothing will see us."

Like flying faster had ever saved a Hessen from the fire. "You think that'll save you?" Archer demanded. He glanced over Astor's shoulder and his heart jumped as he realized: Fowl had never stopped walking. "Forget you," Archer spat at Astor. "I don't care what happens to *you*."

Archer vaulted the railing to race after his brother. "Fowl!"

Fowl turned so quickly that Archer almost ran into him. The locket swung from his neck with the hateful portrait still staring out of it. "Archer, calm down. We're just trying to help."

"You're trying to outrun them," Archer corrected. His blood pounded in his ears. "The last person who thought he could do that was our father, remember? Do you want to end up like him?"

As the crease between Fowl's brows deepened, Archer realized he'd made a mistake.

"If you want me to be different from him so badly," Fowl said in a clipped tone, "I'll prove it. I'll get out safe. And on the *insignificant* chance that you're right, and I'm wiped out, I guess you'll be better off, anyway."

Then he turned away and took off into the sky with Astor following.

Archer stared helplessly after them. His fists opened and closed, like they wanted to snatch Fowl out of the air.

Fowl had sounded too much like their father. Looked like him, too.

And on the chance I get wiped out . . .

I guess you'll be better off.

Something rustled in the trees. Archer's gaze leaped after it and glimpsed a tail vanishing into the brush.

Something had heard.

Archer's heart beat wildly in his throat. He'd never catch up with them, he knew that. Fowl was as fast as a bird of prey, and Astor could outfly Fowl any day. Archer had no hope of keeping up.

But the dragonkin did.

"Somebody!" Archer shouted at Wick and Twill, who stood uselessly in the doorway. "There are still manghar left in the valley. Somebody get one of the manghar! The Scorch won't just let them leave, you know they won't!"

"I'll go." Their male host appeared behind Wick. "I'm the fastest here."

Archer jumped out of the way as the centaur pounded past. Aethan raced into the trees, his hair and tail streaming behind him.

Archer looked around again. Where had that dragonkin gone?

He had a terrible feeling in his stomach, one that was getting too familiar by now. It felt like the moment he remembered he had left Fowl to protect the Hessen house alone. Or ages before, when he realized the manghar were on a manhunt for Wick. When he had first made a fool of that manghar guard and remembered manghar never let go of grudges, not until someone bled. The feeling could only mean one thing; something terrible was going to happen.

Wick stepped off the ramp behind Archer, but Archer didn't have time. Even if he couldn't keep up, he had to see.

Archer threw down his bag and took off up the mountain.

Stupid broken wing. Useless. Worthless. No good.

He heard Wick calling after him, but Archer didn't slow down. He slapped branches away as he raced as high as he could. Still no sign of the manghar. What was taking so long?

He made it to the crest of the hill and scanned the landscape for something higher, settling on a nearby rock formation. Archer dug his hands and feet into cracks and climbed, nearly splitting both his palms on the same sharp ledge as he ascended. Finally, he planted both hands on the rough surface at the peak and hauled his body on top of the rocks.

Heart pounding, Archer searched the skies for his brother.

Two winged shapes remained within view, indistinct in the middle of the horizon. They hadn't slowed down yet.

Movement in another part of the sky caught Archer's eye. Four dragonkin leaped from the trees, speeding toward Astor and Fowl. Neither seraph looked behind them.

Archer sucked in as much air as his lungs would hold. "*Fowl!*"

Fowl didn't even turn.

Then, before the other four even reached them, a fifth lizard sprang from the trees, just ahead of Fowl and Astor. Even from a distance, Archer saw their wings flare out as they desperately tried to stop in time.

Archer saw fire.

Then he saw two sets of wings drop down into the trees. One pair pale grey like his own, one pure white. They disappeared from view.

With a snap of wings, a manghar soared over his head toward the conflict.

How to Say All the Wrong Things

WICK RACED THROUGH the woods after the manghar. The snap of wings and echoing crack of branches faded into silence, leaving Wick with only the sound of his own footsteps crackling through the underbrush. He slowed from a run to a walk, listening.

Did the silence mean that the dragonkin had gone, or that they had killed Fowl and Astor, as well as the manghar?

He walked on toward the place the sounds had come from and noticed something else: the only footsteps he heard were his own.

Wick looked over his shoulder. Archer had not followed him.

That couldn't be a good sign.

He steadied himself and pushed forward. Archer could wait; for now he had to know that no one had died.

Three shapes separated from the dead twigs and branches of the forest in front of him. Fowl supported

Astor's limp as the manghar followed them, gripping his spear and watching the sky. Both Fowl and Astor were criss-crossed with scratches from tumbling through the trees, and Fowl's long hair stuck to a bloody gash on his forehead. The manghar behind them appeared to be completely unscathed.

Fowl slowed as he spotted Wick, making Astor and the manghar slow with him. As the distance between them closed, Fowl muttered, "Nobody died."

The knot in Wick's chest loosened. "That's the important thing. Your plan wasn't the wisest, but at least everyone is all right."

Wick fell into step with Fowl as he passed and noticed with a wince the scorched feathers across Astor and Fowl's wings. "What happened to the dragonkin?"

"Fled." The manghar kept his eyes on the sky. "They were only small ones, and they flew away before I could throw my spear."

"They were watching us," Wick murmured. "Just like Nin said they would be."

If they kept to their word on one thing, could the dragonkin be trusted to give Aro the full month like they'd promised?

What would happen if they didn't?

The four of them walked in silence. The red paint of their host's house appeared in flecks between the tree branches. As they drew nearer, Wick spotted the shape of someone on the porch blocking the doorway, arms crossed, mangled wing dangling.

Oh, no.

"Well?" Archer demanded as they stepped into the

clearing.

Fowl barely glanced up. "Don't start, Archer."

"I don't have to. Look at you." Archer's crossed arms tightened against his chest. "Tell me, did that help? Did you learn anything from *nearly dying*?"

"Yes," Fowl said, stopping stock-still at the base of the ramp. "Now I know that next time, we'll be fine as long as we're sure the dragonkin aren't watching. We came back in one piece; I don't know what more you want." Fowl put a foot on the ramp, but Archer didn't budge.

"I want to know you won't try that again," Archer said, jabbing a finger down the ramp at Fowl. "If that manghar hadn't been there, you could be in big trouble right now. Those dragonkin could have killed you!"

"Someone had to try." Astor broke in, and Archer's stormy gaze swung toward him. "If we run out of other options, we'll need a way to flee the country. Someone had to find a way out."

"And it didn't have to be you," Archer snapped.

"Why not?" Fowl demanded.

"Because *I* told you it was a bad idea. How come whenever I'm right, everyone decides not to listen to me, huh?" Archer let out an exasperated hiss and grabbed two fistfuls of his own hair. "I can't believe you're turning me into the responsible one here. I'm not the older one, I'm not supposed to be the voice of reason. I'm not supposed to be the worrier, either. That's his job." Archer pointed an accusing finger at Wick. "*Not* mine."

Wick wondered if he should intervene. The argument seemed to be getting more heated with every passing moment.

"No one asked you to be the responsible one, Archer," Fowl said, looking up with an icy expression. "Actually, no one asked you to interfere at all. So, if you're looking for the right person to blame, that would be yourself."

Archer's brow folded into a deep valley. "Don't start sounding like our father."

"I'm not. *You* are. Throwing blame? Waiting around just to tell me you're disappointed? That's just like him," Fowler muttered darkly. Then he paused, and spoke again, soft and sharp. "But at least he never yelled at *me*."

Wick watched as Archer flinched. But then Archer took a quick breath, and the words poured out faster than before. "That was his problem. Me, I haven't even *started* yelling yet." Archer paced down the ramp, his voice rising. "You're driving me insane! I don't even know what to do with you anymore."

"Archer, stop." Astor pulled his arm free of Fowl's shoulders and put himself between Archer and Fowl. "You're not helping. You're just making a scene."

Archer stepped forward, directly into Astor's breathing room—his favorite way to intimidate. Anyone else would have stepped back, but Astor just put his fingertips on Archer's chest and shoved. Archer stumbled back a few steps.

The time had come to get involved.

"Archer," Wick said sharply. "Leave it be. He's right; you're only making things worse."

Archer froze, gripping the railings. His eyes darted from Wick to Astor, then back to Wick. "You—you just—"

"Leave it for now. I mean it." Wick turned to Astor and Fowl. "If any of your injuries are serious, you should have them looked at by someone in the valley. If they aren't, stay here and lay low. We've had enough excitement for the day."

They both hesitated, but then Fowl nodded.

Archer straightened, still staring back and forth between Wick and Fowl. His mouth opened as if to argue, but then the crease in his brow abruptly released. "Whatever. Do what you want, but leave me out of it. I'm done with all of you." Hiking his bag higher up his shoulder, Archer skulked into the woods. Fowl just shook his head and returned to the house.

Briefly, Wick considered following Archer, but Archer was clearly in one of his moods. He probably wouldn't take kindly to anyone intervening with it. With a sigh, Wick opted to leave him alone for the time being. Archer would come around; he always did.

In the meantime, Wick had more work to do.

Approaching the doors of the library, Wick found Eland on his way out with his arms full of papers.

"Wick! The house next to mine found a trunk of old journals in a back room," Eland said. "I'm taking the day to go through those instead. I might be back later tonight, but if there are a lot of them, I might have to keep going through them tomorrow."

"Do you want a hand?" Wick asked.

"Only if you don't have too much to study already."

Wick shook his head. He followed Eland across the trodden-down grass toward a path into the hills. "You know," he said as they walked. "Archer was the first to recognize the dragonkin, from an old song. I wonder. . ."

"What do you wonder?" Eland promoted.

"If the dragonkin were somehow forgotten by history, I wonder if our folklore would remember them."

"There are some collections of folklore in the library," Eland said. "We could page through them."

"We could. . ." Wick scratched his head. "I wish we had some experts to ask, as well. Are there any good storytellers among the remaining refugees?"

"I don't know. You could ask Ongel."

"Only once we're done with the journals," Wick said.

"Speaking of journals," Eland said, "do we still have Caihu's journal?"

"I had it in Tor. I was trying to read it." Wick said slowly, thinking back. "It's in our bags somewhere."

"Do you think we need it?" Eland asked. "Did it have information that could help us?"

"I didn't make it far." Wick sighed, running a hand down the side of his face. "It was too confusing. But Caihu predicted all this, so he must have written something useful in that journal."

"Maybe Archer can make sense of it," Eland said.

They turned onto the shaded porch of a small grey house.

Wings flapped behind him, and Astor's voice shouted, "There he is. He's up here!"

"Wick!" another voice shouted, bouncing off the rocks in every direction. Hoofbeats raced toward them.

"Over here," Wick called, turning.

Having done his duty, Astor swung around and dove back down to the valley. The red head of Eland's father appeared around a turn in the path, his eyes wide.

"It's the leshy," Hirim said. "They're here."

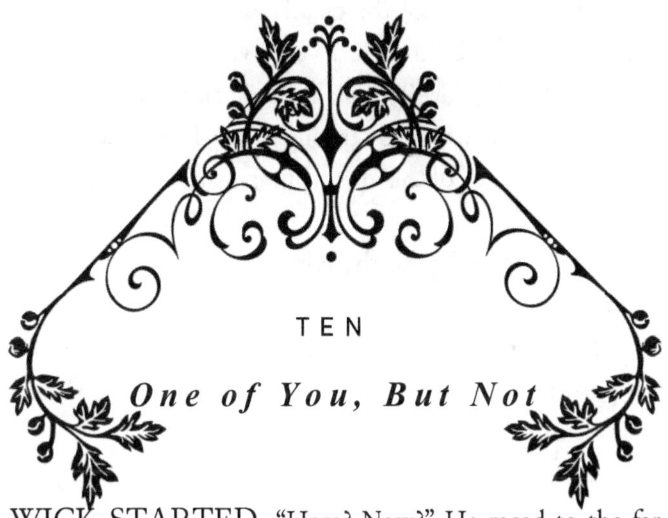

One of You, But Not

WICK STARTED. "Here? Now?" He raced to the far end of the porch. As the valley came into view, he stopped short.

When he'd wondered about the leshy appearing, Wick hadn't known what to expect. He'd thought that when the time came—if the time ever came—they would only see a few leshy. A handful of daring and adventurous ones, like Twill, or a few frightened families. That was, if any leshy showed up at all.

He had guessed wrong.

It almost seemed that the valley had sprouted saplings. The tree people roved across every part of the valley. Groups of them were already seated across the grass like the crowds had been just a few weeks ago, waiting for help.

Waiting for him?

Wick's heart raced at the thought of speaking to any leshy. His last visit to leshy territory played behind his eyes on repeat: a throne room carpeted with autumn leaves; the tight grip of the guard's hand on his shoulder; running for his life through his own village. Hiding in the bushes and seeing Twill's look of disappointment.

The wind whipped through his hair, and Wick rubbed the flesh of his now-human arms to ward off gooseflesh.

Hirim stepped onto the porch beside him. "You look anxious."

"I'm worried this won't go well," Wick murmured softly, so no one else would hear. "The last time I visited their territory, I had to run to get away."

Hirim nodded. "I heard. But this could be your chance to reconnect with them. I'll speak to them if you want me to, but if you ask me, I think you should be the one to lead."

"I don't know if I can." The valley full of leshy might as well have been a pit of snakes, for how daunting they seemed. The knots in Wick's stomach tightened. "I don't know if they'll let me."

"Eland tends to worry about taking charge, too," Hirim replied. He took a few steps down the path and looked back. "Just like him, I'll give you any help you ask for. But I'll also give you the same advice: You may be the youngest person in a conversation, but remember, you represent the valley. You're the one in charge here."

The pain in Wick's stomach didn't leave. But Wick knew that if he didn't move now, he never would. He stepped down from the porch to the path, and the sunlight warmed his face. Through the crowd, he spotted the royals.

No. Not all of the royals. Only two. Wick recognized them by the crowns on their heads—the wicker wrapped around the head of Telf, the eldest prince, and the soft pink blooms that crowned their youngest slip of a princess, Lilt. An attendant at Princess Lilt's side pointed toward Wick.

Wick's feet stopped moving as their heads turned his way.

Maybe he wasn't ready to face the royal family. But there they stood—not in their throne room, not even in leshy territory. In the valley. Weary and in need. And despite all the time that had passed and the many bagfuls of water under the bridge, Wick could help them.

He steadied himself and took another step.

"Welcome to the valley," Wick said to the prince and princess as he approached. He clasped his hands at his front. "What brings you here?"

"Creatures came down from the sky," the prince said. He stood several inches taller than Wick, and the prickling wicker wrapped around his brow lended a serious look to his face. "They burned the forest, and days ago, we found nests of them in the trees."

The little princess took a step forward, out of her brother's shadow. "The people wanted somewhere that they could feel safe." Her chin dropped by a finger's width. "We can't give them that in our territory."

Twill's voice spoke in Wick's mind. *If I'd been through what you've been through, I wouldn't care about them anymore.*

But Wick wasn't her. He made his own choices. "Unfortunately, we can't promise you safety here, either. If you'd like, we can find somewhere for you to go, like we have for the other refugees, but the dragonkin have reappeared here often. The valley isn't safe."

"What about the places you sent the other refugees, were they safe?" the princess asked. She lifted her face to gaze hopefully at Wick.

"I haven't heard otherwise," Wick said calmly. It wouldn't help to tell them that the dragonkin were everywhere, or that they couldn't be kept away, even with magic. Even so, it would not be safe for the leshy to stay in the valley. "Do your people need medical attention?"

The prince shook his head. "All we need is a safe place to stay."

"Then I'll approve this with the centaurs. Give me a moment." Wick turned, then paused. His shield of professional indifference wavered.

Wick swiveled toward the prince and princess again. "I need to know. Is this everyone? Are there more coming?"

My family?

Princess Lilt laughed stiffly. "You know the leshy. All of them want to be safe, but it's hard to decide what's safe since—"

"More survived," Telf cut in. "But the rest stayed behind."

The rest had thought it safer to stay put than to risk the world outside leshy territory. The princess was right: Wick knew the leshy. He should have guessed.

With a nod, Wick left the royals and wove through the leshy refugees toward the Great Hall. Just a few seconds of speaking to the royal family left him feeling like a weight rested on his shoulders.

Easing the door open, he slipped inside to search for Ongel. But when he turned around, he found not Ongel, but Tinor.

Wick had tried to avoid Tinor since arriving in the valley, and until now, he had succeeded. It didn't matter that Tinor had finally sided with them—he had seen the Scorch and had no other choice. Tinor had been their strongest opposer, even going far enough to lie to their allies, and Wick didn't feel ready to discuss all that with him.

He certainly didn't have the strength to do so now.

Tinor paused as well.

"Do you need any help?" Tinor said at last, barely cutting the tension. "There are quite a few leshy out there. Do they need a place to stay?"

"I'm planning to send them to the nixies, if the nixies can take more," Wick responded. The tone of his own voice was strange to him; almost too confident. It was the tone of someone speaking to an equal, not to a mentor he had looked up to for years. "Until then, the leshy have plenty of space and sun. I do need a place for the prince and princess to stay. It would be disrespectful to just leave them out in the valley."

"The pavilion nearest to the lake, with the upper-level balcony, is my personal study." Tinor pointed toward the hall's eastern windows as they poured light. "The royal family can stay there. They should get more than enough sunlight."

Wick paused. Tinor was. . . offering help?

First the leshy had appeared, then the royal family

had asked Wick for help, and now Tinor came offering. . . what? An olive branch? An apology? How many more surprises could he take in one day?

"Thank you," Wick managed.

"You seem tense," Tinor pointed out awkwardly. "Is something wrong?"

Wick raised his head. Even if Tinor meant to apologize, he hadn't done it yet. Wick knew he couldn't look like a child again, not in front of Tinor and not after all that had happened. He spoke frankly at last, his words short and clear. "I doubt you know anything about it, but this is the first time I've seen my people since they banished me. Technically I'm not even supposed to *call* them my people anymore. And now they came to me for help. It's only fair that it feels strange."

Wick fled before Tinor could answer. The two royals waited for him outside the doors. Their spotless robes and crowns made them look out of place in the burned valley. "There's a pavilion beside the lake," Wick said, pointing. "The one with the balcony. I've arranged for you to stay there."

"And what about our relocation?" the youngest leshy princess asked. Her flower crown glittered as she raised her face to Wick's. "We're overrunning this valley already; we'll only be in the way if we stay here."

"Plans are in progress," Wick said. "I hope to move everyone toward the nixie kingdom in the next day or so."

"Wonderful." As Wick beckoned for them to follow him toward the lake, the princess added, "We appreciate your help, Wick."

Wick caught the warning look that Telf gave her.

Clearly his exile was still alive and well, even in catastrophe. The royal family—and likely the rest of the leshy as well—were barred from treating Wick with any more friendliness than they would a stranger.

The silence as they approached the pavilion together wrapped around Wick's neck like a chokehold. Wick shaded his eyes from the sunlight reflecting off the gold columns, but the royals with their inhuman glowing eyes didn't even flinch.

"This is the one," Wick said stiffly, gesturing to the stairs. "I hope you'll be comfortable." As eager as he was to exit the situation and relieve the pressure building behind his temples, Wick stayed long enough to watch the royals start their ascent before he turned to leave.

"Excuse me," a soft telepathic voice said in his ear.

Wick halted and turned, already expecting to see the princess. She stood halfway up the stairs, her hand still resting on the rail.

"Please forgive Telf," she said, her voice soft but pleading. "And myself. You need to understand. You were right about catastrophe coming, but because of your crimes, we're bound by the rules of your exile, just like you are. I believe that you should be pardoned, but I'm the youngest; I have to wait for someone else to speak up first, or everyone will remember that I'm just a girl, and they'll never take me seriously."

"I understand," Wick said stiffly.

"No, listen." The princess shook her head ever so slightly. She stepped down the last stair, and the dappled lake light swam over the bark of her face. "So many leshy have argued on your behalf. Your family has come to us three times, and Twill entreats us each time she's in the city. One of your school teachers sent us ten essays on why your banishment was unjust, and a centaur, Ongel, has sent us page after page spelling out all that you've done for everyone. Your banishment stands for now, but I'm waiting for the first chance to put it away."

"I appreciate that," Wick said, slowly, making sure he meant it. Realizing how tightly his shoulders had clenched, he straightened his spine. "But I think you should know: no matter what happens, I don't think I'll be going back to leshy territory."

"Because of us?" The princess's voice was frank, but kind.

"Partly. It's not the place for me anymore." Wick swallowed. "I'll never fit there again. I don't know if I ever fit in the first place."

The princess thought for a moment, then her eyes rose to Wick's, brighter than before. "You're right, that's exactly what you should do. We leaned on you too much, didn't we?"

Her candor made Wick pause. "Sometimes," he admitted. "I wondered what would happen to the leshy if I didn't work so hard."

"Exactly. You're right to branch out. Twill thinks so, anyway." Lilt clasped her hands in her lap. "Did Twill make it here safely?"

"She did," Wick said, relieved to redirect the conversation. "She's helping a manghar with his explosives."

"Explosives?" the princess said, surprise in her voice.

"They're a lot like our fireworks, honestly. Maybe

she'll let you take a look at them."

"It sounds exciting." Princess Lilt gestured over Wick's shoulder. "There she is now. Let's ask."

Wick turned to find Twill striding toward him in her long, loping gait. "Wick, leshy materialized in one afternoon—your highness?" she said, posing the address nearly like a question. "I didn't know you were here."

"I'm glad you're safe, Twill," the princess said. "Wick was just telling me about your explosives."

"That's why I was looking for Wick," Twill said. She glanced at the princess again, then spoke to Wick in a low voice. "Did anyone else want that black powder?"

Wick frowned. "Not that I know of. Why?"

"Because we've been missing two barrels since last night." Twill gave Wick a meaningful look.

Would the dragonkin steal the barrels? Would anyone else? Aro was in crisis; surely it had been only a matter of time before the people began to plunder supplies.

But why take just black powder, and not anything they could eat?

"I'll ask around," Wick said. "Maybe someone took the powder for their own experiments and didn't tell you."

"Hmm." Twill crossed her arms. Her fingertips tapped against her upper arm. "I hope you're right, because no other explanation sounds that pretty."

Wick turned back to the princess. "It looks like I just became busy."

"Of course," Princess Lilt responded. "Let me know if there's any way we can help you, Wick."

Wick's heart squeezed at the use of his name. He

swallowed, but his voice emerged still thin and choked. "The same to you, your highness." Then, like a thunderbolt, he remembered. "Your highness, is Lelo here? The museum guard. Did he come with you?"

Lilt shook her head. "He said leaving the territory would be no safer."

Of course. Wick's heart sank again.

Lilt's head tilted. "Tell me why you needed him, and maybe I can recommend someone else for the job."

"I remember him swapping stories and lore with my teacher during festivals. I'm going on a hunch," Wick admitted, feeling a little foolish, "but I think I might find some useful information in the old stories."

"In that case," the princess responded crisply, "the next best thing would be me."

Wick's heart thudded. "You?"

"Folklore is a hobby of mine. Your old teacher is a friend of mine, and I swap stories with him, too, when I get the chance. I'm surprised you didn't know that." The laugh entered her voice again, and for a moment, the princess sounded almost like Twill.

"I had no idea," Wick admitted.

"Well, what are you looking for?" the princess asked.

"Anything that could help us with this." Wick gestured toward the valley. "Stories or poems or songs, about the dragonkin, about fire, about the flowers dying and the trees giving up. Anything that would give us an advantage."

"I don't think any of our stories could give you a tactical advantage," Lilt said. "But I'll see what I can remember, and I'll write it all down before the end of the day. Does that sound agreeable?"

"That's exactly what I need. Thank you."

"Of course."

Wick hurried away from the princess and Twill before anything else could happen, and didn't stop walking until he had sequestered himself safely inside Ongel's dim study.

He ran a hand down his face and took a deep breath. "When did life become so complicated?" he murmured to himself.

The door at his side opened, letting in sunlight and chatter as Ongel's head rounded the door. "Is everything all right? You raced in here like someone was after you." Ongel shut the door behind him, and the sound from the hall faded to silence again.

"I've had more uneasy conversations in the last hour than I expected for the whole week," Wick admitted. The day had only just begun, but already exhaustion filled his head, so heavy that he considered laying his heavy head down on the floor. "The last time I saw the royal family, they ran me out of the territory, but I just finished settling them in a nice comfortable pavilion by the lake. Tinor's pavilion. Tinor who I just spoke to for the first time since he accused me of treason."

"Tinor isn't quite who he was when he was working against you," Ongel said gently. "Despite the past, I believe he's trying to change. What did he say to you?"

"He just asked if I needed any help, nothing more," Wick said, shrugging tired shoulders. "But I could hardly talk to him. I used to be more forgiving, Ongel. What happened to me?"

"You have more to forgive these days." Ongel's dark eyes watched Wick's face. "It's harder to forgive open lies and rejection than to forgive an everyday foolish mistake. I don't expect your bond with Tinor will mend quickly."

A sigh remained trapped inside Wick's chest. Or maybe it was a knot to match the ones in his stomach. "Tinor was the first person I met in the valley, I think. I was lost the moment I set foot down here, and he directed me to the main hall where I belonged." The words poured out. "He was always quick to lend me a hand when I needed advice. But when I sided with Archer, Tinor decided to work against me."

"Tinor mentored me when I was young, too," Ongel said. "But I think I've mentioned that before. He's always feared being wrong. I'm sure that makes things especially difficult for him these days."

Wick frowned. "What do you mean?"

Ongel pressed his lips together, hesitating. "Wick, few people know about this, but I trust you to keep it quiet. Tinor's seeing power has run out. He has none left."

Wick's eyes flew to Ongel's face. Ongel's mouth pressed into a grim line.

"His supply was depleted even before you began gathering the Heather Stones, and after, when you escaped from our cells and I joined you in Tor, he couldn't understand it. He was so desperate to see our reasoning instead of understanding it that he used up the rest of his power." Ongel smiled wryly. "Now he can only go off evidence and blind faith, like the rest of us."

Wick's heart felt strangely heavy. All of his life, the grey-haired figure of Tinor had been a person of authority.

Now, knowing that Tinor could no longer see visions gave him a strange feeling. Like he had. . . outgrown Tinor, somehow. "I feel guilty knowing he did all that because of Archer and I."

"Don't think it was your fault," Ongel said gently. "Even if it had been only Archer, or someone else, or if no one had done a thing and the Scorch had arrived anyway, I still believe Tinor would have depleted himself. All of us were confused, but Tinor desperately wanted to know why his skill alone couldn't give him answers. He did this to himself. From the beginning, I warned Eland not to make the same mistake."

Wick's heart thudded. "Is Eland's power depleting?"

"No, but only because I warned him to watch himself. He had to know why you would join Archer when he couldn't see a thing." Ongel paused. "It was a very confusing time for all in the valley."

Wick smiled a bit. "Believe me, it was a confusing time for me, too."

All day Wick worked to keep the leshy comfortable and provide for their every need. Some asked what was happening, others wanted to know if he had their relatives, all seemed uncomfortable outside of the forest. Wick tried to ignore the stares. He carried blankets to keep children warm and assured everyone he met that they would soon be moved to someplace safe.

The royal family stayed in their pavilion most of the day. Whenever Wick walked by, he could pick up tidbits of their conversation. They seemed to be discussing a course of action.

Strangely enough, while serving his people more than ever in his life, Wick felt more like a leader than a servant. The leshy treated him differently, too, looked at him as they would look to a member of authority, not a messenger or a child. Of course, many of them probably didn't know or recognize Wick, but even the prince and princess had *asked* for his help. Visibly, unarguably, something had changed.

With every question he answered and every little problem he solved, Wick experienced a growing sense of. . . something. Something so new and faint that he couldn't identify it. But it felt good.

Like drinking the sun again.

Late in the evening, after he finally decided the leshy could survive without him, Wick collapsed into bed, where he slept soundly until dawn. When he awoke, he remembered the library and all his unfinished work there, so with hardly a word to anyone, he made the hike back to the valley and down the ramp to the belly of the library. He leafed through papers gently, trying to recall where he had left off.

"Ah, yes," he murmured as he found his bookmark. "I was getting a complete education on the manghar trade routes." He rubbed his forehead. "I wonder if this is what it feels like to go insane."

"Seclusion in a dark library sometimes does that." Ongel appeared on the ramp from upstairs. "But is that what you meant?"

"No." Wick swiped at his aching eyes. "There's hardly anything here on the Scorch. Or the Heather Stones. We need a lot more information on both if we're going to make plans, but all I've found so far are. . . surprises."

"Surprises?" Ongel entered the room and leaned over the table. "What kind of surprises?"

Wick tapped the cover of the borrowed deerskin journal. "Aro's history couldn't be perfect, I knew that, but. . . we've fallen on some desperate times, Ongel."

"We have," Ongel agreed. "And yet every time we've survived. It gives me hope."

Wick paused, thinking of the questions he had written in the journal. Would it be better to bring them up now, rather than later? "Ongel?"

Ongel's eyebrows rose. "What is it?"

"There have been many times when the valley had to ignore smaller disasters to stop a bigger one." Wick rolled his pen between his fingers. "Even knowing the future ahead of time, how can you know what to do about it?"

Ongel made a humming noise. "With more care than you think. I can't even see the future, you know, but I do help to make decisions here. Deciding the fate of everyone isn't easy."

"But how can you decide? Especially now?" Wick's mouth made a single gasp of a laugh. "I wasn't even good at making simple decisions as a messenger. These days, every decision I make is more complicated than the last. I could never decide the fate of Aro. How can you make those choices?"

"As well as we're able. Sometimes even with our best efforts, we can't change the future. Other times, we stop one terrible future and create a different one by accident." Ongel sighed heavily, then turned to Wick with a comforting smile that just barely reached his eyes. "If you ask me, changing the future is actually about living in the present. All we can do is assess facts in the moment and do what seems right. The consequences are not under our control." He straightened. "On a similar note, I should find Archer. He seemed anxious before I left, but I haven't had the chance to see him since I got back."

"He's still at the host house, I think," Wick responded. "He wasn't awake yet when I came down."

Ongel's brow creased slightly. "I was just there, and Fowler said Archer's been gone all morning." He paused. "We both assumed he was with you."

A chill crawled up Wick's spine as he realized: "He stormed off yesterday. I never saw him come back."

The twitching of Ongel's tail stilled. "Stormed off?"

"After he got in an argument with Fowl and Astor, he just walked away. I assumed he came back to the house sometime during the night, but I never thought to check." The pricking chill swept up Wick's neck. "I haven't seen him since yesterday afternoon. No one has."

The Pedestal

"NOW, LET'S STAY CALM," Ongel said, but Wick saw a furrow of worry in his brow. "Let someone know that we're leaving, and we'll go to your host house. He might just be hiding in a corner somewhere."

Wick nodded quickly and slid out of his chair to follow Ongel. They passed Hirim on their way out of the library.

"Archer may be missing," Ongel told him. "We'll look for him at Aethan and Dorana's house first, but if he isn't there, we may need to start a search."

"I see." Hirim looked at Wick with a touch of pity in his eyes. "Good luck. I hope you find him."

"Thank you." Wick raced up the path after Ongel. All the way through the forest, Wick's hands clenched into fists by his sides. If he had just gone after Archer, if he had spoken to him. . .

Calm down, you don't know for sure that he's gone. Wait to panic until you're sure.

After what felt like an eternity, the red house appeared through the trees, and Wick sprinted the rest of the way to the ramp. Ongel wasn't far behind him.

Wick threw open the door and shouted, "Archer! Are you here?"

No answer.

Wick strode up to the second floor. Maybe Archer was still sleeping. He whisked Archer's door open. "Archer!"

The bed, in its usual rumpled, unkempt state, lay empty. The light curtains in the window blew slightly in the breeze.

No Archer.

A quick glance around the room yielded no sight of Archer's leather satchel, either.

Don't panic yet.

Wick opened every door in the host house. He checked every bedroom, even his own, in case Archer was hiding somewhere he thought he wouldn't be found. Wick raced back down the ramp to check the kitchen, but found Ongel already there.

"I see he wasn't upstairs, either," Ongel said grimly.

Wick shook his head.

"What's going on?" Fowler appeared through the open front door. "What are we all shouting about?"

"No one can find Archer anywhere," Wick stepped back, out of the kitchen. "I'm worried. Did anyone see him come back last night?"

Fowl hesitated. "No," he said finally. "But he always does. That's his routine. He wanders until it's late, and then he comes back after the rest of us are asleep. He's done that since he was little."

"But this time," Wick insisted, "no one has seen him since yesterday. We have to assume that he's missing. I'll try to convince one of the manghar to help; they're excellent trackers and most of them are looking for someplace to direct their energy anyway." He slipped past Fowl and out onto the porch.

The snap of wings caught his attention. His first instinct: *duck*. His second: *look up*. Wick spotted a manghar passing overhead.

"Hey!" Wick bellowed. "Excuse me!"

Miraculously, the manghar heard. He wheeled a vulture's lazy circle and swooped between the trees to slam down before Wick with a spray of loose earth. He looked vaguely familiar; if Wick was lucky, maybe he'd worked with this manghar before.

"My friend, Archer, is missing," Wick said, "and I'm worried he might be in trouble. I need your help to find him, and quickly."

The manghar paused. "Archer?" A small smirk spread across his face. "The thief?"

Like a bolt of lightning, Wick remembered. He remembered crouching with a snickering Archer as they hid from a manghar guard. He remembered a prickle of annoyance at Archer's carefree, even gleeful tone, whispering that the manghar wanted him dead. He definitely remembered the narrowed eyes and the cold sneer of the manghar in question.

The same manghar now staring down at Wick.

Grinning with a thousand teeth, the manghar spread his wings. "Don't you worry. I'll find him."

"No!" Wick lunged forward. With one hand, he grabbed the collar of fur around the manghar's shoulders. With his other hand, he snatched a sharp spike of metal hanging from the bat man's belt.

The manghar's eyes lit up with something like delight, and he seized the collar of Wick's shirt, too. Locked together with Wick's new dagger jammed against the manghar's gut, and the manghar's talons inches from Wick's throat, their eyes met. Wick hardened his face to avoid flinching as the manghar leered.

The manghar tilted his head and asked in a grating growl, "Are you scared of me, tree boy?"

"Not for myself. No." Wick tightened his grip on the manghar's ruff of fur. "Just for Archer. I hear you're a good tracker, so I know you can find him. But when we do find him, how do I know you won't kill him?"

"Is that all?"

"Unless you give me another reason."

"Good." The manghar pushed Wick away, breaking Wick's grip on him as easily as thread.

Wick didn't lower the knife. "I could hurt you, but I'd rather not."

"You don't have to." The manghar rolled his neck, joints cracking. "I don't plan to kill the boy."

Wick blinked. His knife arm dropped slightly before he remembered himself. "Tell me what you mean by that."

The manghar tilted his head back to examine the sky. "Have you felt the thrill of filling someone's eyes with fear? Watched them face the choice between fighting and fleeing, and choosing to run? Reveled in their flinch when you enter the room? Have you ever experienced that?" The manghar paused and threw a glance at Wick.

Realizing the manghar wanted a response, Wick shook his head.

"I doubt you have. But understand, tree boy; you're good at understanding. I have a wife and two children. I don't have the time or conscience to kill a boy for embarrassing me. But embarrass me, he did. So, even though I haven't wanted to kill Archer for years, I do love to make him run away. Do you understand?"

Wick's knife arm lowered. "If you didn't make him fear the consequences, he would never leave you alone."

"Precisely." The manghar extended a huge hand tipped with talons. "Shake my hand, tree boy."

Wick shook the hand with all his strength. The bones of his hand ground against one another in the manghar's grip. "Let's use names, shall we? I'm Wick."

"My name is Leroy."

Such an everyday name. Archer would have laughed. As it was, Wick had to suppress his own smile. "Would you like your knife back?"

"Never. You rightfully took it. You should keep it always."

"In that case, you should get started," Ongel said, appearing with a suddenness that made Wick jump, nearly dropping his new knife. "Every moment Archer stays lost is another moment he has to find trouble."

Leroy cracked his knuckles with a sound like firecrackers. "I'd rather find him first."

Wick's paranoia prickled once more, but he couldn't afford to be picky. Leroy's tracking skill—and his personal tie to Archer—gave them their best chance.

"Then we should get moving as soon as possible. Ongel, you're needed here, so you should stay in the valley in case he comes back." Another thought struck Wick like a thunderclap. "And the leshy. They should be fine taking direction from the centaurs, but if they need another leshy to talk to them, I'm sure that Twill can take charge until I get back. Tell her I'm sorry for leaving without notice." Wick paused, thinking. What else? "Oh. And you should probably tell Astor where we've gone. I don't know how soon we'll be back."

For the time being, that would take care of everything.

"So Leroy can track Archer, and Fowl and I—Fowl?" Wick turned in time to see Fowl's back retreating into the host house.

"Fowler!" Wick bounded up the steps. Grabbing Fowl by the arm, he demanded, "Where are you going?"

"I thought it was obvious. I'm going inside," Fowl said dryly. "But if you can't wrap your mind around that, I can always spell it out." He and Wick stared at each other for a long, tense moment.

Fowl sighed. "Clearly, I'll have to. As you can see, I'm not coming."

Wick, who could not "see," fumbled for words. He turned to Leroy. "Leroy, could you find Archer's trail while I speak to Fowl?"

"With pleasure." Leroy spread his wings and soared into the forest. Ongel gave Wick a meaningful nod and started off toward the valley.

Wick faced Fowl, who was vanishing again into the host house. Wick chased after him and stopped in the doorway. "Fowl, do you understand what's at stake? Anything could happen to Archer out there."

"No, Wick, you're the one who doesn't understand." Fowl sat on one of the couches with forced relaxation. "Do you know what Archer's doing?"

"Punching someone in the face, if I know him well enough."

"Clearly, you *don't* know him well enough, and you also weren't listening. Do you know what Archer is *doing*? Do you know what he tried to tell us by leaving without notice?"

Wick frowned. "I don't know what you mean."

"You wouldn't, because you haven't known him long," Fowl informed him. "I've known Archer since the day he was born. I've seen this pattern before, and I know what it means. The simple fact of the matter is that Archer doesn't want us to find him."

Fowl sounded so cold, and so certain. Dead certain. Wick took a deep breath to steady his racing heart. "I don't think that's true."

"Because you don't know anything," Fowl said quickly. "Archer is immature; he behaves like a child. If he wants you to follow him, which isn't often, he makes a big show of slamming doors and then he stomps up to an open hallway so you can find him easily. If he wants time to himself, he goes for a wander and comes back after dark to avoid you. He's done that since we were children. But if he's gone for longer than a day, you should give up."

"Why?" The question came out in a sharper tone than Wick intended. The gnawing fear in his gut was making him careless.

"Because, Wick, he's given up on you." Fowl waited a moment, watching Wick's face. When Wick couldn't come up with a response, Fowl went on. "You have to understand the method. Archer doesn't give people chances very often, but when he does, he'll only give you one. The best one and only chance you could want. If Archer decides he admires and trusts you, he puts you on the loftiest pedestal he's got. He thinks you can do no wrong, that you'll never let him down, that you're the only thing that floats in a sea of evil." Fowl shrugged his heavy shoulders, palms up. "And just like that, he forgets that you're mortal. The fall from that pedestal is inevitable, and fatal. By proving that you're fallible, you dash your own temple to pieces, and once you do, you can never go back. Because he'll only offer you one chance."

"So I suppose we've both fallen off the pedestal now?" Wick asked, trying to sound nonchalant as his mind raced. Fowl had to be wrong. Fowl looked at life through the same melancholy lens that Archer often did. But the description of the pedestal sounded much too familiar— too much like how the leshy had rejected him. It opened a hole in the pit of his stomach.

Fowl's smile was tight. "Not quite. I haven't been on the pedestal since the moment he broke his wing. In his mind, I should have saved him—no, I should have built him stronger wings with my bare hands, out of sticks and clay—but I didn't, and that makes me an evil brother. I've been trying to climb back into his respect for years. But yesterday, I knocked myself down from wherever I climbed to, and I took you down with me." Fowl took a deep breath. "So, now he's given up on both of us."

The pit in Wick's stomach only deepened as Fowl finally fell silent. Then, like a beam of light, clarity broke through the cloud of despair. "Fowl," Wick said quietly, "I have to be honest: I don't think either of us understands Archer."

Fowl looked up at Wick quickly, almost angry at the rebuttal.

"We're both doing our best," Wick went on, before Fowl could interrupt, "but Archer doesn't make himself knowable. Since he left Tor, he could have changed in any number of ways from how you remember him. So, you could be wrong. That's one possibility."

"The other is that I'm right, and he wants us to stay away," Fowl said bitterly.

"Exactly." Wick gathered up his courage and spoke quickly, "So if you're right, if he's abandoned us without even a goodbye, I don't think he deserves to get what he wants. I'm going to find him whether he likes it or not, and you're coming with me."

Leroy's voice boomed out from the trees. "I have the trail!"

"Let's go, Fowl." Wick stepped off the porch without another glance back. With surprise and a little bit of pride, he heard Fowl's footsteps behind him.

For now, he had Fowl's attention. If he was lucky, Wick could hang on to that attention and use it to help both the Hessen boys.

Something new once again flowed through Wick's veins. It felt like once again, something had shifted irreversibly, but this time perhaps it had shifted in a good way.

Leroy stalked through the forest, tracking on foot for Wick's sake. He kept his eyes fastened on an invisible track Wick couldn't see. Here and there he tried to point out a clue to Wick or Fowl, but Wick only saw a leaf like any other, a patch of moss like any other. A glance at Fowl's furrowed brow proved that Fowl couldn't make sense of Leroy's trail either.

For the time being, Wick had to trust that Leroy knew where to go.

Leroy kept a relentless pace, but Wick was grateful that it kept himself and Fowl too out of breath to talk. Fowl had come with them, yes. But Fowl still believed that Archer had left them indefinitely.

Wick didn't know what to believe.

If I understood Archer, Wick told himself, jumping over a ditch to follow Leroy, *I would know why he left. And what he plans to do.*

But I don't.

He tried not to think about what might happen if they didn't find Archer. All the same, as they walked deeper into the darkening forest, he couldn't stop thinking about the last time Archer had struck out on his own. That time, Wick had assumed the world would end, and they would both die before they ever saw one another again. But then, after apparently a week of punching everyone he hated, Archer had returned.

Granted, he returned to stop Wick from being murdered by three manghar, but at least he had come back, in the end.

Archer hadn't come back this time. Now, he was the one in certain danger, and no matter the cost, Wick had to be the one to find him.

The sunset had passed over them and sunk into the western sky when Leroy stopped to rifle through the bushes. As the bushes rustled, Wick foolishly hoped that Archer would emerge, but when Leroy whisked his arms out of the shrubs, he instead held a fistful of flapping reins.

A horse, golden and flustered, emerged from the bushes with her eyes rolling.

Sasha!

Nausea stirred in Wick's gut. Archer had abandoned his horse.

"I have a terrible feeling about this," Wick said. He pulled Sasha's bridle closer to rub her nose. Anything to still the tremor in his fingers. "We have to find him, and soon."

"We've lost the light," Fowl pointed out.

Wick shook his head. "That doesn't matter. He's looking for serious trouble, I'm sure of it. If we give him even one extra hour, he might find what he's looking for. Leroy, do you still have the trail?"

Leroy snorted. "As fresh as the moment he passed through."

Wick stepped into the stirrup and swung his leg over Sasha's back. "Then let's keep after him."

They continued the hunt as darkness set in. Leroy kept his night eyes on the ground, but Wick and Fowl switched to calling Archer's name into the night. With every shout, Wick prayed that if they did pass Archer, he would answer.

The hours crawled by, and every mile seemed to go

by slower than the last. Wick continued doggedly forward. After twice an eternity, the night crawled into early morning, and light peeked through the trees.

Archer still hadn't appeared.

Wick realized Sasha had stopped walking. Exhaustion hung heavy behind Wick's eyes and weighed like boulders on his limbs. It seemed to drag him toward the ground. He looked around. Nothing but more unremarkable forest in every direction.

At last Wick allowed himself to think: *What if we never find him?*

A soft sound caught Wick's attention, and he twisted in the saddle. Leroy stood a few paces behind Sasha, his expression almost morbidly placid.

"Your friend is over there." Leroy raised a muscular arm and pointed to a nearby rock formation clutched in a dense thicket.

"How do you—" Wick's words vanished as he spotted pale grey feathers fluttering above a ridge of the rocks. Equal parts relief and fear rushed through his veins, bringing him back to life. "I see him! Thank you!"

Wick slid down from Sasha's back and dashed toward the rocks, slapping branches of pine needles out of his path. The rock formation towered over him. Jutting stones and ledges made easy handholds. Wick barely touched the rocks as he raced to the top.

Ducking one final branch, Wick scrambled onto the flat top of the rock, and the owner of the fluttering feathers came into full view.

Wick froze. The rock was cold on his palms. "Oh, Archer."

Archer lay sprawled across the stones, one arm bent around a jutting rock like a makeshift companion. He didn't look well. His chest rose and fell regularly in his sleep, but his pale face glistened with a sickly sheen. His hair, which usually seemed to stand up on its own, stuck to the dampness of his forehead. Had it rained, or was that shine just sweat? Archer's clothes appeared to be clinging to his skin.

Wick's senses returned to him. He leaned out from the rocks and shouted to the others. "We found him!" Hurrying back to Archer, Wick crouched and shook his friend by the shoulder. "Archer, wake up. We've been looking for you everywhere."

Archer stirred, and his red-rimmed eyes opened halfway. "Wh—Wick? Why're you here?" He pulled himself into something like a sitting position against the rocks and dragged his hands down his face.

Wick put a hand to his forehead, nearly laughing. "What am I doing here? We've been trying to find you all night." Wick looked around the plateau, and at last he noticed all the items scattered across the uneven plateau. "Actually, what are *you* doing here? What were you trying to do?" His eyes stopped on a barrel spilling dark mounds of something.

The stolen black powder. Both barrels of it.

Wick took a deep breath. "What are you doing with those? Were you going to. . . blow something up?"

Behind the barrel, something glinted a familiar green. The Heather Stones? But no, the real Heather Stones were still locked up in the valley, and these stones lay jumbled in a pile without sparking or reacting to one another. "And you have fake Heather Stones?"

"Yes, I was going to blow something up." Archer pulled his knees in and sat cross-legged without looking at Wick. The hollows under his eyes deepened in the sunlight. "And the fake stones are from Astor's house. He was the one who made them for us the first time, so I stashed a bunch in my bag before we left Tor."

"Why?"

"Is this an interrogation?" Archer snapped. "It was bait. Now, will you leave me alone?"

Wick pointed to the fake stones. "What on earth did you think you were going to catch with—" The words died in his throat. Waiting in the middle of the forest, surrounded by a stash of artificial Heather Stones and real explosives, Archer could only be hunting for one thing.

Seeing Wick's dumbfounded expression, Archer muttered, "And so clarity arrives."

His voice woke Wick from his shock. Wick's gaze returned to Archer. "You were going to bait the dragonkin, and then blow them up."

"Give the man a prize," Archer said, meeting Wick's eyes at last. Archer's eyes were tired, glassy, but angry.

Wick blinked as another thing occurred to him. He looked around the plateau once more to be sure he wasn't crazy. "You don't have a fuse here. How were you going to blow up the dragonkin without getting blown up yourself?"

With a dry smile, Archer shrugged.

"Archer," Wick said in a warning tone.

"No. You don't get to interrogate me anymore. My turn: what do you want?"

"To find you. It's not safe out here, Archer. We've searched for you all night so we could bring you back to the valley."

"Nope, nope, nope." Archer struggled to sit straighter and paused, his face pale. "These are some shaky rocks. I'm not going anywhere with the lot of you."

"The rocks aren't shaking," Wick said firmly. "Archer, you don't look well. There are dragonkin out here. Everyone's been desperate to find you—"

"And you found me." Archer spread his hands. "Way to go. Now go away."

Wick's heart beat louder. "Why are you acting like this? Why—" He paused, then swallowed. *Better now than never.* "Why did you leave?"

Archer sat motionless for a heartbeat too long, his eyes resting on the uneven rock by his feet. "You said it. I wasn't helping."

The last words Wick had said to Archer before he had left. "I didn't mean that."

Archer made a flustered noise, flapping his hands dismissively in Wick's direction without looking at him. "It's not about what you *said*," he managed at last. "It's about the facts. I haven't been any help since I got involved with this mess. I've wasted my time, and yours, and anyone else's. So, I'm done. I'm going to stay in the woods alone, because that's what I'm good at. If I'm lucky, I won't ever see another person before the dragonkin come back and end the world."

Wick paused. His heartbeat rattled in his chest. Archer *had* to see sense, he had to. "You can't just stay out here by yourself."

"I can and I will. So, leave me alone, I don't want anything to do with you or your stupid Heather Stones." Getting to his feet unsteadily, Archer pushed past Wick and began climbing down the rocks. Only a few feet down, his hand slipped and he fell the rest of the way, smashing his chin on an outcropping of rock.

Fowl lunged to catch him, but Archer had already picked himself up. He shook his head, discombobulated. Wick scrambled down the rocks, scraping his palms, and reached the bottom as Archer headed for the woods. Wick began to hurry after Archer, but a hand on his arm stopped him. Startled, Wick twisted to find Fowl behind him.

"I'll take care of him," Fowl said softly. Abandoning Wick, Fowl strode after Archer.

Anxiety stirred in Wick's gut as he watched Fowl and Archer walk away from him into the forest.

T W E L V E

The Cruel Deal

FOWL'S FOOTSTEPS caught up to Archer just as he made it to the treeline. "You can't just walk away."

"Why not?" Archer spun around, swayed, and grabbed onto a tree with both hands to steady himself. "I've done it before, I'll do it again, and I'm done here. I'm going."

Fowl paused a moment before he spoke. "Your plan was stupid. It would never have worked. Even with the false stones, you'd have been lucky to get more than one dragonkin. It wouldn't have saved anyone."

"It would make me feel better," Archer snapped.

"After you were dead, too?" The frown line between Fowl's brows deepened. "And why is that?"

"Because I have to burn *something*." The words rolled out of Archer's throat as a growl. The sound made his own blood curdle. "Because I can't burn anyone who did this, not you, not Wick, not stupid Astor, not even some of those chumps in the valley that I should kick straight in the teeth, all because one morning I woke up and I *cared* or something. I keep trying so hard, because everyone wants me to be better, better, better, and what's it got me? Nothing. Everyone keeps leaving me high and dry when I. . ." Over Fowl's shoulder, Wick looked. . . worried? Or maybe scared.

Archer clamped his teeth shut on the remaining words. "Forget it. I tried to help, but it didn't work. So, I'm done."

"What did I do, Archer?" Fowl interrupted the tail end of Archer's rant.

Archer tried to laugh, but the sound that emerged was nearer to a gasp for air. "What did you do? Really?"

"I've done plenty, I know. But what did I *do*, two days ago, that made you leave?"

As much as he wanted to, Archer couldn't let go of the tree. His muscles trembled, maybe with ire, maybe with ground's quivering that no one else seemed to notice. . . it didn't matter. If he let go, he'd fall and look like an idiot. Still clutching the trunk, he leaned closer to Fowl. "You left me first, that's what. You took your huge, beautiful, working wings and your blond replacement brother and you left me behind, just like you've always wanted to."

"I told you I was coming back for you," Fowl said stiffly. "More than that, I was leaving *for* you."

"What kind of rotten excuse is that—"

"Shut up and I'll tell you!" Fowl spat. "I'm scared to death of what'll happen to you when those dragons come back. With my wings, I'm faster than you, face it. So, I was going to scope it out first, find a safe place to escape to, and once I had one, I'd come back for you. But you didn't give me a chance to tell you that."

"You didn't offer, either." Unable to look at Fowl anymore, Archer glared at the ground. "Let's be honest, Fowl, we're nothing alike, so we'll never make sense to each other. We might as well quit trying."

Fowler shook his head. "I don't care about that right now. I just need you to come back to the valley with us." He paused. "I know you don't want to help anymore, so, fine. Don't. You can sleep all day every day for all I care. I'm just not leaving you out here."

Archer hesitated. What if, even then, everything went all wrong? "You won't just say that and then start weaning me back on the responsibilities, like how Father did. Promise me you won't."

"Gladly," Fowl said, too quickly. Judging by the speed of his answer, he would have agreed to anything. Good. "If you come back to the valley with us, I promise you won't be handed any responsibility you don't want. Wick," Fowl called over his shoulder. "You have to agree to this, too. It can't just be me."

From his place near the rock formation, Wick nodded just once. "Of course. Archer won't have to take on any responsibility if he doesn't want to."

Fowl turned back to Archer, and through Archer's hazy vision he thought he saw a challenge in Fowl's eyes. "Can we agree on that, Archer?"

A part of Archer was still tempted to stay in the forest until the end of the world, but his head hurt. His brief stay in the forest had already been miserable, and he hated to admit it, but Fowl was right. His plan would never have worked.

Until he could come up with a better way to exact his revenge on the world, sleeping in the valley for days sounded more comfortable.

It wasn't like someone would come around with a better offer.

". . . Fine." Just like that, the ground moved under Archer's feet. Traitorous gravity heaved him down, striking his head against the tree trunk. Lights flashed. Now on the ground, Archer clutched his throbbing face. "*Why?*"

"Archer," Wick said, his voice suddenly very close, "have you eaten since you left the valley?"

Archer winced up at the bright silhouettes of Wick and Fowl above him. "I don't remember," he lied.

"That's a *no*," Wick corrected. "Archer, it's been two days, and you haven't eaten. You look like you're sick, too. Of course you don't feel right." Wick looked over his shoulder at an unseen someone. "Leroy, could you get Archer's bag? He left it on top of the rocks."

Idiot. You left your bag behind.

Leaves crunched loudly, and behind Wick appeared the last person Archer wanted to see. The teeth and talons gleamed, larger and sharper than he remembered. The muscles swelled a thousand times stronger than Archer's present strength. Despite the earthquakes in his muscles, Archer scrambled backward at top speed, ramming into the tree trunk again. He curled into a ball, clutching his doubly bruised head.

"Calm down. Leroy only came to help us track you down," Wick said, and Archer heard the clanking sound of Wick rummaging through the unfillable bag. "He's not here to assassinate anyone."

Archer stopped rubbing his head and looked up at the manghar. He'd run from this manghar so many times that sitting so near to him made Archer's heart race, like he was running even now. Or was his racing heartbeat related to his shuddering muscles? The manghar crossed his rippling arms and kept watch with a relaxed expression.

Staring up at the manghar, with all of Wick's worrying and rustling in his ears, Archer finally registered the name Wick had used to address this wall of muscle. Archer started to laugh. It only made his head spin more, but he couldn't stop.

"Wonderful, he's going into hysterics," Fowl said dryly.

But Archer kept laughing, even as the face of the manghar grew confused.

"*Leroy*." Tears flowed from Archer's eyes. Still laughing, he ground the palms of his hands into his eyes. "All this time, I was practically wetting myself over you, and all along, your name was Leroy."

◇

THEY QUICKLY DISCOVERED that Archer couldn't stand on his own. He simply did not have the strength left to do it, and no amount of food made any improvement. Archer had come down with something ugly. Leroy hefted the shivering, sweating Archer onto Sasha's back, and they spent the rest of the day on the trek back to the valley. Archer didn't utter a single word the entire journey, and hardly anyone else did, either.

Wick spent the day watching the empty faces of the Hessen boys and thinking again and again on what Archer had said.

It's not about what you said.

I wasn't helping.

The moment the valley came into view, Wick sent Leroy ahead to find Ongel. Leroy returned within a quarter hour with a message: they could bring Archer to Ongel's house on the mountainside. He would meet them there.

Wick took them on the shortest possible path across the mountains. The path was rocky and slanted, as though it wanted to dump them into the valley, and Wick repeatedly turned to be sure Archer wasn't about to slip off of Sasha's back.

The burden of worry on Wick's shoulders slipped away the moment that Ongel's house came into view. The blue-grey stones of the walls became smoother from every rainstorm, but their reliable sturdiness never changed.

Passing into the shadows of the tall peaked gables always brought Wick comfort, from the first time that Eland had pushed an anxious, homesick leshy child through the thick double doors, doors that Ongel always kept open. Just as he had back then, Wick pressed a fist to his chest and felt the knots there loosen. Ongel's house had a purpose: here was a sanctuary. Here, everything would be all right.

The moment that they entered the blanketing shadow of the house, Ongel appeared in the doorway. "You're here safe! Come in, come in."

Archer slid down from Sasha's back, clinging to her

neck as he struggled to gain balance. His eyes didn't look right.

Ongel noticed, too. He stepped closer, his hoofbeats making loud, hollow thuds on the planks of the porch. "Archer, my boy, are you all right?"

" 'M fine, don't worry about it," Archer muttered. He put a foot up on the porch and paused.

Before anyone could catch him, he collapsed sideways onto the front step.

"Archer!" Fowl leaped forward and Wick scrambled up the steps, but Ongel, kneeling over Archer, held out a hand to stop them.

"Stay calm," Ongel ordered, gently but firmly. "I need both of you to do that for me." Drawing Archer's limp form into his arms, Ongel laid a palm the size of Archer's entire face across his forehead. "As I suspected, he's running a fever. Fowler, you can help me settle him here. Wick, I need you to go to the storehouse and bring me a pouch of herbs that's labeled, *for fevers*. Can you do that?"

"Of course." Wick released Sasha to wander and started for the path, his heart racing. A dozen paces away, he paused and looked back.

Ongel and Fowl were vanishing into the shadowy house with Archer propped between them. Archer's mangled wing dragged heavily across the porch.

Wick's stomach churned.

He turned and raced down the path like the wind, silencing all his worries lest one of them turn out to be right.

By evening, Archer was no better. Ongel had put Archer up in his own enormous bed and draped him with piles of blankets while Archer shivered. Ongel knelt on the floor beside the bed and occasionally wiped at Archer's face with a damp towel.

Wick and Fowl arranged themselves on couches and cushions, far enough from the bed to stay out of Ongel's way, but close enough to be available at a moment's notice. Fowl didn't look Wick's way even once. His expression was hard enough to be carved from stone—mouth set, brows clamped together. Only his eyes moved, watching Archer as he flinched and squirmed.

When the light streaming through the windows had changed from white to yellow to sunset red, Ongel turned to face the room. "Listen carefully, boys," he said gravely. "Archer isn't much better, but he isn't getting worse, and it's nearly night. It's time for us to take shifts."

"I'll sit with him first." Wick forced himself up from the couch, nearly stumbling from the stiffness in his legs. "I'll gather some reading from the library, and I'll take over when I'm back."

Gathering materials from the library passed as a blur. Wick stuffed materials haphazardly into his messenger's bag, scarcely looking at the pages. Eland asked him a question or two, but when Wick responded, he heard his own voice as though it were a mile away. Eland slid something into Wick's bag, a rolled sheet of veined white paper wrapped in a ribbon. Wick didn't recognize it. In a flash, his footsteps had taken him back up the hill to Ongel's front door. He passed through the door at the same moment that Fowl came out of it, and they exchanged the briefest glances before Fowl left without a word.

Wick lowered his bag to the floor beside the bed, and Archer flinched again.

"There isn't much to do," Ongel said, taking another blanket from the chest and draping it over his shoulder. "Wait with him, keep half an eye on him. If anything happens, I'll be sleeping in the next room."

Wick rubbed his forehead as silence fell over the dark room. "Ongel, I'm worried about him."

"As am I. He came back very ill."

Not what Wick had meant. "I agree, but. . . I'm worried for him even after he wakes up. When we found him in the woods, some of the things he said were. . . I don't think he's all right. It's almost like we lost a piece of him somewhere."

"What do you mean?"

Wick hesitated, trying to order his thoughts into words. "In the short time I've known him, Archer's changed so much. He's grown into what I would call a close friend. But now. . . now he would only agree to come back to the valley if he didn't have to help anyone anymore. He said he was through with this, and through with us." For a moment, Wick fell silent, knowing exactly what words to say but afraid that if he uttered them, they would be true.

At last the words spilled out in a rush. "Ongel, I'm worried that we did this. That we pushed him too hard and we broke him."

Ongel, too, paused before he spoke. "Not long ago, I thought we'd broken you, too. When Archer had to take over your duties in Eri, honestly I wondered whether I should step in and make you go home for a time."

Wick blinked. "Really?"

Ongel nodded. "I worried that our Wick was gone, and that we might never get you back. If we didn't, I blamed myself. I'm your mentor. It was my job to protect you. But I was lost on how to help you, just as you're at a loss to help Archer now. All I can do is hope that just like you, Archer only needs time and support to come around."

"I hope so, too." Wick cast a glance toward the bed. "The problem is that Archer is more stubborn than me. I can't see him changing his mind about this. And if he doesn't change his mind about it, that means he's been broken in some way that can't be fixed."

"For now," Ongel said patiently, "we can't know what will happen. Just like changing any other future, we have to make our decisions in the present. We'll cure him of this fever first, and the rest will come after."

Ongel left to sleep, and Wick pulled his couch closer to Archer's bedside to read by candlelight.

THIRTEEN

Fever

IT HAD TO BE close to midnight when Archer began thrashing. It began as a faint murmuring in Archer's throat, his left arm twitching violently beneath the covers. Then he cried out, and the blankets on the bed churned like water as Archer's limbs flailed.

Wick leaped forward before Archer could throw himself out of bed. Now knee-deep in blankets, he caught one of Archer's arms, then the other, then caught a wing to the chin that shook his brain. Blinking hard, Wick put a knee down on top of the flailing wing and trapped it. The bent shape of the wing struggled under his weight.

Wick prayed that Archer's weaker bones could take the beating.

Archer's muscles clenched, then released. His eyes snapped open, shiny and wild, and his massive black pupils found Wick's face. "I'm going to burn," he rasped.

A shiver raced down Wick's spine. "What?"

The flickering candlelight glinted in Archer's fevered

eyes. "I'm supposed to," he hissed in the same dry voice. "Just like the rest of them."

Wick let go of Archer's arms and planted a foot on the floor. "Nobody's going to burn, Archer." He swallowed. "Not if we can help it."

Archer's wings flinched again, then he curled into a ball on the bed as Wick stood. He muttered something into the blankets. "That's what he wanted," he said louder, in a drifting, breathy tone. "Should have been a dragon. He should have been."

He isn't lucid yet, Wick told himself, slowly lowering himself back onto the couch. Somehow, the thought didn't make him feel any better.

Archer shivered and muttered incoherently for hours. Occasionally, he seemed to dream, and the muscles of his wings or arms twitched. Each time, Wick thrust his book aside in case Archer began to flail again, but the thrashing did not repeat itself. Every time the candle flame flickered, Archer shuddered.

Wick flicked through his books and papers, more absent-mindedly than he would have liked, every so often remembering the wild look in Archer's eyes as he whispered that he would burn.

Wick's grip tightened on either side of the book.

I'm going to burn.

That's what he wanted.

Who had he been talking about? Nin, the dragon general?

No.

He should have been a dragon.

Moments before, Archer had been talking about *the*

rest of them, about destiny and fire and—

His father.

That's what he wanted.

I'm going to burn. Like the rest of them.

Could that really be what Archer thought? That his parents had burned, and his home, and somehow that meant his father wanted him to go up in flames, too?

Wick glanced toward the bed, where Archer faced away from him, his broken wing bent awkwardly against the wall and his good wing flung out across the blankets. Both cast shivering shadows across the tapestry hung behind the bed, the shadows warped until they looked almost like claws.

I'm going to burn.

Stop it.

Wick shook himself. Speculation would hardly help Archer now. Paper rasped between his fingers and he realized he had gripped the book tightly enough to crush the pages. He tried to smooth out the wrinkles as his mind abandoned the memory of Archer's fevered eyes and instead returned to the things Archer had said in the woods.

I had to burn something. I just couldn't burn you.

Wick stared intently at the candle flame. *Had* they caused this? Archer's fever, his nightmares, his paranoia. Was this their fault?

Or had Archer learned to make false assumptions, just like the rest of his family?

Archer's good wing slid over the blankets, wrapping over Archer's chest like a shield.

"Get better quickly, Archer," Wick murmured. "We

have a lot to talk about."

Sometime in the wee hours, staring emptily into the flame of the night's second candle, Wick recognized with a start the comfortable feeling inside his skull. He was about to fall asleep.

Staying seated would only put him to sleep faster. Wick sprang up from the chair to pace the floor. Before he'd made it halfway to the far wall, something behind him made a mighty thump.

Archer. He's in trouble again.

Wick spun around. Archer had sat bolt upright in the center of the bed, his hair tumbling in his wild eyes. His arms trembled as they struggled to hold him upright.

"Where are you going?" Archer gasped. "Don't leave."

With his heart still pounding from the scare, Wick stepped toward Archer. "I'm just taking a walk around the room."

Archer's eyes darted from one side of the room to the other. "Where's Fowl? Did you stop him?"

"He's sleeping," Wick said slowly. "Don't worry about him. He's all right."

Archer's gaze never left Wick's face. Slowly, so slowly, he nodded, then spoke, cool and slow, like he was caught in a dream. "Don't tell me what to worry about."

A floorboard creaked in the opposite doorway, and a shadow appeared. It was Fowl, squinting and rumpled from sleep, but present. "I'll take over, Wick. You can sleep."

"Fowl," Archer gasped. His breath came out harder now, and his face glimmered with sweat.

Fowl's brow crinkled, the lines deepening into black

crevasses in the harsh candlelight. He stepped over the back of Wick's abandoned lounge and sat on the edge of Ongel's bed. "I'm right here. But you need to lie down again. You're sick."

Archer sank back into the mess of pillows that he had scattered in his struggle.

"You'll be here this time, right?" he asked, in a voice smaller than Wick had ever heard before. This voice belonged to a child, not the snarling force of nature that Wick had come to know.

"If you want," Fowl responded. "You have to go back to sleep, though, or you'll never get better."

Archer curled onto his side, only halfway beneath the blankets. He stared, unseeing, into the dark. "I keep thinking I'm falling again," he said in a distant voice.

Fowl's back stiffened.

"But I don't think I can catch myself this time." Archer blinked at the darkness for a moment more, then his eyes closed. His wings relaxed and sank into the blankets.

"You can go now if you want, Wick," Fowl said, without turning around.

Wick pulled the other sofa closer to the bed and sat. "I think I'll stay. He seemed. . . worried about either of us leaving him. The last thing he needs is more stress."

"You're right."

Wick and Fowl sat with Archer until morning. Fowl kept watch, while Wick fell asleep with his arms draped over the back of the couch. He woke again when Ongel arrived to force another glass of medicinal herbs down Archer's throat.

After only a brief struggle, Ongel stepped away from the bed with the glass, now empty. "Has he spoken to you at all?"

"A few times," Wick said. "But he hasn't seemed right yet."

"He's still quite feverish," Ongel replied with a nod. "The world probably feels like a dream to him. I have faith that he'll recover soon, but I don't know how soon." He turned to Fowl, who was watching Archer with his knuckles pressed against his mouth. "Fowler, why don't you bring us some food?"

Fowl's eyes snapped over to Ongel. "Why me?"

Ongel set the glass on the bedside table and turned to Fowl, wiping his hands on his sleeves. "You look anxious, and anxiety does better with moving around than with sitting still. And it would be a great help to all three of us."

Fowl's wings shifted.

"I'll even walk with you. I want to check on the state of things down there." Ongel moved toward the door. "Follow me, Fowler."

Finally, Fowl moved toward the door. His and Ongel's shadows vanished into the weak early-morning sunlight. Wick got up to pace before sleep could take him away. His eyelids grew heavier by the minute.

At least Fowler would listen to sense when it came from Ongel. Just like Archer did.

Then Wick paused.

Fowl tried to be stubborn, but he crumbled in the face of direct orders. Archer never had; in fact, orders seemed to make him dig his heels in deeper. But the common denominator was the same: the Hessen boys were used to having someone telling them what to do, how to stand, what to say. With that person gone, Fowl adhered himself to the nearest figure of authority, and Archer. . . stole black powder.

Wick rubbed a hand down his face.

Archer had a lot of explaining to do when he woke up. *If—*

No. Stop it.

Wick resumed his pacing.

THE NEXT FEW days continued in the same manner. Wick, Fowl, and Ongel took turns sitting by Archer's bedside. They slept in the room, as well. Occasionally Ongel was called away by questions or meetings in the valley, but at every opportunity, he returned to check on Archer and feed him more remedies. Archer gave up his thrashing and screaming, but it was hardly more comforting to watch him shiver and mutter in his sleep.

During the third night in Ongel's house, Archer's temperature climbed and his shivering worsened, so Fowl climbed under the blankets to keep his brother warm.

Wick took over the watch when he realized that Fowl had fallen asleep.

In the wee hours, Wick found himself thinking back on the pedestal that Fowl had spoken of. On the one hand, the certainty on Fowl's face as he told Wick that Archer had abandoned both of them made Wick shiver. Fowl's description of the fall from the pedestal so aptly described Archer's relationship with his father, with the valley, with the other seraphs—and yet.

Wick had lost Archer's respect once before. When they had parted ways after the nixie kingdom, Wick had assumed he'd seen the last of Archer. Nevertheless, ten days later, Archer had come racing back to Wick's aid.

Wick frowned. Since involving himself with the Heather Stones, he had done nothing but let everyone down—his parents, Twill, his mentors, the leshy royal family, and certainly Archer. But despite Wick's morals and his greying face and his constant politics, Archer had stayed present. He'd argued, he'd sulked, but every time Wick apologized for his mistakes Archer's response had been the same: *I'll wait for you.*

Not the words of someone who gave no second chances.

Wick's left wrist ached from supporting his chin for so long. He replaced his left hand with his right.

In fact, if Fowl was right, it would mean that Archer gave up on people entirely. Fowl, by his own admission, had fallen from Archer's respect years ago. If the fall from Archer's good graces was as permanent as Fowl thought, Archer wouldn't have put in so much effort to get Fowl somewhere safe. He never have taken Fowl out of Tor in the first place.

Fowl had been wrong all along.

The candle at Wick's elbow sputtered, and reality returned.

Even if Fowl was wrong, Archer had still left them. He had still stolen black powder and plotted to blow up the dragonkin, even if he went down with them. He had still cut ties with the valley and demanded to be through with the Heather Stones.

And Wick still felt at a loss on how to help him.

"I'm still right, Fowl," he muttered to himself. "Neither of us understands Archer."

Just then, Archer groaned and sat up. He rubbed both palms against his eyes and sucked in a deep, chest-inflating breath. Then he dropped his hands into his lap and looked around. His eyes stopped on Wick.

"Ah," he said, voice gravelly and dry. "You. I'm back in the valley, aren't I?"

"You are," Wick said cautiously. "In Ongel's house." He studied Archer's eyes, trying to judge if the feverish shine had gone.

"Ongel's house?" Archer peered around the room. He swiped at his face with his sleeve. "I'm sweating all over the place and I don't even feel—" He stopped as his hand bumped against Fowl's wing. Fowl didn't stir, but Archer turned a baffled stare at Wick and jerked a thumb toward Fowl's sleeping form.

"You were feverish for a long time," Wick said. "Fowl was trying to keep you warm."

"Ah." Archer scooted himself a few inches away from Fowl. "I wouldn't have thought... Huh."

"Archer," Wick said. The word came out short and crisp. His heart pounded in his ears. "I need to ask you a direct question, and I need to ask it now. Why did you leave?"

"Right." Archer slouched back into the pillows. His eyes roamed from Wick's face up to the shadowy rafters. "I told you: I wasn't helping. I was worthless, and everybody could tell."

"That's not what I'm asking," Wick said. He set aside his sheaf of papers with more force than he meant to. "What I'm asking is how could you? How dare you? After how hard you've worked to gather the Heather Stones, after convincing me—not to mention the nation—to notice what was happening right under our noses, after walking through the burning forest for *days*, after telling me that you believed in the person I would become, after all that you and I have done together, how could you give up so quickly?"

Archer spluttered for only half a second, then stopped. The candle flickered in the silence. "Because it was never about you," he said in a low voice. He stared down at his hands. "It was about me. Don't be surprised or anything; one day they'll write it in the history books: *Archer Hessen was born selfish.* Look, the moment I opened my eyes, all I've wanted was to be better than my father. To be *different* from him." He spat out the words. "That's why I left home, and why I'm here in the valley when he's not. And that applies to you, too. I only cheer you on for myself. If I could be the person that he should have been after I fell and lost my freedom forever, that I would. . . win, somehow. That I would finally beat him. But the more I think about it, the more I realize: I don't miss him, I never did, I just want to replace him. I'm here in the valley, doing the things he should have done, looking after Fowl the way he should have, doing things he would have done if he ever cared. But he didn't care, and I guess I don't either. I'm just an idiot who thought I did."

"I don't believe that," Wick replied shortly. "Sometimes you are an idiot, but you aren't a heartless one, I know that."

"Or maybe you just think I'm better than I am, like you did with everyone in this valley."

The comment stung, but Wick leaned forward. "You're being unreasonable on purpose so that I'll stop talking. It won't work. A few weeks ago, you couldn't care less if you were anything like your father, so where did this come from?"

"Maybe I can invent trouble for myself, ever think about that?"

"You can, but I don't think you invented this one." Whatever had caused this must have happened while Wick's back was turned. It was the only explanation. "What happened that I didn't see?"

"My father wrote letters," Archer blurted, and fell back into the pillows. He raised his palms to the ceiling. "Apparently. To Tinor. About me."

Wick rubbed his chin. "And how do you know that?"

"Tinor gave them to me. I burned them already, but. . . they weren't. . ." Archer took a deep breath, and then the words poured out. "He always talked to me like nothing I said made any sense. But in the letters, he talked about me like he could predict my every move. And I hate him for doing this to me after he's already gone, but I don't know what to think." Archer opened his mouth and then shut it again.

Wick rallied his senses to respond, but Archer interrupted him before he could get a word out.

"He. . . thought I was something great. I think. But here's the thing, even if he thought I was so great, he still didn't love me." He sighed, but the sound of it was strangled. Archer turned his head and asked the candle flame, "What does that mean about me?"

"It means your father was a terrible man, Archer." Wick turned his eyes to the candle flame as well. "It doesn't mean you have to be as bad as he was."

"I don't know. Maybe it isn't that I'm as bad as him, maybe he was as good as me." Archer growled and rubbed his eyes with a ferocity that looked painful.

As he did, Fowl stirred and raised his head. "Too much talking, Archer is—" He flew upright and skidded out of the bed. His eyes darted up and down as though studying Archer for injury, but aside from old cuts and burns, there was nothing to find.

"The fever is gone? Don't lie," Fowl warned.

Still on his back, Archer shrugged. "I guess."

Fowl skirted the bedframe and whisked Archer upright by his shoulders. For a moment, it looked like Fowl might hug him, but instead Fowl shook Archer sharply by the shoulders. "Don't ever do that to me again."

A clatter echoed from the far doorway, and Ongel appeared, his braided hair swinging. "Archer!" he cried. "I'm relieved." Then he beckoned. "Let me feel your face to be sure the fever is gone."

As Archer complained of everyone hovering over him, and Ongel left to prepare more medical herbs, Wick took his leave. He slipped out of his seat and walked toward Ongel's open double doors, where weak rays of morning light illuminated the grain of the floors.

Weariness clung to Wick's face like a mask as he descended the hill. Through bleary eyes he watched his step carefully lest he trip and arrive at the bottom of the hill the fast way.

The crowds of leshy were gone now, relocated while he had watched over Archer. A voice at the back of Wick's mind asked if he could have at least seen them off?

Was it his imagination, or did the sky look greyer than when he had seen it last?

"Hello, stranger." Twill fell into step beside him.

"How are you and Gregory getting along?" Wick asked.

"We're building up a storm of explosives in the mountains. We just need your mentors to come and approve our designs." Twill cocked her head, apparently thinking. "Greg is a little crazy, I think, but he's good at revamping leshy firework designs into explosives. How's our seraph?"

"His fever is better," Wick responded. "He's still a mess, but he won't die."

"Better than nothing." Twill raised her face to the sky, and her eyes squinted. "This sunshine is disgusting. I've felt lethargic for days. At least the other leshy might have better sunlight out on the coast."

"When did they leave?"

"Yesterday. Are you sorry that you missed it?"

Wick shook his head. "Not really. My first conversation with the prince and princess was awkward enough."

"Speaking of, Princess Lilt said she left a letter for you. With Eland." Twill looked at Wick sideways. "What was it?"

"Oh. *Oh.*" Wick froze. The memory struck him like a lightning bolt. Eland thrusting a roll of paper into his hands as Wick had been rushing back to Ongel's house. The paper had been shot through with veins of gold. *Royal stationery.* "It was the research that I asked her for. She was able to get it to me."

"You asked the princess to help us research," Twill said dryly. "Princess Lilt who helped banish you from home?"

"The same," Wick confirmed. "I don't know how I got this lucky, either. I just thought we might find something about the dragonkin buried in old stories and such. Princess Lilt studies folklore as a hobby, so I asked her if she remembered anything related to the dragonkin or the Heather Stones." He looked back at Ongel's open doors, shining bright in the sunrise. "I haven't even read it yet."

"I just don't know how you do it." When Wick looked back at Twill, she was shaking her head. "I can barely put up with the royal family after they banished *you.* If they'd banished me, I wouldn't talk to them ever again, even if they begged me."

"Because you're spiteful, Twill."

"Only most of the time."

"You sound like Archer." Wick tilted his head toward the center of the valley. "Come on. I've got to get some breakfast for everyone, and then I'm going back to read that letter."

Memories and Other Things With Teeth

WITH HALF A LOAF in one hand and a near-empty jar of fermented carrots in the other, Wick stepped back up onto Ongel's porch and slipped through the doorway. Ongel had opened all the curtains while he had been out, letting sunlight bounce across the bedroom.

The rays of sun illuminated the ceiling-hung shelves ringing the room and the many rocks and dried plants that decorated them: Ongel's "collection," all gifts from the children of the valley. Wick had observed more than one shy child approach Ongel with one of these gifts, and each time Ongel made a show of awe and flabbergastation over their "once-in-a-lifetime discovery" of quartz or fool's gold, all before insisting that the precious stone must be kept somewhere safe.

The children loved it every time.

Glancing toward the shelves once more, Wick wondered if any of the "precious stones" had been a gift from a younger Eland.

Archer had curled up facing the door, fast asleep. No twitching or muttering this time, and color had returned to his face.

A rustle and a moving shadow through the far doorway alerted Wick to Ongel's presence. Wick crept around the bed and slipped through the far doorway into Ongel's narrow kitchen. The windows had been thrown open there, too, illuminating rows of gleaming pots on the walls and an array of herbs spread across the tablecloth in various stages of preparation.

Ongel dropped a pile of blankets and cushions into a corner. Bunches of drying plants above them swayed. "How are things in the valley? Are we making progress?"

Wick deposited the food on the only empty patch of tablecloth, beside a twig resting in a tiny vase. Another twig like Archer's? "Twill and Gregory have built some explosives. Actually, a lot of explosives. Someone should go have a look at those soon."

"I'll make sure that someone takes care of that," Ongel said. He took the chunk of bread that Wick offered him. "I need to check in with the other mentors, as well. Would you stay with Archer? Fowler is gone for now; Astor insisted he could use some exercise, so they're taking a flight around the valley."

"I can do that," Wick said with a nod. "Should Archer stay here tonight, too? Or can we take him back to our host house?"

"That would be entirely up to him." Ongel walked through his bedroom and took a red wool coat from a peg by the door. As he threw it around his shoulders, he added, more quietly, "He can stay here as long as he likes.

I'll be back in a few hours."

The open windows and occasional breeze made the silence in the bedroom somehow seem louder. To drown it out, Wick dropped onto the couch at Archer's bedside and fished through his bag for Princess Lilt's letter.

Flecks of gold glinted from the bottom of the bag. Wick drew the paper out and unrolled it in his lap, gripping it top and bottom to keep it flat.

The letter contained no introduction. Even with her misgivings about his banishment, the princess hadn't known how to address him.

The following contains everything I recall about dragonkin or the Heather Stones from leshy history and folklore.

As you know, the Oak Leaf—our Heather Stone—is quite precious to the leshy. It's a reminder of a time when leshy fought side by side with the rest of Aro, and received equal rewards as a result. The Oak Leaf is only removed from the museum on the eve of each year's autumn festival to crown our Autumn Throne. I've even heard it said that our first autumn festival was meant to celebrate the departure of the Scorch, but I have no sources to know for sure.

Thus ends my recollection of history that may be helpful. As far as folklore goes, I originally thought I had nothing, speaking with a few of our own reminded me of the tale of the Scaly Potter.

In the tale, a third-generation potter despairs in the forest. He has only a few days to create a masterpiece for the festival, but he can find no clay in the stream. He searches long and hard through two days and two nights and he finds nothing but sand. He begins to lament and beg the forest for a chance to prove himself to his father and grandfather, when from out of the forest a lizard appears. The lizard is large and beautiful, and its eyes shine like sunlight. In exchange for a drink of water, it says, it will show him how to make clay from the sand.

It seems impossible, but what else can the leshy do? Of course, the potter brings the lizard a drink of water in his hands, and in return, the lizard teaches the potter to make clay from the sand, clay that is smooth as silk and white as foam on the sea. The potter makes a beautiful bowl, and the bowl is baked in the warm hollow of the lizard's belly.

The leshy potter thanks the lizard, but already he has forgotten the secret to the clay. He asks the lizard to show him again. The lizard tells him, "Meet me here tomorrow, and I will show you again how to make the clay yourself. But take care that you don't forget, for after tomorrow I will be gone."

The leshy potter takes his bowl home to show to his father and grandfather, and they are astonished. They demand that he brings them more of the clay so that they can use it also, but the festival arrives the next day, and the dish made from the foam-white clay sells for hundreds of copper. The potter forgets all about meeting the lizard like he promised.

After the festival, the family sets out to get clay for the next festival's dishes. The father and grandfather, still curious, ask the potter where his clay came from. He leads them to the stream where he met the lizard, of course, the lizard is now gone. The leshy potter and his family return to using ordinary clay, and never again do they make such an incredible bowl as the one baked by the lizard.

Sadly, that is the only story I recall about a creature even similar to the dragonkin, but I hope it helps you. Best of luck.

Wick leaned against the sofa back to think. The princess was right. The lizard described in the tale did seem to be something like a dragonkin. Large body, glowing (like fire), able to cook a dish on its belly with the heat of its body. But did the story give them anything new to work with?

Archer started in his sleep, a violent twitch that shifted the blankets. Wick watched him for a moment, then returned his gaze to the letter.

Then Archer jumped again, hard enough to throw half the blankets away. His eyes flew open. Like before, his eyes found Wick, but this time they weren't swimming in huge black pupils.

Wick sat up straight.

"Sorry," Archer murmured. He looked away and slowly drew his sprawled left arm under his head. "Nightmares. Dreaming about. . . nevermind."

"About falling again?" Wick asked.

Archer frowned and shifted under the blankets. "What do you mean, again?"

"Once, while you were feverish, you told Fowl you were falling again." Wick paused. "That you couldn't catch yourself this time."

Archer hesitated. "Is this another interrogation?"

"Not necessarily." Wick set the letter to the side. "I just want to know if I should be worried."

Archer breathed deeply and rolled back to study the ceiling. A breeze from the open doorway ruffled his hair as he examined the rafters. "Sometimes I wonder if my parents just never loved me," he said with a bitter laugh. He paused. "Or maybe it's worse than that. Maybe that *was* love. Maybe that was the best they could do for me. Wouldn't that be awful?"

"When I snapped my wing," Archer went on, slowly, "I didn't think I would fall. I thought wings were wings, even with my bones. But the wind changed so fast— nobody ever told me it would be like that. The wind snapped me like a matchstick. And when I was falling, all I could think was *I can't die. I can't die, or I'll never fly again.* I was lucky, I guess, because I fell into a tree. Well, through a tree. I bounced off a lot of branches before I finally got a hold on one. It pulled every muscle I had in that arm. I almost let go. But I didn't, and in the end, I pulled myself up on that branch and I called for help." Archer inhaled deeply and blew the breath out. "I picked a busy street so that everyone would see me fly and see how wrong they'd all been, but somehow by the time I fell onto that branch, everyone had gone. Nobody heard me. So, I climbed down part of the way and fell down the rest of it. It hurt like the devil to walk back home with all those sprains and a broken wing dragging in the road, but I did it. I made it all the way up the stairs on my own, too." He fell silent for a moment. "Nobody was there, either." Archer swallowed. "Fowl was racing *Astor* on the other side of the city. And our parents were at some meeting. So, I dragged myself all the way to Eri instead."

"None of them knew you would be hurt," Wick said.

Archer flapped his hands above his face. "That's not the part that matters. The important part is that I *fell*, and when I came looking for people, I couldn't find any. When

I was. . . in the woods, up on that rock, I felt like I was falling again, but this time there was nothing to catch myself on. I just had to keep falling. Except then I woke up here, and I wasn't falling anymore. And I didn't have to go looking. People were *there*." He made an exasperated noise. "I don't know what I'm trying to say. I don't even know what I mean. Forget it." He rubbed his hands down his face. "I'm so tired. Get out of here; you probably have work to do or something."

"No, thanks." Wick took up his sheet of paper again. "It's my turn to watch you, and I have plenty of work to do right here. Just go to sleep."

Archer's arms dropped back into the blankets with a dull thump. "But the world is ending."

Indeed, it was. Wick made his shoulders shrug. "It'll end anyway. It's still my turn to watch you."

◇

CONSCIOUSNESS DRIFTED back to Archer like a leaf adrift on a lake. His skull throbbed, but his mind, restless from sleeping so much, demanded to know what time it was, so he forced his eyes open.

A broad-shouldered seraph with a head of blond curls sat on the sofa beside him.

Archer jumped. "Did you come to kill me or something?"

Astor's brow crinkled. "What? No. What are you talking about?"

"Where's Wick, then?" Archer asked, irritated.

"He's in the other room. Listen." Astor rested his elbows on his knees. "We have things to talk about, and you can't escape before I can say my piece."

Archer shoved the covers down. "Watch me. I'll walk out that door."

"Don't, all right? This is serious." Astor extended his hand. A glass of something amber-colored and sweet-smelling hung from his fingers. "I brought you a peace offering. Let me talk."

Archer pulled himself up to a seated position amid the blankets and gingerly took the glass. He took a small sip. Sweet and tangy cider stung his taste buds. "Where did you find cider?"

"I brought a little cask from home."

Archer narrowed his eyes. "Why do you want to talk to me? You hate me."

Astor exhaled slowly. "I don't. . . dislike you, Archer. I just don't *like* you, because of that time after you. . . you know, broke your wing. When you bit me and then couldn't keep my name out of your mouth since. I think you yell too much, and you hold too many grudges."

"Wow, thanks," Archer muttered dryly. "Good talk."

"I'm not done," Astor said curtly. "I don't like those things about you. On the other hand, you've worked hard to keep Aro safe, and I can only dream of doing something like that. So I admire that. Plus, we both want to keep Fowl from drowning in his grief. We have that in common."

"I guess," Archer murmured into his glass.

"Now," Astor went on, "I want you to tell me what I did to you so that I can either explain it to you or make you get over it, because the end of the world is as good a time as any to make up." He leaned back again. "I'm listening."

Put on the spot, Archer struggled. He had hated Astor for so long, and Astor—well, he'd *thought* that Astor hated him, too. They were enemies, simple as that. Just like Leroy, just like Fowl. . . Archer squinted into his glass as he remembered. Both Leroy and Fowl had come to find him in the forest.

Did they hate him?

Did anyone hate him?

"Are you awake?" Astor asked.

"I—Yeah! Obviously." Archer tried to think of words and came up empty. "I don't know."

"You bit me and you don't know why?"

"No!" Only willpower (and the deliciousness of the cider) kept Archer from throwing his glass into Astor's face. "I. . . Look, I bit you because I had broken my wing, I could barely walk, and you, like a *dimwit*, asked "what was wrong with me this time." *And* because I couldn't find my brother when I needed him because he was off doing something, somewhere, with you."

As Archer furiously downed more of his cider, Astor blinked at the far wall. "I said that?" he asked at last.

"Yeah!"

Astor rubbed a hand down his cheek. He looked at Archer. "I really didn't notice your wing was broken?"

"I guess. All I know is that it was stupid."

"That is stupid," Astor said slowly. He shook his head. "Yeah, that was really dumb. I don't even remember that part, I just remember you bit me and you wouldn't let go."

Archer tried very hard not to smirk. It had felt a bit

too good to lock his jaw onto Astor's arm and hear him scream. He noted that he should bite people more often. "It was funny."

Astor shot Archer a sidelong look. "For you, maybe. But. . . I was an moron when I was younger, I see that." He sighed. "You do know I wouldn't have invited Fowl anywhere if I'd known you'd need him, right?"

Archer shrugged. "He was always with you, or Renn, or any of the rest of you." He leaned carefully against the headboard, trying not to jostle his glass. "What were the lot of you always doing together, anyway?"

"My parents," Astor said. "They. . . watch the children of important people in Tor. A lot of them are overlooked or lonely, like you or Fowl."

"I'm not lonely," Archer broke in.

"Right," Astor said. "Anyway, they would invite all of my friends, or my sister's friends, to come to our house every so often and we'd all just have fun for the evening. Games, songs, good food, sometimes a bonfire. My friends could always come to my parents for advice, although Fowl never did. He just came to have fun. That's all." He reached for the table by the bed and picked up a second glass of cider, this one mostly empty. He held it out. "Now, we've shared stories and drinks together, so we can't be enemies. Can we agree on that?"

Archer hesitated, then reached out to tap his glass against Astor's. "I guess so."

Astor downed the last of his cider, but his mention of stories had made the wheels in Archer's head turn. "Astor, you're a folklorist."

Astor swallowed and set his glass down. "Of a sort. I

like to write songs about old stories sometimes."

"What comes up in the old stories about the dragonkin?" Archer asked. "Or anything like them?"

Astor squinted at the ceiling as he thought. "They're in that old nursery rhyme, the one you mentioned before. *Eyes of fire, skin of flame. . .* all that. I remember one old story about a cloud of fire that touched down on a bare hill and left it green. That was my sister's favorite when we were little."

"They made the bare hill green? That's weird." Archer's fingertips rubbed against the smooth glass. "Anything that might tell us more about them?"

"I don't know. My father isn't here, or I'd get him for you; he's good at telling stories. But if I think of anything, I'll tell you, how about that?"

"Or Wick," Archer corrected, remembering with a flinch that he had removed himself from helping. "Just tell Wick."

"All right."

The night after returning to their host house in the mountains, Archer didn't sleep. It was all the fever's fault for scrambling his normal sleep schedule. All night, Archer tossed in the bed, cycling between staring angrily up at the ceiling and glaring down into the blankets. In between he tried to get more comfortable, but no positioning of the soft pillows brought sleep any closer.

In the early hours of the morning, after a full night of rotating like a roast over an open fire to earn only one short doze, Archer finally gave up. With a huff he launched out of the bed and dragged himself down the stairs in search of the kitchen. Maybe a bit of food would improve his mood, at least until everyone else got up.

A quick glance around from first-floor landing yielded a glimpse of a gleaming tabletop through the opposite doorway. The watery light of oncoming dawn glowed through the thin curtains, just barely illuminating the shapes of cabinets several feet above Archer's reach.

Maybe centaurs believed in stools.

As he entered the kitchen, squinting in the tint of barely-there light, Archer ran face first into something solid. "Ow."

"Shh." The obstruction moved to the side, and Archer realized he had run directly into Fowl's back. "You'll wake up—Oh."

For a moment, the two of them stared at one other without speaking. They hadn't exchanged a word since Archer had returned to the host house.

Suddenly sick of the silence, Archer rubbed his sore nose and skirted around Fowl to the other side of the kitchen. The wide table formed a barrier between the two of them. "Shush yourself while you're at it. What are you doing up, anyway?"

"The same as you," Fowl said as Archer dug through the few cabinets he could reach. "I couldn't sleep because of the nightmares. I'm getting something to eat, instead."

Archer glanced back and spotted a triangle of pie on Fowl's plate. "Where did you get that?"

Fowl opened his mouth hastily, as though he planned to say something curt, then stopped. Archer considered the creases pulling at his brother's face for a moment too long. Those furrows seemed to appear more and more often these days. As though Fowl heard his thoughts, the creases of Fowl's face relaxed a bit. "I found it lying around." Fowl took a quick step across to the counter and pulled the pie tin out of the shadows. "There. Take whatever you want."

Archer fished through drawers until he unearthed a spoon, then picked up the pie tin. "We'd better sit outside if you want it to be so quiet in here."

Silently as they could, Archer and Fowl crept through the cavernous front room of the host house and stepped out onto the porch.

Archer kept an eye on the forest. Sitting exposed on the porch like this would make them easy targets for anything out in the trees. And that dragonkin that chased him could still be out there.

"Can you really eat all that?" Fowl closed the door and descended the steps. The light in the sky had grown bright enough that Archer could make out the red of the berries in his pie tin.

"Can't I?" Archer smiled to himself as he sat on the bottom step.

"You're hopeless."

"I know." Fowl was nothing like Wick, Archer realized. If Wick had called him hopeless, it would have been funny. But from Fowl, it stung. Fowl meant it.

Archer dug into the tin, piling his spoon as high as possible before jamming it into his mouth. The berries tasted sweet, the crust faintly salty, crunching between his teeth. Chewing, Archer eyed a bit of bandage peeking out from the high collar of Fowl's shirt. "How are the burns?"

"They're fine." Fowl didn't look at Archer as he dug

his fork into his own pie. Using his left hand, Archer noticed. Fowl's right hand was still bandaged. "None of the injuries were very serious." Fowl hesitated, then set down his spoon. "I don't think you really want to give up on these people."

Archer twiddled the spoon. "What's that supposed to mean?"

"You care about people here, now, don't deny it. You can't just undo that whenever you want. I don't think you hate them yet, either, because if you did, you wouldn't have come back just because your friend and I asked you to."

"Well, my middle name is Oak, not Consistency." Archer gouged his spoon into the dish and wished the pie crust could scream. "I'm not confined to doing only things that make sense."

"Yes, but this doesn't make any sense at all, that's what I'm saying." Fowl crossed his arms. He leaned back against the stairs to observe the sky.

"I came back here because it was too cold and miserable out there in the forest. I wanted to be comfortable." As if on cue, a chilling wind blew across the porch, making both of them shiver a bit.

"Yeah, right," Fowl retorted. "You're sitting outside in the cold right now because the baby in the house needs quiet."

Archer harrumphed and dug at the pie some more. The air really was too chilly. The breeze blew straight through the cloth of his shirt. He suffered in the freezing silence for a moment longer, then finally relented. The only way he could explain what he really meant was to take the long way around. "Look, Fowl," he said. "Have you thought at all about what our parents left us when they died?"

In the corner of his eye, Archer could see Fowl frown. "Hardly anything. All their possessions burned up in Tor, and I doubt father's empire would respect either of us the way they respected him, so, I guess that's gone, too. I suppose you were right. Their legacy is gone."

"Exactly. I got up to a lot of thinking out there in the woods, and I realized that all that's left of our parents is you and me." His taste for pie evaporated, Archer rested his spoon in the pan. "After my wing broke, I left Tor because I wanted nothing to do with them. I wanted to be anything other than them. But now I'm thinking, I brought them with me whether I wanted to or not. I'm still carrying them around."

"What do you mean?" Fowl asked.

"Look, I learned all their terrible traits, really I did. Father was selfish and conniving and scheming, and so am I. Whenever things went south, he lashed out at people and hurled blame around at everyone else, and so do I. When people needed help, Mother just ignored the problem and kept carrying on. I do that. I'm the spitting, snarling image of both of them, and I never realized it. I'm all that's left of them, and look at me. I didn't carry off anything worthwhile." Archer's eyes prickled, and he blinked quickly to make it stop. "They don't even have grave markers, Fowl. They just have you and me as a. . . memorial or whatever." He quickly swallowed the lump in his throat. "So, if I change, if I become better, then there won't even be an echo of them. And I'll be the one that erased them."

Fowl turned to Archer so quickly that his wing nearly slapped Archer in the face. "You *are* an idiot, do you know that?"

"Hey," Archer said, in a voice that was supposed to be harsh, but came out as a weak murmur.

"I think that was the dumbest thing you've ever said, which for you is really saying something. Our parents neglected us. And even if they didn't, even if our parents were saints, we can't commit our lives to being copies of them just so they won't be erased. Let me give you some perspective, all right?" The furrows in Fowl's brow deepened. "Do you know what Father said about you when you weren't home?"

"How would I?" Archer demanded, finding enough composure to return Fowl's harsh stare.

"Nothing. He said nothing. He never spoke about you, and neither did Mother. You never had a place at the table, and the door to your room was always shut. It was like I was the only son. It was a charade, day after day." Fowl took a deep breath. "Our parents had some good qualities, but they were far from perfect people. You can't warp them into something they weren't just because they're dead, all right? What they were is just what they were. On the other hand, you and I are alive. Even with dragonkin and stupidity and fevers, we're still alive. We have no choice but to keep changing."

The silence stretched for several long minutes.

"We used to get along a lot better than this," Fowler said, abruptly changing the subject. "We didn't fight when we were children."

Archer tilted his head. "Fowl, I think this is the best we've gotten along in years. Don't look the gift horse in the mouth." He tapped the spoon against the pie plate, staring at the miniature portrait dangling from Fowl's neck. The hatred he had once felt toward the portrait disappeared under a wave of something else, something heavier and more suffocating. *Is that really the last picture of all of us alive?* His fingers fiddled around the edge of the pie plate in his lap. "Hey, why are you so invested in what I think all of a sudden?"

Fowl's fingers closed around the locket. Still fiddling with it, he gave Archer a sideways glance and half a smile. When was the last time Fowl had *smiled*? "A few days ago, I wasn't sure if we'd ever get to talk again, that's all."

Archer's stomach clenched. Fowl *wanted* to talk to him? When was the last time that had happened, either? Since Fowl was in a sharing mood, he ventured to ask a question that had been burning at his mind for days. "Hey, I don't know if you remember, but ages ago you said you never wanted me to leave. What did that mean?"

"What I said," Fowl responded. "I've only got one sibling. When you left Tor, I had none. And you left angry, with no warning. None of us knew if you were ever coming back. And I always thought. . ." He stopped and let out a single dry laugh. "I see that I was wrong now, but at the time I thought that we were a team. It was you and me pitted against Father's ridiculous expectations, you and me showing up to appease him, even though we thought his events were a sham. But then you left, and I had to do those things alone."

Archer frowned at the pie plate. Bending, he set the

plate down at their feet. He could feel Fowl's eyes on him.

"You look like you have something to say, too," Fowl said.

"I—" Archer stopped. He looked over at Fowl. The sun had started to notice the time, finally casting a hint of pink glow through the trees. "I never got the impression that we were a team. You never talked to me, Fowl. You were always off with your friends, or reading all those books that I can't understand, and you were never with me. It wasn't just our parents. No one paid attention to me."

"Our grandparents did," Fowl said.

"They were a whole city away, and at the end of the day, I still had to go home to Tor. It never felt like anyone was on a team with me, especially not anyone in our father's city. Do you know how dangerous all those stairs are with no railings, even if they bother to add stairs at all? Do you know how hard it was to watch everyone else fly around?" *Through the treetops, dancing in the sky, taking it all for granted.* "Flying looked better than anything, and I wanted it more than anything, but they told me I couldn't have it." Archer realized he was fighting for breath. When did that happen? And why did his chest hurt? "All I wanted was to *matter*, but no matter what I did or how loud I screamed, I didn't matter. No one wanted me, they just wanted what they could get from me, and *that's not good enough.*"

"I'm sorry," Fowl blurted.

Both of them stopped short.

"No, really," Fowl went on. "I am sorry. I didn't know. I thought you understood that I saw you as an ally.

I never wanted to be in that house, either, not with all the pressure he put on us. That's why my friends were—are—so valuable to me. They see me as a real person, as one of them, not just a display piece, and that became especially valuable after you left and it was just me against Father." He swallowed. "I didn't know we weren't thinking the same way. I really didn't."

Without meaning to, Archer once again glanced down at the locket and the eyes staring out of it.

This time, Fowl caught the look. "Oh. I'll get rid of this thing. It doesn't matter." He reached behind his head for the clasp of the necklace.

Archer shook his head. "You haven't let it out of your sight since you got it, so it does matter. It's just. . . The painting—"

"It's a terrible painting." The latch of the locket came free, and the necklace dropped into Fowl's fist. He held the locket close to his face, scrutinizing the portrait for a moment. "No, really, it's terrible. It makes us look like we had a totally different relationship. And your hair doesn't even look like this anymore." Fowl held the necklace out to Archer. "Here. I only kept it because it was Mother's. But both of us hate that painting, so you should draw something else to go in it."

Archer harrumphed, but he took the necklace. "It might turn out looking terrible anyway, especially if I try to draw something that small." He hesitated, suddenly hearing the prickle in his own voice and hating it. "But if you really want me to, I can try to draw something."

"Good." Fowl turned again to face out toward the forest. "Do you think we can patch things back together?"

Archer sighed and leaned against the porch railing.

"Honestly, Fowl?" he said. The first beams of light broke through the trees, illuminating their different colored eyes. "We were both wrong. Let's start with that."

Fowl nodded. "Done."

More Information, But Fewer Answers

WICK RUBBED at his eyes with his palms, the sweat on his face joining the sweat on his hands. In his dreams, dragonkin climbed out of the library walls, burning away the books, then the walls, then the entire valley. Each time he blinked, the flames reappeared.

He took a steady inhale and slid out of bed. He had decided from the start to sleep in only one corner of the huge centaur bed lest he need to tidy an acre of blankets every morning. Straightening his slightly rumpled clothes, he heaved his messenger's bag over his shoulder and forged on through the living room.

Perched on a couch by the fireplace, her chin in her hands, was Twill.

Wick paused. "Are you waiting for something?"

Twill's golden eyes turned toward Wick, and she sat up straight. "I'm waiting for the boys to finish talking."

"What boys?" Wick asked.

"Archer and Fowl." Twill sighed. "I was about to go down to the valley, too, but I heard them talking out there, and I can't remember the last time that happened. I thought I'd let them finish while they can."

Wick cast his eyes across the expanse of the common room toward the door. When he listened carefully he could hear the murmur of voices, then one of Archer's annoyed grunts.

"You're right," he admitted. "We should leave them for a minute more, at least." He leaned his shoulder against the cold fireplace mantle. Then he frowned. "What even brought you to the house?"

"Not sleep, obviously," Twill said. She adjusted her seat on the couch, pulling up a knee to rest her chin on. "I hit a roadblock with the black powder bombs, but Greg was asleep, so I couldn't ask him what to do. Then I went to the library and finished the stack of reading from you and Eland, but I couldn't ask either of you what to do next, either. So, I wandered around the valley until I was bored, then came up here to see who'd be awake first."

Wick frowned and nodded toward the door. "They were up before I was."

"Yes," Twill agreed, "but when I heard them, I remembered how terrible they both are in the morning, and I avoided them." She shook her head, but her voice was amused. "I should have just gone back to the valley, because I've been waiting for them for a half hour."

Longer than the two of them had spoken since arriving in the valley. "Is it going well, at least?" Wick asked.

Twill shrugged. "I'm not an eavesdropper." She tilted

her head toward Wick. "Enough about them, though. What's your next plan? We're finding nothing in the library, and I heard from Astor that you're looking for folklore now. Is there a method to your madness, or is this a sign that we've run out of options?"

Maybe we have.

Wick crossed his arms tighter so that he couldn't squirm. Worried that his voice would betray him, he put on the perma-assured tone of a messenger. "We'll find something soon."

Twill's eyes narrowed. "Can't fool me. That's your lying voice."

"It's—No, it's not," Wick lied.

"And that's your guilty voice. We are out of ideas, then, at least in the library." Twill clasped her hands around her knee. "So, what happens if we find nothing? If we don't have a plan, do we go out fighting, or do we surrender and wait to see if they spare us?"

"I don't know yet." Wick studied the bricks of the fireplace instead of meeting Twill's eyes. "That decision isn't mine to make."

"What if it was, though? Do you think we have a better chance at fighting or fleeing?"

Wick swallowed. "I don't have a clue."

"Ah," Twill said, her tone strange. "A Wick with no plan. Now there's a scary sight. Do you think we'd actually stand a chance in a fight? Even with the black powder?"

Wick sat on the hearth and raked a hand through his hair, feeling sweat from the nightmares still lingering. "Even if we surrender, I don't know if we'd have a chance. They've got all the odds in their favor; for all we know, they'll kill us either way. We need a plan, but we have no weaknesses or strengths to plan *for*. We don't know anything about them." He sucked in a deep breath, but he sounded haggard, even to himself. "All I can do is hope that I'll stumble on something useful before we all burn."

"Ah, yes, you. Just you, by yourself, with no help." Twill rocked back onto her palms and cast Wick a look. Her voice remained lighthearted even as she said, "Don't forget the rest of us are helping you. Good thing we are, too, because if we all counted on just Wick, we might actually be sunk."

Wick picked at a loose thread of his messenger's bag, unable to answer her.

"There we go," Twill said suddenly, straightening. "I think they've stopped talking at last."

✧

SOMETHING CRACKLED in the forest. Archer and Fowl both swiveled toward the sound.

That dragonkin, Archer thought, his heart thundering. *It's back.*

A patch of thick bushes shuddered. Fowl stood, and Archer darted up after him.

A weasel fought its way out of the bushes. It stood up on its hind legs for a moment as it stared back at the Hessen brothers. Then it raced across the clearing and disappeared.

"Do you hear that?" Fowl tilted his head, listening. "Is someone talking out there?"

As Fowl walked down the ramp, looking for the sound, Archer turned toward the door. He had heard it, too, but it had sounded like voices from inside the house. The deeper murmur was Wick's voice, and the other—with no echo, no reverberation—had to be Twill.

A chance to poke a little fun at Wick. Maybe poking fun would make Wick smile or frown or something, anything other than the stupid creased face he made lately whenever he looked at Archer.

Archer put his ear to the door.

"A Wick with no plan," Twill's eerie voice said. "Now there's a scary sight."

The half-smile fell from Archer's face.

What?

Twill's voice faded into unintelligible muttering for a moment. Archer was. . . too far away for the leshy telepathy to work? Or maybe out of range? Who knew. Archer jammed his ear further into the door as he listened.

Wick's voice came in at last. "I don't know if we have a chance even. . ." Muttering. Wick had to learn to speak louder. "For all we know, they'll kill us either way." His voice faded again, and when it returned, it had a strange sound to it. A raggedness. Archer realized in a heartbeat what it reminded him of.

Wick sounded just like he had after the leshy banished him. Like he'd become hollow, and a breath of wind would blow him away. Wick was close to giving up.

Wick said, "All I can do is hope that I'll stumble on something useful before we all burn."

"What are you doing?" Fowl asked.

Archer yanked back like the door had burned him. "Nothing, I just... Nothing."

"Well, whatever it was must have gone." Fowl crouched on the steps and reached for his pie plate once more. "Are you going to eat the rest of that pie?"

"What? Yes." Archer snatched up the pie tin and sat against one of the posts of the porch. Then he paused, his spoon halfway to his mouth. Crumbs tumbled from the spoon back to the plate.

The dragonkin had offered him information. He'd forgotten all about it in the running and the fever dreams and sleeping in Ongel's house. But that dragonkin was still out there, it had to be. And it *wanted* to talk to him.

Maybe a dragonkin was what they needed.

The door opened behind Archer with a click. "What's going on out here?" Wick asked.

Archer gestured to the pie plate at his feet. "Pie."

◇

IT TOOK a bit of time and plenty of excuses, but eventually Twill, Wick, and even Fowl traveled back to the valley, leaving Archer alone at last.

This was his opportunity to find that dragonkin. Maybe even his only opportunity.

Archer rose to his feet, but a thought stopped him.

Did you forget? You're done with contributing.

Archer paused. He could at least tell Wick and the others that it was out there, and they could be the ones to go and find it.

And if they think it's a trap? Or worse, if they go, and it is a trap? You really want to walk around with that on your conscience?

Archer leaned against the wall of the house and

crossed his arms, studying the grass as he weighed his options.

The dragonkin had offered answers, and even in a selfish way, possible answers could mean good things for him. Answers could ensure his survival, and Fowl's, and Wick's, and Ongel's, and a lot of other peoples'. It would ensure that there would be frutelken, and songs, and good food for decades to come. And since it was so willing to talk, he could find out what it was asking for in return. If it asked for too much, or if it turned out to be a trap after all, Archer could make a quick escape and forget about it.

If you're being selfish, you're not doing a good job.

Archer shook his head. *No, I am. I'm just curious. Curious about how I could save other people's lives. . . Well. Maybe I'm not selfish. I don't know.*

Curse Fowl for being so perceptive all of a sudden. He'd successfully shaken Archer's certainty about making purely self-centered decisions.

Either way, Archer made up his mind to talk to a dragonkin.

He went for a little wander through the Great Hall until he encountered a centaur's suit of armor with a very big sword, and ever so slightly repossessed it, sword and scabbard. The belt, built for a much larger waist, could have wrapped around Archer three times. He slung it over his shoulder instead. The scabbard dangled by his side, so long that it slapped Archer's ankle as he walked. He'd never wielded a sword and frankly had no idea how to, but he'd swung lots of tree branches at a lot of heads, so how different could it be?

With his newly acquired sword in his newly acquired

belt, and nobody around to stop him, Archer started up the track to the mountain pass. That dragonkin seemed to have a knack for sniffing him out. It seemed to show up every other time he'd gone for a walk by himself, with the exception of. . . well. The last time.

Still. Archer squared his shoulders. He was willing to gamble.

After all, he didn't really have any other useful skills. Maybe the way he drew enemies like a magnet could be useful.

Selfish. Sure.

The terrain added odd variety to his travels. Burnt treetops crumbled ash onto patches of frosty moss. Entire sections of the forest had been torched, but only in bits and pieces—three or four trees here, a whole strip of brambles there, then a quarter mile of untouched autumn leaves. So far, the scorch marks hadn't made it to the grass, even after the repeated attacks. The mountainside seemed more like a museum he was walking through than a place for a casual stroll.

A part of him wondered what Wick would think of this plan. Wick probably wouldn't like it. He'd say something about charging into danger, or something like that.

Like Archer hadn't already done a lot of charging into danger. Constantly. Unapologetically.

Archer looked up at the blue sky. He'd already been walking for several minutes, and no dragonkin had appeared. Of course, now that he wanted to find a dragonkin, he might finally get to enjoy a peaceful stroll.

Typical. Archer shook his head.

Then the sound of wings snapped behind him.

Archer looked back. The huge shape of a dragonkin soared over the trees, the shadow of it barreling toward him across the ground. The fire under its skin pulsed red.

Archer's heart skipped a beat.

And it then occurred to him what a terrible idea this was.

Archer took off running. There was still time. If he played his cards right, he could still throw it off his trail.

The dragon struck the trees. The branches crashed and snapped as the dragon plowed straight into them. Then the forest floor shook on impact.

Archer put a tree between himself and the dragonkin and struggled to unsheath his burgled sword. He hadn't expected it to be so heavy or awkward. For a terrifying moment, he thought that his arms might not be long enough to even pull it from the sheath. With a cry of desperation, he forced it free, and the sword's weight drove the tip of it into the ground. Immediately, the tail of the dragonkin slapped it from Archer's grip. Archer jumped back, his hands stinging from the blow.

Then, with the same speed, the dragonkin withdrew and settled a stone's throw away. The fire under its skin flared with each breath, but the look in its eyes didn't *seem* malicious.

Then again, his father had never looked malicious, either.

"You're the dragon from before, right?" Archer said, struggling to keep his voice from shaking. "You wanted to talk to me."

"That I did," the dragonkin said.

Archer studied the dragon. Did it seem a little older than some of the others? Its skin seemed to sag, and its eyes appeared sunken into its face. It made an expression that could have been a smile, but could just as easily have been a sneer or even a baring of its sharp teeth. Archer couldn't be sure.

The dragonkin broke the silence. "Are we going to talk, or did you only come to kill me?"

"No, I want to talk," Archer said. *You sound like a kid. Grow up a little.*

"The weapon could have fooled me."

Maybe it was his imagination, but Archer almost thought the creature was trying to make a joke. The confusion just grated at Archer's nerves. "I thought you were going to kill *me* from the way you plowed into the trees. What are you, an avalanche?" He willed his hands to stop trembling.

"My apologies." The dragon's shoulders shifted uncomfortably. "I didn't mean to frighten you. But in my defense, you keep running away, and the last time, you vanished for days on end."

"I was sick. Pick a different excuse," Archer snapped, then remembered himself. This dragonkin could *still* eat him. Spouting off would not help. "Sorry."

The dragonkin's eyes crinkled a bit. "You're spirited. Are you young?"

The friendliness of the question took Archer by surprise. "Uh, yeah. Pretty young, anyway. If you're looking for an authority, you're talking to the wrong guy. Nobody would put me in charge."

"Why not?"

Archer crossed his arms, his wings fidgeting. "I don't think this is what you wanted to talk to me about. You made me an offer last time; are you actually going to answer any question I ask?"

"That depends on what you ask," the dragonkin said, "but yes, I plan to answer almost anything."

"Huh." The wheels in Archer's head turned. Given enough time, he could extract anything from this dragonkin. But what if he didn't have time? If this was their only chance to talk, he'd have to choose carefully.

But on the spur of the moment, anything essential disappeared from his mind. Blind instinct it was, then.

"What do you want to know?" the dragon asked.

"What do you get out of this?" Archer interrupted. Better to ask the obvious question now than discover the consequences later. "What's it going to cost me?"

The dragonkin settled down, stretching out the claws of its wings as a resting place for its head. "Why does it have to cost you anything?"

Couldn't it just answer the question? Archer started to wonder if the dragonkin would be of any use after all. "Because," he snapped, "nobody just gives information for free. Especially to their enemies, and especially when you want to torch this whole place to the ground."

"I don't," the dragonkin responded. Its tone was even, but the words sounded clipped. Was it angry? "I don't want this, or any other place, to burn."

Huh. Archer eyed the dragonkin for a moment. "Why don't they make more dragons like you?"

"Don't be foolish. There are plenty like me." The dragonkin paused, blinked, then went on, calmer now.

"But the ones like me don't make good soldiers, so they all stayed behind, in our country."

Archer's curiosity got the better of him. He crept just half a foot closer. The dragonkin didn't make a move toward him. "If dragonkin like you don't make good soldiers, why did Nin bring you?"

"He didn't bring me," the dragonkin responded. "I followed the army, just out of sight. If Nin had known, he would have tried to stop me. He thinks I'm not true to their cause. And he's right. I think their plan is too drastic, and their methods are too extreme."

Archer realized that their conversation was getting off topic. This was not going the way he imagined. "That's not the point, though. Explain everything. From the beginning."

"Very simple," the dragonkin said. "We come from another land, across the sea. We used to be your allies, but it seems you have forgotten that. Or maybe you reimagined us into your enemies."

How did they know that? What did their history of Aro look like? Archer's brain threatened to explode from keeping a mental tally of all the questions he wanted to ask. "Keep going."

"We need your Heather Stones to heal our land, but we haven't been able to get them back in some time due to your people driving us away time and time again. Now, with the old leader of the Scorch dead and General Nin now taking over the army, there is renewed vigor to take what's ours."

Archer found the nerve to move even closer, keeping his eyes on the dragonkin, watching for the signs of a creature about to spring. The quick motion of the eyes, the bunching of the muscles an instant before the leap—if the dragonkin looked ready to go after him, he would run and never look back. "I thought you said you didn't believe in what the other dragons are doing."

The dragonkin's eyes flicked back to Archer's face. Its eyes were blue, not steel blue like Archer's, but a true, cloudy blue like the sky. "I don't believe in their methods, but I believe in their cause. We need your Heather Stones, desperately. One way or another, Nin will get them, even if he has to burn you and pluck the stones from your ashes."

A shiver slipped up Archer's spine.

"To be frank," the lizard went on, "he'd rather burn you. Still, he will, if he must. But I want to spare you, if I can."

"Why do you need the stones?" Archer asked, then quickly added, "Do you plan to give them back?"

"That would depend on a lot of things," the dragonkin said. "It is my belief that once we're through with them, the Heather Stones should be given back to you. The ancient agreement was that they were yours to keep and ours to borrow. But it's been so long that our predicament has become complicated; the Heather Stones may not fix it quickly. It may take days, or it may take a year to repair. Until we physically have the stones, it's impossible to know."

"Why do you need them *for*?" Archer repeated, with more emphasis. "You sound like you're dodging the question."

"I'll get to it," the dragonkin said. "To answer that

question, you need to understand the context."

Getting a simple answer would take all day at this rate.

"We need the Heather Stones because perhaps we should have never let you keep them in the first place." The dragonkin adjusted himself slightly, nestling loudly into the dead leaves on the forest floor.

Archer frowned, trying to hear what the dragon wasn't saying. Was something happening back in the dragonkin homeland? Another war, maybe? Or could it be something else?

Even before it spoke, the dragonkin watched Archer's face. "I think you understand, don't you? The stones, your Heather Stones. They were *our* stones first, and we still need them."

Archer's mind buzzed. The cogs whirred. He wasn't a knowledgeable guy, not like Wick, and suddenly he wished Wick was present to fill in the gaps, to explain the confusion away just like he always did. But even so, Archer knew that the stones belonged to Aro, only to Aro. . . right?

"Prove it," he said suddenly.

The dragonkin's eyebrows lifted. "Prove it?" it repeated, slightly incredulous.

"I don't know half the things Wick does, but I know the centaurs have had the stones since forever, and they were the ones that gave the pieces to the rest of us," Archer said. He crossed his arms. "You could say anything to make us hand over the stones. Give me some proof, or I'll walk away." What was it that Wick had said, all the way back when they had first met in the forest?

Something like. . . "If you *are* telling the truth, you're not making a good case right now."

"I suspected you wouldn't trust me," the dragonkin said, eyeing Archer from the ground. Slowly, it drew in its wing claws and picked its head up.

Archer wondered for a moment if he would have to run. He watched the dragon for the quick flinch before the spring.

The dragonkin extended one wing claw with something wrapped tight in its fist. "I came prepared. Maybe this will change your mind."

Archer tentatively held out a hand—his left, just in case he wouldn't get it back—and the dragonkin dropped something cool and smooth into his open palm. It was a small pebble of green stone, green like grass, and riverbeds, and magic. It was just a whisper more blue than the ones Archer knew, but he would recognize the stone anywhere. "Is this a piece of the Heather Stone?"

"Heather Stone the stone, yes, but not one you've seen before," the dragonkin responded. "Our land still has a few veins of it left. They're little more than crumbs, too few to repair what needs repairing, but the stone is there, just the same." It tilted its head slightly. "Does Aro have any veins of the stone?"

Did they? Probably not, right? Or Aro would have more than just eight Heather Stones. Archer flexed his empty hand at his side and wished for the first time in his life that he hadn't bitten so many of his tutors. Maybe if he hadn't, he wouldn't keep reaching for his store of knowledge and coming up empty.

Wait. Something else the dragonkin had said drifted

to the front of Archer's mind.

"You keep talking about fixing something." Archer said, tearing his eyes away from the shining green stone in his palm. "What happened? What do you need to fix so badly that the Scorch would light us all on fire?"

A new look came over the dragonkin's face, something somber that Archer couldn't quite name. Once Archer had seen that same look on his grandfathers' face, the day that Archer had appeared on their doorstep covered in the scrapes and blood and twigs of his furthest fall yet.

It rooted Archer to the spot as the dragonkin answered him in a voice heavy as a mountain.

"Our land is in terrible danger. We need water to cool the fire in our bones, to allow us to keep living. But now we have none." The dragonkin extended its neck, reaching closer to Archer. For some reason, this time Archer didn't feel the need to run. The dragonkin's eyes shone with deep fear and a hint of something else, something heavy and dark.

"Our children's wings are burning."

SIXTEEN

*The Exodus
of the Valley*

ARCHER'S BLOOD RACED cold through his body and tingled down his arms. He didn't want to be tricked. It could easily be a lie, an attempt to invoke his feelings and steal his loyalty. Plenty of people had tried that before.

But their wings. . .

His own feathers shifted against his back.

"Ah. I knew you would understand," the dragonkin said. "You know what it is to lose something so precious as flight."

"Wrong," Archer said. He looked up at the face of the dragonkin. "I didn't lose it. I never had it."

"But it was still stolen from you," the dragonkin said. "And now, the same is happening to the dragonkin children. If anyone was meant to understand the severity of the situation, it would be another creature with wings. When I heard the stories about you. . . I knew you would be the one to help us."

A branch snapped somewhere in the forest. "*Archer!*" Wick's voice bellowed from the trees.

The dragonkin glanced at Archer, a question in its eyes.

Archer paused, frowning toward Wick's voice. This was too soon. He didn't have nearly enough proof to believe this dragonkin or even to pass the job off to someone else.

But if he didn't answer, Wick would probably send out another search party, making everything more complicated.

"We'll have to talk more later," Archer said.

"Fine." The dragonkin reached out and raked a deep gouge in the earth with its wing claws. Archer jumped back, but the dragonkin made no move toward him.

Drawing back, the dragonkin pointed to the mark it had made in the ground. "We'll meet here tomorrow night to discuss more of this."

"Fine by me."

The dragonkin nodded, then leaped up into the sky. Archer watched it go, then started meandering back toward their host house. Soon, Wick's voice shouted again, from much closer this time. "Archer!"

"I'm here." Archer glanced to his right without stopping, and Wick fell into step beside him.

"Twill said she saw you go into the woods. I got worried."

Archer's suspicions had been correct. Wick would have sent out a search party and a dozen sniffer dogs if he hadn't found Archer. "You say that as if something bad happened the last time I went for a walk alone," Archer said. He realized too late that Wick wouldn't appreciate the comment.

Wick gave him a bitter sidelong glance. "Don't even joke about that."

"Sorry."

Wick just shook his head. Then he gave Archer a funny look. "Why do you have a sword?"

Archer squinted into the empty slot of the sheath, frowning. "Technically, I don't have the sword anymore. I have a. . . sword case."

"I thought you said you got chased by dragonkin the last two times you went for a walk," Wick said in his criticism tone.

"I did," Archer said. "That's why I brought the sword."

"For all the good it's doing now," Wick said dryly.

"Ah, but if the dragonkin had tried to jump me before I lost the sword, they would have been in for it!" Archer lied cheerily. If Wick asked how he had lost the sword, or where he had got it, he could make up another story just as easily.

Truly, it was a shame that Wick hadn't learned to see through his lies yet.

"So what did you want?" Archer asked.

"Hmm?"

"You came looking for me." Archer dropped the sheath back to his side, where it swung wildly. "I assume you wanted something."

"Well, yes," Wick responded. They had nearly walked all the way back to the host house by now. Archer could see it through the trees. "There's news from the nixies.

They decided not to go to war—yet."

Archer glanced at Wick. "Yet?"

"They've come up with a new plan. Essentially—" Wick stopped walking while he explained, and with a sigh, Archer stopped with him. "—they plan to create a dome on the seafloor, using magic. Then they'll fill it with as many refugees as they can. The dragonkin are made of fire, and so far, we haven't seen them near water, so I think it's safe to assume that the dragonkin won't go near it."

A nagging feeling itched at Archer's brain. The dragonkin had said something about water. Was it that they needed water, or they needed to stay away from water? It wouldn't make much sense if they needed water, would it? Archer had been too distracted by the comment on their children's wings to remember much else.

Hopefully, that hadn't been the plan all along.

For the millionth time, Archer wondered if it had been smart to talk to the dragonkin, or if he was still walking into a trap.

He had to be sure, absolutely sure that it wasn't a trap before he brought anyone else near it.

Archer glanced up and found Wick's eyes fastened on him. "You had a funny look just now," Wick said, getting a funny pinched and worried look of his own. "What's wrong?"

"Nothing," Archer replied nonchalantly. "What's your point about the nixies? I don't have anything to do with them."

"I'm not asking for your help," Wick replied. "I'm not asking for anything. I'm *offering* you a chance to leave."

"To. . . what?" Archer's heartbeat quickened, creating

a sick feeling in his chest. *Leave?*

"The leshy refugees will go in the first dome, but that's just the start," Wick said. "If the domes do repel the dragonkin, the nixies will make more domes and evacuate more people."

Archer studied the leaves on the ground as they crunched underfoot. "What if the domes collapsed, though? No more refugees."

Wick frowned at him. "The nixies wouldn't let that happen. And even if it did, the leshy don't need to breathe, remember? They can't drown." He started walking again, and Archer ambled after him.

"Anyway," Wick went on. "If it works, you and Fowl could leave the valley. It's your choice. Would you rather stay in the valley, or would you rather go to the nixie kingdom to take shelter in the dome?"

This was a test. Years of living under his father's roof had taught Archer how to sniff out a trick question from a mile off.

The question Wick posed wasn't the question he wanted to ask. It never was, not when the topic was this important.

The question was not *do you want to evacuate?* It wasn't even *do you want to leave the valley for good?*

Wick wouldn't leave the valley even if it burned. Wick would stay there and do all he could until the very last minute. But he had offered Archer the chance to leave without him. So really, it came down to a question of loyalty.

He was really asking, *Are you done with me?*

Do you want to leave me behind?

Archer felt the crease of a frown in his brow. *Did* he want to abandon Wick yet? He seemed to leave everyone in the end—his family, all his old friends, even the one girl that had ever shown interest in him. He just couldn't seem to hang on to anyone. Did that apply to Wick, too? It hadn't been Wick's *fault* that Archer had left—really, that had been everyone's fault—but Wick had been the one who *said*—

Forget about it. Forget what he said.

Why did the question have to be so *hard*? It was a question of what Archer wanted, but what did he want?

Unable to decide, Archer stuffed his hands in his pockets. "What do you think is best? You're the decision maker."

For someone who's done with them, you don't seem too eager to leave.

Wick raised his eyebrows a bit, but pondered for a moment anyway. "If I had my way, no one would be in the valley once the dragonkin come back. But since that isn't an option, I can settle for evacuating everyone from the host house. Everyone that wants to go, that is," he corrected, then took a deep breath. "So, if you want to go, I won't stop you."

Wick was trying to avoid getting to the point, but unluckily for him, Archer was already firmly seated where he could not be moved, and besides, he had been avoiding the question first. "So?" he prompted.

"Think on it, at least," Wick said, directly dodging the question this time. "There isn't much time to make a decision."

"Don't tell Fowl about it, though." Archer kicked a

branch out of their path. "He'll just want to decide for me."

Archer spent the rest of the day in his guest room alone. Fowl had been right; since there was no one in the house to talk to, Archer did little besides doze until the evening.

The dozing turned out to be a mistake. That night, sleep returned to being a far away concept. In between disgruntled tossing and turning, Archer tried to think about the decision Wick had offered him. Wick wanted to empty the host house, but it wasn't that simple. Twill probably wouldn't leave Wick behind, and Fowl wouldn't go unless Archer did.

Unless of course, he lied and told Fowl that he would be going along later.

Archer paused, mid-blanket-tug. Did he really want Fowl to go without him? Did that mean he wanted to stay?

Life had been much simpler before the stones and the Scorch and all the nonsense that went with it. What had life been like before this? Before Wick, even? He seemed to recall a lot of running and punching and sleeping on the ground, but not much else.

A low voice from the hallway caught his attention. Was that Fowl? Who was he talking to?

With a groan, Archer got up to see why his brother was awake.

As he walked down the hall toward the sitting room, the snatches of conversation became louder.

"I'm not worried about my friends, I suppose," Twill's voice said. "Most of them are smart enough to look after themselves, even if things go wrong. But on the whole, yes, I'm concerned for the leshy, especially for their future after all this. In Aro, you have to be seen to survive, but leshy existence is mostly about staying private." A creak echoed as Twill shifted on whatever furniture she sat on. "Maybe that's why Wick was always so interested in transmogrification. Most leshy like to blend in, but not Wick. He always liked being seen."

"Do you know why so few of them left the territory?" Fowl asked. "Wick doesn't talk to me much, but I heard him say that hardly any leshy came to the valley."

"I don't know," Twill responded. "I never really understood them. They might be trying to avoid Wick, with his exile and all that, but honestly, they probably just didn't want to leave the forest."

Their conversation fell silent.

"Eavesdropping is rude," Twill said. "You could at least come in."

Oh.

Archer reluctantly stepped through the doorway. "I wasn't eavesdropping."

"You couldn't sleep again?" Fowl asked.

Feeling oddly like a child interrupting his parents, Archer shook his head.

After a moment of awkward silence, Fowl slid over on the couch so that Archer could sit beside him. Twill adjusted in her seat on the armchair so that they all faced each other.

"It's a pity," Twill went on, once they were all situated. "I could investigate the situation in leshy territory, or just give them the kick they need to get moving, but it was dangerous enough getting here. The Scorch said they wouldn't attack us yet, but I don't trust them to keep their word."

"I wonder why they're even bothering to hold back." Fowl leaned back against the cushions of the couch. "It would be easier to wipe us all out and take whatever they want, so why don't they?"

"Maybe they don't have as many fighters as they say," Twill suggested. "They could be bluffing us into doing what they ask."

"I don't think so." Fowl looked down at his folded hands and chewed his cheek for a breath. "The army seemed big enough when they burned down Tor."

Did Twill's eyes soften in pity? "Right. I forgot about that."

Fowler gave her a dry smile. "I didn't."

Archer pulled his feet up onto the couch, trying not to squirm. Talking about dragonkin was his opening, right? Even without much evidence, maybe Twill and Fowl would hear him out. Even if Archer wasn't too sure about it himself.

He threw out a risky question. "I wonder if we could get hold of a dragonkin and talk to it. Find out what their motive is, you know?"

"They aren't talkative," Fowl said. "Don't get any stupid ideas."

Stupid ideas had already occurred, but Archer shrugged. "It's not stupid if you can walk away from it."

"Yes. It is." Fowl looked over at Archer, and Archer regretted sitting so close. He didn't like being within arm's reach of Fowl on the best of days. "Did you forget that those things killed both our parents and wiped out most of Tor? Or how they almost killed both of us? They're soldiers for an army, Archer. They aren't going to argue with you until you win them over. They'll catch you, and they'll kill you."

"I don't think I'd trust them even if they were the ones offering to talk," Twill murmured. "Not without a lot of hearty defenses. Did you hear their general? I wouldn't trust them not to play mind games with us."

Still, Archer had managed to walk away from his conversation with the dragonkin. Could it be playing mind games with him? Had it been tricking him, even when it let him leave?

Maybe the whole thing was just one horribly bad idea.

But he still had a piece of green stone in his pocket, that had to prove something. And then there was the story it told him. The lizard's eyes had looked—desperate? Or distressed?—as it described the situation in its homeland. If the dragonkin was a liar, it was an awfully good one. As a liar himself, Archer knew that every convincing lie had a crumb of truth in it somewhere.

But how large of a crumb?

His fingers itched, wanting to reach for his pocket. In the morning, he had to find out if it really was a shard of Heather Stone. He could only think of one way to know for sure.

Archer woke up the next morning to discover that he had fallen asleep on the couch with only a crick in his neck for company. After stretching away the sharpest pains, Archer hiked down to invade the Heather Stone cavern.

He found himself blessed with incredible luck, or maybe just immaculate timing, for when he arrived, no one stood within a hundred yards of the cavern's entrance, and enough screaming *hello?* into the cave itself proved that no one was inside. So, as he crossed toward the chamber with the green stone floor, Archer wondered what he would do if the shard of stone turned out to be real.

Wick was the better decision maker. How had Archer ended up with this? Just a few days ago, he'd thought he was done with the valley, but now, Archer was the one who had to test the stone, so Archer had to decide when it was time to explain everything to Wick and get his help. And the time would never be right until he had more evidence.

Until he had enough solid evidence, no one would listen to him, not even Wick.

Archer shook his head. He could worry about all that after he tested the shard of stone. If it turned out to be fake, he wouldn't have to show Wick anything.

He stopped in the doorway to the chamber and eyed the green Heather Stone buried in the floor. Shot through with thick veins of white and glowing like pale green moonlight, the stone could have easily fit a grown dragonkin with outstretched wings. He never could shake the feeling that it was watching him. Evaluating him.

Archer knew he wasn't supposed to be in this room, and he suspected the stone knew it, too.

Archer stuck one cautious bare foot onto the cold,

slick stone, and when it didn't combust he decided it had to be safe enough to stand on. He stepped out onto the stone. From here, the torchlight pouring in from the cavern gave the stone a fiery glow beneath bare feet.

Archer reached into his pocket and found the little shard of green. The moment of truth.

He knelt on the stone and lightly, gently tapped his shard stone to the surface of the Heather Stone.

Explosion.

The force of the stones repelling each other punched Archer's hand into his own chest and threw him three feet in the air. He flinched just in time for gravity to sling him downward again.

Archer slammed face-first onto the Heather Stone. He just had the presence of mind to keep the stone shard elevated so it wouldn't react with the floor a second time.

"Well, there's the answer you were looking for," Archer groaned, and jammed the stone back into his pocket.

"Is that you, Archer?" Twill's voice called from out in the cavern.

Archer grimaced when her voice didn't echo. The leshy's telepathic voices never got less unnerving. "Yeah, it's me." He picked himself up to sit just as Twill appeared in the entryway.

"Wick sent me to find you," Twill said, not even acknowledging Archer's suspicious presence in the Heather Stone chamber. "We've got a journal, and Wick wants to see if you can make any sense out of it."

Archer frowned. "Why me? Wick's better at reading and learning and. . . basically everything. Why can't he do it?"

"He's busy. Eland found something in the documents last night. Or, I guess he technically found a lack of something. However you want to think about it ."

Archer squinted at her. "I have no idea how you can say so many words and still make no sense."

"I just know you need the intellectual stimulation," Twill said, her tone amused. "Ask Eland to explain it. He's the one with the journal, anyway."

Archer hesitated. "Maybe I don't want to," he said at last.

Twill did that thing she always did where she tilted her head a few degrees before speaking. Did she know that she did that? "What would you do, instead? You seem to be very busy taking a nap, all alone. Will that keep you all day?"

Archer frowned.

"Don't look at me like that," Twill said lightly. "All I'm saying is that it's got to be a boring way of waiting for the end. You could at least make believe like the rest of us that we'll survive on our own terms. There's lots to do out here, you could do *something* to pass the time."

Archer weighed his options.

You're predictable. You can't even be selfish when you want to be.

But at least it'll help to pass the time.

"Sure. Whatever." Archer used his palms to push off the floor.

As Archer passed her, Twill bumped her shoulder against Archer's. "I knew you wouldn't want to stay bored."

They hurried across the valley toward the library, almost racing one another. The library was dark even during the day, only dimly lit by candles and a few slits of light from windows placed high up on the walls. Wick and Eland hunched over opposite sides of a small table stacked with teetering pillars of papers and books. The legs of the table had to be crying out for mercy under the weight.

"Journal?" Archer said.

Wick held up the red-bound volume without so much as looking up from the page.

Caihu's journal, from the unfillable bag. Of course. Archer plucked it from Wick's hand, then joined Wick in staring at the stacks of materials. "What did you find that was so groundbreaking?" he asked, trying to sound moderately disinterested.

"Technically speaking, what we found was nothing." Eland straightened a stack of papers. "But that's the problem."

Archer groaned. "Would it kill someone to be clear about this?"

"I'm sorry. I'll explain." Eland placed both hands flat on the table. "I spent all night assessing the library and taking inventory of our historical materials in order. I found out that we're missing one very important piece, right in the middle of our history."

"Right around when we got the Heather Stones," Wick said.

"Yes. There's a portion of history before the Heather Stones are ever mentioned, and then there's another portion of history where the Heather Stones are mentioned all the time. In between there's no documentation for about three years."

Archer frowned. "As in, someone lost three years' worth of history?"

"We did think of that," Eland said. But then he shook his head. "But Wick's speculating that it might be more complicated than that. Based on the signatures on the documents, we know that the historian before the gap is different from the historian after. But that doesn't explain why the information is missing."

Wick rubbed his forehead. "Every day feels like one step forward and two steps back. I'm going to read through what was recorded before and after the gap to see if I can hunt down any clues, but past that, I'm at a loss."

"And we've only got two weeks before our month is up," Eland added.

Archer exchanged glances with Twill.

"Well, I'll help where I can," Twill said. She tugged a chair away from the table and dropped into it. "Where do you want me to start?"

As Eland spoke to Twill and shifted piles of papers around, Wick got up. "Hey, Archer, can I talk to you for a moment?"

Not a good sign. Archer shifted. "Yeah. Sure."

Wick stepped outside the room, pausing on the ramp that led up into the library's ground floor. The stone walls enclosed around them, chilly but secluded. "I want to be clear: I'm only asking for your help if you want to give it. You've read the journal before, so I thought you might have some insights. But I don't want to push you more than I have already. So, if you don't want to deal with the journal, I can call someone else."

Archer huffed out a quick sigh. "We're in a time of crisis; it doesn't matter what I want. If we all die, you'll wish you'd made me do more."

"No." Wick's voice was uncharacteristically firm, making Archer's eyebrows rise a fraction. Wick continued, sure and steady as before. "We *are* in a time of crisis, which is why I have to be careful. Yes, we all could die. But if we survive, I don't want to remember that fear made me a heartless coward." Wick took a deep breath. "I'm rambling now. I just thought I'd ask before I dragged you into my work again."

"It's fine," Archer murmured, almost interrupting Wick. "I needed something to do, anyway." He stared down at a splinter half-sticking out of the floor.

A long moment of painful silence passed. Archer picked over the words in his brain, couldn't guess which of them were the right thing to fill the quiet. He just knew that the sick feeling in his stomach would kill him if he couldn't figure out how to make it stop.

At last, Wick turned and rejoined Twill and Eland at the table.

Archer hesitated, then sat down on the uneven wood of the ramp cross-legged and dropped the journal into his lap. Reading, that he could do, but sitting in the same room with the intellectual people seemed wrong, somehow.

Archer ran his thumb over the front of the journal. The cover was dark and shiny in places from other fingers rubbing it time and time again. Ink stains blotted the pages, visible even with the book closed, and the book warped and bent into waves from age and exposure to who-knew-what inside Archer's bag.

It looked much smaller than Archer remembered. Maybe it wouldn't be helpful after all.

Still, it wouldn't read itself. Archer cracked the cover open.

Just like he remembered, Caihu's sharp-edged henscratch rambled across the pages from cover to cover. The individual notes read more like vague gibberish, many of them discussing things that only Caihu understood: *empty room, hands had veins, why do Trigon's eating habits matter?* Some notes weren't legible at all.

Trying not to sigh, Archer settled his forehead on his fist and tried to decipher Caihu's nonsense.

Are We?

HALF ASLEEP, WICK trudged through the pitch-black woods to their host house. They had to be getting close to a breakthrough in the library. He wouldn't say that he could feel it—he could only feel his gritty eyes and a knot in his shoulders from bending over the books—but if they had been looking this long, they had to find something soon.

And they were running out of time.

Maybe his premonitions of a breakthrough were more desperate than prophetic.

He neared the house and abruptly something large crashed and splintered in the trees behind their host house. Wick remembered what Archer had said about a dragonkin chasing him, and he broke into a sprint. He raced across the porch and slammed the door behind him. Then he listened with his heart pounding in his chest.

The sounds quieted into a rustle, then faded away into silence.

"Could you wake up everyone in the valley while

you're at it?" Archer groaned from the couch.

Wick yanked the front door a few times to test the lock, then edged closer to the couch. The fire dying in the hearth glowed just bright enough to outline a figure on the couch: Archer, curled up on his side with his good wing wrapped over his head like a shelter.

"What are you doing?" Wick asked.

"Ask me what I *was* doing." Archer curled up a little tighter.

"You were trying to sleep. Why out here?"

"Answer your own question, why don't you?" Archer muttered, but he unwrapped his wing from overhead and sat up. "I can't understand a single thing Caihu wrote in that journal. His handwriting is worse than mine, and the notes don't make any sense, either. I'm no help. Again." Archer rubbed a hand across his brow, frowning.

"I'm sorry that I had to drag you back into this." Wick leaned on the back of the armchair opposite Archer. "I know you don't like it."

"At least this time you're talking to me," Archer grumbled. "You weren't the last time you made me do your job."

Wick stalwartly chose to assume Archer didn't mean a word of it. "Harsh. I know you don't like doing my kind of work. But I appreciate your help all the same."

"It's fine." Archer looked toward the fire, and the flickering light illuminated rings of exhaustion surrounding his eyes.

"Have you been sleeping?" Wick asked. "You look like you haven't closed your eyes in a month."

Archer shook his head. "Not very well. It doesn't help

that your friend Twill is up all hours of the night and chatters to whoever is still awake, whether they like it or not."

Twill. Wick sighed. "I'll talk to her about it. She ought to know better."

Archer's mouth pressed tight. "It's only her fault for talking," he admitted. "The not sleeping part doesn't have anything to do with her. I just. . ." He stopped himself.

"Nightmares?" Wick asked.

"Only when I can get to sleep. Even when I'm still awake, it's hard not to think about everything going up in flames. And then sleeping just never comes." Archer shook his head. "Whatever."

Wick hesitated. He clearly couldn't leave Archer like this, but did Archer even want his help?

The crackling of the fireplace filled the silence.

Well. Maybe an animal with its foot caught in a trap didn't want help, but just because help wasn't wanted didn't mean it wasn't needed. Wick sat in the armchair facing Archer before his anxieties could talk him out of it. "You know, I'm worried about you. I want to know if you're all right. Really all right."

Archer didn't even look up. "I'm always all right, stupid tree."

"Right. The last time I just *assumed* you were all right, you disappeared. And by the time I tracked you down again, you were waiting for the dragonkin with a city's worth of explosives." Wick rested his forearms on his knees. "Honestly, I don't care what you think of me; I'm going to get it out of you. How are you really?"

Archer smiled a peppy, false smile and leaned briskly

on the arm of his couch. "I've never felt more lost in my life, thanks. How are you?"

"Concerned. Go on."

"I told you, I'm sick of wasting my time. I'm sick of agonizing over hard choices, just to watch our choices go up in flames. I hate it. I want to go back to looking out for me, just me, and let everyone else take care of themselves." Archer stopped talking and floundered for words for a moment, making inarticulate gestures over the arm of the couch. Finally, he said, "So, why can't I do that?"

"What do you mean?"

"I just want to look after myself. I should be out in the woods in a hideout of my own, waiting for the end of the world. But here I am, in the valley, because Fowl asked me to be. And here I am, reading the blasted journal, because you asked me to. I can't *ignore* everyone anymore. I'm stuck."

The more Archer spoke, a thought dawned on Wick, slowly spreading the first bit of light across his shadowy wasteland of concerns.

"I don't think you're stuck," Wick said slowly. "You didn't just forget how to ignore everyone else. I think you just lost your taste for it."

Archer groaned bitterly. "This has to be your fault."

"Sorry, but I don't think it can be anyone's fault but your own. When you first set out, yes, you were gathering the Heather Stones for selfish reasons, but I don't think you've actually been acting selfish for a long time."

"Well, I definitely wasn't being generous or anything. I was just following along on whatever you were doing."

"Even then, no one told you to save my skin as many times as you have. You chose to do that on your own. No one told you to look after Annalise and her family." Wick willed Archer not to be angry with him as he continued, "Looking after your grandfather's house when the Scorch came back would have been selfish, but Fowl says you were there like a shot when Tor became overwhelmed." Wick spread his hands. "Maybe you didn't mean to, but you've chosen all of this."

"Why would I do that?"

Wick dared to crack a bit of a smile. "Believe it or not, maybe you've started liking people other than yourself."

Archer made a face. "Gross."

Wick shrugged. "I don't think so."

"Wick, are we still friends?" Archer asked suddenly. Wick looked up. Archer stared at his hands as they clasped tightly on the arm of the couch. "And don't lie, please. It wouldn't help. Just be honest."

Wick almost spoke, then stopped. Answering too quickly would be a waste of the opportunity Archer offered him. It wasn't often that he got the chance to be totally honest; every sentence had to be filtered through layers of decorum and indirectness and diluted down to something acceptable. Archer had offered—no, *asked for* an answer that was forthright, truthful.

The door was open.

"Honestly?" he said. "I don't know. Friendship is generally a mutual feeling, and I can't speak for you. But speaking for myself, I think you're the first friend I've made since I was a child, and that's a valuable thing. I don't want to lose it. Even though you try to bully me, and I ask for your help at all the wrong times, I hope you'd like to stay friends."

"I think you're the only friend I've made, ever." Archer laughed, almost hysterically. He rubbed both hands across his face. "Oh, I'm tired. Of course I want to stay friends, that's why I asked. I guess I won't go to hide with the nixies, either, if you want me here. Now, go away, I need sleep."

Relief pumped through Wick's body like ice-cold water.

Archer was staying.

Just like that, Wick's body remembered its fatigue as well. The weight on his eyelids tripled. "I just hope I can make it to my room without falling asleep. Talk more tomorrow."

"Fine by me." Archer flopped back on the couch and wrapped his wing over his face. Wick left him to sleep.

◇

ARCHER THOUGHT more than once about returning to the woods to speak to his dragonkin, but each time he did, he remembered Fowl's face, lit by the light of the fireplace, his dark, dark eyes chilling Archer to the bone.

Did you forget the part where those things killed our parents?

Fowl could be right; the dragonkin's seeming goodwill could all be a trick. Archer didn't want to be the next victim.

As the days passed, Archer kept the others company

in the library, and kept reading the journal. He found a few of Caihu's notes that could have been talking about the dragonkin, or could have been talking about forty other things in creation. In places, the notes even overlapped or drooped down and trampled the next row of words. Caihu had assumed that no one besides him would ever read his journal, that much was for certain.

Or maybe he had known, and he'd gone out of his way to make it completely unintelligible.

A faint slap from Wick and Eland's table made Archer look up. Wick had tossed a book aside and sat frowning at the table.

Eland also looked up. "Are you all right?"

Wick ran a hand down the side of his face and took a long, deep breath. "We need some kind of information, and soon, but all we've found so far is a gaping hole right where the knowledge should be. I just don't know where else to look."

"Then we'll give up on using the Heather Stones as part of the plan," Twill responded. She pushed her own book away and folded her hands on the table. "Greg's explosives are ready to go; we'll give everyone a weapon or a bomb, and we'll fight for it."

"We can't do that, Twill." Wick crossed his arms on the tabletop. "We're at an extreme disadvantage. Whether we try to fight them off or give them the Heather Stones, they might wipe us out either way. We need some kind of secret weapon or leverage. Without that, we're all done for."

"We'll have to talk to the mentors, then," Eland said grimly. "If we don't have anything solid to work with, maybe they do."

"And we're supposed to hear back from the nixies tomorrow about the domes," Twill added. "Maybe we'll get lucky, and we can all hide out in the domes until the danger is past."

Archer ignored them. So, they were desperate now? Archer thought of a lizardly form with cunning eyes. He knew where they could learn more about the Scorch, and if he got lucky, maybe he'd even get a straight answer.

And, so long as it wasn't a trap, he could even get enough evidence to prove that talking to the dragonkin wasn't his worst idea yet.

"I'll let you take over, then," Archer said, and left the library. No one stopped him.

He didn't have a weapon this time. Archer crossed the mountain pass. And the sun was starting to go down; in an hour the darkness would put him at a disadvantage. What if the dragonkin was angry that he hadn't showed up the last few nights? What if it had been a trap all along, and he was walking into a pair of open jaws?

Archer paused under the charred branches of an elm tree. His palms were slick with sweat.

Would it be better to go back?

If the plan had been to kill him all along, the dragonkin would have killed him already. If the plan was to destroy the valley, it would have done that already, too. But if it was trying to help them. . . Well, it seemed to be doing a decent job at that, at least.

Even if it had all those teeth.

Drawing his wings in tighter, Archer forced himself forward.

As he neared the clearing, he saw that the dragonkin was already there, waiting. It didn't *look* hostile. No flaming breath, no darting eyes. Just a dragonkin settled down with its neck in the leaves like it was resting. Even with its eyes closed, its head turned slightly toward the sound of his footsteps.

"I'm back," Archer called as he circled around the clearing, trying to keep out of the dragonkin's reach.

The lizard's strangely familiar eyes opened, then narrowed at him. "This was not what we agreed. I started to think you weren't coming."

Archer sat down on the ground with his back against a tree. "I wasn't."

The dragonkin didn't lift its head from the ground, but the end of its tail tapped gently against the dirt. "Why not? Did you decide you didn't want to survive, after all?"

"Look," Archer said, leaning forward. "I don't really have much of a reason to trust you. Your people have burned the place where I live, and I've lost both my parents because of you. My friend still hasn't found his family. My brother is afraid all the time. *I'm* afraid all the time," he admitted begrudgingly. "And on top of that, I still can't tell if you're lying to me. So, I stayed away for a while."

"All perfectly good reasons," the dragonkin agreed. "After all, a lot of your people have died because of the dragonkin."

Archer's jaw clenched. "You don't sound very sorry about it."

"I *am* sorry." The dragonkin's eyes, usually very shrewd, softened. "I wish that no one had died. But consider. Hundreds of your people have died, but think about the thousands of dragonkin who have died because Aro kept us from the stones that could have saved us."

"How can it be that many?" Archer frowned. "I thought the Scorch came here because the water issue is happening *now*."

"What I said was that the last of our water has dried up. Our country used to be full of wetlands; they dried up slowly over the last century. Many of our elderly and sick dragonkin succumbed to the fire early, and toward the end parents sacrificed their own health to give water to their children. And then there are the soldiers who died every time we tried to get the stones. Your people can be quite a mighty and desperate bunch. After losing so many of my own people, I hope you can excuse my indifference toward a few of yours dying as well."

No. Archer didn't want to excuse the indifference, and he didn't want to be understanding. Not after all he had lost. But the flippant response never made it out of his mouth. After the death of his parents, what had he done but seek revenge?

Archer studied the dragonkin for a moment. The more he thought about it, the more this dragonkin looked much older than the other lizards he had seen. The skin looked a bit more saggy, the snout more wrinkly, the eyes more tired. "Do you have a name?"

"Do you have a heartbeat?" the dragon answered hastily. "Of course I have a name. My name is Gint."

Huh.

The name gave Archer a strange feeling. The Scorch had names, and experiences, and feelings. He couldn't give the feeling a name, but it seemed alike to when he and Wick had first connected back on that hilltop, talking about the sun. If Gint was here to trick him or lie to him, the feeling could be very bad and very dangerous. A weakness. But if he was telling the truth. . .

"And your name is Archer," Gint went on. "I heard the other boy calling for you by that name when he was looking for you in the woods. Is he the friend you mentioned, the one who's looking for his family?"

"Yup. That's Wick. Don't ask me how we're friends, we have nothing in common." Archer felt around in his pocket and produced the slippery shard of green stone. It glinted orange in the light of the setting sun. "I tested this, by the way. It reacted with the bigger stone just like the others do. So it's a real Heather Stone."

"I told you it was," Gint responded with a glint in his eye.

Archer rolled the shard around in his fingers. "I want to believe you."

Gint's brows rose ever so slightly.

Archer forged ahead. "And I hate the idea of anyone's wings burning. So, I want to help you. But if I'm going to get the others in on this, I need answers to some questions that even we can't answer."

Gint tilted his head, making the saggy folds of his neck sway. "Such as?"

"Ever since Nin left with his army, we've been hunting through our records for anything about you."

"Looking for a weakness?" Gint suggested dryly.

"Sure. Call it what you want. Problem is, if the dragonkin used to have an alliance with Aro, we have no record of it. Our records have a gap right around that time in history. If you know why they're missing, I think you could make Wick believe you, at least. Just showing him that you want to help would be a good start."

"The people in the valley are the centaurs, correct? And they still influence the rest of Aro?" Gint asked.

Archer nodded. "Better believe it. If they say we don't fight, we won't."

With his blue eyes still fastened on Archer, Gint tilted his head a bit. "While I think about your records, would you mind if I satisfied my own curiosity a bit?"

"Sure." Archer sat cross-legged on the ground, about ten feet from Gint. "I might not be the most qualified person to talk to, but go ahead."

Gint hesitated, putting thoughts into words. "How are the stones used here? This land had to be flourishing before the Scorch came, so what are the Heather Stones used for?"

"Emergencies, I think." Archer shrugged. "I don't know a lot about them, but Wick made it sound like they were basically only used to keep the Scorch out. Maybe some other emergencies, sometimes. Big stuff."

"You hardly use them." Flame licked around Gint's nostrils as he chortled. "I wondered."

"What did you use them for, when you had them?"

Gint extended a beckoning claw, and Archer tossed him the stone. Gint caught it effortlessly. "Our land is not a healthy one," Gint said, "so, in our time we used the stone—all one piece at the time—to fix many emergencies of our own. Avalanches, replenishing our water and the like. But the stones are good for more than that." Holding the bit of stone in his claw, Gint waved it gently over a patch of moss clinging to a nearby tree. The stone glowed between his claws, and slowly, color leaked through the moss, turning the whole patch to shining, transparent gold, like glass.

Archer stared with his eyebrows scrunched and his mouth gaping. "How did you do that?"

"The stones are wish magic," Gint said. The stone between his claws stopped glowing. "Depending on the blind faith of the spell caster, the options can be nearly limitless. But because they can do almost anything, they can be dangerous in the wrong hands."

Wick had said something about *the wrong hands*, too, but he had never mentioned wish magic. Hadn't he also said that they didn't know much about the Heather Stones and how they worked? Maybe. . . maybe that was even why they couldn't get the stones to work now.

"You're telling me that all this time, we could have done anything with them? Built towers, turned rocks into birds, that kind of thing? No wonder everyone kept them under lock and key," Archer mused. Then he perked up. "If the dragonkin had them, you could even use them to heal your children's wings."

"Precisely. The dragonkin have other minor magics, but our bodies hold a certain immunity to most of them, so our minor magics can't be used to heal. And the drying of the land is too severe. The Heather Stones seem to be the only thing that works."

Archer barely heard. His eyes searched through the burnt grass as he processed everything.

The dragonkin were immune to magic.

That would explain why the centaurs could never see the Scorch coming. Why the dragonkin could crawl through the centaurs' enchanting spells. It wouldn't help them make a plan—actually, it would make a plan of attack even more tricky than before—but in the moment, the little touch of clarity took part of the weight off Archer's chest.

"But if it's all that bad, why didn't Nin just take the stones by force right away?" Archer asked at length. "Why even give us the time to think about it?"

Gint shook his head. "Because he's two-faced and false with my queen. He wants her to believe that he was merciful. He gave you a generous portion of extra time so that she would hear about it and reward him, but if I know Nin, he plans to kill you, just the same."

Archer's heart thudded in his chest. "We should have guessed that, shouldn't we?"

"Never mind that," Gint added, his tone sad but warm. "You won't need to predict his every move; that's what I'm here to do. If you'll just help me talk to your leaders, you can still survive."

"You'll talk to them if I have anything to say about it," Archer blurted. His resolve lit a fire in his chest, so bright it surprised him. "I. . . I really think you're telling the truth, and I'm going to get Wick to listen to me, one way or another."

Gint's eyes softened. "Very good."

"I just need all the answers to the questions Wick will ask." Archer rubbed his forehead. "He never seems to stop asking questions. So, if I was the tree and I was going to interrogate me, what would I ask?" He looked up at the sky, thinking. "He'll probably want to know what your piece of the Heather Stone proves. Answer: it's definitely not a piece from our stone, so it proves that Heather Stone is native to your land."

Gint nodded.

Archer got up and began pacing back and forth as his mind ran wild. "But he's going to ask how the bigger piece got inside of the cavern, because it's always been inside the mountain, and there's no way it was just put there." Archer paused. "I can't answer that."

"We carried the entire mountain from our country," Gint responded without pausing to think. "It was the only way to transport it without shattering the stone. But it can never be moved again. The stone is too fragile."

"You moved the entire mountain?" Archer asked in disbelief.

"Yes. If you look closely at its shape next to the other mountains, you'll see it was never meant to be there. The rock it's made from isn't native to this region."

"Huh."

That sounded like something he could use.

I Didn't Ask For Your Opinion But I'm Getting It Anyway

ALL THROUGH BREAKFAST the next morning, Archer tried to come up with the right way to tell Wick what he had to say. Everyone else ate the meat and bread that the hosts had provided for them, and chatted softly, full of delicate hopes that the nixies' domes were holding up. Archer did his best to stay quiet and keep out of everyone else's way.

Once the meal was over, Wick took up his plate and stood. Archer leaped up after him.

Wick gave Archer a strange look. "Is something wrong?"

"I wanted to talk to you about something, that's all," Archer said defensively.

The look didn't go away, but Wick nodded. "Okay. Let's go outside."

They walked down the steps and circled around to

the side of the host house, where a spot of shade between the trees and the house provided a bit of privacy.

"What is it?" Wick asked.

This was the hard part. Archer hadn't thought about how to start, just what he would say afterward. He floundered for a moment. "You know how you said we needed some kind of information that would help us, no matter what, because now we're running out of time?"

"Yes." Wick crossed his arms, his face freezing into a farce of a casual expression, clearly trying to hide his concern. Archer hated when he made that look. It always made it much harder to get anything through his thick skull.

"And you know how I said if we could just interrogate one of the dragonkin, that would give us all the answers we needed?"

"No?"

"Oh. Right. You weren't there." The conversation had gone much more smoothly in Archer's head.

"Archer—"

"No, listen," Archer insisted. "I didn't interrogate one, exactly, but there was one who offered to talk to me, so we talked."

Wick's eyes and mouth widened. "Archer!"

"*Listen.* Sheesh. He isn't like the other ones. I don't know how exactly, but he's different. And he's told me a lot of stuff." Realizing he couldn't possibly get the conversation back on track, Archer made a mad dash for the most important information before Wick's ears stopped working. "Wick, the Heather Stones were theirs first. They came from the dragonkin land. We agreed to let them use the stones whenever they needed, but they haven't been able to for centuries because we've kept them out."

Wick's look of concern only grew.

Archer kept going. He'd made it this far; how much worse could it get? "Look, what's happening to their land is killing them. We need to help them." He paused.

The stiff casual expression had returned to Wick's face. He had moved into damage control mode.

Archer inhaled. "You don't believe me."

"I don't disbelieve you," Wick said. A careful answer. Always so polite. "But I want to know what kind of evidence they have to prove their story. I also want to know why you would hide it from me. How long has it been since you first spoke to this dragonkin?"

"A couple weeks?" Archer guessed. "Give or take. I know you always want proof, and I didn't have any proof yet. I had to wait until *I* was sure."

"All right," Wick said uncomfortably. Then he paused. "Do I really do that?"

"Do what?"

"Question everything. Make you prove everything you say."

Archer kicked at the ground. "Yeah. Kind of. A lot."

"Oh." Wick sounded deflated.

"You've always been like that, if it makes you feel any better," Archer added, now just as uncomfortable as Wick.

Wick shook his head. "It really doesn't."

Archer shrugged. "Don't look at me. I just got proof because I knew you'd want it, that's all."

"Well, I'm sorry, just the same." Wick crossed his

arms tighter, as though the gesture would anchor him to the ground, but it didn't stop his feet from fidgeting, tapping one after another on the ground. "Look, I trust *you*, but I don't know if any of us can trust this dragonkin. What did it say to make you believe it was telling the truth?"

An easy question. Thank goodness. Archer dug inside his pockets until his fingertips found the bit of smooth stone. "He had a piece of the Heather Stone, a little piece that didn't come off any of ours." Archer held the stone out between his clenched fingers. The blueish green tint of it reflected onto the skin of his hand. "And it works. I took it to the big stone under the mountain to test it out."

Wick's mouth twitched into something like a smile. "So, that's what you were doing in there. Twill told me you were lying on the floor."

"Well, before that I was bouncing off the ceiling. The big piece does the exploding thing just like the little ones, apparently," Archer said. "And if you look at the mountain, really look at it, you can tell it doesn't belong in the valley. It doesn't even match the other mountains. The Scorch brought the mountain here with the big Heather Stone inside, because it would break if they tried to take it out of the mountain."

"It could still be lying." In a rush of wings, Fowler landed next to Archer.

Archer turned to him with a scowl. "*Why* do you think it's all right to eavesdrop?"

"Because you get into all kinds of trouble when I don't," Fowl responded. "You can't trust them, Archer.

They're our enemies. They're desperate to get the stones, and they'll say anything to get them."

"I don't trust the army." Archer turned to Fowl with his face like flint. "I don't trust any of their soldiers. But *this* dragonkin is not a soldier, and I'm pretty sure that he's not our enemy, either. He's just a regular person with a life, and there are lots more like him back in their country. I think."

"And even if there are," Fowl said, "and even if your dragonkin has good intentions, there's no saying that their army will let us live. They might just take the stones and burn everything to the ground. It wouldn't cost them a thing."

"That's what I'm worried about, too," Wick said slowly. "I may have to speak with this dragonkin myself and see what answers I can get."

Wick wasn't convinced, but he wasn't calling Archer crazy. Yet. "I can take you to him," Archer offered.

"Not right now. But soon," Wick said. "For now, I need to see if we've received an update from nixie territory." Wick had been looking at his crossed arms as he spoke, clearly thinking over his own plans. Now, he looked up, his golden eyes keenly fastened on Archer's face. "But I will investigate this with you tomorrow. I don't want to pass up this chance."

As Wick walked off toward the mountain pass, Fowl said, "Archer, you're being an idiot."

"Yes, and I like it that way, thank you." Archer shouldered past Fowl's enormous wings and chased Wick toward the pass. "Hey, tree!"

Wick looked back.

"Look into it if you have to," Archer said. "You know I don't believe just anything, but I believe him. That dragonkin isn't lying to me."

"And I believe you," Wick said. He gave Archer a bit of a smile. "I just don't know that I believe *them*, not after all the damage that's happened here. But I won't forget."

"Okay." Archer let Wick go. He knew he had done his best, but he really wondered if his best was good enough. He still wasn't used to making the truth desirable and pretty and *convincing*. Talking someone to his side was one thing, but keeping them there? Keeping Wick there, after the number of times Archer had messed everything up?

How did he know when to let go and trust Wick to make the right choice?

Managing the truth felt too much like crossing a chasm on a tightrope. Too far to the left, too far to the right. . . either would end in a fall. The only chance of making it across was to stay balanced in the middle.

All he had to do now was find where the middle was.

◇

"WHAT DO YOU THINK?" Wick asked Twill as they waited on the steps of the Great Hall, keeping an eye on the skies. A manghar messenger was due to bring them an update on the nixies' underwater domes, and Wick wanted to be the first one to hear whether his people were safe. "About Archer and that dragonkin, I mean. I don't want to doubt him—I've wasted too much time doing that in the past. The problem is the dragonkin. This could be another sly ploy to get the Heather Stones. I don't want to fall for it."

"I still want to know what they'll do after they get the stones," Twill mused, turning slowly to scan across the horizon. "Will they leave us alone forever? Will they want an alliance with us again, if we even had one in the first place? Or are they planning to take the stones and burn all of us to savory little crisps?"

"Don't make us all sound so delicious," Wick said, trying his hardest not to laugh. "This is a serious conversation."

"I know," Twill said solemnly. "But I also know that people like you would be very savory as a crisped roast. I would just turn into a charred lump, but I imagine you would be scrumptious."

A bark of shocked laughter burst from Wick's throat. Twill laughed, too, catching Wick's shoulder as she nearly fell over. For a moment, they shook together in silent laughter, Wick half-doubled over and Twill clinging to his arm, reality momentarily forgotten.

It was Wick who recovered first. He forced himself to stand up straight even as his stomach muscles tried to cramp again. "All—" He hummed in his throat as another wave of laughter threatened. "With all deliciousness aside, that's my concern too. Even if Archer's dragonkin has good intentions, who's to say that the rest of them do? It only takes a few of them to burn an entire street in minutes, we know that." Wick rubbed his face. "I want to believe him. I want there to be a future where we don't have to go to war. But I really don't know if that future is possible."

"To be honest, I don't know about the dragons,

either," Twill admitted. She looked over at Wick. "But I know more good people in Aro than I know good dragons. Until I know for sure that good dragons even exist, I'll prioritize the people of Aro, no matter what that means for the Scorch."

Wick frowned. "I thought you didn't care about the country."

"The country can go suck an egg," Twill said firmly. "It's just dirt and rocks and trees. What I've always cared about is individual people. They're what matters, not this country. Even if we have to leave Aro altogether, what matters is that we live." She gestured around to the valley. "Look at them all, Wick. They're right here. They're still alive. I'm going to keep them that way no matter what it costs me. That means if we have to fight, I'll fight. On the other hand, if we have to join forces with one of the dragonkin to survive, I'll do that, too. Whatever it takes."

Wick had known Twill for longer than he had known anyone, but never before had he heard her speak with such conviction. He had always known her to be terse, standoffish, with only a small group of friends even at the best of times. But now, hearing her spell out her convictions so clearly, Wick realized Twill had always been champion to anyone she held dear. She always watched out for her friends, and she always kept her family in mind in whatever she did, even if her family didn't understand *anything* she did. Even her criticisms toward Wick's messenger job had only been her way of protecting him from giving up too many things that he couldn't get back. Twill protected her people with everything she had, and would keep on doing it until the end of everything.

Wick glanced over at Twill. She had returned to gazing out across the bright horizon. Their relationship was nearly symbiotic these days; she stood on the sunnier side of the steps, drinking in the golden rays, at the same time shading Wick from the beaming sun. He had to squint his now-sensitive eyes against the sun that shone behind her, but for a moment, as the sun blinded him, her outline nearly looked like his. Then she returned to being Twill, with a chin sharp enough to cut and twigs crowning her head that ruffled in every dry breeze across the valley.

"You're really something, Twill," Wick said.

"Yes, I am." Twill's golden, roving eyes flickered in Wick's direction. "Maybe," she added, softer, "in another lifetime, we even could have been together."

"What do you—" Wick froze as if rooted to the spot. Twill didn't even seem to notice, and she didn't glance toward him again. "How long have you thought about that?"

"Never, I suppose." Twill turned his way at last and crossed her arms, a challenge in her gaze. "But when you enjoy someone's company often enough, you start to wonder why you shouldn't enjoy it always. Don't be upset. I'll never forgive myself if you're upset, but just think about it." She gestured to her own face, then to Wick's.

Realization dawned. "I can't change my form again," Wick said. "And you never would."

"Just because I could doesn't mean I'd want to," Twill said gently.

"No, I think you're right." Wick's heart stung as he nodded. "I don't think you'd enjoy this form, and I wouldn't wish it on you."

"I don't think I'd wish it on me, either." Twill made a sound like a laugh. "Needing sunlight is enough work. I couldn't deal with all the extras you've got going on." She paused. Then she looked his way again, and her eyes sparkled with mischief. "And if I can't be the right one, I'll just have to find her for you myself."

"If you're finding someone for me, I'll just have to find someone for you," Wick responded.

"Good luck." There was a smirk in Twill's voice. "None of them want me, and that's fine."

"None of them ever *see* you. You only leave your house to see your family," Wick pointed out.

Twill flapped a hand. "Psh."

"You need my help. Admit it."

"What I need is to see you happily married with about a dozen children. And for this messenger to show up, it's been an hour." Twill drew upright and pointed. "There he is!"

The manghar swooped over the mountains and dove toward the center of the valley, headed directly for Wick. With a great flapping of wings, he slowed himself at the last second and dropped to the ground in front of them. He stood shorter than most manghar, and stockier, too, with red fur covering his torso. He held out an envelope in a thick-knuckled fist. "This is to be given to Ongel. No one may read it before him."

"Understood." Wick took the envelope. "Thank you." He turned to find Ongel.

A shadow flickered over the steps as he and Twill hurried up them, and when Wick looked up he saw three dragonkin soaring over the valley. It felt like an omen.

Ongel, coming out the door of the Great Hall, nearly ran straight into them as they tried to come in. Wick held out the envelope. "This came for you."

Ongel stepped back inside the Great Hall and let them in as well. "Let's hope that this is good news." He slid his thumb under the flap and tore the envelope open. Two sheets of paper folded out. Ongel took a brief moment to read them through. Wick tried to read Ongel's expression, but Ongel didn't betray himself with so much as a twitch of the lips.

Ongel's eyes reached the bottom of the second page, and he nodded.

"Did it go well?" Wick blurted.

Ongel offered the letter to Wick. "Read it for yourself."

Wick took the papers and scanned them as quickly as he could.

Most respected Ongel,

As agreed, we constructed a dome on the seafloor for the refugees from the valley and from leshy territory. The domes are holding strong, and the refugees seem comfortable.

However, we have another problem.

Only hours after we moved the refugees into the domes, sentries alerted me to something at the base of the domes. The dragonkin are sleeping in the water.

Their breathing is regular and they appear to be comfortable as they sleep. Unluckily, this seems to be a natural state for them. One or two even crawled through the domes and fell asleep on the rocks inside. We have escorted the refugees to areas of the dome that are further from the sleeping dragonkin, but if the dragonkin can crawl inside the dome so easily, the refugees are no safer here than elsewhere.

In summary, the domes will be useless to us. The dragonkin have no issue with the water, worse yet, they even seem to enjoy it. Another course of action will have to be settled on.

Respectfully,
Sanlar, general of the nixie kingdom

Wick's heart sank. "The domes are useless."

"Evidently." Ongel rubbed his forehead.

Twill leaned over Wick's shoulder to skim the letter. "Doesn't this mean we're out of options? That was our last idea."

Wick frowned at the paper in his hand. Twill had a point; the domes had been their best defense, even a last resort of sorts. They didn't have a backup plan, or even a next step.

Unless they spoke to Archer's dragonkin.

Wick's fingers drummed against the back of the paper. He couldn't be sure if the dragonkin was a liar, or worse, part of some trap that Nin had set for them. Maybe a spy, or even an assassin.

The only thing he knew for sure was that Archer, who didn't trust others easily, not only believed this dragonkin, it but trusted it completely.

Wick met Ongel's eyes. "We're not out of ideas yet. Archer's gotten us a meeting with one of the dragonkin, and it sounds like it's a sympathizer."

My Friend, the Man-Killing Beast

ARCHER PUT HIS HEAD into Ongel's study. "You ready?"

Ongel tucked a pair of pencils into the bag slung over his back. His armor clanked loudly with the motion. "I am now. I want to be sure we have plenty of materials to take notes if we need." He glanced over at Archer. "Is our dragonkin getting impatient?"

"I don't know. I haven't seen him yet." Archer shifted on his feet uncomfortably. "Wick is just worrying about our time ticking, that's all." Wick wasn't the only one. Archer's throat seemed to get tighter every second, like something was crawling up from his belly to block his windpipe.

"I understand. The tension in the valley is thick enough to wade through. Everyone is on edge." Ongel closed his bag and followed Archer into the hall. "As it is, I hope that my armor doesn't seem like a threat. But again, if the need arises."

Archer stole another glance at Ongel's armor as they walked up the mountain to meet the others. The armor made him realize just how huge Ongel was. His chest plate alone was twice as wide as Archer's chest, and twice as long. Leather straps as thick as Archer's arm threaded through triangular pieces like large scales to cover his horse-like half, as well. His pointed helmet could have doubled as a soup pot.

The armor also reminded Archer uncomfortably that Ongel would fight, and even bleed if, in his words, "the need arose." The thought of it sent a prickle up Archer's spine.

If Gint turned out to be a traitor and Ongel got hurt, Archer would tear the dragon apart with his bare hands.

"Do you think about what will happen if we can't figure this out?" Archer blurted. Ongel looked over at him, curious.

"If we don't figure out what to do about the dragonkin. If we don't get answers. Right now our options are to either find out why our history is wrong and try to make it right, or buckle down and try to fight our way out. Right?" Archer said. He pointed sharply up at the sky. "There are lots more of them than there are of us. If we can't figure out how to make peace with them or whatever, they'll boil us alive."

"Indeed," Ongel murmured. "It's been on my mind, as well. We have difficult decisions ahead of us."

"Exactly. All I can think about day and night is everything burning, and everyone I. . ." The choking feeling cinched tighter in Archer's throat. "Everyone I know getting killed, just like my parents were. Will any of us even survive?"

"I hope so, Archer. I truly hope so." Near the crest of the hill, Ongel stopped walking. Archer halted, too. "In fact, we want everyone to survive, if it's possible. That's why we're going to meet with this dragonkin friend of yours. With luck, he can help us find a solution. We just have to keep doing the right thing, if we can, and hope that our efforts pay off."

"Maybe hope will cut it," Archer said. The words came out sounding more harsh than he meant them, but Ongel didn't seem to mind.

"In the absence of certainty, I find that hope carries me further than you might think." Ongel placed a hand on Archer's shoulder. For a moment, the weight of his hand banished the choking feeling in Archer's throat. "Currently, we have no certainty, so for now let's count on hope, shall we?"

Archer shrugged. The moment that Ongel let go of his shoulder, reality would come pouring back in. "I don't think I have any."

"Life's difficulties do work hard to kill hope, and you've had difficulties to spare lately." The hand on Archer's shoulder squeezed. "Just give it a bit of breathing room. In my experience, the soul naturally manufactures hope, whether you like it or not. Give it some room, I think it'll happen on its own." Ongel's hand lifted, and to Archer's astonishment, the world didn't come to an end. "Come on, let's join the others."

Archer found that his feet could move again. He followed Ongel.

They crested the hill. Wick, chatting with Eland,

glanced their way and waved. Wind gusted through the trees, making everyone's clothes flap. The time of year for snow crawled nearer every day, but the weather didn't reflect that. The wind today was hot. Hot like a campfire.

"All's well?" Eland asked.

"I had trouble with the armor." Ongel gestured to his getup. "I'm not quite sure, Eland, but I suspect I'm getting old at last."

Everyone but Archer smiled.

"I'll go on ahead and let him know that we're coming," Archer said. "You can talk for a minute or something, then follow along after me."

"Fair enough," Ongel replied.

Awkwardly, Archer took a step back from everyone and set off alone.

Walking with his head down, his hands in his pockets, Archer realized his soul did seem to be manufacturing some kind of hope, just like Ongel had said. Not the kind Ongel had meant, but a hope all the same.

He hoped that he was right.

Right to trust Gint, right to lead people he. . . *cared* about to meet a dragonkin. Not too long ago he wouldn't have admitted, even to himself, that he cared about anyone, least of all anyone from the valley, where rules and authorities and prophesied fate made their rounds like guards. He wouldn't have trusted the dragonkin not to kill them, and he wouldn't have trusted Wick or anyone else to believe him when it came to a crazy plan like this. Trust didn't get any more exercise in his brain than compassion did. Yet here he was, with both of those things running in circles fast enough to make him dizzy.

Well, maybe it was a hope. Or maybe it was fear. In the face of so much uncertainty, hoping for success and fearing failure felt pretty much the same.

Gint's hunched silhouette came into sight through the trees.

"I'm back," Archer called.

Gint's head lifted from the ground. "You're late again."

"I walk slower when I'm thinking. Sorry." Archer stepped over a low bush and joined Gint in the clearing.

"Did you speak to your friend?" Gint asked, resting his head back down on the ground.

"He's on his way here right now, actually, and so are two of the centaurs." Archer hesitated, then sat down cross-legged on the ground. Maybe it was the suspiciously hot weather, or maybe it was the way he'd slept, but his bad wing ached today. "One of them is armed; don't take offense."

"That your friend is careful in dangerous times? Actually, I think I admire him already." Gint's blue eyes rolled up at Archer. "I take it the two centaurs are your friends, too. Are you the type to have friends?"

"No," Archer said with a laugh, then he stopped short. "Or maybe I am." The number of people he could possibly call friends seemed to be growing. A handful of them had even come hunting for him when he had already decided to quit them for good. They'd put important work on hold for him. Was that what friends did?

Unable to reach a conclusion, Archer finally shrugged. "I don't know."

"Interesting."

Archer felt a line in his brow crease. "What do you mean, interesting?"

"I've never heard anyone sound so certain and then so uncertain immediately after." Gint's voice was amused, and the corners of his eyes crinkled. "You make me think of my sister's children. So fiery and so young. Keep that fight in you."

"Not a problem."

Footsteps crunching through the leaves caught Archer's attention. His heart beat a little faster.

Please, let this work.

On the spot, Archer decided he wasn't sitting in the right place. He scooted across the leaves so that he sat closer to Gint, facing the others. That way, he could be a buffer between the others and the dragonkin.

Wick was the first to step into the clearing. Archer recognized his diplomat stance at once: head up, standing tall with his hands clasped in plain view in front of him, his feet planted securely on level ground. Meticulously cordial, but alert. Like a bodyguard pretending to be at ease. "Good afternoon."

Archer almost laughed. Wick was long gone. Only Diplomat Wick had made it to the clearing.

"Greetings," Gint responded in a neutral tone.

As Eland and Ongel stepped out of the trees after Wick, Archer said, "Guess I'll do the introductions. Everyone, this is Gint. Gint, these are the friends I mentioned. You probably remember Wick, and this is Eland and Ongel."

"Father and son?" Gint asked, nodding toward Eland

and Ongel.

"No," Eland said quickly. "Ongel is my mentor, and Wick's too."

Gint eyed Archer. "But not your mentor."

"No. I didn't even know who Ongel was until a few months ago." Honestly, Archer couldn't put into words exactly what Ongel was. Something different from a friend or a mentor.

Something too complicated to think about now.

Another hot wind blew through the clearing. Archer's hair fell into his eyes, and he brushed it back up and out of the way. So far, no one had spoken.

After what felt like a lifetime but had probably only been half a second, Ongel broke the silence first. "Gint, would you mind if I got straight to the point?" he asked. "I hate to waste our little time with too many niceties."

"Directness is good." Gint lifted his head off the ground, resting at Ongel's eye level. "I hear that you have some questions for me."

"Indeed. In fact, I'd like to hear you describe what brings you here. To be sure that I understand."

Gint nodded with a faint smile on his face. "Direct, again." He glanced down at Archer, who still sat cross legged on the ground. "I like this friend of yours. Let's see, in my own words. I, personally, am here to prevent war between my people and yours. Currently, it looks like this conflict won't end until either your people are annihilated, or mine are. Slaughtering either of our people seems. . . unproductive, to put it blandly. I thought some of you might still be sympathetic and willing to help me, but it seems I've underestimated the problem. You don't remember our shared history at all."

"Please," Ongel said. "Describe that history for me, as much of it as you know. I'm hopeful to see your history line up with ours, or at least what we have of it."

Gint's head tilted, and his eyes narrowed. "What do you mean by that?"

"Since the Scorch came back, a lot of us have been hunting through the library for more information on the dragonkin," Eland said, speaking for the first time. His voice sounded uncertain. "We found a gap in our history books, around the time that the Heather Stones first appeared."

"A purposeful gap, do you think?" Gint asked, his voice taking on a skeptical tone. "I don't mean to accuse, but the stones we gave you are powerful magic. People tend to conveniently forget that they weren't always the ones in power."

"We're not sure." Eland hesitated. "I'm sorry."

"Unless you were alive then, it isn't your task to be sorry," Gint said gently. "Make no mistake, I'm frustrated, but my frustration is at the culprit, not at you."

Archer blinked, taken aback at the soft tone to Gint's voice. He had never spoken like that to Archer, but then, Archer never apologized for anything.

"But," Gint added, "I would say it's your job to get to the bottom of it. We may still have time to fix this. Let me see what I recall from my books."

"For reference, what books are these?" Ongel asked.

"Historical documents from our royal library. I am a librarian," said Gint.

Archer, who had never heard this before, began to

wonder if he'd learned anything important at all before he'd brought the others here.

Gint looked up to the sky as he thought, inhaling deeply.

Then he recounted all of dragonkin history, just as he had with Archer. For Ongel and Eland's sake, he included more details, maybe too many details. He went over how the dragonkin had used the stones to keep their land green and their springs flowing, and then how their explorers had discovered Aro in its struggling state and had approached their leaders about lending the stones to Aro. All the while, Eland wrote hasty notes in the book that Ongel had handed him.

"There were countless meetings, according to the records I've read," Gint said. "Between my people, and between my people and yours. In the end, we agreed that Aro had dire needs at the time, and you could keep the stones long enough to bring your land back to life. We agreed that the dragonkin could have the stones back whenever we needed them, and then we would return them to you to keep your land stable. I don't recall anything in our history books that should have changed that. But some time later, when a group of my people tried to borrow the stones back, Aro was hostile to their approach, and the dragonkin were driven away, using your Heather Stones. We were unable to communicate with your people again."

Eland frowned and looked up from his note-taking. "What year was it when Aro drove you away?"

Gint glanced Eland's way. "I doubt our years are recorded the same as yours are, but in our years that would be 1238, the same year as a full solar eclipse and the same year the Sapphire Comet passed overhead."

Eland's face lit up. "I know exactly what year that is! In our recorded history, it would be 1347, but your astronomy would line up exactly with the same year as when Aro recorded the Scorch for the first time." The excitement on his face cooled into surprise. "Although our records record it as an attack."

"Perhaps we brought too many numbers, but it wasn't an attack." Gint stared at the ground a moment, contemplating. "Does the gap in your history come before the first recording of the Scorch, or after?"

"Before, by a few years," Eland said. "It's about a three-year gap. We haven't yet gotten to the bottom of why the gap is there."

"Was there perhaps some kind of propaganda spread around that time?" Gint asked, his eyes still on the ground. "There had to be a reason for Aro to suddenly turn on—oh. *Oh.*"

Archer's eyes darted from Ongel to Gint. "What? What?"

"The radicals." Gint raised his sharp blue eyes to Archer's face. "There was a time when a group of radicals came together, believing that the stones should only belong to dragon-kind and that your people had no right to them. They launched an attack on Aro, and although my queen heard of it and sent the Scorch after them, the damage had been done. The radicals left many wounded and even a few dead. And if my memory serves me, that would fall just around the time that you have a gap in your history."

Eland's pen scratched the page furiously. "I wonder if something happened to the valley's historian in that attack, and that's why there's a blank spot in the books."

"That would make sense, but this is a lot of speculation." Ongel massaged his creased brow with his fingertips. "We'll have to do some digging on the historians both before and after the gap in our history and cross-reference it with what you've told us."

"And then there's another thing." Wick, it seemed, had been thinking something similar. "Please, don't take this as skepticism, but an attack by radicals seems like something the dragonkin could have cleared up in a day. But now we remember the dragonkin as our enemies. One misunderstanding shouldn't be enough to destroy an alliance."

"Ah but remember," Gint said, raising one of his wing-claws. "If we assume that the radicals attacked during the three-year gap you have in your history, it was only a year later when we tried to borrow the stones back once again. If Aro took that as a second attack, it could be reason enough for you to assume the peace agreement was done with."

"That is a possibility." Ongel nodded to Eland. "Make a note to check journals and diaries around the time of the first Scorch attack and see if we can find something like that."

Eland's pen scratched rapidly.

"You should go look for that immediately," Gint said. "I'm committed to staying here as long as needed, and the sooner my story is proven, the sooner we can help each other."

Ongel nodded. "And if we do come to an agreement, will you go to the army and stop their attack?"

"I can't do that. Nin considers himself my personal enemy, and he would have me shut down immediately."

"Then what can you do?" Ongel asked.

"I'll lie."

Everyone, including Archer, looked at Gint in confusion.

"Lie?" Archer asked, frowning.

"Yes. The only thing that can save you now is word from the queen, demanding no attack until we've had further discussion. She and I are old friends, and in the light of your apparently misinformed history, I know she would want more discussion. The problem being that there isn't the time to fly all the way to meet with her and then return with the news. You would be ash long before I returned. So, yes, I would lie." A hard glint came into Gint's eye. "I would tell Nin that I already have word from the queen to hold off. Since I have a copy of the queen's seal, it wouldn't be hard to convince him."

Wick looked at Ongel. "In that case, we should go to the library right away. If we're lucky, we'll find our proof tonight."

"Agreed. We'll go right away." Ongel nodded to Gint. "Thank you for your help, friend. I hope that we'll come back with good news for you."

Gint's mouth curled in a way that might have been a smile. "I'll be waiting."

Casual Conversation With My Enemy

AS THE OTHERS turned to leave the clearing, Archer got up to follow them. Then he hesitated. He probably wouldn't be much use in the library, or maybe even anywhere else. But he did have a question he wanted to ask Gint.

"Hey, Wick?" Archer caught Wick's arm just before he left the clearing.

"You're not coming?" Wick asked.

Feeling awkward, Archer stuffed his hands in his pockets. "I just want to ask him a question. Don't worry about me."

"Honestly, I think I worry about you more than anybody else I know," Wick said. "It's like you go looking for danger."

"And yet, I don't think your worrying has ever made one lick of difference, has it? Maybe you should stop worrying." Archer smiled. "Seriously, though, I'll be behind you in a minute. I won't get in any trouble."

"If you manage not to get in any trouble, make sure you let me know," Wick called over his shoulder as he walked off. "I'll be sure we document it as a historic occasion."

Archer rolled his eyes and returned to the clearing. Gint had laid his head down on the ground once again, his eyes closed.

As Archer approached, Gint's eyes opened and rolled up toward Archer's face. "You didn't care to go with your friends?"

"I had a question." Archer sidled a little closer and sat down facing Gint.

Gint crossed his front claws under his chin. "Go on."

"I still don't understand what you get out of this. Not the dragonkin or the Scorch, just you. I almost gave up on trying to save Aro three different times, and I live here. You don't really have a reason to let us live, and if I were the dragonkin I'd probably want Aro out of the way so we're not a thorn in your side anymore. So, why do you want us to live?" The moment he finished speaking, Archer blinked in surprise at himself.

I sound like Wick.

"Have you ever lost someone dear to you, boy?" Gint asked.

His mother's face flashed behind Archer's eyes, there and then gone in a flash, vivid as a perfect painting. "Yes."

"Did the pain of it make you want to protect everyone in the world from a similar fate? Did their death lurk behind your every thought? Did your heart beat faster at the thought of anyone else dying such a death?"

Archer thought of every time that he and Fowl had screamed at each other to keep out of danger, to keep away from the dragonkin. They went at each other's throats at every opportunity, not because they hated each other, not anymore.

Because they were afraid.

Archer tried to swallow the lump in his throat. Unable to speak, he nodded.

"Once again, you and I understand each other perfectly." Gint's eyes looked on Archer tenderly. It reminded Archer of how his grandfather used to look at him. No pity, like his mother, no unfounded anger, like his father, just tender kindness.

Gint took in a deep breath and blew it out, ruffling Archer's fin of hair. "I have a sister. I don't think we've ever discussed her, but she's here with the Scorch. She tends to lean in the same direction as the radicals did so long ago, like Nin does. She thinks that Aro doesn't deserve the stones anymore and that dragon-kind should let Aro burn." He paused. "She has children of her own to protect now. Their wings haven't burned yet, but they will."

Archer pulled at a loose thread on the cuff of his pants. "Is she here because of her children?"

"Yes, and no. My sister and I also had a brother. We loved him; the three of us were always together. But he was frail, and without water to cool him, the fire in his bones took him very young. My sister and I both watched him die." Gint closed his eyes for a moment. "My brother died screaming. Every day since, I've thought that I would rather die myself than see another child suffer like he did, whether they're dragonkin or human or even your bat-faced people. To answer your question in fewer words, I am here for your children, and for ours. No child should burn again."

Archer nodded slowly. "You're right. We understand each other perfectly."

◇

WICK CLIMBED over a fallen and crumbling log, repeating to himself what materials he had to double and triple check once he arrived in the library. That old manghar journal might have something, and he'd have to scan through a few of the unmarked leatherbound volumes if Eland hadn't beaten him to it.

He skirted the edge of a steep hill, still muttering. He was so caught up in remembering the list that he didn't spot the foxhole in his path. His foot caught in the crevice, and he stumbled—straight down the steep side of the hill.

Wick slipped and skidded in the leaves. A branch narrowly missed clipping him in the forehead. A tree root caught his ankle, throwing him heavily onto his hip. He slid to a stop and lay still, listening to the sound of his own heavy breathing. He assessed himself. He wasn't dead, or hurt.

Wick sat up to check again. Miraculously, he was hardly even dirty, despite falling through so many charred leaves. He'd sustained only one black palm and one filthy pant leg when he had fallen to his knees.

A laugh burst from Wick's throat. "Well, that was lucky, wasn't it?" He pulled himself to his feet and dusted at his sooty hand, but the black only smeared. The trickle of a nearby stream caught his attention. That would do to rinse off, and then he could find a safer, less steep path back up the hill.

The stream swelled against its banks, even though no rain had graced the valley in weeks. Wick stepped over a gouge in the earth—had something torn up the ground? Mounds of rocks and fresh earth littered the dry grass.

Wick made it as far as the pebbles of the stream bank and froze.

A huge dragonkin lay stretched out in the water.

Its tail curled against its side, the tip of it only inches from Wick's shoes. It looked almost like a submerged log, with its head and limbs sunk into the current and only the ridge of its spine breaking the surface of the water. Its eyes were closed, the inflation and deflation of its breathing slow and steady.

For now, it was sleeping.

Wick took a single step back. The rocks crunched underfoot.

Then he paused.

For the next few days, the dragonkin were still honorbound to peace. In theory, no dragonkin could hurt him until the month ran out.

This could be his only opportunity to look for a weakness on a live dragonkin. Even Gint might not be willing to tell them how to kill one of his people.

Wick hesitated, his eyes scanning over the scaly coat of the dragonkin. How would he know a weakness if he saw one? What did a weakness look like?

With every rise and fall of its sides, slits behind the

dragonkin's spiked collar opened and closed, in the exact place where the ruff of flame would be. A stream of tiny bubbles flowed out each time, like gas escaping from a fissure. The scales near the gills were blackened and burned. Just as Martook had said, the dragonkin seemed to be scarred by its own fire.

"They're on fire their whole lives," Wick breathed. "They just can't stand it."

The dragonkin's eyelids snapped open. Eyes like shards of jade swiveled up to look at Wick.

Too late to run. Wick froze as if bolted to the bank of the stream as the dragonkin rose from the water. Streams of water poured from its steaming back and rolled down the panes of its wings. The ruff of fire ignited the moment its head lifted free of the water, and like a bolt of lightning, Wick was struck with recognition.

He'd seen this dragonkin before. Even without the stripes of chalky blue war paint, he recognized its face.

General Nin's mouth pulled into a long shape like a sneer. His nostrils glowed orange. "Have you come to beg, or to die early, before you watch the others burn?"

Wick's rooted feet wanted to run. "You can't kill me," he rasped. "We have an agreement."

Nin's claws crashed down on the bank at Wick's feet. His face loomed over Wick's head, blocking out the weak sunlight. Wick felt as small as a mouse staring into the eyes of a snake.

"Lamentable," Nin hissed the word slowly, deliberately. "Do you have a weapon, little creature? Will you attack me first and force my hand? Please. I would love it if you forced my hand."

Wick swallowed and silently congratulated himself. "I'm not even armed. You'll just have to wait."

"Alas." Nin settled down further into the stream bed with a sigh. Wick took a step back as the movement brought Nin's face even closer. "I'll just have to slaughter you later. It doesn't have to be this way, you know. You could still give up your stones."

Promises, promises. The fear in his heart lit a fire in Wick's blood.

"And then what?" Wick asked bluntly. "You might kill us anyway."

"True," Nin responded lazily. His eyes rolled away from the valley, in the direction Wick had come from. "But think of the alternative. I won't promise you'll survive if you give up your stones, but we both know you won't survive if you don't."

"You can't prove that, either," Wick said, without even a touch of fear in his voice. Confidence pushed him to forge onward as he thought of Gint and the hope Gint guaranteed. "We'll find a way to survive, no matter what you do. *I* can promise you that."

Nin's gaze whipped back to Wick's face, his eyes not looking at Wick, but *into* him. Attentive, too attentive. "What secret are you holding, boy? Something changed. What was it?"

He'd already said too much. Wick swallowed, his heart racing. "You'll just have to wait, like we agreed."

The corner of Nin's mouth twitched. "We'll see, tree boy, we'll see. You can talk, but talk will fail you one day. Time will tell the victor here."

Time to go. It seemed like a mistake to turn his back

on Nin, so Wick took one step backward up the bank, then another.

Nin watched him, but didn't follow. He settled down further into the water, resting his chin on the bank.

Never taking his eyes off the dragonkin general, Wick backed out of the clearing and around the broad trunk of a tree before turning and half-walking, half-running through the trees toward the valley.

Archer met him at the door of the library. "The question is, how did I beat you here when I—did you go swimming in a coal mine?"

Wick took one last look over his shoulder. The distant sounds of crackling flames only existed in his imagination, and the valley was just as peaceful and free of dragonkin as it had been the moment before.

"Wick." Archer insisted. "You look more paranoid than Fowl right now. What's going on?"

Wick leaned on the doorway and took a deep breath. His lungs couldn't seem to hold enough air. "I came across Nin in the forest, that's all."

Archer's head jutted forward. "That's *all*? The actual general of the Scorch army is walking distance from here and that's *all*? Did he see you?"

Worse.

"He threatened me, I think." Finally, Wick's heartbeat began to slow. "He dared me to attack him so that he could kill me."

Archer gave Wick a quick look up and down. "Tell me you didn't have a weapon or anything."

"I didn't. I think that's what spared me." Wick took one final deep breath and straightened. "I don't like that he's this close to the valley, but for now, the only thing we can do is find those records for Gint. That way we can send *him* to Nin and buy ourselves more time." He crossed the room and started down the ramp to the library's lower level. As he shuffled papers at their study table, he muttered, "Finding the records should be easy, finding something *in* the records. . . who knows."

"Do you. . . want help?" Archer appeared at the corner of the table. He glanced at the stack in Wick's hands. "It doesn't look like you have much to go through, though."

"We don't have many volumes from the correct time period." Wick paused, willing his hands to stop shaking. "What did you ask Gint about?"

Archer flipped one of the journal covers open, avoiding eye contact. "I asked him why he wants to help us."

Archer's behavior seemed suspicious. Wick frowned. "And?"

"He thinks it's unfair that kids die here, I guess." Archer shrugged, then said, "If I'm gonna help, I need to know what I'm looking for."

"Anything relating to the historians before or after the historical gap, from the year 1341 to 1344." Wick slid his page of notes over to Archer. "Their names were Valoren and Geniss."

Archer barely glanced at Wick's notes. "I know Valoren."

Wick's chin snapped up so quickly that his stiff neck protested. "What do you mean?"

"I never met him, obviously; he lived ages ago. But I

know of him. Caihu mentioned him while, you know, he was dying and I was sitting around being useless. Valoren was Caihu's father." Archer's eyes bugged out as he realized. "Do you think he went crazy, too?"

Wick's mind raced around in circles. The candle in front of him flickered, adding to his dizziness. "From what we read in his journal, Caihu seemed to be driven mad by the ever-changing futures he saw. I guess it's possible that the madness was hereditary, but we'd have to find concrete evidence." Then his excitement vanished, replaced by emptiness. "It wouldn't explain the gap, though. In fact, I'm not sure if this helps us at all."

Archer leaned both fists on the table and grinned wryly. "It does, actually. Caihu said his father died in a fire that he set himself."

Wick's mouth fell open. "He what?"

"He burned his whole study to the ground, with him in it. Caihu said it was a catastrophe for the valley to lose his work. I didn't ask what the work was, but you said he was the historian around the exact time that we're missing a serious chunk of history." Archer paused. "They probably lost all of his stuff in the fire. It isn't much of a stretch."

All of a sudden, the curly, befuddling handwriting in the records became perfectly clear. "Wait a minute." Wick flipped back a few pages, almost ripping the paper in his haste. "The only information I found on Geniss were complaints of his infamous laziness." He laughed. "I thought it wasn't important, especially since his time as historian begins after the historical gap, but if he didn't like to do more than was asked of him, it wouldn't surprise me if he never looked over Valoren's records. He never would have noticed the gap."

Archer's brow creased. "The other territories don't have records from that time?"

"No. Very few of the territories write physical records of their history even now, and the only exhaustive record of Aro is in the valley. No one else would have a copy."

"I think that's what they call an oversight," Archer said. "When are they going to put me in charge of this place? I'd fix it."

Wick cast Archer a dry look. "Somehow, I don't think you'd fix anything."

Archer clutched his heart in mock distress. "After all this time, you still don't have an ounce of faith in me. It's disheartening."

"You know that's not true." Wick flipped over another page. "In that case, all we would need to find is—"

"Wick!" Eland's hoof beats raced down the ramp, too fast. Archer screamed as Eland nearly ran him over.

"I'm sorry, I'm sorry. But Wick!" Eland shook a sheaf of papers in the air. "I've got exactly what we needed to find. It's barely even a paragraph, but the notes specifically call the first Scorch attack *not* a first attack, but a return! As well as calling it a betrayal of their alliance. This is what we need to prove that Aro once had an alliance with the Scorch, and that what Gint says is true."

Unbelievable. "And we've got the gap explained, too," Wick said. He put a hand to his head, nearly giddy with relief. "I can't believe our luck. We found nothing for weeks, but because of Gint we understood all of it in a single hour." His gaze fell on Archer, and his thoughts returned to the task at hand. "Eland, go get Ongel and tell him we have what we need. Archer, ask Gint for an audience with his queen."

Eland raced back up the stairs with Archer bounding close behind him, and Wick dragged his palms down the length of his face. His breath flowed more freely than it had in months.

They stood a chance now. Aro could survive. And without a doubt, they owed it all to Archer.

Silently, he reminded himself never to doubt Archer again.

TWENTY-ONE

Outrun, Out-fly, Outlive

FOCUS, WICK.

Now was no time to lose momentum. Even if they were done in the library for the foreseeable future, Wick could still make himself useful to Ongel.

His eyes lit upon Eland's notes, thrown down open on the table. At the top, Eland had scribbled a quote from one of the journals.

I learned that the Heather Stones are not a random, abstract magic, but only fulfill the user's expectations for them. If the user believes, even for a moment, that his spell will fail, it will do just that.

I consider myself fortunate to be the right hands to use them.

Below it, written in Eland's same looping, clear handwriting:

Another mention of having the 'right hands' for the Heather Stones, not in a way that implies there are wrong hands, but rather that not everyone can use them.

"The stones need to be used by the right person," Wick murmured.

How did one find the *right person*? Would Gint know?

It can't hurt to ask.

Scooping up Eland's notebook, Wick hurried out the door. Archer couldn't have made it far. As he stepped out onto the bare ground, a dark-haired form pounded across the valley toward him.

"Tree!" Archer cried. "This is bad!"

"What is?" Wick called.

"For crying out loud—" Archer skidded to a stop beside Wick, almost colliding with him. "Look up!" He grabbed Wick's shoulders and tilted him backward, pointing Wick's face toward the peaks of the mountains.

A hot breeze gusted through Wick's hair.

His stomach dropped.

A blazing head as large as a horse rose from the treetops. Wings as wide as the Great Hall flapped twice more, and a long, serpentine body followed the head.

Nin.

Across the distance, his eyes seemed to find Wick.

"Look!" Archer cried, pointing across Wick's chest to the other side of the valley.

Other dragonkin soldiers rose from the trees, their ragged wings beating at the air, their faces set toward the valley.

"What are they doing?" Wick breathed. His heart sank as he remembered his conversation with Nin in the forest.

Had they come because of him?

Nin raised his chin, exposing folds of scaly neck. He blew a funnel of fire into the storm clouds stretching across the sky.

The Scorch lunged over the hills into the bowl of the valley.

Archer seized Wick's shoulder. His fingers dug into the muscle. "Where's Fowl?"

Wick couldn't tear his eyes away from the approaching dragonkin.

"Wick." Archer's voice was hard this time. "*Where's Fowl?* We have to warn everybody!"

Though it filled him with terror, Wick tore his eyes away from the descending dragonkin. Like a miracle, his eyes lit on a circle of trees across from the library, and Fowl's silhouette moving in their midst. "There! Sound the alarm. I have to warn the Great Hall."

Archer shoved Wick away. "Then go!"

Wick sprinted toward the Great Hall. The hot air stung his eyes. "The Scorch is coming!" he screamed. "Take cover!"

An apprentice walking near the Great Hall looked up and galloped for the mountains. To warn his family?

Behind Wick, Archer's voice echoed through the valley. "*Fowl!*"

With the sound of leathery wings growing louder overhead, Wick realized what an impossible feat Archer had achieved when he'd reached Wick before the manghar.

One could never outrun anything with wings.

Wick pelted toward the Hall, watching the shadows of the dragonkin pull ahead of him more and more.

"They're coming!" Wick shouted at the top of his

lungs. "The Scorch is coming! Take cover!"

With a crack of wings, a smaller shadow shot overhead. Fowler, bound for the center of the valley.

"Fowl!" Wick shouted. "Warn the Great Hall!"

"Trying!" Fowl bellowed back.

Wick had never seen a flier so streamlined. Fowl's hair plastered almost flat against his skull. His arms and legs clamped tight against his body with his wings tucked into a tight angle, like an arrowhead. He dove for the center of the valley, where Wick could see the small shapes of the centaurs leaving the Great Hall. Wick's lungs burned from the running, and his legs already threatened to slow down.

People looked upward as Wick passed them. Several took off across the valley, sounding the alarm.

Fowl reached the knot of centaurs outside the Great Hall just as the Scorch blocked out the sky. The first dragonkin swooped down over the Great Hall and blasted flame from its maw.

"No!" The flames blinded Wick's eyes. He skidded to a stop and looked across the valley. Everyone else ran for cover, or rather, whatever cover wasn't already on fire. Many centaurs raced into the mountains, or the cavern, looking for anything that wouldn't burn.

Archer raced out of the smoke and snatched Wick's arm. "Tree, look out!"

The flaming shape of General Nin barrelled toward them like a meteor. A cruel smile curled across his face.

He's glad to burn us.

Archer yanked Wick's arm, pulling him into motion. They ran for a nearby rock formation. There was no time to check if Nin pursued them; they only ran.

The impact of each footfall sent a jolt up Wick's legs. He prayed that his friends were not burning. Eland. Ongel. Hirim. Tinor, blame him. Eland's little siblings that he only met once.

Would the dragonkin kill them all, even if they still had days left?

Wick dove into the shelter of the rocks with Archer close behind him. Nothing hit the ground behind them, so Nin hadn't followed.

Wick crawled closer to the lip of the rocks. He needed a glimpse of the valley before his imagination could convince him that all was lost. What he saw wasn't an improvement.

The dragonkin gleefully sprayed fire across the valley as the flames crawled up the walls of buildings and engulfed whole trees. Walls of fire shimmered in nearly every direction Wick looked.

Archer took a ragged breath. Wick glanced his way. Archer's eyes had the glassy sheen of fear.

Despite his own thundering heart, Wick asked. "Are you all right?"

"I'm. . . Yeah. Yeah. I'm fine." Archer sucked in a breath and whisked a hand through his hair. "Where's Fowl? Do you see him?"

Wick strained his eyes for a glimpse of anything through the flames. His eyes smarted from the heat and ash. The wobbling outline of someone with long, dark hair swooped toward the Heather Stone cavern, carrying something that could have been a small centaur child. "There!"

Fowl disappeared into the shadows. Wick watched, but Fowl didn't reappear from the cavern. Good.

"He should be all right in there," Wick whispered.

The dragonkin swooped over, spraying more flames. Wick and Archer ducked. When Wick looked back at the burning roofs and smoldering treetops, he couldn't help but shudder.

His home was burning.

The place where he had grown up, been taught and cared for and befriended, was on fire. Soon, it would be gone.

Something landed on his left, dragging his mind across the million miles and back to his body with a jolt.

Leroy, the manghar, tightened his grip on his spear and threw Wick a sidelong look of camaraderie. Behind him, four other maghar hefted their weapons in their hands. Wick recognized the jangling earrings of Gregory the bomb-maker among them.

Leroy's eyes glinted. He thrust Wick's knife into his hands. "Come, tree boy, we'll attack them together." Then he gathered himself, ready to spring into the sky.

"*No!*" Archer threw himself across Wick and hooked both of his arms around Leroy's spear. "You can't!"

"They must be stopped!" Leroy tried to shake his spear free.

Archer clung to the spear tighter. "No! And not you, either!" He let go of Leroy's spear with one hand to snatch the wing of a different manghar as he crouched to take off. Archer's head swiveled to look Leroy in the eyes. "They're baiting us. They're just making a giant show of burning the valley, because they can only hurt us if we hurt them first. Don't you get it?" He shook Leroy's spear. "If you try to fight them, you're falling for it. They'll kill you. And then they'll kill all the rest of us."

"If they attack us, I will retaliate," Leroy said.

"Obviously. But right now, you *have* to listen to me." Archer tightened his grip and cast Leroy a pleading look. "Leroy, let me trust you."

Leroy's eyes roamed the sky. His spear lowered, and finally Archer let go of it. Leroy motioned to his companions. "Stand by and watch."

A dragonkin swung its head toward them, eyes set on Leroy's spear.

"No!" Archer shouted. "You keep back."

The dragonkin slithered nearer, faster.

Archer raced three steps forward and put his face directly in front of the lizard's.

Wick stiffened.

"Back up," Archer ordered. "We have a deal. We have a deal! Hurt them and I get to hurt you, and believe me, you do not want that."

The dragonkin hesitated, its reptilian eyes now fastened on Archer.

"We'll fight you later," Archer said emphatically. "But for now, these manghar are safe from you."

Archer took another step forward, too close. Wick's skin crawled.

Archer barked, "This is the part where you leave. Get!"

The dragonkin hissed, then took off into the sky.

Wick glanced at the manghar. Leroy paused, then stepped toward Archer to clasp his hand. "Well done."

Archer's expression was a medley of terror and surprise, but he shook Leroy's hand all the same.

Wick put up his hand to fend off the heat as the manghar returned to watching the sky. As worthless as it seemed, all they could do was wait. Even if it meant watching the valley burn.

The heat increased, making the air shimmer in front of Wick's eyes.

A huge voice hissed, "There you are."

Nin dropped to the ground just a stone's throw from them with an impact that made Wick fight for balance.

"The boy with one wing," Nin hissed. He crawled his way closer, his head weaving back and forth like a snake's. "And the boy with a face like wood. I've been looking for you."

Wick closed his shaking hands into fists, feeling the grit of soot in the cracks of his palms. "What do you want?" he asked in a voice that he meant to sound commanding. Instead, his voice shook, either with fear, or with anger.

"To offer you my congratulations on your last few days of life," Nin snarled with a curve to his mouth that no longer looked anything like a smile. "It's true what I heard about you two; you've been a thorn in my side from the beginning. I look forward to burning you."

"You can't," Archer spat. "We had a deal."

"And we still do. I promised you'd live for another month. I never promised not to interfere in other ways." His eyes slid from Archer to Wick. His smirk increased, then he turned to Archer again. "I think our business here is nearly done. I only came to return something of yours."

The sound of wings thundered louder overhead, and the ground around them fell into shadow. Elsewhere in the valley, someone cried out.

Wick followed Nin's gaze upward.

Above their heads, the rest of the dragonkin circled, blocking out the sun. They were carrying some sort of mass in their midst.

"Nothing of much use," Nin declared. "But I knew it had to be yours. It blew to us on the breeze."

What was he talking about? What were they carrying?

The cloud of dragonkin released their burden, and the mass plummeted toward the valley.

"Look out!" Wick shouted. His voice died away as he recognized the falling shape.

Another dragonkin. And not just any dragonkin. Even from a distance, Wick could make out the ragged crest and baggy hide.

It was Archer's dragonkin.

Gint.

TWENTY-TWO

Fill Your Hands

ARCHER LOOKED up at Wick's cry and saw Gint's body tumbling toward them.

No.

He scrambled out of the way just in time. Gint struck the ground, throwing earth and stalks of grass in every direction. The impact knocked Archer to his knees.

Gint's head ricocheted off the rocks with a sickening thump. He didn't get up.

Archer's heart skipped a beat. On hands and knees, he scrambled toward Gint's slumped form.

Gint's eyes were hardly open when Archer reached him. The Scorch army had torn him up. His body looked like a splintered tree trunk, his flesh carved up with gashes and burns. They must have passed him around to take swipes at him.

And then there was the damage from the fall. Archer took one look at Gint's twisted left wing and looked away again.

"What did you do? How did they find you?" Archer's

legs turned into mush like rotten fruit. He sat down beside Gint with a thump.

Gint's eyes opened once more, just a slit, and they settled on Archer. "I was foolish," he whispered. "I believed Nin would be reasonable."

"You went too soon." Archer dragged a shaking hand down the side of his own face. Then he noticed the blood pouring from beneath Gint's head. "You'll bleed out!" Archer fumbled beneath Gint's head, trying to find the source of the gushing blood. He only succeeded in rearranging it. Red trickled across the dry ground toward his knees.

"Don't worry yourself with me," Gint whispered. "You need to save both our people."

A laugh shot out of Archer's mouth. "You want to save yours, after they did this to you?"

"No, no." Gint struggled to turn his head toward Archer. The gashes on his neck surged with red. Archer's stomach churned. "My people didn't do this. This was Nin's doing. He is the one to blame."

Archer's breath rushed in and out of his lungs, faster and faster. "I don't care who's to blame."

"Get to my queen," Gint said. His voice grew weaker. "I know you can. You're so full of fire. Just like one of us."

"Shows what you know," Archer muttered bitterly. "I might be the most—" He glanced up, and the words died on his breath.

The rise and fall of Gint's sides had stilled, and his eyes turned to glass. The frill of flame flickered behind his head died out, leaving him looking small and naked.

Gint didn't look like a creature anymore. He looked

like an empty thing, a flower pot left out behind a shed.

Like his grandfather's house, hollowed out to sell. Gutted.

Gint was gone.

◇

NIN TURNED BACK to Wick with a self-satisfied look on his face. "I knew you were conspiring with one of us. It could only be Gint, meddler that he is." Flame flared in his nostrils. "Thank you for the hint."

Nausea twisted in Wick's gut.

Nin had guessed. Nin had guessed that Gint was working with them, and the Scorch had hunted him down.

It was all Wick's fault.

"Until next time, boy. I think my work here is done." Nin started to turn away, then paused. "Unless. . ." His head swiveled back, looking past Wick, past the crumpled body of Gint.

Nin spat a ball of flame that arced over Wick's head, over the dead ground, and shot through the open door of the library.

"No! Stop!" Wick cried, but it was too late. The orange glow of fire grew brighter at an alarming rate as the flame dug its teeth into the reams of dry paper. Flames climbed through the library's windows.

What would they do without the records?

Nin spread his wings. "*Now*, my work here is done."

Nin took off into the sky.

Wick raced toward the library, but then Wick heard Archer scream. The sound was raw and torn, like a wounded animal. It made Wick's blood run cold.

A cloud of sparks blew past Wick's face. The library. The library was still burning. By now the flames curled up the windows to the roof.

Wick's heart pounded.

All of this is my fault.

Maybe he still had time to save the library.

Behind him, Archer made another sound, strangled from somewhere deep in his throat.

It's my fault.

I have to fix it.

I have to.

Leroy appeared above Wick's head. "What can I do?" he asked gravely.

"Put out the library. I'm going to Archer." Wick tore his eyes away from the blazing library. He ran to his friend.

GINT. *Gint is gone.*

My chance at living is gone.

EVERYONE IS GONE.

Pressure built between Archer's ears.

His mother. His father. His homes, both of them.

What was left but for them to take him, too?

YOU SHOULD HAVE STOPPED CARING.

Fear, thick, black, and sticky, swirled in his guts.

YOU PROMISED.

The blackness churned thicker until it forced its way down his legs and up his throat.

He fell to his knees and vomited.

His heartbeat pounded in his throat and ears with the force of a military drummer. Something else—not blood or vomit, but hot and wet—poured from his mouth and nose. His eyes were frozen on the place where the liquid wound down into the grass. He couldn't move them.

Archer's instincts screamed at him in roaring voices to fight, to escape. But there was nothing to fight or escape. Just his broken body that turned to shaking stone, bearing him down and trapping him in.

They're gone they're all gone all gone all gone
EVERYTHING IS GONE.

YOU'LL NEVER GET IT BACK.

ALL YOU CAN DO IS LOSE.

Something heavy fell onto his shoulders.

Nin!

Archer's limbs fought back, striking at the attacking weight as he scrambled away.

Through the haze of fear he saw it: a hand. Wick's gripping hand that he'd shaken off his shoulder.

"Archer." Wick's voice was near and far away all at once. Was he angry? Was he afraid? Archer's brain turned into a soup of information. Thoughts ran in rampant circles around the shape of Gint's body but never came within the reach of Archer's fingers.

"Archer, I'm sorry." Wick's voice went on in the distance. "Do you want me to get Fowl?"

What was Fowl going to do? What was *anyone* going to do?

Archer fell back against something firm and jumped again. The corpse?

I need a second, just a second, just give me a lifetime or two and I'll—

His stomach cramped again. Did he have anything left to throw up?

Had he even thrown up at all? Or was it an illusion of his mind? Everything in the past felt like a nightmare of a different lifetime. Nothing existed but *this. This now.* His eyes had frozen again, and wouldn't move from his sprawled legs.

New shapes appeared before his shaking eyes, two lumps of. . . Something. Was that what feet looked like?

A cool. . . other something touched his face, gently lifting his chin. The muscles of his neck had turned to stone, but also to water, and as the century's newest miracle, they let the hands lift Archer's gaze past the knees that knelt in front of him, away from the earth.

Warm, glowing eyes met his.

Wick?

How had he become a tree again?

"Hey," Twill said, her voice soft but firm like a strong hedge, fencing in his scattering thoughts. Gently, she gestured to her right. "He has something to say to you."

Just as gently, just as steadily, she turned his chin. Crouched beside her was Leroy, ash clinging to the skin of his face as his features bent and rounded into an expression Archer had never seen on a manghar.

"Battle is a heavy thing to carry." Leroy reached out and laid a hand on each of Archer's shoulders—first his left shoulder, then his right. His grip was firm, hard even, but Archer found his hands flew to Leroy's arms, clinging to them like they were the only anchor that could save him.

"It's too heavy for one," Leroy continued. "So, we create armies. And we form tactics."

His grip tightened. The grip began to hurt, but if he let go, the scream in Archer's belly would claw its way back up his throat.

Leroy gazed down into Archer's face and spoke firmly. "To bear the weight of battle, we arm ourselves. We fill first our lungs, then we fill our hands. Fill your lungs, boy."

For the first time, Archer realized why his chest felt fit to explode. His breath raced in and out faster than a sprinter's, and it hadn't slowed down. "I can't," he gasped out.

Leroy shook his shoulders. "Fill them!"

Maybe it was the harsh movement, or perhaps it was the lingering terror that someone might kill him, but something shook free. Archer sucked in a sharp breath of sooty air. Promptly, he choked on it.

Leroy slammed a hand on Archer's back until the cough subsided. "Again!"

Air flowed. Archer's body expanded. The racing desperation devouring his mind crested like a wave.

Then, like the heavy rain of a storm, it slowly passed.

I can breathe.

"Good. Now fill your hands." Leroy's heavy hands lifted from his shoulders, and he stepped away. Immediate emptiness flooded Archer's chest. He felt too light, like a wisp of grey cloud. He'd float away if no one caught him. If Archer begged him, would Leroy come back?

A pair of golden eyes, different from the first, dropped into Archer's line of vision again, then disappeared just as quickly as Wick pulled Archer into a hug.

For the moment at least, Archer couldn't float away.

Wick released him, perhaps too quickly, but his hands stayed heavy on Archer's shoulders much like Leroy's had. Over his shoulder, something was burning like a giant torch. Like a bonfire out of control.

"What's. . . What is that?" Archer squinted toward it, trying to bring the swinging periscope of his vision to focus on one thing, any one thing.

Wick glanced over his shoulder a moment, then quickly turned back to Archer, his back hunched. "It's the library."

The library.

The library was important to Wick. And to Eland.

And to their survival, right? The realization arrived like the slow swell of the tide, building up behind Archer and pushing him forward.

He *had* to do something soon, or the need to scream would come back. He had to fight back before the panic devoured him.

Leroy's voice echoed in his mind, again and again.

Fill your hands.

Fill your hands!

"Let me go," he said to Wick. "I've gotta—" He didn't finish, but Wick released his shoulders.

Archer climbed from his knees to his feet. The library blazed on.

At Leroy's feet rested a bucket full of dirty water. Water from the lake?

Fill your hands.

Archer cast his eyes toward Leroy. "You were supposed to be putting out fires." Then he paused as it all settled in. "But you came back for me?"

The library was more important, of course it was more important. A thousand things in the valley were more important than intervening in whatever had just happened to Archer Hessen.

"Why?" The word leaving Archer's mouth wanted to be harsh, but the sound that emerged was plaintive and weak.

"You saved me," Leroy responded. "You stopped that raging dragon. In return, I had to save you."

Archer's windpipe cinched. He managed to rasp, "Thank you."

Then he inhaled.

Fill your lungs.

He forced another breath.

Then fill your hands.

Archer reached down and hefted the bucket of water Leroy had left there. It weighed a hundred times more than he had expected, and yet with an effort, he was able to lift it with only one hand. Balancing to the best of his ability, he staggered toward the inferno. Heat from the library poured onto his face in vicious waves. He blinked hard against the soot that blew into his eyes.

For a moment, he wondered if he could make it another step. But he hadn't dragged himself up from the muck just to freeze looking into the fire.

Archer heaved the bucket higher and pitched his water onto the flames. The water flew through the doorway and vanished.

The bucket fell heavily to Archer's side. A manghar dropped down beside him and threw his bucket onto the flames as well, then vanished, presumably returning to the lake. Archer stared into his empty bucket. The manghar had been throwing water on the blaze this whole time, and it had hardly made any difference. How would they ever put it out?

More water flew into the flames, and the inferno hissed. The manghar at Archer's side jerked his head toward the lake.

"More. Be relentless."

Obviously.

Obviously, Archer.

They would put it out the only way they could. Relentlessly.

Archer heaved the bucket up and walked to the water.

Back and forth he trod, gripping the bucket as the bucket seemed to grow heavier each time. On the ninth journey from the lake—or was it the tenth?—Archer heaved at the bucket, but his muscles betrayed him. The bucket stayed firmly embedded in the wet sand. He heaved at it again, but his shaking arms refused.

He couldn't lift it.

Willpower, Archer.

Archer reached for the handle of the bucket again, but another hand beat him to it, a hand much larger and bonier than his own, with knuckles the size of quail's eggs.

Tinor's tired grey eyes met Archer's. "Let me," he said solemnly. "You've done more than enough."

Archer could only watch in astonishment as Tinor,

Tinor, lifted his bucket and cast a spray of water into the flickering library. The hot air whipped long wisps of his silver hair.

Archer looked at his empty, dirty hands.

What do I fill them with now?

Where was Wick?

Archer looked around for his friend and froze. Innumerable eyes looked back at him. Everyone had followed Leroy's advice to fill their hands. Everyone had a bucket of water, or a friend under their arm, or rubble in their hands, but only their hands were busy. From every corner of the valley, their eyes followed Archer.

Archer swallowed his panic and his shame, and desperately searched for Wick.

In the midst of the crowd, Wick caught Archer's eye and made a *wait for me* gesture. He slipped between tireless manghar bucket-carriers and crossed the charred ground to Archer.

Wick held out a mug full of miraculously clean liquid. "I brought some water."

Archer put his hands into his pockets, feeling the grit on the fabric of his pants. "Find somebody who needs it more."

"More than you?" Wick gave Archer a dry look. "Just take it."

Archer hesitated, then took the mug from Wick's hand. Unfortunately, slightly cool clean water did seem to be what he needed. Archer drained half the cup at a go. Then he remembered the library. "Sorry I couldn't put it out," he mumbled over the lip of the mug.

"Don't worry about it," Wick responded without

hesitation.

"You could have put it out yourself."

"Faster than the manghar? I doubt it," Wick said with a wry smile. "We'll find a way around it. We always do. Besides, I had more important things to worry about."

"Like what?" Archer said, tacking on half an insincere laugh. He took another gulp of water to quell his racing heartbeat.

"Archer, don't be stupid."

"I am stupid." Archer's thumbs tapped against the clay of the cup, making the water inside shiver. "It's just. . . Why do you keep coming back for me?"

Wick frowned. "What do you—Why wouldn't I?"

"Saying that doesn't help." Archer fought himself for half a second before looking up at Wick again. "I don't know what that means. *Why* do you keep coming back for me? You did when I was in jail in manghar territory, you did when I abandoned the valley, you did while the library was burning. What do you get out of me that makes it worth it?"

Wick crossed his arms, looking at the ground as he pondered for a moment. Archer found himself grateful not to have an immediate response. A throwaway reaction could mean nothing, or worse, could mean a flippant lie.

Wick looked up, his expression somber. "It's not because I get anything. That's not the point. The point is that you're one of my best friends, and you've helped me more in the last few months than some people have in my entire life. I don't just think you're worth it. I owe you." He gestured around the valley. "And so do they. You matter a great deal to the people here."

"Ha." Archer scuffed a foot through the black dirt at his feet. "They might like me a lot less after this. Everyone was staring."

Wick's somber expression fell away, replaced by surprise. "You didn't see. They only started looking after you got up."

What? Archer's brow furrowed. "What does that mean?"

"Archer." Wick pointed to the damp husk of the library as it dripped black soot. "I mean it. Of course there were a few stares while Leroy was sitting with you, but when you got up. . . You got everyone's attention."

"Why?" Archer insisted. "The more you talk the less sense you make. Why would I get more attention once I was *done* making a scene?"

"They know who you are. Everyone here knows."

"Great," Archer said uncomfortably.

"I'm not done," Wick cut in, and Archer clamped his mouth shut. "A lot of them have heard about your family, and what you lost during the last attack. They've seen you work your hardest in the valley, even when you didn't know what you were doing. They've watched you fight, and now they've seen you crumble, just like all of us crumble."

Archer rubbed his forehead. "I don't know if this is making me feel any better."

Wick gave him a hard look.

"Interrupting. Sorry."

"What matters is that they saw you do something many of us haven't done. You got back up."

"Because I had to."

"What matters is that you got back up, and that everyone saw. You've inspired them, now. You've got their attention, just you wait and see." Wick swallowed. "You said you wanted to be better than your father. Look. The whole valley just saw you become better than him. That's going to matter."

The words from the letters burned their way to the front of Archer's mind.

One day, I suspect that he may be a greater man than I am, and build something fit to inspire the nation.

It is worth it to let him live.

Wings flapped overhead, and Fowl dropped down beside Archer. "I heard something happened. I got caught up in the cavern helping Astor with his arm—" He took a quick step toward Archer, then pulled up short. His mouth tightened. "Are you all right?"

Archer tilted his face toward Fowl with a false smile. "Never been less so. How's Astor doing?"

"A tangle of people fell over the bridge inside that cavern. A few of them landed on top of Astor and he twisted his arm. He could have done worse."

Archer flexed his fists, resisting the urge to look back at Gint's corpse. *It could definitely be worse.*

"How are the others?" Wick asked.

"They were trying to find a medic when I left."

"They could probably use help," Wick murmured. Archer caught the worried glance cast his way. "If you'll be all right, I'll see who I can find for them."

Archer clutched his cup tighter. His stomach felt both sick and hollow, but he said, "Don't worry about me. I'll be fine."

Wick hesitated, but he left all the same.

Now with only his brother, Archer turned his head just enough to catch a glimpse of Gint again. Strangely enough, the screaming voice in his mind had quieted, clearing room for an inkling of a thought.

"Fowl, we don't know how much longer we've got, and I have nothing better to do," Archer said. He looked up at Fowl. "I say it's about time we had a proper burial service. For Gint, and for our parents. All three. What do you say?"

The After

THE FOREST was deadly quiet on the day that Archer Hessen buried his parents.

Well.

There was really nothing to bury. Only the memories and the bitterness. But all the same, he and Fowl took great care with the ceremony. They had to.

They selected a clearing where the sun came through the trees almost prettily, despite the muddy ground. They hardly debated about it. In fact, it might have been the first time the Hessen boys had agreed on anything. On the only knoll with any grass, they cleared away enough branches and fallen leaves to fit three graves. They peeled strips of bark from opposite sides of the same tree and dug them into the earth until the markers would stand on their own.

A few bright orange leaves took the place of the flowers they couldn't supply.

And that was it.

Archer and his brother stood side by side in silence.

Archer stared blankly at the three markers they had pulled together, nothing more than pieces of bark with names written in pencil. Fowl had written the names, of course. Archer's writing was barely legible, even to him.

The pencil marks would wash away with the next rainfall, and the orange leaves they had used to decorate would soon curl and turn brown, but they had done their best.

"I think usually people say something at this point," Fowl murmured.

Archer hesitated. "Like what?"

"They talk about the deceased, what they were like. You know."

Archer let out a rasp of a laugh. "I think we both know what our parents were like." He froze, realizing too late that Fowl's relationship with their parents had been nothing like his. "Sorry. I . . . just don't know what I'd say."

"No, it's fine. I don't know what I expected you to say." Fowl glanced over at Archer for a second, the brown of his eyes visible and then gone. After a moment, he went on, "What was Gint like, then? I never met him."

"Crotchety." Archer smiled wryly, looking at Gint's name on his headstone. Gint wasn't buried under his gravestone any more than their parents were. Carrying his corpse here would take more time than anyone currently had to offer, and they would have been all night digging the hole for him, but Leroy had promised that he and his friends would get the body out of sight.

"He didn't like to be questioned." Archer paused. "No, actually, I think that was an act. He always acted offended, but he'd answer anything I threw at him, every time. He said I reminded him of his nieces and nephews." Archer paused, then swallowed. "He was the only one of them that wanted to save us. I wonder if it was lonely, being at odds with the rest of them."

With surprise, Archer realized that he had already reached the end of what he knew about Gint. They'd never talked about anything but plans and schemes. No personal details.

Would he have remembered to ask about Gint's life, if he'd had the chance?

Selfish.

Archer struggled to think about something else. Anything else.

"I know I already asked this," he said to Fowl, "but do you miss them? Our parents?"

"Less now, maybe." Fowl stared straight out ahead. "But yes."

Fowl didn't have to ask, and Archer didn't have to answer. The unspoken words rang loudly. Maybe the loss of his parents stung, and maybe Archer would rather die than lose anyone else to the flames, but Archer had known a world without his parents for a long time. He didn't have much to miss.

Fowl, on the other hand, had hardly known a day where he didn't walk one step behind them.

"I have a better idea." Fowl turned to face Archer fully. His long hair blew in the hot breeze. "If the idea is to be true to our parents' memory, I think it's better if we speak about them honestly. Think about it: our father was conceited at best, and I don't think it does his memory any good to lie about him. Let's just think of him as who he was. The same for Mother."

"I don't think Mother was any more selfish than the rest of us," Archer said. He shrugged. "She never did anything really wrong. I'm just not sure she did anything at all. She never spoke up for either of us, she never stood up for herself, she just played happy family every day."

"She was trying to survive, same as the rest of us," Fowl said quietly. "I hope you realize that."

Do I?

Archer thought of his mother, and could only recall the same impenetrable wall of pleasantness he'd run into a thousand times. Their mother had put on her best smile every day, until it began to look threadbare, at least to Archer's eyes. But was that all there was to it? When had she put on that smile for the first time? Did she plaster it on every time Archer's father entered the room, or did it only appear once they had their children to perform for?

What else had she painted over with that pleasant contentment? Their dinnertime tension, certainly. Their arguments at midnight, constantly. But what other cracks had she hidden from the rest of them, from Archer? Cracks in her marriage, in her own happiness, in her relationship with her own parents that she never spoke to? In the relationships between her three boys that circled around her like planets around the sun? Or had their circling been more like vultures?

Archer's confusion only grew.

Do I really know anything about my own mother?

The uncertainty began to spiral, bringing back that familiar feeling of a giant hand squeezing his chest, suffocating. Before it could panic him further, Archer clamped a tight mental grip over the feeling, clamping it in place.

"It's like you said before, Fowl," Archer said quietly. "They're gone now. We can hope they were better than we remember, but there's no point in trying to make them into something they weren't."

Fowl's expression barely changed, but Archer saw the disappointment as it flitted past.

SELFISH.

Oh, shut up*!*

Archer dug through his mind for words. "Maybe one of these days, I'll think about someone else for a change, and society will advance a hundred years. I'm sorry I say stupid things like that." Archer searched for some way to lighten the mood he had created. "Tell me what you miss about Mother."

"I'd sound silly."

"Some things you remember from when she was alive, then."

Fowl's mouth hovered, open, for a moment before he spoke. "She always dressed her best, even when no one would see it."

For Father and his ridiculous expectations. Archer caught the comment and smothered it before it could reach the open air.

Fowl continued, unhindered. "She was sick once and I brought her breakfast because she couldn't work up the energy to come downstairs. She couldn't get out of bed, but when I walked into the room, she had put her hair up for the day, like she couldn't look any less than her best even then. It was endearing." He took a breath. "She always let me go to see my friends, even if it was late. I can't imagine living in that house with Father if it wasn't for her. I never would have made it without her." Fowl turned toward the graves again quickly, but Archer saw the clench of Fowl's trembling jaw.

"She was the best cook in the territory," Fowl said in a voice that only trembled a little. "No one's frutelken tasted like hers."

Archer's vision blurred, but a quick swipe of his hand across his eyes fixed that. "Hers was the best in the world."

Then Fowl's frame began to shake, and the best Archer could manage was an arm around his brother's back as they stood just around the corner from armageddon, mourning what little they once had.

WICK FACED the blackened husk of the library. Despair crept into his bones like the chill, making a shiver race down his spine.

Only the skeleton of the building remained. The nearer side, where the door had been, was reduced to knee high stumps of framework now. Wick could see straight through into the rooms. A pile of drenched charcoal, blocked by a fallen beam, marked the grave of their research tables. Where Wick and Eland had once sat for hours into the night, poring over record after record, only mud and ash remained.

Still, Wick splashed through the ankle-deep muck and into the wreck. The remaining eaves creaked and crackled above his head.

Something must have survived.

The creaking grew louder.

"Wick!" A firm hand on Wick's arm pulled him back.

Eland's ash-streaked face appeared between the slats of the wall. "Wick, there's nothing left. The structure is ready to collapse. Just leave it."

Wick looked around.

Eland was right. The thing that surrounded him could no longer be called a library or even a building, but a wreck. The black paste that stuck to his shoes was all that remained.

Wick took the hand that Eland offered and climbed out of the wreckage. His arms dropped heavily to his sides. "Eland, we grew up here."

"I know."

"Now, it's all gone."

"I know." Eland took a deep, steadying breath. "We'll just have to build it again."

"And what until then?" Wick ran his hands through his hair, feeling sweat and soot stick to his fingers. "The Scorch is coming back in the morning. We have no plan and no means to survive once they come."

"I don't know yet, either," Eland said. "The mentors are going to meet again to discuss a course of action. I plan to sit in to listen, and you can, too, if you want."

"Better than staying here," Wick said.

"Come on, then. They're starting soon." Eland pointed across the valley to a group of centaurs gathering by the lake.

Wick noticed that Eland waited to follow until Wick

had passed him and put several yards between himself and the crumbling library.

The centaurs sat in a circle on the blackened ground, their faces drawn and their hides streaked with dirt and ash. A few were crusted with remaining blood from treating injuries, or from injuries they had sustained themselves. Dark circles ringed every pair of eyes.

Aldor, a dark-skinned centaur that Wick barely knew, was the first to speak. "As far as I can see, all we can do is find places to hide our people and have everyone lay low until the Scorch returns in the morning. I doubt the creatures plan to be merciful, so the best we can do is hide."

"Dragonkin," Wick said softly. "That's their name."

Aldor hesitated, then nodded. "All right. The best we can do is hide from the dragonkin. Whoever they can't find, they can't kill."

Eland's father, Hirim, cleared his throat. "It might be time to consider if there's any advantage to handing over the stones like they asked."

"There doesn't seem to be," Ongel said. "If anything that Archer's dragonkin told us was true, the Scorch is out to destroy Aro no matter what we choose. As grim as it is, our options seem to be to fight or perish."

Sitting beside Ongel with blood plastering his hair against his forehead, Tinor shook his head. "And the Heather Stones are useless to us."

"They might not be," Eland said.

The circle turned to face them. Even though they sat outside the ring, Wick felt surprised to learn that he and Eland were a part of the discussion. Before all this, he would have felt that they were intruding on the meeting by even listening. A great number of things had changed since he met Archer.

"What do you mean?" Ongel asked, his voice taking on a tense edge. The situation was taking a toll on all of them. "Did you learn something?"

"There wasn't any time to tell you," Eland said. "And I wanted to find more information on it before I did. But without the library, I can only tell you what I remember." He glanced back at the ruin of the library.

"Incomplete or not, it may still help," Ongel said. "What did you find?"

"One particular scribe left notes in the margins of the historical scrolls," Eland said. "All the notes were lost in the fire, but they implied that one can use the Heather Stone magic without using all of the stones at once."

"They've been known to be used in threes or fours in the past," Aldor mused.

"Yes," Wick said, interrupting Eland. "But when Archer and I were gathering the Heather Stones again not too long ago, we wondered if using fewer was possible, since we didn't think we could convince everyone to work with us." Without meaning to, Wick glanced toward Tinor. Tinor could only meet Wick's eye for a second before looking away. It almost made Wick lose his train of thought. He fumbled for a moment. "But—that theory fell through. The stones only worked once we brought them all to the cavern."

"And maybe that *is* the only way we can use the stones now," Eland continued. "But the book I found implied—no, *stated*—that the Heather Stones have to be used with no doubt in the user's mind. The one who uses the stones has to have absolute certainty both in himself and in the magic he's casting."

"Because it's wish magic," Archer's voice said behind Wick's head.

Wick twisted around quickly. Archer stood only a few paces behind Wick and Eland with both hands gripping the strap of his bag. Judging from the blackened leaves still clinging to his clothes, Wick guessed he had just returned from the forest with his brother. Fowl passed by, headed for a knot of refugees. Fowl's shoulders slumped, Archer's brow hung heavy. The funeral had wrung them both out.

"What do you mean?" Aldor asked.

"The Heather Stones are wish magic," Archer repeated, looking at each of the centaur mentors in turn. "There was a dragonkin who volunteered information. Gint. He explained some of the Heather Stone magic to me. According to him, depending on the faith the spell caster has in the stones or whatever, you can do just about anything with them."

Wick didn't remember Archer telling him this before, but then again, he hadn't asked for it, either.

"My working theory right now is that we're the problem." Archer hefted his unfillable bag further up on his shoulder. He gestured around. "Think about it; it all started out with me and Wick trying to use the stones, which didn't work because Prentiss planted a fake stone on us. Later we tried again, but since we remembered them failing the last time, the stones failed again. And we went and told all of you that the stones hadn't worked for us, so that gave you doubts of your own, meaning the stones wouldn't work for you, either. What I'm saying is, the stones are fine. *We* just can't use them." Archer took a quick inhale and said, "The doubt is spreading like an epidemic."

Aldor held up a hand. "I don't know much about this dragonkin. What else did he tell you?"

"A lot of things, honestly," Archer said with a shrug. "Mostly stuff about his people. They used to have the Heather Stones themselves, and they used the Heather Stones to keep their land healthy. But according to Gint, the dragonkin gave the stones to us because Aro was in need. We agreed to share the stones with the dragonkin and take turns using them. I don't know what happened to that, but now we don't let them use the stones at all, and their land is the one that's dying. Their people are burning up over there. They're desperate enough now to do anything." He paused. "That's why they know so much about the stones; the stones were theirs a long time before they were ours. As far as how to use them. . ." Archer made an *I don't know* gesture with his hands. "All I know is what he told me. But if we're assuming that he told the truth and the centaur who wrote Eland's book knew what he was talking about, we can combine them and guess that you have to absolutely believe that the stones are going to work in order to get your wish fulfilled."

Hirim spoke up. "In theory, the stones would work if the person who used them had no doubt, correct?"

"That's what the book said," Eland answered. "Someone with unshakable faith in what they're doing and what the stones can do."

"And I know that I can't live up to that standard," Eland's father said slowly. Several of the other centaurs nodded in agreement. Hirim continued, "But I may know someone who can."

He turned to Ongel.

It took Wick a moment to understand. Then he realized that Hirim was right. Ongel was always the first to believe in the people around him, and the last to give up hope. Even when everyone else had been against Wick, Ongel had been willing to listen. He had never abandoned Wick, or the Heather Stones, or even Tinor in all his confused yammering about Wick's downfall. Even now, after the stones had failed them time and time again, he never expressed any kind of despair in their failing abilities.

Wick knew that even he himself would fail. He doubted everything constantly, even himself. But Ongel. . . Ongel might be the one they needed.

No one disagreed.

Ongel looked faintly surprised. "I'm sure I can try. But first we need a plan of action. Do we plan to use the Heather Stones to set up a barrier rather than go into hiding?"

"Actually," Aldor said, rubbing his chin as he spoke, "it might be best to do both. Your faith in the Heather Stones may be an asset to us, since even I wonder if the dragonkin have somehow weakened the Heather Stone magic. I suggest we try to cast the barrier spell, but until we do, we should have all our people go into hiding."

"Should we cast the spell now?" Tinor asked. "Surely it would be better to try it as soon as possible."

"No," a woman said. Wick recognized her as Cohn, the copper-skinned centaur woman who had come to their aid in Tor. "In the past, the barrier spell usually worked for only a few hours and then died away. In theory we could put it up a second time, but imagine if we can't. I suggest testing the stones using a different, smaller spell. If they work, we'll prepare to put up the barrier *only* once we have the Scorch in sight." She glanced around the circle.

Again, no one disagreed.

"In that case, we'll—"

"But they know we only cast the spell from the cavern," Archer said, close over Wick's shoulder.

Surprised by the uncharacteristically dismal tone, Wick twisted toward Archer. Archer still had his hands stuffed awkwardly in his pockets, but his shoulders hung slack as he stared emptily toward the circle of centaurs.

"They likely do, yes," Cohn confirmed, sounding confused.

"And you're only going to cast the spell once we're looking the dragonkin in the eye," Archer added in the same black tone. "What if they try to take us by surprise?"

"We'll have to be careful, I agree."

"Yeah." Archer bobbed his head once, mechanically. "That'll cut it." Turning quickly, he walked away.

"Archer!" Wick scrambled up from the soaked grass and hurried after Archer's retreating back. "What is it?"

Archer's good wing swung aside like a curtain as Archer looked over his shoulder. Shadows ringed his eyes. He hadn't been sleeping again. "Being careful isn't going to cut it. We're pushing our luck even trying to cast the spell at the last minute."

Wick struggled to find the point Archer was trying to make, but Archer's train of thought was as far from Wick's understanding as he stood from the moon. "Yes, I know that."

Archer spun fully to face Wick. "Don't you get it? They think Ongel is the only one who can do this, and they think their way is the only way, the same as always. Can't you tell what's happening? Our chances of casting the spell in time are small. Ongel's chances of survival are way smaller than that."

The phrase hit Wick like a stab to the gut.

Archer's steely blue eyes stared Wick down, wide and hard as they'd ever been. "They're going to put him square in the middle of the danger and step away. If anything goes wrong, he's dead."

Ongel's Mission

BEHIND WICK'S BACK, the circle of centaurs fell silent.

They had heard.

"They know so much." Archer's voice was sharp. "But they can't come up with anything better than this. We can't just let him go. All it'll take is one wrong move for the dragonkin to snatch him like *that*. The end of him means the end of all of us, and this is the best they can come up with?"

"May I interrupt?"

Wick turned and saw Hirim stand in the middle of the circle. The moonlight glinted on his red hair.

Archer inhaled deeply. "Do what you want."

"I agree with Archer that this plan is too risky," Eland's father said gravely. "If Ongel is our only spellcaster, we need more measures to keep him safe. I think we need to think it over while we help everyone hide."

"I'm not happy to put Ongel in danger," Aldor said. "And doing so is no small risk. But if there is no other choice, so be it."

Wick glanced back at Archer.

Archer looked no less uncomfortable. He turned on his heel and strode away from the group of centaurs.

Wick raced after him, hurrying to match Archer's quick step. "We *will* come up with something that works."

"You don't know that." Archer quickened his pace, his movements sharp and erratic. "And neither do they. With all their smarts, they couldn't predict anything that's happened so far; not the Heather Stones failing, not the Scorch coming back, nothing. They don't know what to do now, either."

"I know that," Wick agreed. Archer's hurried stride had taken them a good distance from the circle of centaurs now. "But we can't solve this by losing our tempers."

Archer wheeled on him, and on the spot, Wick remembered what it was like to see Archer angry. He would kick and scratch and spit and swing with all his might. He'd stabbed a manghar once. A furious Archer never held back and he never backed down. Not until the whole world burned.

For the first time, Wick realized how useful it could be.

"You're not listening to me," Archer hissed. "Ongel's been there for me in ways that my father never even thought about, and I won't lose him. I won't do it."

Wick found a spark of a challenge in his heart and blew it into a flame. He met Archer's eyes and stepped closer, staring Archer down. "No, you're not listening to *me*. Ongel was the first mentor I ever had. He's filled space in my life, too, spaces that nobody else could ever fill. If we lose Ongel, I don't have the first idea how I'll cope. But listen." Wick swallowed. "The centaurs are in a difficult position, they always are. They have to make choices that you or I could never make. They don't sleep well at night, and their minds are never easy. Believe me, I've been neck deep in the affairs of this blasted country longer than I've been able to read, and I know that the centaurs don't make any decision lightly."

The look in Archer's eyes didn't change. The torchlight behind him blazed around his silhouette, like he was on fire. "That doesn't make them right. If we do this their way, it'll never work."

"Then don't do it their way. If you don't like their plan, you won't get them to make a better one by walking away. If you care about Ongel, and I think you do, you need to be *in* the decision making. The centaurs can only do things the way they know how. So, if you want to do things any other way, you'll have to help them. You wish you could have somehow prevented your parents' deaths, don't you?"

Archer struggled for words, then shrugged. "I hope so."

"No one could save them, but we *can* save Ongel. This is your chance: help us come up with a better plan. You've made your way in and out of places that everyone else called impenetrable. You made the Crowned Head your personal friend. Archer, you're not as useless as you think you are. If you can do all that, you can help us find a way to armor Ongel so that he'll survive this. You can do that."

Archer's fingers clutched the strap of the unfillable bag like they had a thousand other times before. His brow furrowed in the flickering torch light.

"I might as well do it myself, right?" He glanced up at Wick.

A feeling like a warm summer breeze inflated Wick's chest.

How far they'd come since bickering over a branch in the forest.

How far Archer had come.

Archer turned on his heel and paced back toward the circle of centaurs as they began rising to leave one by one. "No, hold on," he said, his voice uncharacteristically steady and loud. "We're not done here. I want to help with—no. I'm going to be the one *in charge* of Ongel's safety."

Aldor turned to him, surprise and perhaps a touch of suspicion warping the features of his long face. "Why?"

As Wick returned to Archer's side at last, he saw that Archer's expression remained calm, but stoic. Stubborn and immovable as rock. "Because I care about him being safe more than anything right now. I'll make sure nothing happens to him."

Aldor paused, then wet his lips before he spoke. "Respectfully, I don't know if you're qualified for that job."

"Wrong," Archer responded shortly. "I am the second son of Ochre Hessen, the one who left him because he was using me. I'm the one who was working to save Aro while you were still scrambling to learn why you were in danger. I got the manghar and the nixies to join us, I've escaped from just about every jail in Aro, I've survived every attempt on my life so far, and I've outwitted *prophecy*. Your prophecy. So not only do I think I've earned a tiny bit of your respect, but I think if there's anyone qualified to keep Ongel out of danger, it's me." He inhaled sharply. "Tell me I'm wrong."

Aldor's expression reshaped into something more amiable, curious. He glanced at the faces around the circle, many of whom wore similar expressions.

"It was you that tried to befriend one of the dragonkin, wasn't it?" Cohn asked. "Before its own kind killed it. You mourned it."

Guilt twisted in Wick's gut. He saw Archer's relaxed slouch clench into a hunch. "Yeah, that was me."

"You had some kind of fit."

Archer breathed deeply, and his posture straightened by a fraction of an inch. "I had a moment; that happens to all of us. Then I got past it."

Cohn's usually stern expression softened slightly. She almost looked. . . impressed.

"So. Can you tell me I'm unqualified to do this?" Archer repeated, harder this time.

Aldor turned to Archer again. "No, I don't think I can. I'd be very willing to hear your ideas."

"Good, because I've got plenty." Archer sat on the ground, and one by one the centaurs sat with him, reforming their circle.

Archer pulled one knee up and propped an elbow on it as he explained. "First of all, I want to test the stones like you said, but *everyone* should try them."

Ongel raised his hands. "Archer, my boy, it would be

no better to make someone else take my place."

"That's not the point. That would make me feel better, but it's not the point." Archer's fingers wove patterns in the air as he seemed to struggle for words. "If. . . if the *worst thing* happened, we'll need someone to fall back on. Or maybe to go to the cavern with you. It's just better to have more than one plan."

Aldor thought, then nodded. "I can agree to that." The other mentors agreed one by one. Tinor was the last to nod his assent.

Aldor crossed his arms contemplatively, then looked to Archer. "What else?"

The next hour gave way to plotting their survival.

From the endless circles of theories, two necessary actions emerged: the people needed to be warned, and the valley needed as many layers of backup plans as they could muster. Even if the sky fell down and the bottom of the earth fell out, the stones had to make it to the cavern, and the spell had to be cast.

With Gint now gone, they had no other choice.

Messengers went out in every direction, to each major territory and city. Most carried the same letter of instruction, scribbled hastily on charred paper: *Spread the word: before morning, hide in a place that will not burn. Remain hidden until one full day has passed without seeing a dragonkin. Do not be seen, do not try to fight. You cannot win against the dragonkin. Have no fear; the valley will protect you.*

Others, traveling to the nearest cities, carried a far more urgent message: *To the leaders of Aro: send whoever you can spare to protect the valley. Our survival depends on it.*

The messengers were instructed to find their own unburnable hiding places before dawn and to go into hiding before the dragonkin could arrive. The valley would rest easier without their messengers attempting heroics.

"I just hope that the people in the further parts of Aro will know to go into hiding without being told," Wick mentioned to Archer at one point. "Even if we sent the fastest flier we could find, they'd never make it in time. Let's just hope the people have the good sense to take cover on their own."

"Ah, but that plan requires people to have *sense*," Archer pointed out. "And have people ever had any of that?"

A strangled sigh emerged from Wick's chest. "I suppose miracles can happen. . ."

As Wick handed the last of their letters to a chalky-pale human named Rewin, Archer made an important observation: The barrier spell seemed to be good at removing the Scorch from Aro, but they needed a plan to *keep* them out once the barrier spell had run its course. After trying and failing to describe his idea for a good half hour, Archer returned to Wick in exasperation.

"I don't have the words for this," he grumbled to Wick.

Wick held out his pen. "Have you tried drawing it?"

"I—no." Archer plucked the pen out of Wick's hand and swept some scraps of paper out from Wick's pile.

Some time later, Archer went back to the mentors with a stack of paper.

◇

ARCHER STRODE across the crackling grass, following the crowd of centaurs toward the Great Hall. Surprisingly, the dragonkin had only scorched the roof, leaving most of it still standing. The burnt grass, on the other hand, seemed to be sticking to the soles of his feet in dense layers. It made him want to scream.

Wick fell into step beside him. "Time to try the stones. Not nerve-wracking at all, is it?"

Archer barked a dry laugh. "Not even a little bit." His brow scrunched. "But we're doing it. They listened. That's insane."

He glanced over just in time to see Wick's suppressed smile. "Just like I knew they would. Now, am I still stupid?"

Archer adjusted his weight, struggling to find something to say that wouldn't make him sound like an idiot. "You'll be stupid until the day you die, tree. But you have a heart."

"So do you," Wick stated.

Archer's steps slowed. *Do I? After all this, do I?*

But Wick hadn't stopped talking. "Maybe start acting like it."

"That sounds a little like something I would say," Archer said. A glimmer of a smile pulled at his mouth. "Either you're copying me, or we might be cut out of the same cloth, after all."

Wick laughed dryly. "We aren't, and you know it." Then he tilted his head. "But maybe we're getting cut into the same shape."

"I can agree with that. Come on." Archer started walking faster, suddenly very aware of the soot on the soles of his feet again. "Let's prove to them that the stones do work."

Inside, the huge bodies of centaurs filled the vaulted hall, proceeding single-file through the tall doorway and packed one by another into the small square of the holding room.

Wick immediately stepped back outside of the hall. "Too crowded in there already. Tell me how it goes."

Archer cocked his head. "Really?"

"I don't need to be in the middle of everything all the time. Sometimes I don't deserve it." Wick made a face that looked something like a nervous smile.

He was thinking too much about something. Archer switched his weight to his other foot. "What do you mean?"

"Archer, I want to apologize. I. . . think it was my fault that Nin found Gint."

Slivers of cold raced down Archer's spine. "What?"

Wick inhaled deeply. He wouldn't look Archer in the eyes. "When I ran into Nin in the forest. I was afraid, and I babbled. I must have tipped Nin off that something was going on. And now Gint's dead."

Archer considered. Feelings of unknown shapes and sizes squirmed in his stomach. At last he looked Wick in the glowing eyes and asked, "Did you *tell* him we were talking to a dragonkin?"

Wick shook his head. "No, but—"

"Interrupting. Rude." Archer breathed deeply. "Did you mention Gint's name? Yes or no?"

"No," Wick responded, still looking somewhere behind Archer rather than at him.

"Did you tell him anything about our plans at all?"

"I don't think so."

The feelings squirming in Archer's gut lessened. "Then, tree, you didn't do anything at all. Stop worrying about it."

Wick struggled for words. "But Nin said. . . He said I helped him."

"Because he fights dirty. He wanted you to feel guilty. But he figured it out on his own, and Gint got caught because he wasn't being careful enough. It wasn't you." Archer hiked his bag higher on his shoulder, even though the bag didn't need it.

"How do you know it wasn't me?" Wick asked, with just a whisper of misery in his stoic tone.

Archer thought. "Look, tree. I don't know that it *was* you, either. So, I'm just going to forget about it, and you should, too."

Wick rubbed his forehead. "You're sure?"

Irritation flickered in the space between Archer's ears. "Stop asking me that. Would I say it if I didn't mean it? You want forgiveness, and I'm giving it to you. Now, do yourself a favor and take it, okay?"

Wick paused. "Okay." He glanced behind Archer, toward the stream of people entering the Great Hall. "Tell me how things turn out, then."

"Fine." Archer followed the crowd of centaurs as far as the holding room. He leaned his temple against the doorframe and watched the centaurs rifle through. Occasionally, their tall backs blocked his view as one by one, each of the centaurs grasped the stones, or laid their hands on them, or merely leaned over the table in the holding room, willing the stones to work to their will. Each time, the crowd in the room held its breath.

Each time, the stones glittered in the light of the torches, but did nothing.

Archer chewed on his thumbnail, watching Eland as he held two stones in his fingertips, like a stronger grip would shatter them. A collective exhale of breath echoed through the room as Eland set the stones back down. Archer saw the slight droop of Eland's shoulders; disappointment.

As Eland, defeated, passed Archer to rejoin the crowd outside the room, Cohn looked around with a crease in her brow. "Was that everyone?"

"All of the mentors, and all of the apprentices," Hirim said. With a shake of his head, he said, "I'm not willing to try any of our children."

"I agree." Cohn sighed, then turned her eyes on Archer. "You or Wick might stand a chance. The last ones to cast the spell were Wick and Eland, weren't they?"

Wick.

Of course.

Here were all the centaurs, gathered and watching the stones refuse to respond to any of them. Each of them had watched the candidates before them fail, knowing the same would likely happen once it reached their turn.

They were only spreading the epidemic of doubt. But Wick hadn't been present for any of it yet.

And he'd done it before.

Archer moved just as Eland started for the door. "Don't. I'll get him." The last thing they needed was someone telling Wick he was their last shot at a backup.

Archer slipped out of the Great Hall and took a quick look around the valley. With the sun already gone below the horizon, the shapes of trees and people blended into similar smudges. He squinted into the dark and finally realized one of the shadows was moving closer.

"How are the tests going?" the shadow asked in Wick's voice, and at last Archer could make out a mess of dirty blond hair.

"It's fine." He couldn't tell Wick how bad things were, or Wick would never get the stones to work. Archer grabbed Wick by the shoulders and steered him through the doors of the Great Hall. "You're up next to try the stones out. You've done it before, remember?"

"I did. . ." Wick said absently.

"That's the spirit. Come on!" Archer pushed Wick down the hall and through the thinning crowd of centaurs into the holding room. "Wick's gonna give it his best shot, everybody."

Wick shook his shoulders free of Archer's shoving hands and took a cautious step toward the table with the Heather Stones. Over Wick's shoulder, Archer watched the stones twinkle. The stones were in the right room, charged and still charging, ready to go, but unresponsive.

With all that magic within reach, it drove Archer to near-hysteria that they just couldn't get to it.

Wick's hands hovered above the stones. "Are we going for any specific method?"

When no one responded, Wick glanced back over his shoulder at the others.

"Just do whatever you think will work," Archer said quickly.

Maybe if Wick already thought it would work, that would lend them a scrap of a chance.

Maybe Wick believed in the stones, even if he didn't believe in himself.

Wick took a deep breath. "All right, then." He reached for the leshy stone and the seraph stone.

Archer started to hold his breath, realized he would suffocate like that, and started breathing again.

Wick turned to face the room, the stones cradled in each of his hands. The light of the torches gleamed from the surface of the stones, making them glow orange and green like an opal. Wick stared down at the stones with the intense glare of a harrowed wizard.

For a long moment, the room went deathly silent.

Wick stayed with the stones, his posture still tense and his thick brows clenched.

Archer willed Wick to make it work.

Four breaths. Five.

At last, Wick's shoulders slumped. "I'm sorry. I can't do it."

"In that case, Ongel," Aldor said from his place beside Archer in the doorway, "it's your turn now."

Archer's heart beat faster. If Ongel could still get the stones to work after he had seen everyone else in the room try and fail, it would be a miracle.

It would also prove that they *had* to put him in the way of danger.

With his heart pounding in his chest, Archer rubbed the corner of one eyebrow in tiny, rapid circles.

Ongel squeezed Archer's shoulder reassuringly as he passed by. Wick moved clear of the table, looking defeated. As Ongel approached the table, he gently rearranged the stones to sit a little closer together, in a cluster. Then he rested his fingertips on the edge of the table and lowered his head. His braids gently fell forward over his shoulders as everyone in the room held their breath.

Then things started happening.

Something touched the top of Archer's head.

Archer jumped and smacked at the top of his head, startling the people nearest to him. His head was wet. Something wet tapped at his shoulder, and finally it occurred to Archer to look up.

Snow was drifting gently down from the ceiling.

Archer elbowed Eland next to him. "Look, look."

Eland looked up, and several of the others in the room followed. "Snow!" Eland whispered.

"Ongel," Archer replied.

Across from them, Ongel's head lowered further.

Every shutter of every window in the hall behind them swung shut with a series of solid, profound *thuds*. In a flash, all the snow in the room transformed into tiny dots of light that winked out instantly.

As Archer looked back toward Ongel, he saw a faint green glow surrounding Ongel's form, making the shape of him somewhat hazy. It only took him a moment to recognize it.

Ongel was proving he could cast a barrier spell.

Ongel raised his head, and the green haze vanished like mist. He lifted his hands from the table, and the glow of the Heather Stones faded away. The orange flicker of the torches seemed duller now compared to the bright green light. Ongel looked over his shoulder, the wrinkles of his eyes creasing deeper with his soft, encouraging smile. "I think that should do."

And so Ongel's fate was sealed.

Archer leaned against the ridges of embossed wallpaper as the remaining centaurs filed out of the room, murmuring to one another about the next steps that needed taking.

"Aren't you coming?" Wick asked, noticing Archer hadn't moved. "There's still a lot of work to be done before morning comes."

"I'll be there in a minute," Archer responded, without taking his eyes off the ground. "I just need a moment to think."

Wick hesitated only a moment. He took a step toward the hall, and then stopped with his hand on the doorframe. "You know, you worry me sometimes. You've got to stop doing that."

"Or you could stop worrying," Archer responded, without even thinking. "It'll make your hair go grey like all these people if you don't."

When Wick still hesitated, Archer smoothed the sharp edges from his voice and said, "Seriously, I'll be right there. I need a second without people talking in my face, that's all."

Wick nodded. "I'll be outside with Ongel when you're done."

"All right." Archer waited until Wick's footsteps faded and the *boom* of the double doors closing echoed down the hall. Then he pushed off the wall and approached the Heather Stones.

Nestled in black velvet, the stones glimmered faintly. Archer didn't spot any glow of green magic, though. Just reflections of the torchlight.

Not like when Ongel had been near them. With Ongel, the stones had reacted right away, like they had been waiting for him. They didn't react at all as Archer approached.

But he had to try.

Just for the sake of it, Archer reached for different stones from the ones Wick had tried. The manghar stone, and the fair folk. Two of the biggest turning points in the last few months of his life. Who knew that putting a river in a bag would have led to all this?

"You can do this," he muttered to himself. "You've done it before, right?"

Have you, though?

Archer pressed his face against the cool surface of the stones, jamming them against the space between his eyebrows.

Come on, Archer, he told himself. *If you've ever believed in anything in your life, believe in this. You've got a crumb of conviction somewhere. Believe for Ongel.*

With his eyes screwed shut and the stones still pressed up against his forehead, Archer willed for the temperature of the room to change, for snow to fall like it had for Ongel. Inside his head he felt around blindly for the sensation of certainty.

Please.

Twelve heartbeats later, still no change in temperature.

The exasperated sigh flew from Archer's mouth as his

grip on the stones loosened. He opened his eyes, just in time to see a fading green glow.

A Night Worth Writing Songs About

A REACTION!

Archer yanked his hands away from his face and stared at the stones. They appeared normal now. Unresponsive.

"No, come on. Do it again." He shook the stones.

Nothing.

Archer considered smacking the stones together, just in case, but even if that worked, an explosion would only hurt the valley, not the dragons.

I failed, after all.

Archer walked out of the room and down the empty hall. Throwing open the doors of the Great Hall, he found himself face-to-face with Wick again. Wick had his hand at eye level already, ready to push the doors open.

A faint glimmer of annoyance flitted through Archer's head. "I told you I was fine—" He started to say.

"No, look!" Wick turned and pointed across the

valley. "A friend of yours is here."

Not fifty yards away stood Crowned Head Theodore of the manghar, strapped tightly in leather armor and bristling with blades from every point of his muscular circumference. Behind him, their brutal plate armor glittering in the torchlight, milled at least a hundred other manghar. Among their numbers, armored in layers of coral and slathered in blue war paint, nixies stood at the ready with spears in their hands.

Wick's voice was thick with relief. "They brought warriors to protect the valley."

Archer started down the steps at a run. "They'll be able to protect Ongel."

Theodore turned Archer's way with a grin as Archer dashed toward him. The lamplight glittered on his long teeth. "At last, a fellow warrior!"

"You don't know how bad we need you," Archer said. His chest felt strangely light, like a sort of iron band had fallen away. Was this relief? Why relief, when at least a hundred *quite lethal* warriors had just appeared in front of his eyes? A lifetime ago, the sight would have sent him running in the opposite direction.

All the same, the sight of the Crowned Head's pink nose wrinkling into a grin brought Archer more relief than he had felt in a fortnight.

Then, he remembered. "You have people, too," he said, stopping short before his giddy heart could make him hug the bat king. "Don't they need to be protected, too?"

The king's head tilted back to roar laughter into the night. "They would rather face execution than have someone else fight their battles for them. They'll protect their own homes and families as they see fit. I," he went on, more sober now, "have a debt to fulfill, and I will see my task carried out."

"To the centaurs?" Archer asked.

"Certainly not. To Archer, the winged thief, who once stole my throne from my throne room and escaped execution."

Archer flinched.

Then Theodore turned gleaming eyes on him. "Archer the thief now turned Archer the friend to the Crowned Head, and to his guard."

Archer's confusion spread like a mist in his head. "Huh?"

"One of my most fierce and dedicated servants sent a messenger to me, stating that you had saved an entire group of my people from death by the fireworms," Theodore said. Instead of booming or hissing as he usually would, his voice was now firm, earnest. "A debt like that cannot go unnoticed. Until we defeat these beasts or armageddon takes us all, I and my finest guards are at your disposal. Where would you have us fight?"

With the help of the manghar and nixies, plans expanded. The Heather Stones had to stay in the holding room until the last minute to give them maximum power. Then Ongel would take the Heather Stones to the cavern an hour before the sun rose to prepare for the dragonkin. A dozen of the manghar and nixie's finest warriors would accompany Ongel, and a dozen more would guard the entrance to the cavern.

Twill and Greg had put their heads together and decided on two areas to set up explosives—above the cavern entrance, where they could collapse the opening if necessary, and surrounding the lake, where the dragonkin were likely to be, but those protecting the valley would not be.

Manghar would patrol the skies and try to take down the dragonkin before they reached the ground. Whatever dragonkin made it past them would have to face the nixies and the centaurs, who would be armed with bows around the perimeter of the valley, and swords and torches on the ground. The torches had been Wick's idea.

"You said the dragonkin need water to survive, so we'll block off their access to the water with the explosives. We'll also arm ourselves with torches. If they're already burning up, I'd think that the extra heat from the torches could be useful to us." Wick rubbed his forehead. "Although it is a shame it had to come to this. We were making headway with Gint."

Ongel laid a hand on Wick's shoulder. "I agree. It would have been better if we could get an audience with their queen. But since we lost Gint, the only dragonkin left are the ones who aim to kill us in the morning. Self-defense is our best option."

Watching from the steps of the Great Hall, Archer crossed his arms tighter against his body and said nothing.

Self-defense was easy. Defending himself, that he could do. Defending the valley? He could probably do that, too.

But. . .

Gint had talked about ending things without a slaughter. He had worked hard and traveled far to keep the armies from killing one another.

But now he was gone, and all Aro could do was fight for their lives with everything they had. Not to mention Ongel. For Ongel, Archer would fight as many desperate and dying dragonkin as it took.

"Hey, Ongel?" he asked, shifting his feet rather than looking Ongel in the face.

"What is it?"

"Shouldn't you take my bag with you into the cavern? It's. . . it's meant to be with the stones, technically, and you'll need it more than me tomorrow. And if you need a place to hide, you can just tuck yourself inside the bag. . ." Too late, Archer realized that his pointless rambling made him sound like a worried mother. In one sharp movement he whipped the strap of the bag over his head and thrust it toward Ongel's astonished face. "Just take it. It'll make me feel better."

Ongel's eyes crinkled at the corners. His hand closed over Archer's for a reassuring squeeze before he grasped the strap of the bag. "I'd be honored. Thank you."

"Don't thank me yet," Archer said quickly. "Thank me after we've survived." Then he took off after Wick.

"I almost went with the other messengers to spread the word," Wick admitted later as he and Wick prepared a shelter, mostly to protect against the wind and the blowing ash. Once fire came. . . Well, no shelter would matter then. The centaur mentors had split off in different directions, making sure that the rest of the valley found safe hiding places. Without anything else to do, Wick and Archer had begun constructing small shelters for those who wanted to sleep until the morning came.

Even with the sun long gone and darkness stretching

out in every direction, the wind on the side of Archer's face was hot, like chimney smoke.

Wick slid a piece of half-charred wood across the top of the shelter and swiped his sleeve across his brow. It left a streak of black across his forehead. "It's funny how there was a time that going with the messengers would have been my thing to do, simple as that. Now. . . I don't think I'm cut out for it anymore."

Archer nudged the structure with his foot, pleased to see that it didn't fall. "You were always better than that, anyway."

"All the same," Wick went on, "it's the only thing I'm trained to do. I don't have many other opportunities lined up." He paused. "It makes me wonder what I'll do after all this."

"Literally anything." Archer scoffed, relieved when Wick cracked a smile. "You're the guy who cast the last barrier spell with a dragonkin breathing down your neck, they should give you any job you want."

Still smiling, Wick shook his head. "My ego would be the size of the valley if you had your way. It sounds like all I have to do is pick a job."

"That's what I'm saying."

"You're absurd." Wick rubbed his neck, wincing. "Well, if I'm going to be up any later, I'll need something to eat." He set off toward the middle of the valley, where their remaining supplies were gathered. Archer wondered if they'd live to run out of supplies in the next few days or whether they would die with a stockpile of food they would never need again.

Fowl dropped down to stand by Archer's side. "I

brought you food." He thrust some sort of hardened cake into Archer's hand.

"Thanks?" Archer stared at the cake in his hand for a moment, trying to discern what the confused feeling was in his belly, then gave up on it and began to gnaw at his dinner. After Fowl left again, Archer took another of the charred scraps of paper and began to sketch the sharp outlines of his brother's face.

The preparations dragged on into the night. Whatever weapons that could be found were distributed to anyone who could carry one, and all remaining scraps of material from the buildings were built into ramshackle shelters.

At some point in the haze of activity, a blond nixie boy, perhaps Archer's own age, approached to offer him a choice of weapons. After studying the choices of a knife or some sort of spear with spikes on one end and a club on the other for the span of a single blink, Archer said, "You should probably keep them. I'm probably just going to use a piece of wood or a sharp stake or something."

The nixie boy's shoulders slumped. "All right," he managed.

Wrong choice.

Archer jumped forward and took the odd, spike-encrusted spear. "Actually, I'll hang on to this. Just in case, right?"

The boy's shoulders squared once more, and his mouth tightened into something like a smile. As he began to turn away, Archer remembered something Wick had said some time ago, and he called after the boy again.

"Hey, think you can find me a mace?"

The boy raced off, armor flapping, to fulfill Archer's request, and Archer returned to the sketch that was nearly done.

An hour later, with the spear slung over his shoulder and a mace leaning dangerously out of his pocket, Archer approached Fowl with a sketch just small enough to fit a locket.

It had to be near midnight when something strange happened.

Archer, who had been sitting uselessly beside Fowl for some time with Astor sprawled across the grass behind them, looked up from his lap and realized that no one in the valley was moving. The centaurs gathered beside the food stockpile, the manghar perched up in the hills, the nixies clustered around the borders of the lake. . . Every person in the valley stood still, hands hanging empty at their sides.

The preparations were complete.

They couldn't do anything more.

The somber air made Archer's stomach clench.

Wick appeared at Archer's elbow. "I suppose there's nothing left to do but wait. Maybe sleep."

The sickening feeling in Archer's stomach intensified. "Is that all there is? Really?"

Fowl glanced at Archer. "What would you have us do?"

Archer's foot tapped against the ground as he tried to think of something but came up empty. "I don't know. But if this is Aro's last night to live—"

"It isn't," Wick said, gently but firmly. "We'll make sure of that."

"But if it is." Archer turned to Wick and pointed out at the valley. "Actually, scratch that. If this *isn't* our last night, especially if it isn't, is this how you want to remember it? Scrambling for the best chance at survival and then standing around hoping for something else to do? Maybe sleeping, probably not even that? Laying there scared?"

Astor, still awake as Archer had suspected, raised his head from the ground. "He's right, it's anything not worth writing songs about."

Archer pointed to Astor. "Exactly. Seraphs sing songs about all sorts of battles in history, and the people who fought them."

"Astor's written some songs himself," Fowl added.

"But look at this." Archer waved out at the valley again, at all the centaurs settling down under shelters and the nixies leaning their chins on their spears as they waited the night out. "This isn't worth writing songs about. It isn't even worth remembering. And what's more, I'll never get any sleep with the tension out here."

"If we could convince everyone, it would help our morale to do something together," Wick agreed. A ghost of a smile flitted across his face. "And what luck that one of Aro's most infamous party throwers is in this valley."

Archer felt the crease appear in his brow. "Who?"

"He happens to be your personal friend." Wick jerked his head to Archer's right, where Crowned Head Theodore sat on a rock, polishing a sword as long as Archer was tall.

Archer's mouth dropped open. "You're kidding."

Wick shook his head, grinning a bit. "Ask him. He'll

know exactly what to do to raise our spirits."

A miniscule chance remained that Wick was trying to fool him, but Archer was too desperate to destroy the gloomy mood to hesitate any longer. "Come on, then."

Archer marched across the stubs of burned grass with Wick close behind him. "Theodore," he said as he got closer. "Everyone's too tense and gloomy. What can we do to fill some time and make everyone a little less dismal?"

"Preferably nothing tiring," Wick added quickly. "We need our strength for tomorrow morning."

Crowned Head Theodore rose from the rock with a gleam in hiseyes. He slid his sword back into its sheath with a snap. "I was just thinking the same. We'll never battle with all our spirits if our people worry the night away."

Archer grinned. "Exactly. What do you think?"

"Normally, I would suggest a rigorous dance around a bonfire, but since the battle will come early, I think I have a better recommendation." Theodore twisted, almost knocking Archer over the head with one of his wings, and shouted to one of his manghar attendants. "Bring out the wine!"

"HOW MUCH WINE?" Wick asked uncomfortably as the attendants flew off. Wine could be trouble if they let it get out of hand.

The Crowned Head thumped Wick on the back, nearly knocking him over. "Don't worry, boy, we were only able to carry a few bottles. Not nearly enough for anyone."

The Crowned Head led Wick and Archer toward one of the campfires and took a seat on the grass. Archer sat down as well, with Wick on his other side. As the other manghar approached with faceted bottles of dark wine, Archer leaned out of the circle to wave for Fowl and Astor to come over, too. They seated themselves on Wick's far side. Fowl cast a wary glance at the Crowned Head, but sat beside him all the same.

The Crowned Head dug his fangs into the cork of his wine bottle and tore the cork out. He spat it over his shoulder, where it bounced off the grass. "Traditionally, my people share a bottle like this after a funeral. It's good for lifting the spirits. We drink together, we talk, and we seek ease. The only rule is that no one talks about anything somber. We're here to enjoy one another's company."

With that, the Crowned Head put the bottle to his lips and tilted his head back. Lowering the bottle, he passed it to Archer. "Take a drink and pass it along."

Archer grabbed the bottle and took a swig. His eyes visibly watered. Wick fought down a laugh. Clearing his throat, Archer said, "'S pretty good."

The Crowned Head nodded. "It was the oldest in my storeroom. It seemed the right one to bring."

Archer passed the bottle across to Wick. "Try it."

Wick tilted the bottle, studying the sloshing liquid inside. The color seemed different from any other liquid he had seen before, both darker and more vivid than other drinks. "I think this is the first time I've had alcohol."

Archer shrugged. "Good thing there's not a lot of it."

"I saw someone put wine in their food once." Wick

tipped the bottle back and took a sip. The wine tasted of berry and pine wood; probably aged in pine from the very trees growing around the manghar palace. He'd expected a strong taste from Archer's reaction, but the manghar wine burned. It flamed its way down his throat and lit a blaze inside his belly. Wick's jaw clenched as he quickly passed the bottle to Fowl. "You didn't tell me it would do that," he hissed to Archer. His eyes watered, too.

Archer grinned with glee. "It wouldn't be any fun if I had. What did you think?"

Wick rolled his tongue around in his mouth, tasting. "I liked the flavor. It was interesting. The burning will take some getting used to, though."

Archer leaned back on his elbows. "I'll have to get you something even stronger next time. That could be really entertaining."

As the bottle moved around the circle, the circle only grew. Nixies and centaurs gathered from their places around the valley. Weapons were laid down outside the circle. Reserves of dried fruit and even candy surfaced from pockets. A few fair folk Wick hadn't even noticed appeared at Fowl's knee, and later on, a satyr sat cross-legged on the opposite side of the circle.

As the circle grew, so did the sounds of conversation. The manghar shared stories and laughed uproariously among themselves at the public humiliation they had caused their foes. A few of the centaurs shared ancient tales and fables. One of the fair folk had studied poetry in years past, and she shared an epic recitation in the center of the circle, using a piece of a burnt stick as her sword. As time passed, the peoples of different territories mingled more, shared more, laughed with one another. A few changed seats so they could talk to people in other parts of the circle. Even Twill, strange as she was, spoke avidly with one of the manghar guards across the circle, switching between excited explanation to intense argument to hysterical laughter in a matter of minutes.

In the middle of listening to their satyr tell of his mother's journey across the breadth of Aro, Wick realized with a jolt that he had been utterly at ease for well over an hour.

Imagine. Archer of all people bringing the valley together and putting them at ease. Archer of all people wanting—*trying*—to create a better atmosphere for people around him.

After all this time, how did Archer still manage to surprise him?

Not long after, the conversation gradually waned, and the circle thinned. Ongel was the first to leave, patting Wick on the shoulder. "I'm about to turn in for the night. We'll all need our rest for tomorrow, and I'm not getting any younger."

"I probably won't be much longer," Wick promised. Then, "Good night, Ongel."

One by one, the centaurs left for the night. At some point the fair folk and the satyr disappeared as well, back to wherever they had mysteriously appeared from. Wick wondered if he would see them in the morning.

Astor was the last to leave them. He threw a half a smile in Archer's direction and said, "I might get a few songs out of that. Thank you."

Archer shifted uncomfortably beside Wick. "Sure.

You're welcome."

At long last, the rest of the crowd disappeared as well, and only Wick and Archer sat with the Crowned Head under the pitch black sky.

The Crowned Head drained the dregs from the final bottle and Archer flopped down with an arm over his eyes as Wick stoked the fire.

"They were a hearty group," the Crowned Head said with a toothy smile. "I'm proud to fight alongside them."

"I agree." Setting down his stoking stick, Wick plucked up a piece of charred grass and twirled it between fingers already coated with black. "Although, I wonder if I'm really much of a fighter. I think I'm better cut out for strategy."

Archer lifted his arm a few inches away from his eyes. "That's what you think. You just pick your moments. But you fight pretty well, so that means people who end up on your bad side will remember not to do it again."

Wick smiled. "Are you calling yourself forgettable?"

"No, I go for quantity over quality." Archer pushed up onto his elbows. "Lots of fights, lots of punches. I beat the tar *and* the pitch out of everybody. Can't be forgettable if you're haunting dreams."

"I wonder about you sometimes, Archer."

"Many do. I'm a delightful enigma."

"Or maybe you just make no sense. Have you ever thought of that?"

"Nope. And I won't start now, either." Archer finally got up. "I'm going to bed." He hesitated before he finished taking the first step away. "I guess I'll see both of you tomorrow, then."

The Crowned Head nodded. "Whether in the flesh, or from the grave."

Archer walked away, and Wick realized that it was just him and the Crowned Head. As the fire died, the night wrapped around them like a thick curtain, without even crickets or birdsong to break up the silence.

Was this what the end of the world felt like?

The Crowned Head stretched his wings lazily and tilted his head in Wick's direction. "You look like you have something to say, tree boy."

Wick wasn't sure what he had to say. In all his years of serving and assisting Aro's leaders, he had never been personal with any of them. It hadn't been his job or his place. Of course the Crowned Head of all people would be the one to ask for his thoughts so freely. Tonight was a night for the unexpected.

"Do you think we stand a chance at all tomorrow?" Wick asked. He looked at the Crowned Head, who was all muscle and bristle and teeth, but now seated on the ground beside him, almost like a friend. "I don't want sugarcoating or wishful thinking; I don't think I could take it. You're one of the strongest fighters in Aro, and your people are our surest allies, so I would think you would know. Will we make it?"

The Crowned Head breathed deeply, and his brow grew heavy. "If you want honesty, I truly don't know. This life is strange and unpredictable, and battle is even more so. In another time, I would have been glad to die for a noble cause, but this is another thing entirely. If we are killed tomorrow, it won't be a glorious sacrifice for the greater good. It will only mean unexistence."

The anxiety in Wick's chest wriggled just a bit as the Crowned Head put into words exactly what Wick had been thinking all day.

"That's the philosophical answer." The Crowned Head's eyes, less frightening and orange in the dim light, turned toward Wick again. "But you're a man of strategy. If we plan to win, our only hope is the element of surprise. We have to strike hard and fast. If we can get Ongel to the chamber and cast the spell the moment the Scorch comes into sight, Aro will be safe. But if we don't succeed, or the Scorch strikes us down before Ongel reaches the cavern, or even if they produce some surprise of their own, I can't say what will happen."

Wick nodded. "That's what I expected you would say."

"But don't forget, tree boy, that we can be unpredictable, too," the Crowned Head said. "We have a chance up until the very moment we fall."

"Skorffv," Wick murmured.

"What's that you say?" the Crowned Head asked.

"It's a seraph word," Wick said slowly, gazing into the embers of the fire. "Archer told me about it. Skorffv is the moment where failure is imminent, but until failure happens, anything is possible. We're at a skorffv now. Until we fail or succeed, anything can happen."

"The seraphs are poetic." the Crowned Head said with a nod. "My only concern is about what happens after we drive the lizards away. How do we know that they will be truly gone this time? Has the valley come up with a plan for that, if we do survive?"

"We have." Wick hesitated. "Well, actually it was

Archer's idea. He's really something else these days."

"Indeed. Let's hope that we live to see other such wonders." The Crowned Head thumped Wick on the shoulder. "Until then, we strike hard and fast, and we watch the light die in the lizards' eyes when we run them through. And when we succeed, I'll be sure that you see a *real* manghar celebration."

Wick stood. "You've got a deal."

◇

SOMETIME BEFORE Wick returned, Archer fell asleep in their little shelter.

His dreams were filled with fire and floods and something big that was always behind him, always coming, trying to bite his head off. In his dreams he lost arms, and legs, and friends, and he couldn't make any of the right choices. In one nightmare, he lost his parents all over again. He woke up at some point, when the valley had gone silent for the night, the torches still flickering as a few people on the night watch kept an eye on the sky for any dragonkin. Wick leaned against the flimsy wall of their shelter, apparently also asleep.

"This plan better work," Archer mumbled to himself, and taking the comfort stick that Ongel had given him out of his pocket, he held it close to his chest and fell back into a fitful sleep again.

Decision-Making Isn't My Strong Suit

IN THE WEE HOURS of the morning, the ruckus began.

Archer jerked awake as a shout rang out, not far off. He yelled back, a half-asleep inarticulate *"baaaagh."* Darkness still shrouded the camp, and the hour was much too early for this kind of nonsense.

Then he heard what they were shouting.

"They're here!"

Archer bolted upright on the bare ground. Though a part of him didn't want to see, he looked up at the sky.

Near the mountain peaks, the sky glowed orange.

This is it.

Leaning over, Archer gave Wick a shove. Wick jolted awake. Before Wick got a chance to speak, Archer hissed, "They're here, now. Get ready."

Wick's eyes focused with alarming speed. He must not have been fully asleep, after all. "It's not morning,"

Wick whispered in confusion. "They weren't supposed to come until the morning."

"Morning doesn't mean daybreak." Archer hunted around on the ground, and finally his fingers found the shaft of the strange spear-club weapon the nixie boy had given him. "They're trying to catch us off guard. Hey. Take this." He snatched up the mace that lay at his feet and thrust it into Wick's hands. They had talked about getting Wick a mace, and Archer had looked forward to the chance to hand him one since. Up until now, it had seemed so funny.

Now that it was happening, though, it didn't feel funny at all.

Archer moved as close to the open side of their shelter as he dared, hunching over because of the low ceiling. Where were the dragonkin?

Something huge hit the ground in front of him with enough weight to shake the walls of their shelter. A tail lashed not twenty feet away. Teeth glinted in the pale light of the moon. Several more impacts shook the ground simultaneously as more dragonkin touched down.

The ground. The ground was shaking like an earthquake. The plants were already long dead. The flowers had all crumbled. The trees had turned grey with ash.

Just like he'd known they would, back in the beginning.

"No time like the present to move," Archer muttered, and dove out of their hiding place.

Archer used all of his body weight to swing his weapon above his head. It cracked the nearest dragonkin in the side of the skull. The dragonkin spun toward him, and Archer hollered, "Come at me!"

It tried to dart at him, and Archer swung again. The club end struck the dragonkin once more, between the eyes this time, and it fell and couldn't get up.

For a moment, Archer stood still and scanned the valley.

Despite the suddenness of the attack, the valley seemed to be keeping up. The nixies at the entrance to the cavern fended off two dragonkin from opposite sides. A few arrows darted through the air from the archers in the hills. Several dragonkin snaked toward the cavern, and a group of manghar dropped out of the black skies to take them down.

Finally, Archer saw what he had been watching for. A knot of shadows broke free from what remained of the Great Hall and raced toward the Heather Stone cavern. Nixies guarded the flank, bristling with weapons. The manghar flew so low over them that their wings nearly brushed the heads of the others. The knot of them looked almost like a single creature, like a centipede with dozens of limbs. In their midst, barely visible through the muscles of the warriors, was the shape of a large black centaur. Archer caught a glimpse of him, his streaming hair and tail reflecting the light of the torches.

Archer didn't spot it, but he knew that the strap of a worn leather bag wrapped around Ongel's shoulders, carrying the Heather Stones in its impossible depths.

The dragonkin spotted the movement immediately, and a half dozen lizards dove toward them. The dragonkin on the ground darted at the warriors racing toward the cavern.

Time to move.

"Come on!" Archer bellowed, and snatching up the nearest torch with his free hand, he charged toward the chaos. The nearest dragonkin didn't even get a chance to spot him before he jabbed the torch straight into its ear.

Ongel's group were nearly to the cavern now, the manghar guards over them knocking back attacking dragonkin as they went.

More of the Scorch descended on the valley every second. Wings filled the air, and flames raged in every part of the valley, streaming black smoke and casting flickering shadows across the ground.

Something huge jumped at Archer from the left, and before he had time to react, Wick smashed into the dragonkin with both his mace and his body in the same tackle. The dragonkin fell. It shook itself and leaped off the ground again, flying for a different part of the valley.

"Thanks." Archer strained to see Ongel. A centaur's shape disappeared through the entrance of the Heather Stone cavern, and the manghar soared in behind him. "He made it in. No, wait!"

The horde of dragonkin shot toward the entrance to the cavern, faster than anyone could catch up.

No.

Archer raced toward the cavern, his feet burning from the heat of the ground. In the general direction of the cavern, he yelled, "Lower it! Lower it! *Lower it!*"

Someone heard. A lattice of metal bars, shoddily fused together the night before and wrapped in oiled ropes, dropped upright from above the cavern's entryway.

The lower spines of the lattice buried themselves in the ground. As the dragonkin drew closer, Twill, stationed above the entrance to the cavern, dropped a lit torch.

The ropes wrapping the lattice caught and blazed.

The dragonkin pulled back with shrieks of fury. Just as Archer had suspected, they wouldn't try to pry away the lattice as long as it was on fire.

Maybe it wouldn't last for long, but maybe it would buy Ongel enough time that he could cast the spell. And if it didn't, Greg knew what to do.

Wick shot Archer a look of relief and pride. "See! He made it, thanks to your ideas."

Archer laughed nervously. "Don't thank me until it works. We still have to keep all these things at bay until Ongel casts the spell."

Wick hefted his mace over his shoulder. "Then let's go."

Wick and Archer raced across the valley, weapons in hand, to defend the cavern's entrance. From all parts of the valley, the others closed in as well. The manghar roared as they grabbed any dragonkin within reach. The nixies swung their torches in wide arcs. The sight of it filled Archer with a grim gratification. Even if everyone else was driven by loyalty to Aro or whatever other people tended to fight for, Archer didn't care. Either way, Ongel would stay safe.

Archer threw himself forward with a mighty battle cry and latched onto the hindquarters of a dragon getting too close to the cavern. It spun around, trying to latch onto him with its teeth, but Archer hung on. He clubbed at its spine with the sharp end of his weapon, trying to do some damage. Finally, with one hard *thwack,* he caught purchase between the bones, and the dragonkin screeched. Throwing Archer off, the dragonkin reeled away, writhing and twisting in pain.

"I sure hope it hurts," Archer spat, and took a few running steps back to the knot of other fighters gathering at the burning lattice before something could decide to pick him off. Compared to the blazing dragonkin that swooped through the air, there seemed to be a distinct disadvantage to fighting on foot. Archer felt like a rubber duck floating in a festival pond, with only a matter of time before something snatched him up.

Wings sure would help right now.

Just as he thought that, something with feathers swooped over his head. Fowl dove toward one of the dragonkin, fists clenched, yelling bloody murder. Archer always managed to forget that Fowl had fight in him just like their father had, as Archer still did. Fowl just hid it away behind his unwavering indifference.

Fowl rammed himself into the face of a dragonkin just as it reared to spew fire, and it was then that Archer spotted another dragonkin on the ground, headed directly for them.

As everyone bunched together to fend it off, movement to his right caught Archer's eye. He glanced that way and saw a smaller dragonkin, no bigger than a pig, snatch one of their fair folk defenders and skitter backwards, dragging the screaming fair folk with it.

"I don't think so." Archer dashed after it, his heavy weapon gripped in his fist. For a moment, he thought he had lost track of it. The smoke and dancing shadows played tricks with his eyes, and he squinted blearily, watching for the dragonkin that had stolen their fair folk. Then he glimpsed it through the smoke, dragging the fair folk off toward the mountains somewhere. The fair folk whacked at its snout with the sword he carried, but to no avail.

Archer raced toward the dragonkin and leaped onto its back, clubbing it over the head with the blunt end of his weapon. The dragon dropped its victim and rolled, trying to throw Archer off, but he clung to it like an angry burr. They rolled together across the ground in something of a tussle, and all the while Archer kept his grip, wincing every time a burnt stalk jabbed into his back or arms. Eventually, he managed to move his grip higher on the dragonkin's neck and pinned its head down so he could hit it several more times. It collapsed to the ground, disoriented and probably concussed.

Archer stumbled away from the dragonkin, his arms and legs stinging from the sharp grass and palms throbbing from touching hot dragonkin skin. One of his legs splashed into something wet, and he realized he had ended up at the edge of the lake. Next to his ankle were the open jaws of a dragonkin.

With a squeak of alarm, Archer lurched back a few steps, only to notice that the dragonkin wasn't moving. The water lapped and steamed around its head, leaving only the nostrils and eye sockets above the water. The slivers of grey-blue eyes peeking from under the eyelids were fastened on Archer. Several deep gashes in its neck and ribs leaked ribbons of blood into the lake, staining the water orangey-rose. Since it hadn't already grabbed hold of

Archer's leg, Archer wondered if it didn't have the strength to move, or if it was planning something else for him. On one of its nearer wing claws, Archer spotted something faintly glinting.

Despite knowing that he should run, despite knowing how near he probably stood to Twill's hidden explosives, curiosity managed to get the better of him. Glancing around to make sure nothing else was sneaking up on him, Archer edged closer. The thing wrapped around the dragonkin's claw was a string of beads, molded from clay and polished as brightly as the artist could manage. The beads ranged severely in shape and size, and the knots separating them varied from tiny and tight to huge and knobby. It looked like the handiwork of a blind man. Wick's voice in the back of Archer's mind told him that perhaps the dragonkin were just bad at the arts, had he thought of that?

Why, no, Wick, I hadn't. Thank you very much.

The dragonkin still didn't move as Archer studied the bracelet. Archer glanced back at the dragonkin's face. It was still watching him. Come to think of it, its eyes looked familiar: a sharp grey-blue in color, keen and perceptive.

Like Gint's had been.

Hadn't Gint mentioned a sibling? Someone who had sided with the radicals. A sister, maybe?

Gint had been worried that his sister would join the fight.

The dragonkin's eyes, still fastened on Archer, had a sad look to them. Resigned. It appeared to be waiting out its demise.

Then something behind Archer screeched. He jumped and scrambled to the side as a different small dragonkin dashed into the water, splashing water as it ran to the adult. The little dragonkin's wings were too small for the rest of its body, Archer noticed with confusion. They couldn't have been longer than his forearm. How could it fly with wings like those? And its head was nearly the same size as its body. Why was it so small and disproportionate?

Oh.

As the smaller dragonkin tentatively stuck out its neck to sniff the wounds of the larger dragonkin, Archer realized what an idiot he was. Its wings and head were out of proportion because it wasn't fully grown. The smaller dragonkin was a child. Wick would have noticed it in an instant. Fowl would have known from the beginning. Unlike either of them, Archer remained clueless.

The smaller dragonkin made quiet cooing sounds, rubbing its face against the larger dragonkin's cheek. The mother never took her eyes off Archer, like she was waiting for him to make even a single wrong move.

It had to be Gint's sister. And she had brought her baby with her.

The bracelet with the badly made beads had to be something the baby had made, that the parent wore for luck, or out of love. Archer had never been a parent, and he didn't comprehend their interest in keeping badly made presents, but that was what parents did. Before the house had burned, Archer's mother had stored every doodle and figurine from her boys in a box in her bedroom. Archer had never understood why she kept them.

The dragonkin let out a long and painful sigh, hitching at the end like the pain had increased. The muscles along her sides twitched and contracted, and more blood poured from the slices on her throat.

The mother dragonkin was dying.

Another dying dragonkin. By the same lake.

Archer's stomach cramped. He started to turn away, because the parent dragonkin could never be at peace while protecting its baby from him, but then something else caught his eye.

The baby dragonkin seemed more comfortable in the water. Despite its distress, the baby's relief was clear as it curled up at the side of its parent, tucking most of its body into the water. But even as it did so, its wings splayed into the open air, just in time for a ball of flame to erupt no more than a dozen yards from the lake. A wave of heat and sparks blew across the surface of the water, and the flames flared up just in time for Archer to spot something happening to the tiny wings.

The baby dragonkin let out a smothered squeak as a new hole stretched wide across the flat of its wing.

Gint's voice came to memory immediately.

Our children's wings are burning.

A ripple of goosebumps ran across the back of Archer's arms.

The parent dragonkin's eyes began to slip shut. "This won't be the end," she rasped faintly. Her voice was husky, warm. She sounded like anyone's mother. "For our children, we'll keep coming back until we eradicate you or you give us your stones. It doesn't matter what it costs us. You'll never win."

Archer hesitated. Who knew if this dragonkin was still dangerous? Then he shook himself. Even if she was still a threat, when had he ever shied away from danger? Especially when it came to dragonkin?

Archer crouched down beside the dragonkin's head. "Do you know Gint?" he asked quietly. A quick glance around proved that they were still shrouded in smoke, and no one had even spotted them yet.

For a few moments more, at least, the lake wouldn't explode.

The mother didn't answer him, but her sides still moved with her breath. The baby dragon looked at Archer with large eyes.

"I knew Gint while he was still alive," Archer went on. *Obviously while he was still alive, stupid!*

Just keep going.

As the water soaked into the legs of Archer's pants, he went on. "He said he had a sister in the Scorch army. He was worried about her. Are you his sister?"

The mother's voice came out as a struggling whisper. "Gint. My beloved, traitorous brother."

Archer's temper threatened to flare. After her brother was murdered by her own people just a day ago, she still talked about him like that? After everything that Gint had done for her and for her babies?

"He wasn't a traitor," Archer said, his voice tight. "He was doing everything he could to save your people because he knew you'd—" He paused as the statement really sunk in. "He knew you'd never stop."

In that moment, the nature of the fight shifted in Archer's mind.

He would have so willingly given up a thousand things just to keep Ongel from harm, Ongel who wasn't even his blood. Ongel who was almost like the father Archer would have wanted. Archer knew nothing of parenthood, but he knew parents protected their children, no matter what it cost them. For Ongel, Archer would sacrifice the entire valley. How much more would a parent do?

As smoke billowed between them, bringing with it a burning sensation in his throat and eyes, Archer realized that Aro had never had a chance. Not like this.

And so Archer's decision was swayed.

The mother dragonkin opened her eyes and looked directly at Archer, almost through him, and spoke in a quiet, dangerous voice, like a threat. "Don't hurt my baby."

Hefting his weapon in his hand, Archer made possibly the stupidest decision of his life. Turning to the mother dragonkin, he told her, with certainty, "I'll do you one better. Come on, baby!" He wrapped his arms around the body of the baby dragonkin and scooped it out of the water. It screeched and squirmed, but Archer hoisted it out of the water. "Sorry, sorry, but I can't leave you here, this place is rigged to blow. I'm not kidnapping your baby, by the way, I'm just—" Archer stopped short.

The mother dragonkin had stopped moving.

Archer breathed deeply, and his grip tightened on the baby dragonkin. His heartbeat stabbed at his chest, but he didn't have time to think about how much her body looked like Gint's. He didn't have time to think about anything other than what he had to do next.

"Let's go, baby." He raced back through the smoke, dodging debris and fire, and deposited the baby under the nearest rock. For a second, he shook out his burning palms, hissing and blowing on the raw skin. Then he addressed the baby. "I've got to go, so you have to stay here." It looked up at him with fearful eyes. Did it understand? Archer repeated himself. "I can't check on you. So, stay *right here.*"

Then he raced back toward the entrance to the Heather Stone cavern. One dragonkin overhead snapped at him, but Archer ducked, covering his head, and kept running. The grass was so *hot*. Never before had he genuinely wished for shoes.

Wick stood with the others at the portcullis with his mace gripped in both hands. Archer raced to him and grabbed his arm. "Wick!"

Wick jumped and half-swung the mace, but in such close quarters, Archer easily caught the handle of the weapon in time to stop it.

"Archer," Wick gasped. "Don't do that to me."

"Wick, listen," Archer said, in a voice low enough that the others wouldn't hear. "I'm about to make a really stupid decision, and you're going to let me."

Wick turned to him, his eyes face lit sharply in the orange light. "Why am I going to let you?"

"Because if I don't do this, the lot of us will never make it." Archer panted for a moment, floundering for the right words. Why could he never have the right words? "Think about it, Wick. Remember what Gint said? They're desperate for their land to be fixed, and without the Heather Stones, their children's wings are going to keep burning. They're at the end of their rope, and they're desperate. It doesn't matter what we do. They'll just keep coming back until they get what they need to save their children."

"Archer, they're burning everything in sight. They're trying to kill us."

"I know. But it's not just about them. It's about us, too," Archer said. "I have to make sure they stay gone for good. I don't like it, but if it's for you, and for Fowl, and for Ongel, and for Annalise, and. . . Forget it, I guess it's for everyone. I'll do whatever it takes to keep us safe."

Wick stared at Archer, long and hard. In the dim light the gold of his eyes lit up brighter than usual, like a cat's. Finally he wet his lips and nodded hard. "All right, then, all right. If you believe it, I believe you. What do you need?"

This was the tricky part. Archer braced himself. "I need to give them the Heather Stones."

Rather than overreacting or protesting, Wick just sighed heavily. "Your plans are never straightforward, are they?" He shook his head. "Well, how am I incriminating myself this time?"

"Don't worry, you don't have to be involved. I think I can convince Ongel to believe me." Archer glanced up at the sky, where countless members of the Scorch circled between the churning fire and the wheeling shapes of manghar and seraphs.

Oh, no.

Fowl.

Archer swallowed the sour taste in his mouth. "I need you to do something else for me. Wick?"

"What is it?"

Archer turned back to Wick. His shoulders felt very, very heavy. "You can't let Fowl learn about this, or he'll never let me go."

Wick nodded once again. "He won't find out."

"He'll be furious that you kept him from knowing, so watch out. He can be really something when he's angry."

Wick cracked a strained smile. "I know; I've seen it. It's a lot like you."

Archer laughed, feeling a fluttering emptiness in his chest, just like when he had first spoken to Gint. It was empty, horrible fear. He was afraid.

"Wick," he said before he could stop himself, "I know I haven't known you long, and I haven't been very good to you, but you've been a better and truer friend to me than anyone I've ever known." He took a breath, trying to steady the racing of his heartbeat. "Thanks for that."

Wick's eyes fastened on Archer's face, and his caterpillar eyebrows furrowed, now afraid himself. "Don't say that. It sounds like you're saying goodbye." Wick's voice tightened in a way that Archer had never heard before. Wick caught Archer's hand and grasped it tightly, so tightly that it hurt. Archer clung to the grounding force, even as he thought his hand might snap.

"Don't treat this like any kind of goodbye." Wick swallowed and steeled his brow, but his voice still trembled. "Archer, I *will* see you again."

Archer wanted to promise, to swear to his good—no, his *best* friend—that everything would be all right. But he couldn't lie right now. "I hope so." Then he snatched his hand away and pushed through the crowd of defenders around the entrance to the cavern. They recognized him and let him through. The gap between the burning metal bars and the lip of the cavern was just barely wide enough to let Archer slip through. Free at last, Archer raced down the pathway with all the energy he had left in his body.

He had to do this or nothing would go right ever again. Or this would be the end.

No matter what the cost was, he would pay it. Aro, and all the people in it, had to go on. Even if it meant something else wouldn't.

Fools Don't Make Heroes and Heroes Aren't Fools

FOR NOW, there were no dragonkin in the cavern. Archer knew it was only a matter of time before one broke the line at the entrance or found their way through from above. The cavern was empty, but not quiet, as he raced down the stone walkway. His footsteps pattered, and the sounds of the fighting echoed through the cavern from the outside. But here, there was no flickering fire light, only darkness and the dim, still light of the Heather Stone chamber ahead.

He couldn't spot any guards surrounding the chamber. Had that really been *all* the bodyguards, stationed back there by the makeshift portcullis?

Ongel might have already placed the stones.

"Ongel!" Archer shouted.

Something moved in the chamber, like someone coming to attention. As Archer skidded to a stop in the entryway, Ongel appeared on the other side. Archer's fear of the coming conversation swallowed any relief he could have felt at seeing Ongel. What would Ongel say when Archer told him what they had to do?

"What's wrong?" Ongel's brow furrowed with concern. In one hand he held what appeared to be the last of the Heather Stones, the manghar piece.

Archer breathed deeply, trying to regain his breath. The spear point of his weapon dug into the floor as he leaned on it. "Ongel, we need to change our plan."

"What's gone wrong?"

"Nothing, nothing." Archer's words were a jumble in his brain. He was already explaining himself so badly. And time was running out. "Ongel, you've got to realize that this will never work. Even if we do set up a system to keep the dragonkin away after the barrier goes up, it won't matter. They won't give up. They're running out of patience, and whether we admit it or not, we're running out of options."

"Archer," Ongel said in a guarded tone, "is this because your friend Gint—"

"Yes, because he said their wings are burning. But it's more than that. We need to survive more than we need these stones. And if Gint's right, the dragonkin need the stones or they're going to eventually kill us all for them. They've got us beat on fire power. We're playing a long game right now, but pretty soon, we're going to lose."

Ongel's face became grave. "What are you suggesting we do?"

His tone was calm, too calm. Not a question, but a test.

"What should have happened decades before either of us were born." Archer sucked in a deep breath to steady himself. "I want to give them back the Heather Stones, and I'm willing to do it myself."

Ongel's brow furrowed.

He disagrees.

Archer began to babble. "Look, I know all I've done since day one is screw everything up, and nobody has any good reason to trust me with this, but believe me, all I'm trying to do is keep everyone safe. Please, I just—"

Ongel cut off everything Archer was trying to say by placing a heavy hand on his shoulder.

Archer looked up at Ongel's eyes for the first time in several minutes. They were green, sagging at the corners, and full, *overflowing* with such warmth.

"My dear boy," Ongel said softly. "In all this time, you have never once given me any reason to disbelieve you."

"Right." Archer laughed bitterly. "I lie, and I take things, and I don't do anything I'm supposed to. I've never given anyone any reason to believe in me."

"You were right about the dragonkin long before Wick convinced the rest of us to believe you." The corners of Ongel's eyes crinkled as he smiled gently. "I don't know how you do it, but you always know exactly what we need to do. Tell me your plan so that I can help you get the stones to the dragonkin."

Relief flooded Archer's head. "I need to get Nin's attention first. I'm going to offer him the stones in exchange for a meeting with their queen later down the road. If what Gint told me is true, the queen can be reasoned with. We might be able to make new alliances with her if she'll listen to us."

Ongel and Archer hurried to collect the stones from their stands, and Archer shoved them into the unfillable bag. Inside the bag, Sasha snorted faintly, and Archer remembered with a jolt that his horse hadn't left the bag in days. Rushing to the entrance of the chamber, Archer tipped the bag and released Sasha onto the walkway in a bundle of nerves and hooves. The horse looked more than a little disgruntled and whinnied deafeningly into Archer's face.

"I'm sorry, girl. I'm sorry." Archer gave her forelock a quick rub with his knuckles and kissed her on the nose. "Ongel, take care of my horse, would you?"

"Of course." Ongel leaned past Archer and took Sasha's reins in his hand. With his other hand, he deposited the manghar Heather Stone into Archer's palm. "What will you do if the dragonkin won't let us speak to their queen?"

"Don't worry, I have a backup plan." Archer released Sasha's reins and waved Ongel out of the chamber. "You just find somewhere safe to hide or something. I'll take care of this."

Ongel gave Archer a quick nod. "Take care of yourself."

"Doing my best," Archer murmured as the sharp footsteps of Ongel and Sasha faded away into the cavern. The sound of them vanished behind the distant clangs and shouts of the fight outside.

Archer rolled his neck and cracked his knuckles. The time had come for the next part of his plan, one that he couldn't ask permission for. He heaved his weapon up over his head. Then, with the collective force of every muscle in his body, he smashed the weapon down onto the Heather Stone floor.

The floor shattered. Chips of green skittered out the doorway of the chamber. The larger pieces collapsed and slid under one another. Archer fought to keep his balance as the stone moved his feet in opposite directions.

He grabbed the nearest shard of the newly shattered rock and stuffed it into one of his pockets. The sharp edges threatened to cut through the lining of his pocket and into his leg.

If Wick and the others were smart—and they were—they would realize that shattering the Heather Stone left them more than enough pieces to protect Aro if Archer's plan went south.

Archer planted a foot in the doorway and climbed out of the pit of Heather Stones. Outside the chamber, he looked for the best way to climb the cavern wall. Leaving through the cavern's entrance wouldn't do any good. He needed to be where Nin could find him easily.

Hadn't Wick said something about the dragonkin climbing down into the chamber from somewhere? At last, he spotted a section of wall with enough handholds to climb up.

He glanced back once more, hoping to catch a glimpse of Ongel somewhere in the cavern. Instead, all he saw were rocks and the faint flicker or red light far off near the entrance.

"All right, let's go." Archer slung the unfillable bag behind his back and got a good grip on the wall.

Clambering up the outside of the Heather Stone chamber, he spotted a crevice in the ceiling through which he could glimpse a tiny leak of light. He shoved his head and shoulders into the crack and squirmed his way inside the mountain.

The crack was a tight squeeze, but he could just scrape his shoulders and wings through the shaft. Archer inched his way up through the crack. The new Heather Stone in his pocket nearly slipped free, but he managed to catch it before it could fall and stuffed it down his shirt instead.

Still crawling, he murmured to himself. "It was always going to be me in the end, wasn't it?"

A jutting piece of rock cut into his shoulder, but Archer pressed against it and used it to push himself further up the hole. As he climbed, his mind kept swirling.

Bracing himself against the rock, Archer paused for a breath. "I bet I knew that trying to fix the bag would change things." His footing nearly slipped, and he readjusted. "But I didn't want to think about that, did I?"

A small chink of orange light glowed somewhere above him. The way out.

This is it. This is where I find out what Caihu saw.

Archer swallowed hard.

How things had changed since he had taken the fair folk stone, since he had met Wick. The nature of the adventure had changed altogether. This, going after the Scorch and putting himself in danger, not for himself, not to prove anything, but for the sake of people he *cared* about. . . It felt different. It felt darker, realer.

In the slit of space in the belly of the mountain, with ash on his face and smoke in his lungs, Archer tasted something bitter in his mouth and felt an ache in his wing and in his chest. And he knew.

"I was never looking for danger, was I?" He made a sound that could have been a laugh, or could have been something else, something born from the deep ache currently burrowing into his chest. "I was looking for someone to care that I was *in* danger."

But he had that now, didn't he? Wick, who hunted him down, Fowl, who kept him warm in a fever, Twill, who kept him looking toward hope and aid, Leroy— *Leroy!*—who abandoned what should have been his duty to save Archer from the trap of his own mind. They were many. They were everywhere.

Didn't think it through, though, did I? I didn't realize I'd have to care about them, too.

I really didn't think I'd be so scared to leave them.

Then the explosion shook the mountain. Ash poured down on Archer's shoulders; the walls of his little crevice shivered.

They did it. They blew up the entrance.

The walls of his crevice shuddered some more, but didn't collapse in on themselves. Archer sucked in a deep breath.

No other way out now.

Archer felt the surface getting closer before he saw it. The air in the shaft grew much hotter, hot enough in the tight space that sweat sprang up on his face immediately. A bit of ash fell down the shaft and skittered past him to the bottom, bringing with it the strong scent of smoke.

Hot sweat slipped down the side of Archer's face. "Come on," he muttered to himself. "Get going."

Archer reached up and felt for the edge of the hole. There it was, covered in burned grass and hot as Hades. Gripping an edge with each hand, dead grass cracking under his fingertips, he hauled himself up and out of the shaft. He found himself sitting under an outcropping of rock somewhere on the top of the mountain. Getting on his hands and knees, he shimmied out from under the rocky overhang and got to his feet.

The air shimmered, hotter than any he had ever felt. Everything around him was black with soot or blazing with fire, the shapes of the terrain all but lost under the flames. Dragonkin swooped in every direction, even low over his head, making him duck down, but so far, none of them seemed to have noticed him. Good.

Archer clutched the strap of his bag and searched the sky for General Nin.

◇

DOWN BELOW, Wick coughed and clung to his mace. He squinted through the rolling clouds of dust and ash raised by the explosions. The Scorch looked like little more than hazy shadows in the sky.

Wick tried to take comfort in knowing that even if he couldn't spot Archer himself, the Scorch would. And while that in itself was not a comforting thought, the Scorch could help him spot Archer.

He focused his smarting eyes on the shadows of the dragonkin milling in the sky above, but as of yet, Wick couldn't spot any change in their behavior.

He also watched the sky for Fowl. He had promised Archer that Fowl wouldn't find out, and if Fowl spotted Archer too early, he would panic. Wick double-checked the sky. Leroy was well within sight. If necessary, Wick could send him to tackle Fowl at a moment's notice.

As Wick thought all this, a bright green glow flashed through the smog at the top of the mountain, and the shape of the dragonkin swarm in the sky changed. They all started moving toward the mountain, swirling and churning where they gathered like some terrible storm.

Wick hoped Fowler hadn't seen the change.

Something touched down beside him.

"How much longer can it possibly take to cast the spell?" Fowl asked, watching the sky himself. He didn't seem to have noticed the change now that the green glow had faded. "It seems like we've been waiting a long time."

The flash of green was the only indicator Wick needed. Archer was putting his plan into motion. "It shouldn't be much longer. We just have to keep holding out."

◇

THERE.

The silhouette of a huge dragonkin soared high above Archer's head, just a hazy outline in the smoke.

General Nin.

A quick glance around found him a large fallen tree trunk, resting across the rocks almost like a ramp. From there, even a blind man couldn't miss him. Archer scrambled up onto the carcass of the tree and held the unfillable bag full of Heather Stones up over his head with both hands. "Nin!" he bellowed. "I have what you want!"

As if to help Archer's cause, the Heather Stones glowed, shining glowing green even through the designs of the bag and shooting beams of grassy green from every open slit. Immediately the heads of all the dragonkin in the sky turned toward him. Their swirling, churning swarm in the sky shifted, moving toward Archer slowly, steadily, like they were one great beast in the sky. Archer clutched the bag to his stomach as the swarm settled above him. Wind buffeted the mountain top. It tore at Archer's clothes and blew his meticulously kept hair in every direction. His bangs flapped at his forehead.

The massive shape of General Nin descended from the cloud of dragonkin and plowed into the ground not twenty yards from where Archer stood. The tree Archer stood on shook with the impact.

Archer tightened his grip on the branches and straightened his spine. From his elevated position, Archer stood nearly at eye level with the general. General Nin slithered closer, his eyes fastened on Archer. With their faces now only a stone's throw apart, Archer became acutely aware that the general's jaws alone were the size of Archer's whole body. He didn't remember Nin being quite so big.

A cloud of smoke blew past Nin's face, temporarily reducing the dragon to a pair of green eyes floating in the dark. In that moment, Archer realized why he recognized the keen, confident gaze. The same gaze had watched him from the opposite end of the breakfast table all his life. It had challenged him from the center of every crowd and fastened onto him the moment he entered his native city.

Nin's gaze was the same as his father's.

All at once, memories of his father's letters—ones that he had tried to banish to a cobwebbed mental cupboard forever—resurfaced with a speed that was almost blinding.

He may be a foolhardy boy and an enigma, but Archer is still my son, and I find that he burns quite bright.

It sounded like a promise.

Archer's mouth gathered into a hard line. "You might have been right; actually, you might have been right a lot," he muttered as the smoke began to clear once more and Nin leered ever closer. "But if I've got anything to do with it, *I'm not going to burn.*"

"You choose to surrender the stones after all," General Nin said, his voice taking on a self-satisfied tone as his paint-slathered eyes narrowed.

"Wrong. There's no surrendering happening here." The wind whipping around Archer was now so hot that it was painful to keep his eyes open, but he wasn't about to close his eyes while he was surrounded by the Scorch. Archer changed his stance to steadier footing.

He is wild enough to look death in the eye and demand a deal.

"Nin—"

— Death—

"—I'm here to make a deal."

Nin's gaze never changed. "We're past deals."

"You might want this one." Archer's heart beat faster. He tried to push down the fear as he held up the unfillable bag. "You want the stones. I'm going to give them to you.

But in exchange, I want to meet with your queen."

Nin's head did that uncanny tilt, just a few degrees too far for comfort. "Why would you want to do that?"

"We've been fighting over these stones for centuries. If Gint was right, you're here because you're burning and you're scared. But killing us is stupid. And unwarranted. So, if I'm going to believe you and let you have these stones, I want proof that the destruction in your land is real. Then I want to talk to your queen and get a new alliance put in place, so that this never has to happen again." Archer held up the unfillable bag and shook it up and down. The stones inside, wrapped in chunks of thin fabric, clinked musically inside. "I've got them right here. I'm offering you the stones, all yours forever, in exchange for one conversation with your queen. If she won't see me, you and I will never have to talk to each other again. That's the deal."

"Hmm." General Nin slowly lifted a wing claw and extended it, reaching for the unfillable bag.

Archer swung his arm behind his body, blocking the bag. "You don't get the stones until you agree."

Nin's claw crashed down just short of the log Archer stood on, shaking the ground again.

Archer struggled to get his footing back.

Smoke curled from Nin's scaly lips and his eyes burned as he said, "You know, I'm tempted to turn you to a cinder for how we've suffered. You don't have the slightest clue how many of us have died. Compared to our fallen, the death of one boy means nothing to me."

Archer forced a confident smile onto his lips. "I don't think you want to do that." Time for the great bluff.

Archer pointed down toward the mountain. "Fun fact, there's enough Heather Stone down there to throw the Scorch out of Aro and keep the lot of you out every day for the rest of time."

Nin's eyes gleamed. "They could never cast their spells fast enough to stop me from burning you."

"Yeah, I doubt it. That's why I brought this with me." Archer slipped a hand into his shirt and pulled out the freshly-shattered shard of the Heather Stone. One of the sharp corners bit into the web between his fingers. "We've learned a lot about these stones recently, so I know that I can do a lot of damage with just one. I'll take it when I go to see your queen, too. If I think for a second that you're going to pull something, I'll vaporize your precious Heather Stones and cast a shroud of smoke around Aro so thick that nothing can make it back in." He swallowed. "Including me."

"You could never cast a spell," Nin said carefully.

"Look, I may look like a faithless scoundrel, but out of everyone in this valley, I'm one of the two people who *can* cast spells with these rocks." *If I can work up an ounce of conviction on time.* Archer held Nin's eye fiercely. If he wavered for even an instant, Nin would know he was bluffing.

General Nin sat motionless for a long, agonizing moment. Then he spoke, quickly. "Very well."

Archer dug into the unfillable bag and drew out a fistful of Heather Stones. The little silk bags that held them wadded and tangled together. Archer quickly removed one from the bunch. Even through the thin silk, he could see a rose carved on the surface; the seraph stone.

The same stone that Archer's grandfather had safeguarded for so many years, that had changed Wick's mind for the better.

Archer held it up, gripped between his fingers. "You get this one after I've spoken to your queen." Archer cast the unfillable bag aside, and it fluttered away into the smoke.

He held out the remaining stones to General Nin.

In a smooth movement, the general reached out and took the cluster of little bags hanging from Archer's fist. The heat from his skin stung Archer's hand before the general pulled away. Studying the little bundle for just a moment, General Nin extended his claws and dangled the stones over the ledge beside them. One by one, the delicate silk bags burned in his grip, and the stones fell. As the stones dropped, other dragonkin swooped below to catch them. The multi-faceted manghar stone was the last to fall.

Archer watched it vanish.

General Nin's face drew ever nearer. "I still don't like you, seraph. I trust you no more than you trust us. If I suspect this is some sort of trap, I promise you that I'll burn you until nothing is left but ash on the wind."

From the look in Nin's eyes, Archer believed it.

The heat emitting from the general's face, the face so close to Archer's own, had increased to an almost unbearable temperature. Archer was finally forced to take a step backward to get away from the heat.

"But before we decide whether to destroy one another, first I must know." General Nin watched Archer's face closely as he spoke. "I've heard the stories about you:

the broken seraph who couldn't fly and instead chose to cause havoc in every corner of your country. They tell me you are no easy one to persuade. What did Gint say to convince you of our plight?"

Archer's eyes grew dry in the heat. He had to squint to see, his eyes smarting with every blink against the smoke. "He told me the truth: your children's wings were burning. He knew I couldn't stand kids losing their wings."

Nin's eyes flickered to Archer's single mangled wing. "I suppose you want your wings mended in exchange," General Nin said, sounding disinterested. "There's a chance, you know. The dragonkin are still better with the Heather Stone magic than your people are. There are those who might mend your bones so that you could fly again."

For a moment, Archer's heart pounded harder at the thought. He had never expected that anyone could work that kind of magic. Briefly, he reveled in the thought of seizing his own flight and finally getting to experience what all the other seraphs took for granted.

But then he returned to the moment, where he stood on a mountain top, burnt grass in his hair and soot ground into his face, eye to eye with a dragon, and countless nights of thinking took hold.

"No. Thanks, though."

The ridges of the general's brows rose. "No? You don't want to fly again?"

"It's not that. I'm not a big thinker like Wick is, but I've thought about this a lot. I had a lot of time." Archer shifted on his feet. The enormity of the dragonkin general made him feel so small. "I never really flew, y'know. I was born with weak bones. They wouldn't let me fly, and even when I said *forget them* and tried anyway, I didn't fly. I just fell." He looked up at the huge dragonkin. "But here's the thing. For one perfect moment, I was coasting, and I finally got to see what all the fuss was about. I understood. I fell in the end, but before I fell I got to wrestle just one moment of perfect flight out of my whole life."

The general looked interested. "Then why—"

"I'm getting there," Archer insisted. "Be patient. Flying was worth it, *so* worth it. But after I fell, I changed. I had to learn how to live with no wings, and no flying. It put me in a category where I wasn't a winged creature, but I wasn't a wingless one, either, and it meant that I had to live differently from anyone else in Aro. I got mocked for it and I got underestimated for it. Some of the winged people hate me for it, I swear they do. And I won't reverse any of that. Who I am now is because of the wings. Getting them back would be like erasing all that, like it never happened. But it did happen, and it mattered. It still matters. This is who I am." Archer lifted his fist with the glowing Heather Stone and pointed to Nin. "I won't let you take that from me."

Nin's eyes gleamed with a look Archer couldn't quite place. "You have a lot of fire in you, seraph boy. If you're lucky, it might even help you survive."

The general lifted his head and roared out an order in words Archer didn't understand. Then the swarm of dragonkin plunged toward them, and the fire closed in around Archer.

TWENTY-EIGHT

After the Fire

WICK HIKED RAPIDLY up the foothills on the far side of the valley, ducking to avoid the Scorch at intervals. Too much time had passed since he'd seen Archer. He needed a better view. At last, climbing a rock, he got a glimpse.

The sight made his stomach drop.

On the mountain top across the valley, a crumb of color clung to the trunk of a fallen tree. Only the fluttering white-grey of his wings and the glint of something green in his grasp distinguished Archer from the ash and smoke. The Scorch, wrapped in their fire and flames, swirled around the shape of Archer on the tree trunk, suddenly blocking him from view.

Wick's stomach dropped. He had only just caught a glimpse of Archer. Now, he couldn't see anything.

Fowl, who was supposed to be waiting by the cavern, lighted next to him and followed Wick's gaze. "What's happening up there? Why haven't they cast the spell yet?"

"I don't know," Wick lied, straining his eyes for any sign of Archer. Any moment now, something had to happen.

The funnel of dragonkin swirled tighter, and the entire army of the Scorch lifted off, leaving the valley the same dark grey color as the sky. A few dragonkin darted down to lift up their dead and carry them away.

Archer had succeeded.

The Scorch were leaving. The rush of triumph and relief surged through Wick's veins.

Then he saw it. In the knot of dragonkin, almost hidden in the flames, there appeared a flash of grey feathers, falling. The sight lasted for only the blink of an eye before the dragonkin snatched the feathers up again and darted off into the clouds quicker than Wick could think what to do.

Fowl's head swiveled quicker than a snake's to stare into Wick's face. "What was that? They carried someone away. I saw it. Who was it?"

The last tail disappeared into the smoggy sky, leaving the valley strangely silent. The Scorch had gone. And so had Archer.

A thunderous cheer went up from below.

"That was. . ." Wick swallowed, his head reeling. "That was Archer."

He glanced at Fowl and stared. A change came over Fowl's face so quickly it made Wick's blood run cold. Fowl's eyes emptied, and the rest of his face went not slack, but rather blank, relaxed but cold. Placid as the eyes of a shark in the sea.

"He put you up to this, didn't he?" Fowl asked.

"Archer's making you say that to scare me. It's a trick."

He's denying it. "It's not a trick," Wick said gently.

Fowl let his weapon down to the ground at their feet. "It is. But I'll forgive you if you tell me where to find him. It just isn't funny, not today."

Wick spoke more firmly. "Fowl, Archer didn't tell me to say anything."

"Admit you're lying," Fowler insisted, in a harder tone now. "Tell me it's a lie, right now. You're lying. Archer is off behind a rock somewhere laughing because he likes making a fool out of me. Tell me you're lying!" Fowl screamed.

"I can't," Wick said, his voice shaking. A prickle of chill ran up his spine and raced down the back of his arms. "I'm not lying. They took Archer."

Fowl's wings snapped open to take off, but Wick moved faster. He clamped his arms around Fowl's shoulders and held him tight, pinning both Fowl's arms and his wings to his body. He was physically stronger than Fowl—a comfortable life of wealth and literature had been no good for building Fowl's muscle—but Fowl writhed like a serpent, nearly worming his way out of Wick's grasp. Wick tightened his hold. Where was Leroy?

He searched the sky and spotted the familiar glint of . . . *some* manghar wearing armor.

"Leroy!" Wick bellowed.

Fowl's head whipped back, and lights exploded behind Wick's eyes. Wick's nose felt like it had lit on fire. Fowl squirmed all the harder, and finally lurched forward. Wick's feet jerked away from the rocks. The sky rolled by in a flash, and Wick slammed down onto his back. The air leaped out of his lungs.

Gasping for air, Wick rolled to the side, expecting a foot to the ribs or a fist to the face, but. . . nothing came. Fowl glared down at him with a burning fury, hair fallen in wild strands over his face, but try as he might, Leroy's firm grip would not let him free to strike again.

Wick pulled himself up to his knees and pressed the heel of his palm against his throbbing nose. "I'm sorry, Fowl, really."

"Why didn't you tell me?" Fowl demanded, now bent over Leroy's arms as he shouted. The necklace he'd dug out of the rubble in Tor swung wildly from his neck. "I could have stopped him! I could have protected him! You knew where he was going, and you didn't tell me!"

"I didn't tell you because he asked me not to. That's what he told me to do," Wick said. The throbbing of his nose had not stopped. He checked his palm for blood but found none. "He knew you would try to stop him."

"I would have," Fowl said, straightening his spine. Leroy's grip around him tightened. "And if I had, he would be here right now. Imagine that."

"What would you have me do?" Leroy asked Wick, indicating Fowl with a tilt of his head.

"We've got to lock him up for a few hours, at least," Wick said. Guilt twinged in his gut. "Otherwise, I'm afraid he'll try to follow the Scorch."

Something huge landed behind Wick, and he swung around. Behind him stood Crowned Head Theodore, covered in wounds and smelling of smoke. Blood oozed down his chest from a cut above his collarbone.

"I'm forming a party to pursue Archer," the king

announced, and Wick's stomach did another flip of panic. "If you want to come as well, perhaps two of my strongest—"

"You can't." Wick's own voice felt like it was betraying him. His hand dropped to his side. "We have to let them go."

Fowl's eyes widened. "You won't go after him at all?"

Wick forced certainty into his voice as he met Fowl's eye. "You see why we can't, don't you? They picked up and left peacefully, which means that Archer struck some kind of deal with them. He gave us a chance. If we chase after the Scorch, we ruin that chance." Wick swallowed painfully. "And we waste whatever he sacrificed to give it to us."

Fowl's gaze never wavered. "I think we all know what he sacrificed."

Wick turned to Crowned Head Theodore. "I can't stress how important it is that we don't give them a reason to come back. Tell your warriors. We can't risk going after the Scorch."

To Wick's surprise, the Crowned Head bowed his head. "I'll tell them."

The Crowned Head took off again, and Wick was left with Fowl, whose face full of teeth was suddenly much closer than Wick remembered.

Fowl made one final struggle and gained a step closer to Wick. His voice came out soft and sharp, like a knife hidden behind his back. "If we never speak to one another again, I want you to remember this. Archer was the last of my family, and you took him from me. You did that." He paused. "I wish I'd never met you. Have a miserable and long life. That's my last word."

"I am sorry, Fowl." Exhaustion weighed on Wick's brow as he turned to Leroy. "Lock him up in Eland's house, it's the grey one across the valley from us. They keep the key to the back bedroom on top of the doorframe."

"It will be done." Leroy spread his wings and lifted off without much struggle. Carrying Fowl like a log of wood, he coasted down to the valley.

With everyone gone, Wick's legs finally stopped holding him. He sat down on the ground, so hard it sent a jolt up his spine. Something slipped out of his hand and he realized he had never let go of his mace.

Archer was gone. And Wick had let him go.

No.

Once they knew Archer was dead, then they could mourn him. No sooner.

Wick shoved the fear down and got back to his feet.

"Wick!" Eland skidded to Wick's side. "Are you hurt?"

Wick took a deep, fortifying breath. "I'm fine. The Scorch is gone. We need to get with the mentors to figure out what to do next, and to count our casualties."

As he spoke, a stripe of red lit up across the mountains.

The sun was rising. They had survived to see a new day.

TWENTY-NINE

Crooked Wing

"NO! *NO!* I don't want to go *now*. Take me back!" Archer scrabbled at the claws that gripped his right arm, trying to pry them off. He lost his grip and swung wildly from the claw, his shoulder screaming from his own weight. The hot, hot grip of the dragonkin only dug in tighter.

"You're burning me up! *Let go!*" Archer screamed.

The claws released.

The relief of cool air on his burning arm washed away in panic at the fall.

The mounds of little hills and trees far below rushed closer.

Then something else caught his opposite arm. The back feet of another dragonkin. It swung him up and around, throwing him to a different dragonkin, which grabbed him by the back of the shirt, tearing his last good shirt. Archer slipped from its grasp, slamming back-to-spine against another dragonkin, which rolled to throw him free.

More screaming, more falling.

Another catch. This grip was firmer, hotter, but at least secure.

Archer's arms burned with the blinding hotness of the claws gripping his forearm. He didn't know if he should cry in relief or scream in pain.

His pounding heartbeat made its home in his throat. Grabbing the crook of his own arm to lessen the strain on it, he struggled to get breath and calm himself. The air surrounding them—freezing air—seemed to be getting thinner.

It's just to get to their country, Archer. Stay calm. Just put up with the—

AGONY

—for one flight.

"Hey. Hey!" he shouted toward the dragon's head. "How far is it? How long will it take to get there?"

The dragonkin didn't look at him. It gave no indication that it had even heard him. But since there was nothing else to hear but the whistling wind, he guessed that it was ignoring him.

The air only grew colder, and it became harder to breathe. It seemed ironic that while his lower body slowly went numb from the chill, all Archer could think about was how hot he was from the glowing underbelly of the dragonkin.

They tossed him back and forth many more times during the next hour. Archer's throat grew raw from screaming, but each time they dropped him, he couldn't help himself. The grey clouds gathered on every side made it impossible to tell how far they had flown. He could only see glowing lizards on every side, and in the distance, the biggest, meanest dragonkin of all, puffing out a ball of fire every few minutes. To indicate their direction? Archer could only guess.

No one came after them. No manghar tried to take them down.

Archer winced, realizing that no rescue was a good thing. If anything came after them, Nin would probably just kill them and then Archer.

Only later, much later, did Archer realize he had never bartered for the return journey. If their queen was kind or at least fair, she would probably send him back home. But if she was spiteful or bitter. . . anything could happen to him.

General Nin dipped his head and dove down through the clouds. The rest of the Scorch followed him, Archer swinging painfully from his arm as his dragonkin tilted and rushed down through the clouds.

The clouds cleared, and below them appeared the sea. Grey-blue waves crashed and threw foam.

They were already outside of Aro? The Scorch flew like lightning.

He frowned.

Then why—

The dragonkin dropped him. Archer plummeted, his raw vocal cords grating from the screaming. This time, no dragonkin immediately appeared to catch him. Did they plan to ditch him in the middle of the ocean?

Then something flashed below him, and he smacked into the broad span of a wing. The membrane bent under his weight, and a tilt of the wing sent him rolling and bumping down onto the lake of coals that was the dragon's back.

Once again fighting to control breaths that wanted to turn into desperate gasps, Archer forced himself onto scathing hands and knees. The wind ruffled through his feathers. "Hey," he said, wincing, "how much further is it?"

The dragonkin's head reared, and on the spot, the sheer size of the dragon registered to Archer's mind.

General Nin.

"Not far." The general's sharp eyes watched Archer over his shoulder. "Know this, you and your friend with the golden eyes were worthy opponents."

Archer hissed and blew on one stinging palm, then the other. Then he paused. "Okay. What are you saying?"

"I only want to congratulate you before we part ways," Nin said coolly. "It almost seems a shame."

Despite the heat, a chill ran down Archer's spine. He repeated, more insistently, "What are you saying, Nin?"

Nin turned his eyes forward again, and his face vanished from view. The sound of the waves rushed below, closer than before. "Farewell, broken thing."

Then his wings tilted, and in a lazy, slow barrel roll, he cast Archer off.

This time, no one caught him.

The sea rushed toward Archer's face. He plummeted for the span of two heartbeats, just long enough to tuck his limbs in, before he hit the waves.

Just long enough to think:

How many more times can I fall?

To his feet, which hit first, the water felt like a pit of

gravel, first rock-hard, then yielding. To his burned arms and legs, it was like a thousand ice-cold knives. To his sinuses, the water was like red-hot metal pouring into every crevice.

To his bad wing, it was hands of iron, wrenching the bow of his wing up and away from its rightful place.

PAIN.

The dark ocean swam in and out of darkness around him. The wing was agony, transformed into a thousand points of razor-sharp pain. If he moved, the agony would only grow.

But if he didn't, he would drown. His lungs already twitched, trying to force out water that didn't belong in them. But the glow of the surface was still far above him.

Fight or drown, Archer.

He stretched his arms toward the surface and swam.

His wing rippled with screaming pain, his lungs threatened to burst, his bruising legs wanted to give up, but the surface was so close.

Archer burst through the surface of the water. He gasped frigid air. Then he searched the sky.

He couldn't tell which way was back to Aro. He had no way of knowing which way it was to the land of the Scorch. The only way to keep from drowning was to swim for it, in whatever direction the Scorch had gone.

The last of the orange glow disappeared into the clouds to his right.

"That way it is," he muttered through gritted, chattering teeth.

He clawed through the waves after the dragonkin.

Within minutes, it was a battle against his own mind.

There would be no way to keep up with the Scorch if he were *running*. Swimming would be no quicker. And who knew how much further it could be to land?

But he couldn't give in to the alternative.

"Come on, Archer," he muttered to himself as his limbs flailed ever slower against the sea. "You can never beat Nin black and blue if you don't swim."

Can't talk to the queen, either. Can't keep Aro safe.

The only thing is to keep swimming.

His shoulders began to burn.

Archer threw out his arms to swim further, and his bad wing jostled. The muscles of his back seized around it, forcing a cry out of his mouth. Every kick of his legs and stroke of his arms only made it worse.

I can't swim.

I'm going to drown.

Even as he struggled against it, the water began to pull him down.

Something large hit the water beside him, throwing water into his face. Archer spluttered and scanned the dark water. Where had it gone?

Then a moving object, perhaps even the same object, struck him from below. The blow to his injured wing shot him through with blinding pain.

And the world went dark.

Warmth. Heat, but not comfort. Whatever Archer lay on was hard, not comfortable at all. What sort of bed had he fallen asleep on?

And his wing throbbed. What had he done to it?

Something clamped around his wing, too tight, too

painful.

Let go!

Archer thrashed, but he moved too late.

The grip on his wing tightened and *wrenched.* Something in his wing made a horrible *pop* that he felt in every rib.

Relief rushed through him like wind as he realized that he could move without agonizing pain to his wing. Then, crowding in behind the relief, was more pain, this one different. Where the first pain had been awful, terrorizing agony of something being wrong, so horribly wrong. This new pain was like the largest ache of a sore muscle, multiplied triple. The wing hurt, oh it *hurt,* but he no longer needed to scream.

Darkness once again became his friend.

Some time later, a prodding. Pain spiked through the sore wing and flamed in the marks of his burns.

The prodding came again.

"You have to get up," a nasal voice said with annoyance. "Or you can stay injured for longer."

The ground this time was softer than the last time. Archer tried to push against it and it shifted under his hands. He finally remembered to open his eyes, and wincing, he saw that the shifting ground was sand.

A beach?

Archer cast his eyes up. Not a dozen paces away, a line of fringy tropical trees and thick vines swayed in the breeze. He was on some sort of island. Certainly far from Aro.

"Sit *up,*" the voice repeated, still irritated, as though the speaker thought it was more annoying to wake someone up than to be the one woken.

Archer looked back, over the joint of a wing that looked far too ordinary to be causing so much pain, and spotted a glowing lizard's face. A face mere inches away.

Archer scrambled away, but his smarting limbs gave out. He collapsed face-first into the sand.

"Stop running. You're being very rude," the dragonkin said, and the sand hissed as something slid closer to Archer. "If there was something to be afraid of, it would have happened days ago, while you were still unconscious."

The ache, the ache. Archer rolled onto his side and wrapped his hand around the joint of his wing. The heat of his burnt palm warmed his injury, but scarcely did anything to ease the pain in his muscles. "Thanks, I think?"

The dragonkin sat up and shrugged his shoulders. "You really shouldn't thank me. I didn't even know if I put it back in the right socket; your shoulders are very different from mine."

In a flash, Archer remembered: *the stones.*

He pulled himself upright and began to dig through his pockets. His left came up empty.

I lost them.

Then his right hand found something firm in the very bottom of his pocket. Slowly, he pulled it free.

A carved rose glinted in the sunlight.

He still had the seraph stone.

Archer glanced up at the dragonkin, and though it was only a bit taller than he was, the flare of fire in its throat suddenly seemed much more threatening, the slits of its green eyes more sly.

Archer released his grip on his pockets. "Why would you save me? Obviously, you don't want to eat me, and you didn't take the stones from me, so what can you possibly want me for?"

"You flatter yourself." The nose of the dragon wrinkled, perturbed, then smoothed as the dragon forced a cool expression again. "*I* don't want you for anything. If it were up to me, I wouldn't even be carrying your flightless carcass." He breathed deeply, and the fire in his belly surged brighter. "*But* I've done nothing the past few months but report to my queen about you in case you would be useful, and since Nin tried to throw you into the ocean, I supposed you must be." He sniffed. "Will you let me bind your wing now, or will you suffer with it until we arrive in my country? I fly faster than the Scorch, but every minute we aren't flying is a minute I have to make up if we plan to catch up with Nin."

Archer eyed the length of vine clutched in the lizard's claws. He knew as well as another that his dislocated wing would have to be braced or it might never recover. But that would require turning his back on the dragonkin to let it bind his wing.

The lizard's eyes glinted. "Don't make me pounce you again."

Then Archer realized why he knew those eyes. "You're that dragonkin that I saw in Tor! The one that knocked me down!"

"I am. Like I said, I'm a scout. A scout for the Scorch, but mainly a scout for my cousin, the queen." The dragonkin shifted onto all four limbs and skirted to

Archer's back. "I'm going to bind your wing now, before you lose us more time with your gawking."

The vine tightened around Archer's chest, binding his hurting wing tightly against his body. The ache of his wing lessened by a degree.

The dragonkin finished tying the knots with a jerk too harsh for Archer's liking and circled to Archer's face again. "You'll want to bandage your arms and legs as well, or you'll cook further."

Archer held up his raw and shiny palms. "They'll just stick."

"Then we'll soak them off when we arrive," the dragonkin said impatiently. "You need the extra layer of protection."

"Fine." Archer forced a dozen steps to the tree line and tore some of the fronds from the trees. Every movement hurt, but he slowly managed to wrap individual strips from the leaves over his hands and tie them into messy knots that, for now at least, might hold. Probably.

The dragonkin paced on the beach, tossing sand with every step. His wrinkled, perturbed snout turned toward Archer. "Are you ready to go now?"

Archer inspected his hand wraps anxiously. They might just burn on those hot scales. "Guess I'm as ready as I'll get."

The dragonkin nodded and lowered his belly to the sand, putting his back in better climbing range.

"Wait, wait." Archer held up both bandaged hands. The dragonkin frowned.

"It'll be quick," Archer promised. "I just have to be sure. . . You know my name, don't you?"

The dragonkin snorted, and the glow inside its nostrils flared. "Of course. You are Archer of Tor."

"Close. Archer of Aro." Archer swallowed. "And you're Ryga, the queen's cousin."

Ryga watched Archer closely. "I am."

"Just had to be sure. Let's go." Archer threw himself up Ryga's blazing hot side and onto his back. The sudden movement jostled his wing. Black dots skittered across his vision. He squeezed his eyes shut and leaned his forehead on his wrists, feeling the heat from Ryga's skin even then.

"Are you well?" Ryga asked, hesitantly.

"Yeah, I'm good. Let's get moving before Nin beats us there."

The journey took four more days. Ryga flew with sickening speed, like an arrow with wings, or a streak of lightning. Archer's ears began to ring from the noise of the wind rushing past them. Draped across Ryga's back and trying to only touch Ryga's skin with something covered with leaves or clothing, he regularly slipped in and out of sleep. Being awake was too difficult, anyway. If it wasn't the noise and the buffeting of the wind, it was the heat coming from within the dragonkin beneath him, and if it wasn't that, it was the pain from his burns and his wing humming at the back of his mind every time Ryga's beating wings jostled him.

Sleeping helped to pass the time, too. Ryga was poor company, reserving all his energy for break-neck speed and responding to only the most important questions. Archer was able to glean that they were keeping up with the Scorch despite their stop on the island, but only if they stayed on track. He also learned that after fishing him out of the ocean, Ryga had flown with him for a full day and a half before finding an island where he could rearrange Archer's wing.

Past that, Ryga refused to talk to him.

When Archer wasn't sleeping, he watched the ocean shoot away in stripes beneath them, and when even that lost its luster, he resorted to singing folk songs to fill the time.

Ryga didn't stop him.

The only problem with the folk songs: every verse made him think of Tor.

Archer had long since lost track of the days and nights and quick stops for food and drink when Ryga finally spoke to him, waking him from a doze.

"Wake up, Archer of Aro. We've arrived in my country."

Scorch land.

Archer sat up quickly. His wing and many burns protested the movement.

Leaning over Ryga's side, he caught his first glimpse of the land of the dragonkin.

It was a land of devastation.

No matter how far he cast his eyes, Archer couldn't find a single patch of green. A flat grey plain stretched in every direction with barely a differentiation to elevation or color. The stalks of dead trees cropped up every few yards, tiny patches of mud shimmering occasionally shimmering in between. All of it grey. Details came and went in a flash as Ryga shot over them toward the horizon.

"There," Ryga said with a sigh. "Civilization at last."

Dots of what Archer had thought were trees and

rocks in the distance rose from the dust, expanding into spires and domes as Ryga flew closer.

With a pang, Archer thought, *If only Wick could see this. That guy loves cities more than anyone I know.*

Despite the aches in his body Archer leaned further over Ryga's side, trying to commit every detail to memory.

If—*when, it's* when—he saw Wick again, he'd tell Wick all about this city. If he was lucky enough to make allies instead of enemies, maybe he'd even take Wick to this place.

The buildings were tall, layered like cakes. Rather than the grey of the landscape, the buildings were red, a saturated, orangey red, like clay. Pillars of a different, more pinky red held up each layer of the buildings, creating shadowy lairs where Archer could often spot movement as they flew past. The base of each building curved into a bowl shape inside the ground, and squinting into these bowl-shaped basements, Archer could see the pattern of tile. In a flash like divine inspiration he realized—the basements were meant to hold water.

But every one of them was empty.

"Look ahead," Ryga warned. "And keep your head down if you want to keep it."

As it happened, Archer felt quite attached to his head, so he ducked down against Ryga's neck and cast his eyes forward.

The largest dragonkin structure, obviously the palace, towered in the center of the city, so large that it blocked out the descending sun. Layer upon layer of overlapping tiers stacked to the sky, higher than a mountain and deeper than the cavern that housed the Heather Stones.

Unlike the other buildings, most of the palace appeared to be enclosed, with the overlapping exterior layers serving as balconies and walks wrapping sections of the walls. Torches glimmered within the many large windows, and through a few Archer spotted brightly colored tile set in the floors and ceilings.

Archer guessed that the extra walls were probably for security. In his experience, most rulers had enemies. At least one of those enemies was usually Archer.

But the palace, in all its impressive enormity, was not the most ominous thing up ahead. Surrounding the palace, perched on balconies and the roof or resting on the ground, roosted hundreds upon hundreds of flaming lizards.

The Scorch had beaten them.

The Skorffv of Archer Hessen

"THEY'RE ALREADY HERE," Archer breathed. "They beat us."

"By only a few minutes." Ryga growled. He stretched out his neck, angling their trajectory toward an open window that really should have been too small to fit them. "Hold on."

"We're not making a plan first?" Archer called as his heartbeat climbed into his throat.

"No time. Think quickly, broken seraph."

They passed over the heads of the Scorch army, who barely had time to look up before Ryga and Archer shot through the open window into the hallway beyond.

Now in the hallway, it was far too late to slow down. Archer's fingers gripped Ryga's scales.

We're going to crash.

Archer caught a glimpse of massive doors at the far end of the hallway and the upturned faces of two dragonkin before Ryga and Archer collided with the floor.

Archer flew off. He bounced twice, then rolled, colliding with the wall. Stars lit up behind his eyes.

His skull. His arms. His ankles. His blasted wing. Pain seemed to lance through every bone. But through the searing pain, he heard voices echoing down the length of the hallway.

One of them he recognized.

"My queen, I've returned to you triumphant." Smug self-satisfaction rolled from Nin's distant voice in waves.

"Move, little seraph, move." Ryga grabbed the back of Archer's collar and pulled him onto his knees. Archer's hands slapped down on the bumps of the floor. The floor was made up of individual clay tiles, stamped with floral designs.

Art. The dragonkin had art.

"Come," Ryga's voice urged, and the claw on Archer's collar pulled again, pulling Archer upright and dragging him down the hall.

Archer smacked at the claw. "Let me go!" Ryga's claw released him, and he stumbled away. Archer straightened his shirt with chagrin.

Ryga looked at him in surprise. "I didn't mean any harm," he grumbled.

"I know. You're helping. Thanks. But I want to walk by myself." If he didn't, he'd never make a good impression on the queen. Archer fought against his throbbing injuries to fall into the tallest, most confident gait he could muster, which was really closer to a hunched shuffle. He approached the huge green doors and the dragonkin that guarded it on either side.

Rolling flames gathered across the doors as the guards moved to block his way. Their wings spread like owls, making them look twice the size.

The heat in the hallway doubled as Ryga's head jutted over Archer's shoulder. "He's with me. Let us through."

The dragonkin parted again, leaving the barest crack of the door open, just wide enough for Archer.

Nin's voice boomed from the far side. "Indeed, my queen, we had a scuffle or two, but they surrendered the stones reasonably without much fight. A few of my soldiers succumbed to the fire on our journey, but we suffered no losses in their country."

Lies. Nin was telling the queen one lie after another, all to cling to his position of power.

Archer's blood boiled.

He pushed through the gap in the doors and roared, "Liar!"

As his voice echoed, nearly a dozen flaming heads turned toward him.

The throne room was enormous. Bigger than an underground cave, large enough to hold a few hundred flying seraphs with room to spare. The vaulted dome stretched higher than the treetops of Eri had once been. Marble tiles the size of dining tables made up the floor, shining milky reflections of the room into Archer's eyes as he stalked toward the figures across the room.

Nin, still smudged with ash from the battle, turned narrowed eyes on Archer. Sitting on Nin's far side atop a platform decorated with more stamped tiles sat another lizard the size of Nin.

Without a doubt, the queen.

More dragonkin, probably advisers, flanked her on either side, ranging from a stocky brown dragon adorned with a gleaming gold medallion to a tall and wiry blue one with darting eyes and painted claws.

Towering in the midst of them, the queen sat tall. Her pearly white scales glimmered with fleeting shades of blue and rose. Swaying lengths of gold chain draped across her body, and the decorative bangles decorating her folded wings clinked together as she leaned down toward Archer. Eyes the color of a stormy ocean regarded him. Was the expression in them kind? Or was it only watchful?

Archer swallowed the pounding heartbeat that still lived in his throat and limped across the deliciously cool stones of the floor toward the dragonkin. It took him four strides to cross even one.

Never had he felt so, so small in a room.

Archer jabbed a finger at Nin, whose nostrils flared. "You're a liar, Nin, and you're a murderer. You didn't take those stones fairly *or* peacefully. You're a murderer and a sneakthief."

"I'm sorry to interrupt," a deep feminine voice broke in, not overly loud, but husky and faintly rumbling, like it came from somewhere deep in her chest. The queen of the dragonkin extended her neck to look more closely at Archer. "But who are you?"

Archer struggled to flare out his wings. The vine binding his injured wing stopped him. He scrabbled at the vine, but the knot was somewhere far behind him, out of reach. "Ryga, get this vine off of me. You know exactly who I am. I'm the broken seraph, the jerk that stole every one of my people's own Heather Stones *twice* to keep them safe from *him*." He jerked a finger back at Nin. "I haven't met a dragonkin yet who didn't know my name, so I *know* you know who I am. And your general made a deal with me before he tried to drown me in the ocean." Ryga's claws tugged at the knot behind Archer's back, and the vines slipped away, freeing Archer's wings. Muscles screaming, wing aching, Archer pulled himself upright. He raised his chin at the queen. "You have to make things right."

"He tried to kill you?" The ridges above the queen's eyes rose in question. "That's no light accusation."

"He let me fall." Archer met her gaze and raised the crooked shape of his bad wing. "I don't joke about falling. I'm only alive because Ryga came and fished me out of the sea."

The queen gazed at him for a moment, her narrowed eyes unreadable. Up close, she seemed. . . not frail, but. . . delicate? Archer could all but count her bones through the translucent parts of her skin. The fire beneath her skin glowed brighter than the other dragonkin, as though it could burst out of her body. Like Nin, she was massive, but unlike him, she was no fighter.

"You made a deal," she said at last. She raised her head high again. In the corner of Archer's eye he could see Nin watching him with a smug expression. "That was what you said. What was the deal you made with Nin?"

"To talk to you," Archer said, pointing. One of the leaves wrapping his wrists shifted, cutting into his burns. He hissed and wrapped the wrist in his other hand. "Aro made mistakes. We got our history all scrambled, and that kept the Heather Stones away from you when you needed them. I needed to tell you that, so I could clear the air. And maybe even make a new alliance."

The queen frowned. "I—"

"I'm not done," Archer interrupted. The dragons flanking the queen stirred, perturbed. Archer couldn't care less that he'd just cut off a queen. "I came here to make an offer, but now I've got something else to add. I want to make a new alliance with you. . . And I want you to get rid of him." He stretched out his arm, pointing toward General Nin. "He can't be in charge of the Scorch anymore."

"You have a lot of requests for a stranger," the queen said. Archer blinked at the sharp edge of anger in her tone. "Why should I listen to you?"

"Why shouldn't you?" Archer shot back. "I came all the way here. We need an alliance to protect both of us, so that we don't go killing each other again. Gint told me how terrible it's gotten here, and I want to help you fix it. That's why I gave you the stones. But you took from us, too. My parents are both dead now, and my home is burned."

Which home? Eri? Tor?

Aro?

"Archer," the queen said.

The use of his name pulled Archer up short.

The queen drew herself up. "I don't think you understand. Aro is not my enemy, but it isn't my friend. You don't understand the damage that's been done here." She turned slightly, watching Archer over her shoulder, then stretched out her wings.

For a moment, Archer thought she meant the

gesture as a threat or a status symbol, like the way that the Crowned Head used his wings as a display of power. But as the folds of the queen's shining wings unfurled, stretching to the width of the riser she sat on, Archer's blood ran cold.

Her wings were ruined.

Holes gaped across each panel of her beautiful wings, holes as big as doorways. Archer could have walked through them without bending his head. The chains and tinkling charms that draped her wings diverted the eye for a moment, as they were meant to, but Archer couldn't look away. Through the gaping holes in her wings he could see the jewelry on the opposite side.

A delicate, swinging charm plucked against one of the redder holes, and though the queen tried to hide it, Archer saw her shudder.

The injury is fresh.

She only just lost them.

At last, Archer remembered to catch his dangling jaw and looked at the queen's face.

Her eyes watched him closely, her posture guarded, waiting for his response.

Archer cleared his aching throat and spoke into the silence. "You can't fly."

The queen sat and crossed her claws at her chest, her wings no longer hidden. "Not now," she said softly. "They burned."

"I'm sorry," Archer said.

"So am I." The queen's eyes flicked to Archer's wing. "We understand each other, don't we?"

Swallowing, Archer nodded.

"Well, then." The queen eyed him with a keen gaze. "If you're going to say something against my general, it had better be convincing. He was recommended by two members of my council. His unfitness is their unfitness, and if he's a liar, they are, too."

Ryga landed on a raised platform at the queen's side, elevated, like he was a parrot on her shoulder. The queen turned to him.

"Ryga, you pulled him out of the ocean," she said sharply. "Did Nin leave him there on purpose?"

Ryga cast a slightly uncomfortable glance at Nin, who had turned to silent seething. Archer realized Nin stood only a dozen paces away and fought down anxiety. If Nin turned on him, no one could save him in time.

"It looked that way, my queen," Ryga responded. "The Scorch left Aro with Archer as a prisoner, but once out of Aro, Nin threw him into the ocean and left him there."

"He tried to stab me," Nin interrupted. "I thought I was in danger, so I dropped him."

Archer's blood boiled. "Liar! I even left my bag when I left Aro. I didn't have anything!"

"Hush," the queen said sharply. "Interrupting me will be a vote against both of you if it happens again." She turned to Archer. "What else do you have against my general staying in power?"

A test. Archer thought hard. "He's not a general; he's a bully. He doesn't know when to stop. If he was just after the stones, all he needed to do was fly in and take them, but he set fire to Aro at least three times before he even mentioned the stones. He murdered Gint."

The smallest cinch of the queen's mouth betrayed her surprise. "Gint? My historian?"

"Yes. Nin killed him. He likes destroying things, and no one like that should stay in power." He thought further and flinched. It would help to take Nin down, but it would hardly help his own cause. "And he's a liar. He lied to me about keeping our deal, and what's more, I heard him lie to you, too. He said that none of the Scorch died in Aro." He took a steadying breath. "And we killed dozens of them. So, he lied to you, his queen."

"He also betrayed his soldiers," a voice broke in.

A warm, husky voice. A voice Archer remembered.

Archer swung around in time to see a familiar dragonkin soar in through the doors of the throne room. Gint's sister landed just short of Nin's feet, jostling the baby dragonkin clinging to her shoulders, and thrust her face close to Nin's. "Even the seraph boy did better than you. He looked after my baby. You, *you* left me for dead, you snake."

She lived.

An unfamiliar surge of hope rushed through Archer's veins.

Gint's sister had lived.

The queen turned to Ryga again. "Are they telling the truth?"

Ryga cast his eyes down. "Many soldiers died," he murmured. "That part is true. What Nin said is not."

The fire in her throat flaring, the queen turned on Nin.

Nin sprang back, thrusting his wings forward into a defensive stance. "As if it wasn't your own fault! As if you didn't keep me waiting for *months* appeasing a bloodthirsty army while you. . . *deliberated*. While your little cousin ran himself ragged flying across the ocean again and again. Your wings are gone now and it's your own fault. You would still have them if you'd just listened to me!"

Archer saw the queen subtly signal the guards with a flick of her tail toward Nin. "What you're saying is as good as treason, Nin. You can't speak to your queen that way."

Nin's tail lashed, just for a moment. "You," he growled, "are no queen of mine."

Then everything happened at once. Nin made a sharp, echoing cry—a signal. The shifty-eyed adviser and the one with the medallion sprang up and lunged at the queen. The guards from the doors flew toward Nin.

Nin leaped on Archer.

Archer tumbled backward. His bad wing rammed against the tile first, and writhing pain shot up his spine. Then blazing heat struck his face.

Nin crouched over him, mouth open, lungs sucking in air, the furnace deep in his throat blazing bright.

Archer struck out with his foot, connecting with the soft underside of Nin's chin. Nin's dozens of teeth clacked together. The motion of the swift kick carried Archer into a roll backwards, away from the heat. His own weight turned his wing into a long lance of pain that snatched the strength from his limbs.

Archer froze on hands and knees, panting and blinking back the pain. His reflection in the marble floors panted back at him.

His heart pounded. Nin would come after him at any moment. Archer struggled to get up, to look behind him.

But the pain from his mangled wing turned his muscles into water. His arms collapsed.

Archer's cheekbone struck the cold marble and stayed there, and from his side he watched Gint's sister spring onto Nin's back. He collapsed, snarling. The guards forced his head to the floor. Across the reflections on the marble, Nin and Archer locked eyes.

"I'm not done with you, boy," Nin hissed.

Archer's hand found the stone in his pocket. Wincing, he pulled the stone free. His hand and the stone thumped against the floor in front of his face.

Between Archer's fingers, the stone glowed jade green. From so close, Archer could hear it humming. Ready.

At last.

"No," Archer responded. "You really are."

The guards dragged Nin away.

Pearly white claws tapped down onto the stone by Archer's head.

"Are you all right?" the deep voice of the queen asked.

Archer breathed deeply and pushed on the floor again. This time, his muscles let him up. Despite the lance of pain still stabbing into his wing, Archer pulled himself up to a hunched upright position.

It almost felt like the pain lived inside his skin. Everything *hurt*.

Oh, he was so tired.

"I'm as all right as I'm going to be," Archer managed in a tense gasp. He sucked in a deep breath and stood. "This is yours, too. I promised I'd hand it over once I got here." He reached over and set the seraph Heather Stone on the edge of the platform. It gleamed in the sunlight.

"Thank you," the queen said.

"Welcome."

"I'll make a thousand apologies for my general," the queen said, casting a bitter look toward the guards as they dragged Nin away, screaming and spraying fire. "The two members of my council will go on trial as well, since it looks like they were plotting with him." Over her shoulder, the rest of the council held down the two council members as Ryga watched them from above.

"It's fine. Respectfully, he attacked me, but that's not the part I care about." Archer tilted his head up at the queen. "What I want is an alliance. Will you make that alliance with Aro?"

"Respectfully to you as well, we already have the stones we needed. My land can be restored, my people can be healed, and when all is said and done, I may be able to regain my wings as well. What can Aro offer us on top of that?" The queen watched Archer keenly.

Another test.

Easy.

"A lot," Archer returned. The knowledge he'd absorbed from Wick over their months together flowed to the forefront of his mind like a comforting breeze. His confidence swelled. "Culture, we've got a lot of that. Gemstones. Materials. Glass." His burnt wrists twinged, and inspiration struck. "But you also have to think about what you owe *us*. Aro looks a lot like your country now; the Scorch burned most of it. Nin burned our records, too. Now our history is lost. Nin did all that. And he represented you. It's like I said before: we've lost a lot, and you have to make things right."

The look on the queen's face was still unreadable.

Archer frowned. "Your majesty, Gint sang your praises for weeks to get me to come here. He believed you were a just ruler and a good person. He thought you were fair. I want to believe that he was right to say those things about you. Prove that you're a fair queen, your majesty. Make things right with Aro."

How to Summon Everyone In The World

THE CASUALTIES were few but painful. Before anything else was accomplished, the valley took a day to bury and to mourn their three fallen.

Farris, the centaur with the close-shaved hair who had been their messenger in Tor.

Alfonso, one of the crowned head's warriors.

And Astor.

Wick found Astor's funeral the hardest. As he stood in the middle of the crowd with his eyes resting, unseeing, on the covered litter that held Astor's body, he could feel Fowl's angry eyes on him, as though this was his fault too.

Wick couldn't see how, but maybe it was his fault.

Astor would never get to write his songs about their victory. He would never write songs again.

The day after the funerals, once gravestones had been erected with names written in ink until tools were found to engrave them, the centaurs began work to bring the valley back to life.

Crowned Head Theodore couldn't stay, as he had his own territory to return to, but a handful of his warriors remained as guards until the Heather Stones could be sent out. The nixies offered the same, and the two sets of warriors covered all sentry duties day and night.

Everyone else in the valley was divided into groups and assigned different tasks in shifts. There were supplies to hunt down, wounds to care for, sentry shifts to maintain, and an endless list of things to repair, starting with the Heather Stone. The new chunks of stone had to be smoothed down and sent out to the territories, this time not just as symbolic tokens but as a new defense system. A defense system suggested by—of all people—Archer. The very plans he had sketched out on scrap paper during their planning phase.

His idea would require some testing, but everyone had high hopes that it would work. With the right protective enchantments, towers could be built around Aro's borders to house the new Heather Stones. With thirteen pieces this time, the territories had more than enough to go around.

Each tower would have a guardian-spellcaster to look after it. If the unthinkable were to happen and the Scorch made another appearance, there would be no mad scramble to gather the pieces. The guardians of the towers, like the keepers of lighthouses, could react independently to threats. In time, Wick hoped they might even learn to heal the land from natural disasters.

Aro would never be the same again.

Wick was put on a single gathering shift and told to spend the rest of his time answering questions and directing helping hands to where they were needed. He couldn't tell if his assigned tasks were things the valley thought he was suited to, or if they wanted to give him something simple to do in the wake of Archer's disappearance.

Fowl wasn't assigned anything at all. As the days turned into weeks and messengers returned from every direction to report damages, Wick heard little and saw less of Fowler Hessen. The rumors about him were always the same: Fowl stayed in the hills alone, holed up in some broken-down shack, and responded to all contact with either silence or random outbursts of anger.

As the weeks slipped by, Wick watched the sky. Every day, like a mantra, he reminded himself that Archer would come back, that he was sure of it.

Every day, his surety slipped just a little bit more.

At the end of the second week, reconstruction officially started on the Great Hall, and that was when wonderful things began to happen.

The fair folk arrived first, flooding over the mountains in great numbers. With them they carried reserves of food, fabric, and medicine, all taken from their personal stockpiles. Fair folk were master foragers; they had been almost too prepared for a disaster. They brought not only supplies, but overwhelming enthusiasm. With their help, the foundation of the Great Hall was dug in an afternoon.

After them came the satyrs. From the singed fur, it was obvious that the flames had taken their toll, but the fire hadn't dampened their resourcefulness. The satyrs brought the valley's original building plans, dug up from deep in their archives. They presented the plans to the centaurs and immediately set out to scavenge the hillsides. The workload of the hunting and gathering shifts lessened incredibly.

Mere hours after the satyrs appeared, Wick looked up from his digging and spotted something moving through the blackened hills. Unlike the mountainside, the moving things were green, and leafy.

A little thrill of awe raced through Wick's veins.

The leshy.

Like a tidal wave of green, the leshy had returned to the valley to help.

Wick clambered up from the hall's foundation to greet them. He recognized the faces of Prince Telf and Princess Lilt in the crowd. Lilt raised her arm to wave to him. The small part of him that usually flinched at the sight of the royal family seemed unfazed. No anxiety filled his chest, only the cool rush of gratitude as the royals started toward him.

Princess Lilt tilted her face up toward Wick's, her new crown of autumn leaves blowing in the wind. "I'm glad to see you safe. We came to offer our help to the centaurs, and to you, if you need it." She paused. "I'm sorry that there aren't more of us, but the rest of the leshy are rebuilding their homes."

To Wick's surprise, Telf didn't speak at all, but let his sister do all the talking. Had it been Lilt's idea to come in the first place?

"We appreciate it," Wick said. "I'm sure one of the mentors can tell you where we need the most help."

Prince Telf nodded and waved the leshy behind him

toward where Tinor and Ongel stood poring over blueprints.

Before Princess Lilt turned away, Wick asked, "How bad is the damage to leshy territory?"

The princess stopped and turned to him, her hands folded tightly. "The larger landmarks survived, but the forest was heavily burned. Lots of the gardens are, as well. Trade might be difficult for a while, but that's only a problem for our trade partners."

"Any casualties?"

"None that we've discovered so far. Our people are resilient. You should give us a visit sometime; your village misses you." The princess turned to rejoin her people.

As she did, a smaller, more wiry leshy broke away from the group and ran toward Wick. The moment before she reached him, Wick realized it was Reesa.

His sister had grown taller at last.

His parents hadn't come. The sour taste of recurring disappointment was quickly beaten back by warmth. His parents hadn't left home—they never did—but his sister had come. His sister had come, and the royal family, and a hundred others.

The leshy were moving forward at last.

Reesa's hard shoulders rammed into Wick's chest, and her arms clamped around his ribs. Wick squeezed her tightly. Her firm grasp anchored him. He couldn't let go, or the wave of emotions he'd been outrunning for weeks might finally catch up.

Like she understood, Reesa tightened her grip, pressing into Wick's ribs. "You're safe," she said into his shoulder. "There were dragons everywhere. I was scared."

"I'm sorry. I was trying my best to keep everyone safe. I'm sorry." Wick realized with a jolt that she hadn't mentioned his parents at all, and he pulled back. "Are Mother and Father all right? They aren't hurt?"

Reesa looked up at him with bright eyes. "Wick," she said, "they're here."

Reesa turned toward the crowd of leshy and pointed.

Wick froze.

Two leshy emerged from the crowd, their faces streaked with ash, their arms laden with crates of vegetables. As their eyes found Wick, they, too, stopped in their tracks.

Wick's mother dropped her crate of vegetables to her feet. Wick lunged forward to help her gather up the goods. Before he even stood up straight, his mother's arms wrapped around his shoulders, pulling him up and into her embrace.

As the shock faded, Wick remembered to hug her back. Her arms were warm, not stiff, like he remembered.

His father's hand on his back brought him back to reality. "How are you here?" Wick asked into his mother's shoulder. "Traveling is so dangerous."

"That doesn't matter. We might never have seen you again." His mother pulled back, her hands reaching up to rest on Wick's shoulders. She focused intensely on his face, as though she was looking for something. "We came to help you."

A ball of huge emotion churned in Wick's chest. "I'm just so glad you're here, Mother."

His mother pulled him back into her embrace. "We're glad we came. We'll look after you."

The leshy put themselves hard to work in the valley and the surrounding hills. They had brought sacks upon sacks of seeds and pods from leshy territory, and for days on end, they worked hard at replanting. They began in the gardens of the valley, but quickly spread outward to the trees and shrubs as well. At one point, Wick spotted a few dozen of them scattered across the hills, apparently spreading seed and fertilizer to help the grass regrow.

As more volunteers poured in every day, Wick had fewer and fewer responsibilities. Three weeks after the departure of the Scorch, Wick approached Eland with a proposal.

"We need to rewrite the records."

Eland's brow crinkled. "Do you think we can?"

"I don't know if we can or not," Wick said. "But I think we have to. The valley's records were the only complete compilation of history in Aro. And better now than never. We'll forget more by the day."

Eland nodded. "I'll see who I can borrow some paper from. You should get Twill, too. She was in the library almost as often as we were."

"That's what I thought, too. I'll get her while you get the paper."

After some searching, Wick finally found Twill with the two royals, talking about plans to plant a hedge of trees around certain buildings. Twill said her goodbyes to the princesses in her usual informal way and walked away with Wick.

"I can't promise that I remember things very clearly," Twill said. "I was skimming more than anything."

"So was I," Wick admitted. "But the three of us are a

living library now, so we've got to write down everything we can while we still remember."

"Should write down what we remember of the past few weeks, too, I'd say. We probably want to avoid another gap in the history books." Twill rolled her neck, stretching it. "I could use some sun first, though."

Wick nodded absently. "I'm a little tired myself."

"Wick?" Twill said hesitantly. "How are you doing? With everything that happened."

A loaded question. Wick swallowed. "I'm fine, I guess."

"You guess, do you?" Twill asked dryly. In a gentler tone, she said, "The whole valley is burnt to the ground, and we lost three of our own. Maybe even a fourth. None of us should guess how we're feeling, least of all my childhood friend who drowns himself in guilt over every mistake."

"I'm not sure I made a mistake," Wick said. He hesitated. "But all the same, I wonder what I could have done better."

Twill nodded slightly. "Such as?"

Wick shrugged. "How could we have prevented those casualties? How could I have convinced the valley to join us in the beginning? How could I save the records in the library?" He took a deep breath, and his heart pounded. "I also wonder. . . at what point do we assume that Archer won't come back?"

"That would be a question for a mentor," Twill said after an awkward pause. "I don't know the answer to that. But I do know that dwelling on *what ifs* won't help one lick."

The sick feeling in Wick's stomach felt no better. All

the same, he said, "We'd better focus on the records, then."

Later that day, alone for the moment while Eland went for fresh air and Twill got some sun, Wick wrote on. A friend of Eland's had offered them the use of his study, which had been buried in the mountainside and therefore had escaped the fire completely. Wick took comfort in having a roof over his head again, and in sitting in a real chair at a real desk to write. The study was just spacious enough to seat all three of them comfortably, as well as Reesa, who glued herself to Wick's elbow every chance she got.

Wick rubbed his wrist and glanced around the room for the first time in hours. Every surface was covered in little piles of paper.

They had made it as far as drafting up a master timeline, which had proved to be an arduous and complicated process. After much debate and calling the mentors twice to look over their notes for accuracy, they felt confident that their timeline held true. Reesa brought them food and drink and news at intervals.

Despite his aching back and wrist, Wick worried about forgetting details from the last few weeks. For the last hour, he had been scribbling down everything he remembered. Now, with sunset light shooting in over his shoulder and his eyes swimming in and out of focus, he was forced to set the rest of the work aside for the day.

A soft sound broke the silence of the room. A quiet clearing of a throat, coming from behind Wick. He twisted in the seat with a start and found someone standing behind him.

Fowl.

THIRTY-TWO

I Can't Heal Yet,
I'm Waiting

FOWL'S FACE, WHICH had been so full and rosy before they left Tor, now tinged a touch more grey and a decade more tired. His heavy eyes looked on Wick with resignation as he fiddled with the locket around his neck. Wick noticed that the portrait inside was changed. The new portrait was simpler, just ink sketched on paper, featuring the faces of Archer and Fowl side-by-side.

Archer's handiwork?

Fowl swallowed and spoke at last. "Is there anything I can help with?"

There wasn't. But Wick knew that this chance was fleeting. If he turned Fowler down, they might never speak again.

Wick scrambled for something to do. "I was just about to see if the satyrs wanted any help," he said, gathering his remaining papers into a neat stack and dropping his pen into the inkwell. "They're erecting the frame for the Great Hall; they'll probably need all the help they can get."

"All right."

Wick and Fowl stepped out of the study and made their way down a dirt path to the valley.

The silence was excruciating.

Fowler broke through the quiet first. "I think it's better if I try to help than if I stay holed up in a cave by myself."

Wick, uncertain of how to answer, just nodded. Hesitating, he asked, "What changed your mind?"

"I asked myself what I would do now. My parents are gone, and my best friend, and it's time all of us accepted that Archer is dead, too, so really, I only have myself to worry about. My father left a legacy I can never hope to uphold, so I can either build a legacy that's better and kinder than his or I can let his name fade away into history." Fowl paused. "I think I'll do the first. I could use something to work toward, otherwise I might lose my mind."

"I think you'll do a fine job," Wick said cautiously, still uncertain what he could say without getting a knock over the head.

"Look, I behaved badly before," Fowl said suddenly. "I shouldn't have attacked you, and I'm sorry."

Wick blinked. "It's all right. I'm sorry things went the way they did."

Fowl laughed dryly. "You should be."

Wick glanced in Fowl's direction, worried that the apology hadn't been in earnest, but even with the wrinkle in his brow, Fowl's attitude was more contemplative than hostile.

"I still hold you responsible." Fowl's wandering fingers reached for his locket again. "He was always fine on his own. Even wandering around the countryside by himself, he was safe, even if he wasn't happy. Even if he wasn't good." He gave Wick a bitter sidelong glance. "But you had to go and make him *kind*. He didn't need to be kind; he just needed to be safe."

Fowl breathed deeply, and his tense shoulders slumped an inch. "But now he's gone, so I guess there's no reason I can't forgive you. Anyway, you two were busy saving the world. With that on the line, your decisions didn't have anything to do with me, did they?"

Wick's heart grew heavier.

I don't like it, but if it's for you, and for Fowl. . . And Wick? Don't let Fowl find out.

He'll try to stop me.

Keep Fowl safe.

Wick glanced over at Fowl. "Actually, I think you had everything to do with it. Archer wanted to keep you safe more than anything; that's why he had me keep it from you. Neither you nor I like that he's gone, but I promise you, he didn't forget about you."

"Maybe one day I can accept that he thought about me, but not today." A sour note snuck into Fowl's voice. "Right now, the simple truth is that he's gone, and we have to learn what to do without him."

That knocked the conversation down for good. They were getting close to the building site, anyway. Wick stopped mid-step. "Well, I know what *you* can do," he said. He gestured to the building site, where the satyrs clustered around stacks of new timbers. "You can help us put up that frame. And then after that, you can help Twill and Eland and I rebuild the records. You're more well-read than any of us; it'll help us just as much as it helps you."

Fowl sighed, a weighty sound that nearly had Wick prepared for a rejection before Fowl said, "Better than nothing, eh?" He began walking again. After a heartbeat's pause, he said, "Now that we have something for me, we just have to find out what you'll do without him."

Wick didn't have any words to respond to that.

As more days passed, Wick did his best just to focus on each task at hand. Carry a beam, pass a hammer up the frame, lend a hand over here, get out of the way over there. Eat and work some more. He worked hard and excelled wherever he could. In between building and writing, he returned to stay nights with his family, where Reesa always had more stories to tell and his mother always had food to put into his hands.

As strange as it was to see his family in the valley, Wick found himself floored each day by the warmth they had brought with them. Warmth that they had never shared before the world had nearly ended.

Their warmth was the only thing that let him sleep at night as Fowl's words ate at him.

The simple truth is that now he's gone.

Fowl was wrong, simple as that. Fowl turned to despair as easily as Archer turned to violence. It had already been three weeks, certainly, but who knew how long it took to travel to dragonkin territory and back? Maybe it would take twice as long as that.

And of course, there came a point where faith turned to denial, but Wick knew he hadn't yet crossed that threshold.

Right?

Right. Of course.

"I will see you again."

He believed it. Wick knew by now to take Archer at his word; Archer would be back. The Scorch had taken him, but there was no proof that he had been killed. Maybe the dragonkin needed him for. . . Wick couldn't guess that part yet.

But Archer had to be alive.

He had to be.

On his way to the shelter where he kept his bed, Wick found a familiar length of stick on the ground. He picked it up and twirled it between his fingers, trying to remember where he had seen it before.

"I gave that to Archer," Ongel's voice said, and Wick looked up to see his mentor standing only a few feet away. A faint smile pulled at Ongel's lips. "He must have dropped it."

Wick nodded. "I'll give it back to him when I. . . when I see him again."

Pain filled Ongel's eyes, but all he said was, "Good. In the meantime, you should keep it."

Wick kept the stick in his pocket, and as he lay down to get some more sleep, he twirled it in his fingers again. Mysterious calm crept over him like a thick blanket. He quickly slipped into a deep sleep. His first peaceful sleep in weeks.

The following few days passed in about the same way.

Wick rested when he was told and helped when he was told and did little else. There was so much work to do, anyway. When he wasn't working on the records with the others, structures needed building, and some of the houses in the hills needed repairs. The lake had to be cleared of wreckage and ash.

When a funeral was mentioned, Wick dismissed the idea right away.

"It's too soon," Wick told Eland's father when he asked. "We can't have his funeral just for him to show up the day after; he would enjoy it too much."

Eland's father hesitated, like he wanted to say something more but didn't know what it was. "All right, then."

As Wick had expected, Ongel eventually appeared with a stack of letters. Other messengers had already spread out to the various territories, carrying building instructions for the towers and inquiring about damages and repairs. Wick, along with Eland and Twill, had moved their study into one of the valley's new buildings. It was only the second of many. Soon, more would be erected like it, and the valley would be restored to its former glory. Soon shelves would fill the empty space, and they would sit at tables and chairs instead of hunched on the floor, but for now, the library existed, little more than walls and a roof smelling of fresh wood and hope.

"I'm supposed to ask if you'd carry this letter of advice to Queen Frey," Ongel said, setting a heavy envelope down beside Wick's pages of notes. "Your messenger position is yours again if you want it."

Both Eland and Twill tried to look very busy as they

listened for Wick's answer.

Wick smiled and shook his head. "I'd rather not. I think my days of doing messenger work are behind me. It would seem too repetitive now." *And passive. And empty.*

"That's what I expected you'd say." Ongel tucked the letter back into the pile in his arms. "I'll let the others know."

Wick wet his lips. "I'm turning down the council position, as well."

Ongel's eyebrows rose. "Oh?"

In the corner of Wick's eye, Twill's head tilted as she dipped her pen in the inkwell.

"I've changed a bit since you first offered me the position," Wick explained slowly, thinking carefully about what words he chose. "I think now I'd like to pursue something else. I'm still deciding what, but I think I want different things now than those jobs can offer me."

"I understand," Ongel said, but he didn't seem a bit surprised.

"I have recommendations for a replacement if you need one." Wick rolled his pen between his fingers as he looked up at Ongel. "Princess Lilt, the youngest of the leshy princesses, is a very resourceful person, and she has good ideas. Since there are seven leshy rulers, I think they might be able to spare her sometimes."

"They might," Ongel said. "I'll speak with the other mentors and see what they think."

"Twill could also be a good choice," Wick went on, and papers flew across the dirt floor as Twill jolted upright. Wick didn't need to glance Twill's direction to know her burning eyes were fixed on the side of his head.

"Either as an alternate to the princess or as a councilor all by herself. I can always count on her to give me an honest opinion, and she can easily hold her own in a group."

"Hey!" Twill shouted, shuffling forward rapidly on her knees to smack the back of Wick's head. "Don't make my life decisions for me!"

Wick turned to her at last. "I'm not making any decisions for you. The decision is between you and the centaurs. I only recommend you because I trust you and I think you could do a lot of good work here. . . *if* you chose it."

Twill sat back on her heels, arms crossed pensively. "I'd have to think about it."

"And you should," Ongel said. He gave Wick a smile. "I'll tell the other mentors about your ideas. And if you need guidance, or a place to stay while you make your own decisions, you're always more than welcome here."

With that, Ongel left the building, and after a moment, the three went back to their work.

Then the sound of cries came floating through the walls.

Wick's ears pricked up at the commotion outside. Something was happening. Were the dragonkin back already?

His stomach dropped. Maybe Archer's plan hadn't worked, after all.

Wick raced out of the little building and looked up at the sky. Three dragonkin descended from the clouds and lighted on one of the lower hills. They didn't appear to be hostile, but what if—

A figure slid down the flank of one of the dragonkin.

A figure with thin grey wings.

Wick's heart jumped. And his legs started running.

Archer looked up at the dragonkin beside him and said something to it. It spoke back. Then the three dragonkin lifted off and circled up into the clouds.

Wick's pumping legs brought him closer. Close enough to see that his eyes weren't fooling him. It was Archer, with the fin in his hair and the bow in his wing and a look in his eyes that said he would never think twice before leaping into the fray.

A shadow passed over Wick's head. At the same time, Archer looked up at the air over Wick's head and started running down the hill. Wick craned his neck to look up.

Of course, it was Fowl.

With a raw cry, Fowl slammed into Archer. Archer barely managed to keep his balance as Fowl squeezed him tight. White knuckles dug into Archer's shirt. Even from the distance, Wick could see Fowl's shoulders were shaking.

Wick slowed to a walk. It wouldn't be fair to take this moment from them. Not after how Fowl had suffered.

Without loosening his grip even a little, Fowl must have said something, because Archer laughed. Pushing Fowl back a little to look him in the eyes, Archer said something back, and grinned even wider. Fowl shook Archer by the shoulders, looking just a little angry.

Maybe it would be better to give them their space. Wick hesitated, then started back down the hill. He would get a chance to talk to Archer later.

"Tree!"

Wick looked back just in time. Archer raced down the hill, arms open. The impact of Archer's chest slamming into him made Wick's feet skid back, but Wick grabbed onto Archer and squeezed tight.

Archer hugged him back fiercely. "Don't you dare walk away from me."

Wick's vision swam as his eyes prickled. He tightened his grip around Archer's shoulders. "Never, *ever* disappear like that again. That wasn't fair."

"Now, listen here, tree, if I'd known I was going, I would have told you, wouldn't I?" Archer snapped, pulling away and jabbing a finger at Wick. Torn makeshift bandages wrapped his arms from palm to elbow. Gauze padded one of his shoulders, as well.

"Everyone thought you were dead, Archer." Wick's chest ached from weeks of straining for hope. Now that Archer stood in front of him again, the relief was so potent it hurt. "*I* wondered if you were dead."

Archer paused before speaking, then swallowed. "To be fair, tree, I almost was. But look, here I am." He jabbed Wick's shoulder with his fingertips. "Real as anything. Nothing to worry about."

Wick swallowed hard. "Was it a kidnapping, then? That's what we thought."

"More or less." Archer tilted his head back and forth. "Someone had to go see the queen, but I figured that anyone who met with the queen had a fifty-fifty chance of being killed on the spot. If anyone was going to take that chance, it was me."

"Where did you go?" Wick asked. "And what on earth happened to your arms?"

"Same answer for both," Archer said. He pointed up at the sky. "They carried me by the arms and almost cooked me like a potato. Maybe it's better that Nin tried to drown me in the ocean halfway."

Wick's heart thudded. "What did you say?"

"I'm not being funny. He tried to drown me, Wick." Archer's expression was somber. "I'm lucky one of the dragonkin fished me out. But that just gave me more to use against Nin once I met with the queen. She's a good queen, Wick. With enough hard work, we can form a solid relationship with them so that this never has to happen again. After that, they wanted me to watch while they repaired their land with the stones, so I had to stay a little longer."

"Without telling anyone?" Wick asked judgmentally. "I can think of at least three ways you could have sent word that you were all right."

"Maybe you can, tree, but I couldn't." Archer shuffled his feet stiffly. "I thought if any dragonkin showed up, everyone would go into hiding and no one would listen to what they had to say. So, I didn't send anything."

Wick shut his mouth again.

"And Wick," Archer said earnestly, "they have an offer. For you and for me." He reached into the pocket of his pants and produced a pitch black, leathery envelope.

Frowning, Wick took it and broke the gold seal. The paper inside had a strange sheen to it, with a similar dense and gummy texture to the envelope. The lettering was bright gold.

Atlanta, the queen of the dragonkin and leader of the

Scorch army, extends her greetings.

I have heard endless stories about the tree messenger and the damaged seraph that were so ready to protect their country that they would die for it. Having met the seraph, I want to offer you both positions within my personal council.

If the place within my council will not do, I would like to offer you both the job of ambassadors. It seems that your people's records were missing pieces, and are now entirely reduced to ash. My deepest condolences, as knowledge lost is not easily replaced. I am more than willing to offer your people copies of our own records to reference as you rebuild your own. As ambassadors for the dragonkin, you would be the primary record keepers of our two people's history, and as I understand you are quite apt at settling conflict, you would also be responsible for diplomatic conversation between our two peoples.

I would very much like to see our lands in alliance once again. I think we can help one another in countless ways.

Take all the time you require to make your decision. But please consider our offer. What you and your friend have done for my people is something I would like to repay in any way I can.

With the deepest respect,
Queen Atlanta, Royal Leader of the Dragonkin

Wick looked up at Archer. "Ambassadors?"

Archer shrugged. "I think I'm getting better at it. Wick, I talked a *queen* into an alliance with us. If nothing else, I can keep track of the records like she asked. My handwriting is terrible, but I can keep a story straight." His eyes gleamed. "And you should see their land. It's nothing like Aro. It's like a pretty swamp all over, and they build these houses out of clay that hold water inside. You would go crazy."

Wick blinked. The offer seemed almost too good to be true: an actual position of importance, just when he thought that he would never want a job like that again.

The immediate rush in his bloodstream seemed to give him an answer.

"We should go," he said.

Archer grinned. "I knew it."

◇

WICK TUGGED and tugged again on the hem of his crisp white coat. "I don't think I've ever felt this anxious to meet someone."

Archer shook his head as he tucked in his brand-new scarlet shirt. His glass buttons glittered in the torchlight. "You're more scared to meet a fire-breathing lizard from halfway across the world than you were to meet the Crowned Head? You're ridiculous, tree."

"This is totally different than that, and you know it. This is more important than anything I've ever done before."

Archer shrugged. "Stress if you want, but think, you'll be the *second* person alive today who's ever met her." Archer rolled his neck, his spine cracking loudly. "Well, I'm ready if you are."

Wick turned to face the curtain of leaves that hung between them and the throne room. "I don't think I'll ever be ready. Why wait?"

They pushed through the curtain. The brightness of

the room beyond was almost blinding, but Wick pushed down the flinch. Facing them on the far side of the colossal throne room, a pearly white dragonkin wrapped in golden chains bowed her head to welcome them.

Wick took a step out into the room, his new boots clicking on the polished floor. "Good morning, queen of the dragonkin. My name is Wick of Aro."

ENDE.

TURN THE PAGE TO READ A
SHORT STORY FROM

AND EVERYTHING IN BETWEEN:
A SCORCH ANTHOLOGY

COMING LATE 2025

A GAME

FOWL SUDDENLY looked down the bench at Archer. "Care to play a game?"

The lingering rays of warm sunshine had carried Archer to the brink of sleep. He forced his eyes open. "What?" he groaned.

"If you're that disinterested you don't have to play," Fowl said. He settled back further and crossed his arms over his chest. "But I'm curious. What if just for a moment we pretended that we liked each other?"

"What," Archer responded, "act like we've never fought in our lives, like we get in trouble together and can reminisce on fond memories and never had a problem with each other in the first place? Act like we care and look out for each other the way that good siblings do?"

Fowl tilted his chin down a degree, staring at the clouds through the window opposite them. ". . . Yes."

Archer twisted to look at his brother straight on. "Why?"

"Because I want to know if we could," Fowl said. He then added, "I don't think you could."

Archer felt a little stab of hurt, quickly replaced by a touch of anger. "I could just as well as you could."

"Well then, I dare you to try." Fowl got up and walked down the hall. He nearly disappeared into the shadows. Just past the first doorway, he turned on his heel and walked back toward the bench where Archer sat. "Why, hello, brother."

Archer had to curb the instinct to give a snappy response. "Hello," he said at last.

Fowl sat back down beside him. "And how are you on this particularly fine day?"

Archer floundered for two full heartbeats. "I guess the only correct answer is *fine.*"

Fowl faked a jolly expression and thumped Archer on the shoulder. Archer leaned away. "Come on, we're proper siblings. We can be honest with each other."

"Fine, in that case I'm tired and I wish this 'proper brother' of mine didn't make me wake up to play this game," Archer said. He saw the clench in Fowl's brow and inhaled quickly. "But since we're such great companions, what do we normally talk about, brother?"

Fowl's mouth twitched. "I don't know. Anything, probably. Everything."

"And we would know, since we're such great siblings."

"Obviously."

The setting sunlight winked skeptically between the leaves outside.

"Here's a topic: what did you think of the roast we had for lunch?" Archer sat back and crossed his arms.

Fowl's brow furrowed. "It was fine. It was good," he corrected. "Very good."

Archer raised his eyebrows. "I thought we were being honest. It was dry. She always overcooks the meat."

"She does, doesn't she." Fowl propped his chin on his hand and stared at the opposite wall. "Drat, now I'll always notice it."

Archer tried not to grin.

"No really, how dare you," Fowl said with a faint laugh. "I'll never eat dinner again without noticing that the meat is overcooked."

Archer snickered.

"Go on, laugh," Fowl said. "It's fine for you, you don't live here anymore."

His statement broke the spell. Their game of pretend

faltered, and suddenly they were a strange pair again, strangers in a wide city, sitting uncomfortably far apart lest they ever knock shoulders.

For a breath, silence.

Fowl noticed it, too. He spruced up his cheerful expression and rose from the bench. Archer copied his action.

"But we won't talk about things like that, because we're good siblings and are never apart," Fowl said. "Isn't that right?"

"Never been apart in our lives," Archer replied, a little less brightly. "I can't even imagine us apart." That time he sounded almost sarcastic. Archer cringed.

But Fowl wasn't paying attention. He was staring out the window. "Look at the sky," he said softly.

Archer turned and looked. "Oh."

Together they stepped to the window. The sunset was at its climax. The last sliver of sun hung just over the lip of the horizon, casting beautiful oranges and purples across the treetops and dying the clouds a pale pink. Every glass window across the city gleamed gold.

Archer pressed his fingers against the glass. "How do I always forget that the best sunsets are up here," he murmured.

"I haven't seen many elsewhere," Fowl responded, still looking at the sky, "but I think you're right."

They watched the colors of the sky deepen and fade, and this time, the silence that stretched on as they watched didn't feel as suffocating as usual.

Archer glanced down in time to see the last light slip away from the street below them. Then he squinted. "Look down there. Those are the rocks we used to play on with your friends, aren't they?"

Fowl looked. "Those are the ones."

"Hmm. Somehow I didn't think they'd be there anymore."

"I remember that time you got your foot stuck in those rocks," Fowl said quietly. He smiled. "Mother thought you'd lost your whole leg the way you hollered."

"Not as loud as you when I shut the front door on your hand," Archer said. "I'm lucky I'm not deaf in that ear."

Fowl's expression turned suspicious. "I think you shut that door on purpose."

Archer made a shooing motion with one hand. "You were being annoying."

"Of course, of course." Silence. "Is this what normal siblings talk about, do you think?"

"Maybe."

They stood in silence, watching and waiting, until even the clouds vanished and the sky turned deep blue.

It was Fowl who broke the spell. "I think," he said, taking a step away from the window and sitting down on the bench once more, "this may have been the first humane conversation we've had in a long time."

"Yeah." Archer turned away from the window. "Does that mean we win?"

Fowl shrugged. "I don't know. I don't know the rules to this game." Then he smiled. "I really didn't even think you'd play."

COMING 2025

ACKNOWLEDGMENTS

The story is over, so that means it's time for a credits reel! Many hands and voices have been a part of creating this story, and thanks are owed to them all. And maybe some cupcakes. I should make some cupcakes. . .

I owe my Lord and Savior enormously for every book I craft. Unless he were to build this house, I would labor in vain.

Yet again I must shout out my editor, Angela: for being in my corner, for being a hype woman, and for being clear but kind, as all good editors should be.

As ever, I must mention my family. Thanks to Papa for all the pep talks and sound business advice, to Mama for reality checks, to Rachel for being a sounding board, and to Jeremiah for that one time he called Aro the Holy Roman Empire.

Don't think I've forgotten that.

I haven't.

A toast to my friends, muse with a thousand faces. Naomi, Kristin, Willa, Autumn, Sam, Mahlah, Justin, Danielle, and dozens of others. You have all my love.

All my Instagram and business buddies, fellow authors and otherwise, bless you. Thanks for the memes, for the art, for making me laugh, for caring. Most of all, thanks for being here for this ride.

And here's to you, person who reads acknowledgments pages. What a weirdo. <3

ABOUT THE AUTHOR

Bethany Meyer is an indie fantasy author (which you've probably guessed since you're reading her book right now). When she's not writing, she's probably watching anime and scribbling in her sketchbook. She loves the Lord, graphic novels, and yelling enthusiastically about storytelling.

THANKS FOR READING! PLEASE ADD A
SHORT REVIEW ON AMAZON AND LET ME
KNOW WHAT YOU THOUGHT!

YOU CAN ALSO JOIN MY MAILING LIST AT

MEBETHANYDANNI.WIXSITE.COM/BETHANYMEYER-1

TO KEEP UP WITH THE NEWS ABOUT
FUTURE BOOKS!

www.ingramcontent.com/pod-product-compliance
Lightning Source LLC
Chambersburg PA
CBHW061050210726
48294CB00001B/86